"LORD. ALEXANDER. MALLORY."

Rankin spit out each word as if it were an unwanted seed stuck between his teeth. "Trust you to disturb our progression."

"The rest of the world continues unimpeded, Rankin," Lord Alexander said. "It appears I've only disturbed you."

Alexander Mallory. Is there a lovelier name in all God's creation?

Rankin cast a dark frown at Lucinda's hand in Lord Alexander's, startling her out of her bumfuzzled musings. Her cheeks flared with heat again. She pulled her hand free and crossed her arms over her chest in indignation.

"A gentleman's timely reflexes can hardly be named a disturbance, milord," she said, a little vinegar slipping into her tone. "Lord Alexander merely saved me from a quick tumble."

"Have a care then, Mistress," said Rankin with a leer. "For a *quick tumble* is one of the things Mallory excels in, I'm told."

More from Mia Marlowe

Touch of a Thief

Touch of a Rogue

Touch of a Scoundrel

Plaid to the Bone

Published by Kensington Publishing Corporation

Plaid Tidings

MIA MARLOWE

ZEBRA BOOKS
KENSINGTON PUBLISHING CORP.
http://www.kensingtonbooks.com

ZEBRA BOOKS are published by

Kensington Publishing Corp.
119 West 40th Street
New York, NY 10018

All Kensington titles, imprints, and distributed lines are available at special quantity discounts for bulk purchases for sales promotion, premiums, fund-raising, educational, or institutional use.

Special book excerpts or customized printings can also be created to fit specific needs. For details, write or phone the office of the Kensington Special Sales Manager: Attn.: Special Sales Department. Kensington Publishing Corp., 119 West 40th Street, New York, NY 10018. Phone: 1-800-221-2647.

Zebra and the Z logo Reg. U.S. Pat. & TM Off.

ISBN-13: 978-1-4201-2973-1
ISBN-10: 1-4201-2973-2
First Printing: October 2013

eISBN-13: 978-1-4201-2974-8
eISBN-10: 1-4201-2974-0
First Electronic Edition: October 2013

10 9 8 7 6 5 4 3 2 1

Printed in the United States of America

"Three hundred years seems a long time when one is looking forward. Looking back, it's but a watch in the night. Our chance of redemption slips away with each passing sunrise. Until a son of Scotland who has once disowned his true self finds that self again, the curse on Bonniebroch Castle canna be lifted."

From the secret journal of Callum Farquhar,
Steward of Bonniebroch Castle since
the Year of Our Lord 1521

Chapter One

December 1821
Somewhere off the coast of Scotland

The *Agatha May* rolled with a monstrous swell. Lord Alexander Mallory splayed his hand across the coins and banknotes in the center of the table to keep them from cascading to the plank floor. It was good that the table was bolted to the teak or the whole thing might have toppled over.

"That's one hundred pounds to you, MacMartin," he said. The stakes of this poque game were ridiculously high, but Alexander had his reasons for allowing it to spiral out of control.

Sir Darren MacMartin dabbed his face with a perfumed handkerchief. At any other time, Alexander might have had sympathy for MacMartin since he suffered so from mal de mer; the man had spent the better part of the voyage leaning over the gunwale. But MacMartin's seasickness made it more difficult for Alexander to read him when he bluffed.

MacMartin tossed down the required bet and stared at his cards, his face immovable as Gibraltar despite the pinpricks of perspiration blooming on his brow. "So what will you do with yourself in Edinburgh, Mallory?"

"Clarindon and I will help Lord Rankin prepare for the royal progression next August," Alex said cautiously. "What's your interest in a Christmastide visit to Scotland?"

"I've an estate there which requires my immediate attention," MacMartin said, frowning at his cards. "Bonniebroch. Means 'lovely tower,' or some such silly thing. All in all, it's a tidy barony, though."

Alexander already knew that. The estate was the whole point of the game.

"So while you're in Scotland, you'll go by Lord Bonniebroch instead of Sir Darren?" Alexander asked.

"I should, especially once the king arrives next summer, in order to show that I hold honors on both sides of the border. He likes that sort of thing, I'm told," MacMartin said. "I suspect Lord Rankin picked you for this assignment because of your Scottish connections. Should smooth the way, what? If memory serves, your mother was a MacGregor, wasn't she?"

Alexander's mouth tightened. The man knew damned well she was. His friend Clarindon tried to change the topic of conversation, but MacMartin returned to worry it like a dog on its last bone.

"Surely that whole sorry business doesn't still distress you, Mallory. My apologies, if it does. Didn't mean to bring up . . . I mean, I didn't think you'd be bothered after all this time."

Of course, you did. Distracting other players from their hands was MacMartin's gaming strategy. Alexander waved away the false apology. Besides, it really shouldn't matter anymore.

Except that it did. And for a blinding second, he was four years old again, weeping over the bit of unconsecrated ground that was his mother's grave.

"Stop your sniveling," his father had growled at him. "She doesn't deserve your tears. Remember, your mother *chose* to leave us."

Alexander ran a hand over his eyes and consigned the memory back to the vault where he kept all such disturbing recollections. Occasionally, they crept out to torment him, but he always shoved them away. Someday he hoped he'd be able to make sense of his mother's end, but he doubted it.

Clarindon tossed in his hand, leaving just Mac-Martin and Alex still playing. Alexander upped the bid by another two hundred pounds.

"I shall give you my vowels," MacMartin said as he pulled out a scrap of paper and began to scribble an IOU.

"Sorry, old chap," Alexander said. "We agreed to a cash-in-hand game." Then he purposely scratched his nose, the gesture he'd been using as his tell throughout the game and hoped Sir Darren would rise to the bait.

The man scowled furiously, twisted off his signet

ring, and slammed it down on the pile of bank notes. It was a barbaric piece, fashioned of heavy gold with a cabochon ruby carved intaglio style. "I will not allow you to buy this pot. That ring signifies the title and estate of Bonniebroch, which is better than cash. Now throw down." He tossed his cards onto the table face up.

"Three queens," Alex said with a gulp. "A formidable hand."

Sir Darren flashed an oily smile. "Show your cards, sir."

Alex laid them down one at a time, four eights in a lovely row, which handily beat three queens. Then he picked up the signet ring and slipped it on his forefinger. It was much heavier than he expected.

Scottish titles at the rank of baron weren't dependent upon bloodlines. They could be bought, sold, or won in a game of chance, as Alex had just done. The estate at Bonniebroch would give him the pretext he needed to remain in Scotland till the royal visit next August. And would mask his true purpose for being there.

Sir Darren stared at the cards in disbelief. Then he rose shakily to his feet, his eyes narrowing. "Enjoy your winnings while you can, Mallory, much good may they do you."

"That sounds suspiciously like a threat. Do you feel yourself ill-used? If it's satisfaction you crave, as soon as we reach dry land, I'm at your disposal."

"My satisfaction will come from seeing how poorly you fare as Lord Bonniebroch," MacMartin said. "Just don't say I didn't warn you."

Alex chuckled. "Warn me of what? Is the 'tidy

barony' nothing but a tumbled down croft with sheep grazing on the roof?"

"You may laugh now. You won't be laughing after you've spent a few nights with the weeping woman. You may not believe in Scottish curses, but I promise you, they are real. Clarindon, I bid you good day." He bowed to Alexander's friend and weaved from the cabin, looking greener around the gills than usual.

"Hope he makes it to the rail this time," Clarindon said as he helped Alex scoop up the impressive pile of winnings. "What do you make of his talk of curses?"

"We're within spitting distance of Scotland, aren't we?" Alex glanced out the porthole, catching a glimpse of the hazy coastline of his mother's homeland before another swell washed over the heavy glass. "I'd only be surprised if there was no talk of a curse."

"Mr. Farquhar, sir, are ye all right?" Mr. Lyttle stood frozen in place, wringing his hands with fervor.

"Of course, I'm no' all right," Callum Farquhar replied. "I'm still dead, ye ken." Indeed, Farquhar had not been counted among the living for almost three hundred years.

While few people could actually see Farquhar, the old steward of Bonniebroch Castle made sure the butler of the estate was one of them. Over the centuries, Farquhar had learned to approximate the normal motion of the living to an uncanny degree. When he moved across the room, one had to look very closely to see that his high-heeled boots didn't quite touch the broad plank floor.

"But, for a moment, ye seemed . . . more dead

than usual, beggin' yer pardon. Ye faded so I feared ye were about to wink out entire."

Even though Farquhar was a ghost, he was still the steward of the castle. Barons came and went, but since 1521, Farquhar had remained. Lyttle and the rest of Bonniebroch's residents depended upon him for daily direction in the running of the place.

"There's been a disturbance of our plans, a transfer of sorts," Farquhar said, a hand pressed involuntarily to his chest. "Bonniebroch has a new baron."

"A new baron? We didna even have a chance to get used to the old one. What does this mean? Will he still come for Christmas?" Mr. Lyttle shifted his weight from one foot to the other like a squirrel on a slender branch, not certain it would hold him. "We havena much time."

"Peace, Lyttle. Let me think." The impending deadline for the curse's fulfillment hovered over them all like the Sword of Damocles. Farquhar had pinned his last hope on Sir Darren MacMartin. He had Scottish roots, but his family had moved south when he was a child and he'd lived as an Englishman all his life. He met the curse's requirements on the surface. But now the man had somehow let the castle and the title slip from his index finger. A new name formed in Farquhar's mind.

Lord Alexander Mallory.

"I need to discover what I can about the new Lord Bonniebroch," Farquhar said. "Carry on, Mr. Lyttle."

Then, quick as lightning, Farquhar shot across the room and passed through the silvered glass of a long mirror as if it were water. The surface wavered for a heartbeat after his passage, and then went still as a becalmed sea.

* * *

"I hate the English." The muttering masculine voice curled around Lucinda MacOwen's ear. She and her sisters, Aileen and Mary, huddled under an oversized umbrella waiting at the quay with the assembled gentry. The trifling drizzle wasn't enough to send them inside. The chance to see a king's envoys, even an English king's envoys, was too delicious to pass up over a few raindrops.

"The Sassenachs used to turn up when a body least expected them," the voice went on, *"but now when they give notice of their intent to appear and ye can prepare yerself a bit for the insult of it, the bloody English canna even be bothered to arrive in goodly time."*

Lucinda resisted the urge to tell Brodie MacIver to be quiet, but she held her tongue. It wasn't as if anyone else could hear him and she didn't fancy letting her sisters know *she* could. Besides, the poor ghost had enough to worry about what with the wind threatening to blow him into the next shire.

"Your teeth are fair chattering, Lucy." Her sister Aileen was ten months Lucinda's junior but that didn't stop her from trying to manage the other MacOwen sisters as if she were the eldest. "It doesna seem that cold to me. Would ye take my shawl then?"

"No, I'm fine," Lucy said. It wasn't the soft rain that chilled her. It was Brodie MacIver's invisible hand on her shoulder, cold as naked iron in January, which was only natural since one couldn't expect a ghost to be warm. She really ought to be used to it since the specter had been her companion since she was a child.

When she was six, her brother Dougal and his

friends had locked her in the cellar because she wouldn't stop dogging them. In the dark and damp, Lucinda had cried herself hoarse, but no one came to free her. Then just when she was about to go wild with fear, a soft burr of a voice whispered, *"Och, little lassie. Ye dinna have to cry so. Ol' Brodie's here wi' ye."*

When Dougal finally came to set her free he'd expected to find her thoroughly cowed, but she and Brodie had passed a tolerable time together there in the dark. The spirit had been with her ever since.

His presence was sometimes annoying, sometimes a comfort, but just now his spectral hand on her was merely cold. She shivered again.

"Are ye sure ye dinna want me shawl?" Aileen said. "A chill might give ye a case of the sniffles."

Lucy hated to cover her pale blue muslin gown and rabbit-trimmed pelisse with Aileen's garish red shawl, but she accepted it. Her sister's redingote was of thick wool so she could spare the shawl.

Lucinda should have been warm without it from sheer excitement. Today she'd meet her betrothed for the first time. He was a passenger on the *Agatha May* along with the English envoys.

Betrothed. Even now she scarcely believed it.

Though the marriage contract was as firm as a gaggle of Glaswegian lawyers could make it, she didn't want her husband-to-be to look upon her with disfavor at their first meeting on account of a drippy nose.

The *Agatha May* wallowed up to the quay and ropes thick as a man's arm were tossed to waiting dock men. As soon as the vessel was made fast, passengers crowded elbow-to-elbow along the ship's rail. A short fellow in full Highland regalia made his way to the front of the ship where the gunwale was constructed of neatly spaced spindles instead of solid wood.

"Oh, look. There at the prow. Could that be the king?" Lucinda exclaimed. The man was portly, as the English monarch was said to be, and was swathed in a belted plaid of startling Stewart red.

"Canna be," Aileen said. "King Georgie isna due till August. Must be one of his men. Dearie me, what's he wearing beneath his kilt then?"

Lucinda's youngest sister Mary squinted up at the Englishman. "Looks like . . . bright pink pantaloons, tight enough to mold to his knees."

"But everyone knows a man should sport nothing beneath a kilt but what the Lord God gave him," Aileen said. All the MacOwen girls were green-eyed redheads, but only Aileen's eyes perpetually sparked with mischief. "And if those pantaloons are meant to be the color of his flesh, the fellow must be part lobster."

"I, for one, consider the pink pantaloons a mercy." Mary laced her fingers primly before her, fig-leaf fashion. "That kilt is far too short for modesty. Especially from this angle."

"Weel, since the English are to be among us for so brief a time, the more we see of them the better," Lucy quipped.

Aileen giggled, but Mary shot them both a withering glance that would have done credit to their decrepit great-aunt Hester, who *had* let the foul weather keep her safely indoors. The old biddy was fooling no one. The girls knew she wasn't sweet enough to melt.

Lucy stood tiptoe to peer over the shoulder of the

rotund matron in front of her. The MacOwen family wasn't sufficiently important to rate a place directly before the cordoned-off disembarkation space.

"Which one do you suppose is *him*?" Lucinda didn't need to explain who she meant by *him*. Her intended was foremost in all their minds since her pending marriage affected the entire family.

"'Tis no' likely he's a handsome braw lad, worse luck for ye, Lu. The best ye may hope is that he's still got his hair." Aileen crossed her eyes and stuck out her tongue. "And maybe his teeth."

"I dinna think that matters." Though Mary was the youngest MacOwen sister, she was also the most frightfully practical. "Even if he has a hump like Old Man MacClintock, Lucy will still have to marry him."

Lucinda's spine stiffened. "It was to be Maggie, remember, not me. Have a care with your ill wishes, sisters dear, lest I leave my bridegroom to one of ye."

Mary gave an unladylike snort. "Maybe Margaret saw a miniature of Lord Bonniebroch and that's what sent her haring off."

They hadn't heard from their oldest sister, Margaret, since she took flight with the man-of-all-work from a neighboring estate.

"I doubt it, but 'tis fair awkward for me, and that's God's truth," Lucinda said. "I'll no' say I blame her though. Maggie loves Duncan Fraser and there's no help for it."

"And there's no help for the fact that one of us has to wed this Lord Bonniebroch, either," Aileen said. "Even if his kilt hides a forked tail!"

Intermediaries had negotiated the marriage agreement in secret, combing through the particulars about grazing rights and stud fees for the two families' combined herds, about Erskine MacOwen's patents for improvements to the weaving loom, along with Lord Bonniebroch's financial support of the invention. Then their father and the laird had finally signed the contract and that was that.

Fortunately, Erskine MacOwen hadn't stipulated *which* "daughter of the house" would be offered up on the matrimonial altar to seal the deal.

"I'm glad 'tis ye and not me being trotted out to honor Father's word," Aileen said to Lucinda. "But honestly, he might have spared his daughters a passing thought before he made this bargain."

"'Tis no' Father's fault, really," Mary said, loyal as a basset.

"Whose fault it is that he canna manage his own affairs?" Aileen gave a little sniff of disapproval.

"'Tis a small matter now. The deal is done," Lucinda said, lifting her chin. She wouldn't let her sisters see how she chafed at being an unspecified commodity in the transaction, of less import than the prize-winning Blackface ram Lord Bonniebroch also demanded. The sheep, at least, had its long pedigreed name specified in the documents.

But if the family was on firm financial footing and she bore a "Lady" before her name, then the chances of Aileen and Mary making happy matches shot up like a flock of pheasants rousted by a hound.

"Weel, it isna as if ye had a beau, Lu," Aileen said. "There's a mercy."

Lucinda flinched as though her sister had slapped her, but Aileen was right. She'd never had a beau. Brodie MacIver ran off every lad who tried.

This "made marriage" was the best she could hope for and she knew it. And since the contract was binding, Brodie couldn't do a thing about it.

Which probably accounted for the ghost's general surliness of late.

She was all he had.

"Just because I havena got a beau doesna mean I won't hand Lord Bonniebroch to ye if he turns out to be the hairless, toothless wretch ye've wished on me," Lucinda said with a sidelong glance at Aileen.

"Ye'll not be leaving Lord Bonniebroch to one of us, and ye know it. 'Tis not your way. Even before she met Duncan Fraser, Maggie was always the flighty one. But ye've grit enough for ten sons, Lu. Father always says so." Aileen pointed toward one of the Englishmen leaning on the ship's gunwale. "But I'll take your Lord Bonniebroch if he favors that fine fair-haired laddie there. Are there any pictures provided in that *Knowledgeable Ladies' Guide to Eligible Gentlemen,* Lu?"

Before her engagement to Lord Bonniebroch was finalized, Lucinda had pored over the leather-bound listing of bachelors and wondered at the sometimes outlandish advice the book's author recommended for capturing one of them. Now she supposed she'd have to hand the book over to her sisters.

"Dinna point, Aileen," Mary said, batting at her sister's upraised arm. "'Tis impolite."

Lucy followed the invisible line from the tip of her sister's finger. When she spotted the young man Aileen pointed to, her jaw went slack.

She'd never seen such a dazzlingly handsome

man. Or one who could set her heart a-clicking from such a distance.

His skin was fair after the manner of wellborn Englishmen, his sandy hair a bit on the longish side, which made it more striking. The severity of having it slicked back by the wind accentuated his bone-deep good looks. A plaid sash in blue and red, proclaiming a clan affiliation, was draped over his broad shoulders so he must have some Scottish blood as well. If someone had asked Lucinda to conjure up a prince for the Folk of the Hollow Hills, he'd look exactly like that stern, forbidding, utterly beautiful man.

Her belly fizzed as if she'd downed a frothy syllabub in one gulp.

The man stood a few inches taller than the dark-haired fellow at his side, but they both carried themselves with the dangerous grace of fighting men. The brunet said something and the handsome man laughed, a smile bursting over his features like sunrise on a cloudless morn.

Something threatened to burst inside Lucinda as well. She was suddenly hot and achy beneath the bones of her stays. She usually didn't give a man's appearance much thought, but now that she faced the prospect of crawling into bed with one, the subject had pushed itself to the forefront of her mind.

Would it hurt anyone in the grand scheme of things if Lord Bonniebroch turned out to be a man who made her pantalets bunch like this one did?

Aileen turned her sly gaze on Lucinda. "Well? Isn't he fine?"

Lucy released a pent-up breath. "He sets me belly a-jitter, for certain sure."

"Och! That's indigestion, most like," Mary said. "Ye've been off your feed for days. More parritch tomorrow, I'm thinking. That'll set ye to rights."

The stout man in the red kilt turned away from the gathered crowd, and waddled toward the gangplank. It was probably disrespectful to imagine the king's envoy waddling, but Lucy thought he resembled nothing so much as a fattened gander as he strutted along. Her gaze didn't linger on him though. Instead, Lucinda tracked the handsome Englishman's progress along the ship's rail as he followed in the kilted fellow's wake.

"Weel, when you do meet Lord Bonniebroch," Aileen said, "just be sure you dinna mention Dougal till after the knot is tied good and tight."

Lucinda's lips drew together in a tight line. "I thank ye kindly for your advice, Mistress Readily Apparent."

It was clear during the nuptial negotiations that Lord Bonniebroch had no idea Dougal MacOwen was mixed up with the Radicals' cause. The less said about their felon of a brother and his troubles the better.

Once Lucinda was safely married, she'd expect her powerful new husband to help his brother-in-law avoid the noose. Since the laird of Bonniebroch was traveling home from London on the same vessel as the king's advance party, it stood to reason he'd acquired some valuable connections during his recent trip to the English court.

"There's the boggle I've been waitin' for," Brodie MacIver's voice rumbled in her ear again. *"He's the spit of Cormag MacGregor, the thrice-cursed offspring of a diseased swine."*

"Who?" Lucinda whispered. It made her seem a trifle daft when she answered Brodie while others were present, but sometimes the ghost was hard to ignore.

"Only the man who damned me to this half-life of misery," Brodie went on. *"This must be one of his spawn or else Cormag made a deal with the devil to live on in this world forever unchanging. Wouldn't put it past him, stinkin' offal of a mangy dog that he is."*

"Who?" she said a little louder this time.

"The blatherskite wearing the sash of MacGregor plaid over his shoulder, o' course. Is it blind ye are?"

Attaching specific tartans to specific clans was one of Sir Walter Scott's brainbrats. Lucinda loved the blue and green Black Watch plaid that marked the MacOwen family as part of the Campbell clan, but she hadn't had leisure to commit all the other distinctive weaves to memory yet. Brodie, for whom time was no object, obviously had.

"Who?" she hissed again.

"Who, who, who? Fancy yourself a wee owlet, do ye?" Aileen said. "Patience, sister. I'm sure Lord Bonniebroch will make himself known to ye."

The man in the red kilt paraded by and the crowd surged forward to get a closer look. Kilts had been outlawed since 1746, so this one excited much notice. Lucinda only wished a finer figure of a man was wearing it.

Brodie's grip tightened on her shoulder. Then before Lucinda could stop him, he propelled her forward, shoving her between Lady Beaton and Lady Dalrymple. Aileen's shawl slipped from her shoulders. The thick velvet cording that nominally held back the crowd didn't impede her momentum one tiddly bit. She stumbled forward onto the scarlet carpet, a blur of blue and red tartan and a pair of shiny black boots filling her vision.

Then at the last moment before she would have landed with a splat on the wet wool, a pair of strong arms snatched her up. She was yanked back upright and clasped to a chest so muscular she could feel the hardness and strength of it even through the layers of clothing separating them.

"Alexander, my lad. Found a lass already, I see," the dark-haired gentleman chided. "Why am I not surprised? Women in London throw themselves at you with regularity. This Scottish miss undershot the mark a bit, but you seem to have the matter well in hand."

Lucinda's cheeks burned with embarrassment as the gentleman erupted with laughter. She looked up into the face of her rescuer. It was that impossibly handsome Englishman.

If only she could melt away into one of the standing puddles, she'd never ask for another thing in all her life.

> *"Romance is all well and good if one is reading Ivanhoe, but put not your trust in a man's fair words. The informed daughter of Eve insures that the particulars of her marriage contract are spelled out in indelible ink."*
>
> From *The Knowledgeable Ladies' Guide to Eligible Gentlemen*

Chapter Two

"My friend Clarindon exaggerates. You're the first woman to *literally* throw herself at me." The man's chest rumbled with a deep baritone as he looked down at her with amusement. "Is it a Scottish custom or is this charming welcome particular to you?"

"Neither," Lucinda managed to squeak.

Brodie latched onto her hem and it billowed along with him in the stiff breeze. She swatted at her skirts, trying to tamp them down.

Is it possible for a body to die of shame?

She'd have been better off if the fine man had let her land face first on the soggy ceremonial runner. At least then she wouldn't be all atingle at the way her breasts were pressed against the hard planes of his chest. In fact, all of her was flush against his body, with the tips of her toes barely brushing the ground.

"You're trembling," the Englishman said, the teasing light leaving his eyes. They were the gunmetal gray of the North Sea before a storm. "Are you quite well?"

He lowered her to stand on her own two feet but kept hold of her. A tingle raced about her ribs like a caged squirrel.

She ought to pull away. She ought to deliver a stinging cut direct. The man was *English,* for pity's sake.

She could only stand there and look up at him, trying not to let her mouth gape like a codfish.

"She'll no' be needin' assistance from the likes o' ye, MacGregor," Brodie growled.

The man gave no sign of having heard Brodie. He covered one of Lucinda's hands, which was resting on his chest, with his. Warmth flooded her entire body, clear to the soles of her feet.

"You aren't hurt, are you?" His eyes darkened with concern.

"I've suffered no hurt but to me pride." Lucinda managed to slip out of his embrace and tried to collect herself. It was difficult when he didn't release her hand. His grip was firm and comforting and a wicked part of her didn't particularly want him to let go. "I was jostled by the crowd, milord. If I startled ye, ye have my deepest apologies. Someone pushed me, I fear."

She shot a poisonous glare over her shoulder at Brodie. The ghost released her hem, letting her gown settle to earth, and clapped a spectral hand on her elbow instead. Lucinda's glare melted into panic as, through Brodie's hazy form, she saw the man in the red kilt turn and stride back toward them.

"What is the meaning of this?" the kilted man said, giving Lucinda a slow perusal.

She was wearing her best gown save for the one she planned to don for her wedding. She'd thought the pale blue muslin especially fine and well-suited to her coloring, but the man's curled lip made her feel a hopeless rustic. Then he flicked his gaze to the handsome fellow.

"Lord. Alexander. Mallory." He spit out each word as if it were an unwanted seed stuck between his teeth. "Trust you to disturb our progression."

"The rest of the world continues unimpeded, Rankin," Lord Alexander said. "It appears I've only disturbed you."

Alexander Mallory. Is there a lovelier name in all God's creation?

Rankin cast a dark frown at her hand in Lord Alexander's, startling Lucinda out of her bumfuzzled musings. Her cheeks flared with heat again. She pulled her hand free and crossed her arms over her chest in indignation.

"A gentleman's timely reflexes can hardly be named a disturbance, milord," she said, a little vinegar slipping into her tone. "Lord Alexander merely saved me from a quick tumble."

"Have a care then, Mistress," said Rankin with a leer. "For a *quick tumble* is one of the things Mallory excels in, I'm told."

The crowd around them sniggered.

Lucinda rarely disliked anyone at first sight, but she decided she'd make an exception for Lord Rankin.

A light mist began to fall again and she shivered. Lord Alexander must have noticed, for he removed his jacket and draped it over her shoulders. The wool carried some of his warmth with it.

"I'd introduce you to Lord Rankin, miss," he said. "But unfortunately, though I managed to catch you, I failed to catch your name."

"It's Lucinda." She dipped in a small curtsey. "Lucinda MacOwen."

"Not just Lucinda MacOwen an' it please ye," Aileen interrupted, dragging Mary behind her as she pushed into the circle of onlookers that tightened around Lucinda and the two English lords. "My elder sister will be Lady Bonniebroch within a week, so she will."

Lord Rankin arched a wiry brow at Alexander Mallory. "Indeed? This must be a record, even for you. Not five minutes in Scotland and already you've acquired a fiancée. Surely a coterie of mistresses cannot be far behind."

I must be hearing things. Lucinda edged away from Lord Alexander. Being near him made her a bit light-headed. Nearly falling at his feet was bad enough. A swoon would mark her as hopeless.

"I fear there's been a misunderstanding, Lord Rankin. My intended isn't Lord Alexander." *More's the pity.* "My betrothed is Lord Bonniebroch."

The crowd of Englishmen around her laughed again, but Alexander Mallory paled visibly.

"We'll leave you to sort out this *misunderstanding,* then," Rankin said to Mallory. He cast a calculating gaze over Lucinda and both her sisters. "But our quarters at Dalkeith could no doubt benefit from additional local ornamentation. Mistress MacOwen, you and your charming sisters will join us at the palace as guests for the duration of our stay."

Lucinda and her sisters dipped in low curtseys, murmuring their awed thanks. Perhaps she'd been hasty in her estimation of Lord Rankin. Never in all her livin' life, did Lucy MacOwen dream of the honor of sleeping beneath the same roof that would house a king come next summer.

Even if it was an English king.

"If I'd thought it would get me an invitation to Dalkeith, I'd have launched myself at the man too," Lady Beaton whispered to Lady Dalrymple.

"Our guests will no doubt require transportation," Lord Rankin said, snapping his fingers at Alexander Mallory and baring his teeth in an expression no one would mistake for a smile. "Oh, I beg your pardon, Mallory. I've been remiss in not calling you by your new Scottish title. See to the ladies' comfort, if you please, my Lord *Bonniebroch*."

"But ye're *English*." Lucinda MacOwen managed to make being English sound worse than if he carried the plague.

"Guilty as charged," Alexander said. He narrowly resisted the urge to swear at Rankin's retreating back. How was he to ferret out Radicals if he was saddled with this addlepated chit and her sisters?

Undoubtedly, that was Rankin's aim. He routinely cut out anyone who managed to insinuate themselves into Lord Liverpool's inner circle like a sheepdog culling the herd. If Alex failed here in Scotland, he might never be called upon to serve the prime minister again.

As a second son, he wasn't encouraged to make much of himself. His father's estate was flush enough to support a dozen dilettante dependents. A military career would have been appropriate, but Alexander's distinguished service in the military was what brought him to the prime minister's attention in the first place. Alex had earned a reputation for getting things done, devil take the hindermost. Lord Liverpool needed men like him.

If Alex didn't have this clandestine work, he'd be stuck in London dancing attendance on the latest crop of debutantes or wasting his allowance in gaming hells.

Without purpose, he'd go mad. Something rather frowned upon in his family.

It was deucedly inconsiderate of the previous Lord Bonniebroch to fail to mention that he was engaged to marry a woman he'd obviously never even met. He glanced around hoping to see MacMartin on the dock, but the fellow had made himself scarce.

Lucinda MacOwen was a tempting armful, but from the way she gawked up at him openmouthed, it was obvious she was a bit balmy as well. Alexander made it a point of honor to avoid women who were a peck short of a bushel.

"I dinna understand. You're English . . . and yet you're Lord Bonniebroch," she sputtered. The rest of the crowd flowed around them in Lord Rankin's wake as if they were a pair of stones in a stream.

"So it would appear," he said, cupping her elbow to guide her through the throng. Her sisters trotted behind them, cheerful as spaniels.

"Remember what I said, Lucinda," one of her sisters sang out. "I'll no' have ye sacrificin' yourself on my account. I stand ready to honor the word of Erskine MacOwen and—"

"Hush, Aileen," Miss MacOwen snapped, and then she turned back to Alexander, a tremulous smile tugging at her peachy lips. "'Tis honored I am to meet ye in truth now, my lord, though the manner of it was less than dignified."

"The story of how you two met will make an amusing tale for your grandchildren one day, I shouldn't wonder," Clarindon said at Alexander's other elbow. "Come, your lordship, allow me to introduce myself to your betrothed."

Alexander shot him a glare that ought to have reduced him to a bubbling puddle of suet. The girl was bad enough without Clarindon encouraging her in this fantasy of an engagement.

"Sir Bertram Clarindon, at your service." Clarindon made an obeisance over her proffered fingertips and pronounced himself "charmed."

"These are my sisters, Misses Aileen and Mary MacOwen, sir." Lucinda's voice was pleasingly low and musical, but Alexander steeled himself against the growing attraction he felt for her.

He didn't have time for this sort of complication.

"Well, ladies, I'm sure you must have simply boatloads of trunks and portmanteaus that will need to be transported to Dalkeith Palace," Clarindon said. "Shall we hail a cab and see about collecting your effects?"

"Leith isna London, Sir Bertram. We can walk to our great-aunt's home from here quite handily. 'Tis on the next street but one," Miss MacOwen said, nodding in the direction they should proceed. Then she slanted a gaze at Alexander. Her green eyes were quite lovely and her nose had an appealing upward tilt. "I hope Aunt Hester will give ye a fair welcome, my lord."

"My lord? Why stand on such ceremony, Miss MacOwen?" Clarindon grinned hugely as he offered his arms to both the younger MacOwen sisters. "As his betrothed, you ought to call him Alexander, I should think. At least until you find a suitable sobriquet for him. I understand Lady Wattleston refers to her husband as 'His Muchness' and he calls her his 'soft little rabbit.' Isn't that too precious for words?"

"A few come to mind," Alexander said darkly. *But none that bear repeating in feminine company.*

He narrowed his eyes at his friend and Clarindon wisely decided that discretion was the better part of valor. As they walked on, Bertram confined himself to observations on the weather and the coming Christmastide festivities.

Her slender hand resting lightly on his forearm, Lucinda MacOwen was still blushing to the roots of her red hair. Alexander wondered if it was "His Muchness" or "soft little rabbit" that brought out the flaming color. In any case, she didn't say another thing until they reached a venerable gray stone house that listed only slightly toward its easterly neighbor.

"This is the home of my great-aunt, Hester Mac-Gibbon." Miss MacOwen's mouth tightened in a half-apologetic grimace. "She'll no' be expecting to learn ye're English."

She made *English* sound as if it were the culmination of the Seven Deadlies.

"Or that ye're a MacGregor, come to that." She looked askance at his plaid.

MacGregor fared only slightly better than *English* as she spat the word out.

"This?" He ran a hand over the plaid draped on his shoulder. "My mother's maiden name was Mac-Gregor. That's all."

Most of the men at court had scrambled to fetch up some sort of Scottish connection so they could indulge in King George's kilted pageantry. Alexander would have been happy to loan them his. And the connection that came with it.

"It seems I'm both English and Scottish," he said. "If either of those attributes are an impediment to our betrothal, we can—"

"No, no." Her eyes flared in alarm. "I'm sure Aunt Hester will come round." She ushered him through the faded green door. "Eventually."

As the party crowded into the MacGibbon home's small vestibule, Alexander noticed no servant appeared to welcome them, or even to inquire after their business. If they'd been a gang of ruffians bursting into the house with mayhem on their minds, there was no one to say them nay.

"Weel, did ye see the English envoys?" A voice like the scrape of a fingernail on slate called from an adjacent parlor. "Their leader is a fat, wee toad of a man, is he no'? Told ye, I did. Got it from Lady Kilgore who met Lord Rankin herself once in Londontown when she was a slip of a girl and he a spotty-faced boy from Eton. People dinna change that much o'er the years. Might've saved yerselves a drenching, but ye wouldna listen."

Miss MacOwen cast Alexander a self-deprecating grimace and turned to her sisters. "Hie yourselves upstairs to pack. I'll introduce Lord Bonniebroch and Sir Bertram to Aunt Hester and be with ye directly."

Aileen and Mary disappeared up the stairs with a rustle of petticoats and flurry of skirts.

"Dinna stand there dripping on the threshold, ye wee ninnies," the scraping voice came again, more strident this time. "Catch yer death, ye will and ye'll no' see me shed a tear. Nary a one, because I told ye so and ye wouldna heed me. Now, trundle yerselves in here."

On second thought, perhaps not having servants for security was no hardship, Alex decided. Knowledgeable ruffians undoubtedly gave Hester Mac-Gibbon a wide berth.

Alexander followed Miss MacOwen into the dimly lit parlor. Heavily swathed in a lap rug and shawl, an old woman was cocooned in a cushioned chair near the smoky peat fire. Her face was the color of candle wax and seemed to have melted like one as well. Heavy jowls dripped onto her neck and the skin beneath them was crumpled as a crepe funeral wreath. She turned her head toward them, that slight movement the only indication that the wrinkled flesh bundled in wool was still alive. Pale eyes that might once have been blue narrowed in speculation when her gaze fell on Alexander and Clarindon.

"Ye'll never guess who we met at the ship, Auntie," Miss MacOwen said, forced cheerfulness making her voice tight.

"Ye silly girl, ye met these two eejits, o' course. I may be old, but I'm no' blind, ye know."

"She's really quite precious once ye get to know her," Miss MacOwen whispered.

"And I'm no' deaf either," Aunt Hester said, threading the tasseled ends of the shawl through her gnarled fingers. "May the devil come to claim me on the day I count myself 'precious.' Now tell me why ye've darkened me door with the likes of yon MacGregor. Ye know I've no truck with such."

"He's no' a MacGregor. Weel, he's no' *only* a MacGregor," Miss MacOwen said, bending to straighten the lap rug over the old woman's knees. "He's also laird of Bonniebroch." She looked at him with such a winsome smile, Alexander's chest constricted. "My betrothed."

"About that," Alexander said. He'd as soon whip a pup with a newspaper as dash a lady's hopes, but the quicker he put paid to this ridiculous notion of a betrothal the better. "I fear there's been a terrible mistake."

"Oh, aye?" Aunt Hester's brows wriggled like a pair of wooly caterpillars meeting over her bulbous nose.

"Aye—I mean yes." It irritated him how quickly Scottish-isms sprang to his lips. He'd always tried to distance himself from his Gaelic side, but it poked out its head with disturbing frequency. "You see, I have only just become Lord Bonniebroch. I won the title from the previous owner, Sir Darren MacMartin, in a fair game of chance. As I was not informed of this . . . arrangement, doubtless the original Bonniebroch intends to honor his agreement," Alexander

explained. "Surely MacMartin is the one to whom
Miss MacOwen is betrothed."

In the silence that followed, Alexander was aware
of the loud tick of the long case clock in the hall,
the hissing gasses escaping from the peat fire, and
the sharp intake of breath from Miss MacOwen.

"Weel, we'll just see about that, shall we?" The old
woman's features contorted into an alarming expression Alexander feared might be an attempt at a
smile. "Lucinda, trot ye back to the kitchen and
fetch some refreshments for the gentlemen. Tea and
bannocks, I'm thinkin' and a tot of rum for me. Rheumatism, ye know."

She held out her twisted fingers for Alexander's
inspection, but he suspected she'd have the rum re-
gardless of his opinion of her need for it.

"But before ye go, lamb," Aunt Hester said to
Lucinda, "be a dear and take the key from me neck.
Do ye unlock the desk and bring me the copy of the
marriage contract. We'll sort this out, aye?"

Alexander had stood before a French brigade
without cowering. He'd slipped behind enemy lines
and liberated battle plans from a general's own tent
while the man slept on his cot. Once he'd planned
and executed a successful jailbreak in time to save
one of the king's cousins from an ignominious
hanging in France.

No one doubted his courage.

But the way in which Hester MacGibbon said
"marriage contract" made Alexander's balls tighten
and try to climb back up into his body for protection.

* * *

Oh, God, he doesna want me. Lucinda's belly coiled in knots as she fled the simmering turmoil in the parlor for the homey safety of the kitchen.

Aunt Hester had let all her servants go on holiday when Lucy and her sisters arrived in Edinburgh. The old skinflint thought to save a little money by putting her great-nieces to work instead. For once, Lucinda was grateful there was no one else in the kitchen. It meant there was no one to whom she'd have to explain her glistening eyes and high color. She lit a fire in the cast-iron stove and filled the kettle at the sink, working the pump handle with ferocity.

Once she set the kettle to boil, Lucinda reached into her pocket and pulled out the book she'd picked up in a shop off Leicester Square when she'd visited London with her father. It was a silly extravagance. Books were so very dear, but she couldn't resist using the last of her pin money for this one. She ran her fingertips over the title.

The Knowledgeable Ladies' Guide to Eligible Gentlemen.

She flipped immediately to the "M's" and located the information about Alexander Mallory.

"Lord Alexander Mallory, b. 1794. Second son of the Marquis of Maldren," she read silently.

He'll have more than two coins to rub together, I'll be bound.

Lucinda shook her head. No good could come from imagining more about the fellow. Hadn't he already made it apparent that he didn't want her?

There was no point to reading on, but she couldn't help herself.

"Near the top of every marriage-minded mama's short list of eligibles, Lord Alexander's name occupies a well-deserved spot. He is courtly, quick of wit, and has an excellent seat on a horse. The excellent seat of his trousers is not to be lightly dismissed either."

Lucinda's cheeks heated. She hadn't encountered listings of such an earthy bent before this when she leafed through the guidebook. But the creeping blush didn't make her stop reading.

"When Lord Alexander sets himself to charm, any woman in his path will be hard-pressed not to be swept along by his dangerous allure."

Lucinda could testify to that. The man had quite taken her breath away. Thank heaven his less remarkable friend was there, too. Sir Bertram Clarindon was a comfortable sort.

Still, her gaze was drawn back to the guide for more information about the decidedly *uncomfortable* Lord Alexander.

"However, the young Mallory has never, to this observer's certain knowledge, debauched a virgin or ruined an otherwise reputable widow. That in itself is hearty commendation for someone so closely attached to the dissolute court of King George IV."

Not having debauched a virgin or ruined a widow is setting the bar for good behavior rather low. Seems they're damning him with faint praise.

But it didn't stop her from reading on.

"Well-informed readers will recall the unpleasantness about his mother years ago, but in truth, the least said about that, the better. Neither of the marquis's sons has shown any propensity for madness. Lord Alexander may be safely regarded a thorough catch by one and all."

Madness in the family is no impediment, eh? I wonder

what it would take for The Ladies' Guide to Eligible Gentlemen *to disqualify someone.*

Then Lucinda's gaze fell on the last line of the entry.

"However, Lord Alexander shows no signs of allowing himself to be caught."

"That he doesna." She closed the book with a snap. "No' even when he's presented with a legal betrothal."

Her chest had swelled with bewildered happiness when she learned the fine lad she'd admired turned out to be her betrothed. A small candle of hope flickered in her heart. Now that he claimed the betrothal was a mistake, that flame was completely guttered. She leaned against the sink, bracing herself with both arms to keep from collapsing to the stone floor.

"No' just a mistake. A *terrible* mistake, he says." A small sob escaped her throat as she swiped away an angry tear.

"Now, now, lassie, ye ought no' to cry. No' over the likes of a MacGregor," Brodie MacIver said, hovering comfortably above the plate rail that ringed the small room near the ceiling.

"What makes you think I'm crying over him?" she hissed.

"Are ye forgettin' how well I ken yer mind?"

"'Tis apparent I've sought your counsel too often over the years, but I'll no' be needin' it the now. I'll thank ye to tend to your own business, Brodie."

"Fine. Have it yer way, lass. I'll just nip back into the parlor and scare the living lights out of the lad. He'll no' be makin' ye cry again if I have anythin' to say about it."

"Ye'll do no such thing."

"Ye wish me to tend to me own business." Brodie sank

down from his reclining position near the ceiling, coming to rest with the soles of his booted feet almost, but not quite, touching the flagstones. His belted plaid billowed in a nonexistent breeze. *"Seein' to yer protection is the only business I have."*

Lucinda turned from him to arrange fresh bannocks on a plate, lest he see what his support meant to her. Brodie had made no secret of the fact that he wanted her match to fail, but his devotion to her was a balm to her bruised spirit in any case. She'd have hugged him if such a thing were possible with a ghost.

However, for her family's sake, Lu had to find a way to go forward with the marriage. Her father desperately needed the financial settlement specified in the contract. Lucinda's elevation to "her ladyship" would increase her sisters' chances for good matches. And most especially, Dougal might be saved from a hemp necktie by virtue of this union. The marriage *must* proceed, whether she had a willing bridegroom or not.

Whether her ghostly protector approved or not.

"Hear me well, Brodie MacIver," she said softly. It wouldn't do for anyone to catch her talking to herself in the kitchen. A body could get a reputation for being touched in the head in short order. "Ye'll no' show yourself to Lord Bonniebroch. Ye'll no' set his boots afire nor send your cold breath down the back of his neck. If I hear ye've played even one of your fox's tricks on him, I'll . . . I'll—"

"Ye'll what?" Brodie swirled around her, his bearded face gleaming with smugness. *"No' much ye can threaten a ghost with, is there? I'm already deid, ye ken."*

"If ye haunt Lord Bonniebroch," she said evenly, "I'll never speak to ye again."

Brodie stopped circling and paled whiter than his usual spectral self.

"Ye wouldna."

"Try me."

Brodie pressed his lips tightly together and steam spewed out his ears. To someone who didn't know him well, it would have seemed a horrendous sight. Lucinda merely arched a bored brow.

"Dinna think to scare me with a tantrum," Lucinda said tartly as she poured up a bit of rum for her aunt. "If ye wish my good opinion of ye to continue, help me instead. What am I to do to make Lord Bonniebroch take a liking to me?"

Brodie grumbled under his breath about ungrateful wenches and their persnickety ways as he floated back up to the ceiling again and made a slow circuit of the room.

"'Tis no' that there's anything wrong with ye, ye ken. Ye're a right fetching lassie. Even yon dunderheid in the parlor canna keep his eyes off ye."

She looked up at him in surprise.

"Oh, aye, a lass might take no' notice, but a man can tell when another fellow fancies a girl."

Lord Bonniebroch didn't fancy her. He'd all but rejected her entirely. "Ye're no' a man, Brodie. No' any more. Ye dinna ken what ye're talking about."

"But I was a man. And some things dinna die with the rest. I tell ye, yon Lord Bonniebroch may be fightin' on the hook but the way he looks at ye when ye dinna see . . ."

"What about it?"

"Let's just say 'tis a look filled with imagination."

"Imagination?"

"Aye. Ofttimes a woman's best asset is a man's imagination and yon laddie is imagining ye fit to burst."

Lucinda considered this astounding idea as she fetched some clotted cream for the bannocks and milk for the tea from the cool larder. "Imagining me doing what?"

"Doin' most anything long as ye're bare as an egg whilst ye're doin' it."

"Brodie MacIver! I'll thank ye to keep a civil tongue in your head. I'm sure Lord Bonniebroch thinks of no such thing."

The ghost made a derisive sound. If he'd been alive, Lucinda would have been hard-pressed to guess which end of him it issued from.

"If he doesna fancy seein' ye parade around in naught but yer skin, then he's no' much of a man. Answer me honest, lass. Can ye tell me truly ye havena wondered what he looks like beneath his blasted MacGregor plaid?"

Heat crept up her neck and flamed her cheeks. What was hidden under Alexander Mallory's plaid-swathed jacket and tight-fitting trousers *had* tickled her imagination even before she learned he was her intended. She turned her attention back to the tray and furiously rearranged the napkins.

"If, as ye claim, he's doing this imagining about me, why is he trying to cry off on our betrothal?"

"That I dinna ken, but 'tis no' because he doesna like ye. Part of him likes ye fine."

Lucinda sighed. She knew she ought not to hope for anything more in an arranged match, but mere liking seemed such a pale imitation of what she really craved.

Love. Ungovernable. Overturning. All-else-be-damned love.

Finding it in a union with Lord Bonniebroch

seemed as unlikely a prospect as sprouting a pair of wings.

"How do I make certain he sticks to his word and honors the contract?"

"Have no fear. Yer aunt will see to that." Brodie shivered, his diaphanous form shimmering in the air. *"No man can stand before that auld dragon."*

"That's no good." She'd steeled herself to bear a loveless marriage, but one with an unwilling bridegroom was beyond her comprehension. "I'll no' force the man to the altar."

"A lass doesna have to force a man to marry her. She only has to torment him into it."

"Torment him? That sounds lovely. Shall I sharpen the pruning shears and snip away at him then?"

"Nay, lass. If he were no' a cursed MacGregor, I'd tell ye to flirt with him like a little tart. Ye need only tease and please and drive the man wild with kisses and—" Brodie stopped himself. *"But he is a MacGregor and therefore ye ought no' to sully yerself with his ilk. Forget what I said about flirting and—"*

"Too late." Lucinda picked up the tray and headed back toward the parlor. She'd already thrown herself into the man's arms once.

How hard could it be to do again?

"On the subject of masculine fashion, we aver this truth. If one wishes to know what's truly on a man's mind, even skin-hugging knee britches, such as those worn at Almack's, are a poor second when compared to a Scotsman's kilt. However, close attention to a man's trousers can prove most illuminating to the knowledgeable lady who uses the eyes God gave her."

From *The Knowledgeable Ladies' Guide to Eligible Gentlemen*

Chapter Three

"And so ye see," Hester MacGibbon said with a shake of her bulldoggish jowls, "the contract is duly signed and notarized right here."

"But that's not my signature," Alexander protested.

"Are ye no' laird of Bonniebroch?" she asked.

"Well, yes, but—"

"That's how the contract was signed. Lord Bonniebroch. Plain as the nose on yer face. It doesna signify a flibbet what yer Christian name might be. Only yer title and ye've already admitted to that."

"She has a point," Clarindon put in unhelpfully.

"But a marriage contract cannot be enforced between an unnamed woman and a title."

At least, not in England. Scotland was undoubtedly another matter. Alexander paced the room, nervous energy crackling off him. As an unattached covert agent, he was prepared to take risks a married man would shun. There was no place in his life for a wife. It wasn't safe, for him or the lady.

"This is no' a private agreement, ye ken. 'Tis more like . . . two goin' concerns joining forces with the added blessing of a Christmastide wedding thrown in," Hester said.

Lucinda MacOwen glided into the parlor then, her kid-soled slippers making soft swishes on the threadbare carpet. Without a glance at Alexander, she set the tray on a low table, served her aunt the tot of rum, and settled before the tea service to pour out.

"How will ye be takin' your tea, Sir Bertram?" she asked with a smile of such luminous glory, it nearly took Alexander's breath away. She certainly hadn't smiled like that at him. Winsome, hopeful smiles, yes, but nothing like this dazzling display. He forced himself to look elsewhere, but his gaze kept returning to Lucinda MacOwen's graceful white hands as they fluttered over the tea things.

Clarindon told her he preferred tea with milk and made appreciative noises over the fresh bannocks. The fact that she gave preference to his friend by serving him first was not lost on Alex, but he supposed he *had* injured her feelings rather badly. After all Clarindon's needs were met, Lucinda MacOwen finally turned her attention to him.

The smile that had been an expression of unabashed pleasure and welcome became brittle. "One lump or two?"

He wondered if she were thinking of lumps she'd rather deliver to his head instead of the sort that would sweeten his tea. On the off chance she'd had time to add a bit of hemlock to the brown clumps of sugar, he decided to err on the side of caution and asked for his tea without embellishment.

Hester MacGibbon quaffed her rum with a satisfied slurp. Then once she upended her glass, she leaned forward and resumed her lecture on the finer points of Scottish law.

"So the main consideration is this, my lord. It matters no' a morsel what ye may call yerself whilst ye're on English soil," Hester MacGibbon said. "Ye accepted the mantle of Bonniebroch with all the benefits and encumbrances thereto. Here in Scotland ye be Lord Bonniebroch and as such, ye're betrothed to me great-niece. Many is the man that would count himself fortunate to ally with a sept of the Campbell clan, though I'll admit the fact that ye're a MacGregor means we'll have to hold our noses to see the pair of ye wed. Still, a contract's a contract and there's an end to it. We'll hold up our end of the matter."

"Might we continue this discussion privately, Mrs. MacGibbon?" Alexander cast a glance in Lucinda MacOwen's direction. He didn't want to wound her again if he could help it.

"Why? As this touches on Lucinda's future, she has every right to be present."

The girl smiled at him again, a different sort of smile this time. She turned her head in a feline tilt, for all the world like a tabby eyeing a mouse hole.

"As I've need to learn my intended's mind about things, I see no reason to betake myself elsewhere."

"Very well. Since my being a MacGregor is so distasteful to you, surely we can come to a mutually satisfactory agreement to void the contract," Alexander said, wincing inwardly at having to say such things before his nominal bride. He wasn't used to being such a lout.

"Certainly, ye may void the contract an' ye wish to," Hester MacGibbon said with every appearance of affability. "There's a provision that stipulates how the contract may be broken. The party wishing to do so merely forfeits all his holdings to the other party."

"That might be agreeable," Alexander said. He'd wondered how to divest himself of the Scottish estate once he no longer needed it. The least he could do for the jilted girl was gift her with Bonniebroch.

"Are ye no' hearin' me, lad? *All* yer holdings, both here, and in England and wherever else ye may have property or interest in moneymaking ventures of any kind."

"Oh," Alex said slowly. As a second son, he wasn't heir to the marquisate, but his father had settled several unentailed properties on him and through his own industry, he owned half the shares in a fleet of three merchant ships. Even though his needs were small while he remained in the service of his country, he couldn't in good conscience walk away from the private wealth he'd amassed.

"I can see ye've had a bit of a ponder on that point and come round to my way of thinking," Hester said, approvingly. "It's a wise man as knows when to quit a losing position. There may be hope for ye yet."

Lucinda studied the tea set as if she'd never seen the like before. Her lips were clamped in a hard line, her cheeks florid. The girl was quietly livid and Alexander couldn't blame her.

"Miss MacOwen," he said. "We've started out on the wrong boot. Allow me to make amends. Of course, you and your family will be welcome to stay at Bonniebroch after the king's envoy returns to London. That way, you and I can get acquainted with a nice long engagement."

Twenty years or so should do the trick.

"Oh, aye, take all the time ye like." Hester gave a cackling laugh. "The wedding's no' set to take place till Christmas Day. Check the contract. Ye'll find it spelled out nicely. But dinna worrit. A man and a maid can ken quite a bit about each other in a short time. I advise ye to get started whilst I see what those other two wee ninnies are about. Come wi' me, Sir Bertram, and we'll see if an Englishman can haul down a Scottish lassie's trunk without damaging either himself or the baggage."

The old woman levered her bulk out of the chair and moved ponderously across the room. Clarindon, the traitor, followed in her wake, as eager to please as a blasted lapdog.

Once they were gone, silence descended on the parlor like a shroud. Alexander had always prided himself on being able to negotiate the rounds of small talk that passed for brilliance with members of the ton, but for the life of him, he could think of nothing appropriate for this occasion.

What did one say to an unwanted bride?

Fortunately, she didn't seem upset by the silence, though she was looking distractedly beyond his left ear instead of meeting his gaze. Then her eyes flared in alarm and she jumped to her feet. He glanced over his shoulder, sure from the sudden panic in her face that someone was stalking his unprotected back with a drawn blade, but there was no one there.

"Will ye be pleased to take a turn in the garden with me, my lord?" she said, nearly tripping on the words in her haste to spill them over her tongue.

"Of course, but what about the rain?"

"'Tis likely ended, or about to start again. If we stayed indoors for every wee mist, we'd never have a breath of fresh air."

"Very well. Why not?" One place was as good as another for the soon-to-be-leg-shackled-for-life. Even if he dispatched a letter to London immediately, it wouldn't reach his solicitor in a timely fashion. He'd have to figure a way out of this betrothal on his own. Preferably one that didn't involve beggaring himself.

He offered Miss MacOwen his arm and she led him out of the room and down a corridor so narrow, his shoulder rubbed against the faded wallpaper on one side. Still, he was relieved to quit the stifling parlor and hopeful something suitably botanical would spring to his lips once they stepped outside.

"Are ye always this quiet then?" she asked as they pushed through the back door and into a small walled garden.

The rain had ceased and eased the sense of perpetual dampness. As befitted the home of a thrifty Scottish matron, most of the garden space was given over to herbaceous borders gone brown with the cold of December. A trio of rosebushes climbed a trellis in the far corner, the vines dry-leaved and prickly with forbidding-looking thorns.

"No' that I'm complainin', mind ye," she went on. "A quiet man is a restful man."

"I confess I've been rendered speechless by this turn of events," he said. "You must admit it isn't every day a man finds himself unexpectedly betrothed. Please don't take that as a slight, Miss MacOwen."

"And how should I take it?"

She was right. His behavior had been abominable, but he couldn't seem to stop saying the wrong things. Silence was the safest course.

She released his arm and strolled ahead of him a few paces on the meandering path. A rare ray of sunshine broke through the clouds and backlit her in its shining glory. The brisk breeze whipped her skirt against the curves of her calves and shapely thighs. At least his betrothed was a fetching bit of muslin. Part of him thought things could have been decidedly worse.

Then suddenly they were.

A man wearing a cutaway jacket was unable to disguise what might be occurring beneath his trousers. Alexander's tented rather obviously, making room for his growing bulge.

Damn. She'll think me a complete cur. Resisting an engagement was one thing. Doing it while sporting a raging cockstand was quite another.

There was a stone bench in the center of the garden and he made for it quickly, taking position behind the granite back that rose high enough to hide him from the waist down.

"Would you care to sit for a bit?" he asked.

She shrugged and came over to plop down on the

bench. Her slippered feet didn't quite reach the ground, so she hooked her ankles and let them swing back and forth with nervousness.

He began to regret asking her to sit. From this angle, he could see down her bodice into the shadowy hollow between her breasts. They were plump and sweet and likely to fit his palm to perfection. His body would never settle with this sort of feminine distraction so near.

"I wonder," he said, casting about for anything to fill the silence that yawned between them, "if this betrothal isn't a bit easier for you than for me."

"Why should it be easier for me?" She crossed her arms, pressing her breasts together and deepening the cleft between them. Alexander ground his teeth, but couldn't drag his gaze away. "D'ye think I want to be saddled with a man I didna even ken?"

"No, I suppose not, but at least you knew you were betrothed." He moved around the bench and sat down. If he leaned forward, elbows on his knees, his arousal should be less obvious. "When I won Bonniebroch from its previous owner, I had no idea you'd come with it."

"Read the contract, my lord," she said in a biting tone. "Ye're also getting a prize Blackface ram."

He chuckled. "Well, that makes all the difference in the world."

She obviously didn't find that as absurdly funny as he did, for she shot him a searing glance and then looked away.

"This is every bit as difficult for me as ye," she said. "I might've had another beau, ye ken."

"Do you?" If she was pining for a Highlander somewhere, perhaps Alexander could convince *her* to negate the contract. His problems would be over. He'd even foreswear the clause that forfeited her family's wealth to him if that was what kept her from balking.

"That's no' the issue. Even if I did have a beau, I have two more sisters. Ye could take yer pick between Aileen and Mary in that case." She turned to him and he felt himself in danger of tumbling into her green eyes again. He couldn't decide if those shaded glens were a balm for the soul or a hideaway for bandits. "That's no' a bad idea. Would ye fancy one of my sisters, then? I'll be pleased to step aside, if that's the case."

As if he needed another way to wound her. "No, I don't fancy one of your sisters."

"Is it that ye dinna like women, then? I've heard whispers of such men, but never did I think to meet one."

Indignation made his hackles rise.

"Trust me, I like women." He was tempted to unfasten his trousers and show her just how much he liked women. Her delectable form especially, at the moment.

"I simply didn't intend to marry . . ." *ever,* he finished silently. Now to avoid it, he'd have to find a quick husband for not only Lucinda, but both her sisters. It was a daunting prospect, but not impossible. He latched onto the idea as the only hopeful one he'd had all morning.

"Ye dinna want to wed at all?"

"I'm counted young for it still." He was not yet thirty, but the depth of his pockets meant he could well afford a wife if he wanted one.

"Ye seem old enough to me." She folded her hands

in her lap, lacing her fingers so tight, her knuckles whitened. Alex was trained to notice minute ticks, small tells of deception or subterfuge. Lucinda might try to project an image of calm, but she was like a duck, skimming lightly over the surface of the pond with hardly a ripple and all the while paddling furiously underneath. "Perhaps ye feel guilty over winning Bonniebroch in a game of chance."

"No, poque is more skill than chance." For better or worse, he'd earned his new Scottish title.

"So ye fancy yourself a knowledgeable betting man. Perhaps ye'd care to make another wager then, based on something else in which ye may be skilled," she said.

"What do you have in mind?"

"I told ye I didna have a beau. In fact, I've never had one. Many a gentleman caller, o' course, but none I cared to keep. In fact, I've never even been kissed."

Alex snorted. "Perhaps *you* don't like *men*."

A russet brow arched. "I like men fine. But I'm particular, ye ken. I'm no' one to be had for a little light wooing."

His curiosity, along with other parts of him, was thoroughly piqued about what it might take to have her. "What's the wager then?"

"I'm fair peeved with ye now, milord, what with ye no' wantin' to wed me." She leaned toward him. "I think it would take considerable skill on your part for ye to convince me to allow ye a kiss."

A smile tugged his lips. Nothing could be simpler. "What stakes will you wager?"

"How about me brooch?" She fingered the ivory cameo at her left shoulder.

"You rate yourself too cheaply. That's not nearly enough for your first kiss." He eyed her mouth and was reminded again of a ripe peach. He'd bet it was as sweet as one too. How had she gone unkissed this long?

"What would ye consider a fair penalty should I lose then?" she asked.

"Actually," he said, an idea for finding her an alternate bridegroom taking root in his mind, "I'd hate to think we'll be wed without you having anyone with which to compare me. If I win this little wager, I expect you to kiss two, no, three other men between now and our wedding day."

All he'd have to do was make sure she was caught kissing someone else by a busybody tongue-wagger and the ensuing scandal would break the engagement for him. Lucinda MacOwen would be shuffled off to the preacher with the other man she'd kissed quicker than she could say "Bonnie Prince Charlie."

Her lips quirked. "A most original penalty. I accept. And if I dinna allow ye to kiss me, what should ye forfeit?"

"How about ownership of that prize Blackface ram?"

"Done," she said in a businesslike tone. "A princely wager, sir. Grand Champion Black Watch Farrell Loromer has been the making of the MacOwen herd. My father once turned down two hundred pounds for him. Now, after offering me such a rich inducement not to succumb, how do ye propose to convince me to allow ye a kiss?"

Damn. He'd never considered that a sheep would be worth so much.

"You're thinking about this all wrong," he said. "A

kiss isn't a prize for a man's enjoyment only. A woman well-kissed is a thoroughly contented creature."

"Oh, aye?"

"Aye, I mean, yes." He was an Englishman, dammit. It shouldn't be so easy for his Scottish roots to pop out. "A kiss is more than the mere touch of two pairs of lips. It's sharing a breath. It's holding each other's souls."

Her lips parted softly. "Ye make it sound almost a sacrament."

"If it's done right, it almost is." He moved closer to her on the bench, one arm slung casually over the granite back.

"And I suppose ye know how to do it right."

"So I've been told." He leaned toward her.

She leaned toward him too, till their faces were a hand's breadth apart. Then she pulled back. "That's still no' enough for me to allow it."

"The question of who allows a kiss isn't really relevant. Both parties have to want it, need it, for a kiss to be truly magical. There's no allowing. A real kiss just happens."

"It catches a body unawares, then. Sort of like our betrothal, aye?"

"Aye." He didn't correct himself this time. *When in Scotland* . . .

He reached up to brush her cheek with his fingertips. She leaned, catlike, into his touch. Her eyelids fluttered closed, her lashes sooty crescents on her cheekbones. Alex thumbed her mouth and her jaw went slack, the warmth of her breath spilling onto his hand.

To his surprise, he ached to kiss her with a need that almost burned. He bent his head to capture her lips, but she gave herself a little shake and broke the spell. She scooted to the farthest end of the bench. Then she slanted him a gaze that dared him to try again.

"Magical kisses, ye say. Magic is for a child's bed-time story, Lord Bonniebroch, no' for adults fully grown such as we."

"Call me Alexander," he said.

"Not His Muchness?" she asked archly.

"Not until you've seen if I deserve it."

Her eyes flared and she flicked her gaze to his groin for the space of several heartbeats. It was as if she'd stroked him. He'd mistakenly thought he couldn't get any stiffer.

"A lass can make an educated guess, and it appears to me, ye're much of a muchness," she said coolly, as his trousers betrayed his roused state again. "Remember, I'm farm raised, Alexander. I may never have been kissed, but there's naught on a male frame as will shock me, be it on man or beast."

This Scottish girl was a constant surprise.

"I'm gratified to hear it. But back to magical kisses." He still needed to win this bet, so he moved over next to her. "Adults need magic more than chil-dren, you know."

"Adults fully grown," she repeated with another wicked glance at his lap.

His cock responded with a deep throb.

He'd started this day by winning a Scottish estate. Then this strange woman had all but flung herself into his arms, keeping him from his business of pro-viding an advance guard for the king's coming visit. And finally, as unlikely as it seemed, he found himself unexpectedly in possession of a fiancée. After a morning like that, any man would lose his temper over such unrelenting torment from said fiancée.

"All right, woman, do you want to hear it baldly? Yes, I want you. You're as tempting a young lady as I've ever run across and I'm fair bursting with the need to kiss you."

"Weel, then," she said, palming his cheeks. "Since ye put it like that . . . let's see if there be any magic between me and ye."

She closed the distance between them and before he knew what she was about, her lips brushed his. He didn't move as she gently explored his mouth.

He'd always avoided virgins, preferring the company of courtesans and ripe widows. Even as worldly as his other partners had been, none of them had kissed him first.

The sweetness of Lucinda's kiss made his soft palate ache to taste her more deeply. It was time for him to show her what a real kiss was. He palmed the back of her head, wrapped his other arm around her and drew her closer.

Alex traced the seam of her mouth with the tip of his tongue and she opened to him, warm, wet, and wonderful. Her hitching breaths made his balls ache. He swallowed her low groan of need as he stole the air from her lungs and replaced it with his own.

A shared breath. Holding each other's souls. Those words had been calculated to pique her curiosity. He never dreamed they might feel true.

He tongued her softly, letting her suckle him. Then he encouraged her to slip hers into his mouth as well. She teased him with it for a bit and in frustration, he showed her exactly why a French kiss was but a rough parody of another sort of joining. He thrust into her mouth in long strokes, his groin aching because only their mouths were so engaged.

Long before he was ready for the kiss to end, she pulled back and gazed up at him, wild-eyed. She rang the pointed tip of her tongue over her kiss-swollen top lip. Then she smiled.

A satisfied smile that told him somehow he'd been royally hoodwinked. He might have won the bet, but she'd make him regret it.

"Well, Your 'Much of a Muchness,' it appears I lose," she said. Her breaths still came in short gasps, but her eyes gleamed in triumph. "You'll still be in full possession of a Blackface ram once we wed and I get to kiss three more men before Christmas Day."

> "'Tis often said one never really knows a gentleman until one marries him. To remedy this, the uninformed might suggest that the bride should mark how her prospective bridegroom treats her family before the nuptials are celebrated and be either reassured or forewarned thereby. However, the knowledgeable lady understands a more reliable indicator of future husbandly behavior may be found in how the gentleman treats his horse."
>
> From *The Knowledgeable Ladies' Guide to Eligible Gentlemen*

Chapter Four

The sobbing never ended. Alexander stopped his ears, but he could still hear it. Whoever the woman was, she was beyond desperately unhappy. She keened like the biblical Rachael who would not be comforted because her children were no more.

He rose from his pallet and padded toward the sound, his bare feet cold. When he looked down at them, he saw that they were impossibly small, the feet of a child.

The woman sobbed louder.

If he could only find her, maybe he could make her stop. He climbed a curved set of stone stairs, the circular motion turning round and round in his head, all tangled up with *the rhythm of the sobs. The steps led to a corridor that stretched into the distance, dimly lit by a knife-thin blaze of light stabbing the stone floor under the closed door at the end.*

He trudged toward the arched door. The ceilings were so tall, disappearing into the shadows over his head. He'd have had to reach up to grasp the heavy iron latches on the closed doors he passed. He was a dwarf in a land of giants.

A man's voice growled from behind the last door, urging the woman to be quiet. Alexander stopped. He couldn't make out all the words, but the tone was one of undeniable authority. If the man couldn't make her stop weeping, what could Alex do?

He stood still, paralyzed with indecision. The weeping grew louder, echoing inside his own chest now. She was in such agony, he ached for her. No one should have to carry such grief.

Then suddenly the sobbing stopped. The door at the end of the hall swung wide and a bright light blinded him. But just before the world went startlingly white, the after-image of a man carrying a body slung over his shoulder was burned on the backs of Alexander's eyes.

Alex sucked in a hissed breath and was instantly awake. He sat up quickly and realized he wasn't in the strange hall near the weeping woman. He was in Hester MacGibbon's kitchen. The old lady had insisted he stay on with them in the interests of thrift, but she didn't truly have a bed for him. He'd stretched out on the pallet where her footman usually slept.

Could this strange dream be "the weeping woman" Sir Darren MacMartin warned him about?

The nightmare had been disturbing enough. Waking from it was almost worse. He felt helpless, frozen with anxiety. He couldn't do anything for the woman. Worse, he recognized the fear that had made him gasp when he woke.

Alex had felt that before. He hoped the fear was dream-induced too, but his memories of the distant time when his mother had left him were a jumbled mess. He wasn't sure what was a true memory and what was a dream.

It could be classified as a nightmare either way.

The sky outside the small window in the kitchen was lightening to a dirty gray. Alex lay back down and waited for his heart rate to return to normal.

He tried, without much success, to conjure his mother's face. He'd been four years old when she died, but she'd left him when he was much younger than that.

She'd had long dark hair. He remembered that clearly. He remembered the feel of it between his baby-fat fingers, the long strands curling around his childish fist. And the way she smelled, soft and powdery, sweetly infused with attar of roses and honeysuckle.

But he couldn't see her face in his mind's eye. Oh, he knew what she looked like. When Alexander was twelve he'd discovered the only portrait of her his father hadn't destroyed up in the attic. It was a small painting, no bigger than his hand. The miniature had probably been sent to his family when the match between Wentworth Mallory, Alex's father and the future Marquis of Maldren, and Finella MacGregor, was being arranged. Alexander's older brother told him the families had joined forces so each of them would have a claim on land on either side of the border.

Alexander always thought his mother was pretty enough that his father should have wanted Finella for herself, not for any land that came attached to the match.

She peered solemnly from the small canvas, her gray eyes serene, her mouth just a little tight. Had she ever smiled? Alex had no recollection of it.

He shook off the memory and scrubbed a hand over his head, standing his hair on end like a startled hedgehog. He didn't have time to fret much about the past. Especially one as shadowy as his. The present gave him enough to worry about.

With any luck, he'd see the MacOwen sisters to Dalkeith Palace. Lucinda would find another beau among the Christmastide revelers and he'd be free of this unexpected encumbrance.

Alex had no clue what would free him from Sir Darren's weeping woman.

Moving Lucinda MacOwen and her sisters to Dalkeith Palace turned out to be as complicated an enterprise as organizing the flight of the Hebrews from Egypt. Clarindon, the turncoat, had made good his escape to the palace, which was located some miles south of the city.

Of course, Clarindon protested that someone needed to be in residence there to begin seeking out any Radical sympathizers among the Scottish nobility, but Alexander knew the truth. His friend didn't want to miss any of the festivities leading up to Christmastide—hunting in the surrounding countryside capped by evenings filled with drink, card playing, and, if Clarindon were lucky, a bit of wenching on the side.

"Even though you're officially spoken for, old chap, it won't hurt for me to get a running head start before you get there," Clarindon had said.

So shepherding the MacOwen ladies to their new holiday quarters fell completely on Alex's shoulders.

For a thrifty Scottish family, the MacOwen girls weren't short on personal effects. There were enough trunks filled with feminine frippery to warrant their own conveyance. Alexander dutifully arranged for a sturdy cart for the baggage and a coach to transport the women.

He decided to buy a horse for himself.

"Best ye let me bear ye company when ye do," Lucinda told him while he hauled one of Aileen's trunks down the narrow staircase. "If an Englishman tries to buy a horse in Edinburgh, he'll likely find himself getting skinned by the dealer."

"Just because I'm English?" Alex was beginning to think the king's proposed visit to this backwater country was not only a bad idea, but a dangerous one. "Do all Scots hate my countrymen so?"

"'Tis no' exactly hate, ye ken. More like mistrust, I'd say. There's a long history between our peoples and it willna vanish from folks' memories simply for the wishing."

She stacked a hatbox on the trunk he'd deposited by the front door and followed him back up the staircase to fetch the next bit of baggage. Alexander had tried to hire porters to do the lifting, but Great-Aunt Hester wouldn't hear of it.

"There's no call for me to allow strangers in the house," the old woman had protested. "No' when me great-niece's betrothed is a healthy young man and sound of limb."

So if Alexander wanted the MacOwens to move, he had to do it himself.

"It would go easier on ye if ye wore that MacGregor plaid sash when ye buy a horse," Lucinda said.

Damned if he was going to hide behind a scrap of fabric just to fool the locals. "I'm not a MacGregor."

"Aye, ye are, if your mother was one," Lucinda said. "And I've noticed ye dinna seem eager to present yourself as Lord Bonniebroch, either. A Scottish laird always commands respect."

But I'm not Scottish. I'm English, he thought furiously as he stomped back up the narrow staircase. She seemed to vacillate between his two nationalities depending upon whether it suited her argument to consider him as one or the other.

There was no ambiguity for Alex. Any part of him that might have been the least Gaelic had been drummed out of him by his father's resentment toward the woman who gave Alexander birth. "I've been a Mallory much longer than I've been a Scottish laird."

"Well, then, I'll go with ye when ye buy your horse to protect the Sassenach from being hoodwinked by the locals," she said with a curt nod, as if that ended the matter. "Dinna fuss with me. 'Twill ease your way."

But being near her gave Alex no ease. He had to keep in mind that he was trying to rid himself of his betrothed, in the kindest possible way, of course. So there was no point in developing any sort of attachment to her. No need to court or even befriend her. He hunkered behind stiff courtesy to disguise the fact that his gaze kept drifting to Lucinda whenever she was near or that she crowded out even thoughts of his mission for the prime minister when she was not.

But he realized she was right about Scottish attitudes toward his kind. So when Alex headed for the public stables, Lucinda MacOwen's arm was looped around his elbow and her hands were shoved into a white rabbit-fur muff. The brisk cold painted her cheeks a becoming peach and her pelisse hugged her bosom in a snug embrace.

It was enough to make Alex envy the woolen garment, but he shook the thought from his mind. She might be his fiancée now, but that was an exceedingly temporary situation.

So long as he didn't do anything to make it permanent. Like seduce the girl. Which unfortunately was an idea that entered his mind several times a day.

That was another reason he needed a horse. The exercise of riding hard would distract him from thinking about the delectable young woman wrapped in several layers of muslin and wool by his side.

And how best to get her out of those layers.

"I generally dinna trade with the likes of ye," Mr. Gow, the local hostler, said, his wiry brows waving above his deep-set eyes like dozens of insect antennae. "Meanin' no offense, I'm sure," he added as a grumbling afterthought.

"Be easy, Mr. Gow," Lucinda said. "Lord Alexander is half Scottish on his mother's side. And Himself is the new laird of Bonniebroch, so he is."

"Weel, be that as it may, ye're fortunate that a daughter of Erskine MacOwen vouches for ye, your lairdship. Ye've the look of a Sassenach about ye."

Mr. Gow's pinched expression relaxed a bit. "But if Lucinda says otherwise, I'll take yer money."

"Not until I see your wares," Alex said. The man's condescension pricked his temper but he needed a horse.

"Ye've come at a low time o' year for horseflesh, ye ken. Spring is the best. All the lads come down out of the Highlands with fine beasties to trade then."

"I can't wait for spring." Alex was no closer to locating any Radicals than he was when he first disembarked from the *Agatha May*. He'd already lost two days waiting while the MacOwen girls packed. "I need a mount now."

"Weel then, ye'll be wantin' Badgemagus." Mr. Gow led them to a stall where a shaggy-coated beast stood, rocking its weight from side to side. The horse was black as a lump of coal. It glared at them from under a shock of unruly mane.

"He's plagued with some bad habits." Alexander noted that the gelding had nibbled all around the wood slats of his stall. As if to prove Alex's assessment of his temperament, Badgemagus gave the back slats an ill-tempered kick with a saucer-sized hoof. "And riddled with vice to boot."

"Aye, he is that. But since the Fall, aren't we all? His last owner fair ruined his mouth too, poor beastie. Might be that's what's made him so tetchy," Mr. Gow said. "But he's broad of beam and stout enough to pull any conveyance ye'd care to put behind him. And if he'll let ye ride him, ye'll find Badgemagus has a sweet gait."

Alexander snorted. *If he'll let me ride him.* He'd never met the horse he couldn't subdue.

He opened the gate and entered the stall. The

horse had one blue eye and one brown. "Is he blind in the blue eye?" He approached the gelding on that side.

"I wouldna do that, were I you," Gow said.

The horse swung his head around in a blink and nipped him on the shoulder.

"Ow!" Alex rubbed the spot. No skin had been broken, but he was sure it would bruise later.

"I warned ye, did I no'?" Mr. Gow spat a glob of phlegm onto the straw-strewn dirt.

Alex grasped the horse's headstall and gave it a quick jerk downward.

"None of that now," he told the beast in a low, commanding tone. Badgemagus stamped his foot and whickered, sending dragonish puffs of breath into the cold air, but he didn't offer to bite Alex again.

Mr. Gow chuckled. "Guess that proves Badgemagus can see just fine."

"Hmph!" Alex said, realizing the sound was a common Scottish one, but not caring enough to censor himself. "Hmph" was better than the curse that was his alternative.

There was a lady present, after all.

Lucinda had climbed up to stand on the lowest slat so she could peer over the top of the stall at him.

Her brows drew together with worry. Evidently, Badgemagus had a reputation for mayhem.

Well, Alexander had a reputation for horseman-ship and no sorry excuse for a Scottish horse was going to ruin it. He ran his hands over the beast to check his conformation beneath the shaggy coat.

The gelding was horribly foot-shy and resisted all efforts to check his hooves.

"If you don't behave yourself, my four-footed friend, I'll personally see that you are shipped off to France, where they like horses very much indeed— so long as it's boiled, stewed, or fried."

As if he'd understood every word, Badgemagus stood still as stone after that while Alex inspected each hoof. The horse was not up to Alexander's usual standards, but judging from the beast's surly disposition, Alex didn't meet with his approval either.

"Very well," Alexander said. "Since you've nothing else, I'll take him."

"Good," Mr. Gow said. "'Tis either him or shank's mare for ye, laddie. But dinna ye want to see can ye ride him or no' first?"

"Dinna—I mean, don't worry about that," Alex said. "I can ride him."

"I think ye ought to heed Mr. Gow and give the horse a try," Lucinda said.

"Aye, lad. Listen to the lady. The last man I sold Badgemagus to brought him back after a day. O' course I took him off his hands, kindhearted fellow that I am."

Alex snorted. "For less than the man paid for the beast, I'm sure."

Mr. Gow spread his hands before him. "To be honest, I've sold and bought Badgemagus back three times. And at a profit each time, to be sure." The hostler cackled at his own wit, but at least he was forthright about his method of making money.

Since both Lucinda and Mr. Gow seemed set on seeing him ride the beast, Alex gave in. "Saddle him up."

Mr. Gow fitted the horse with its tack and led it outside the stable to the cobbled street. Alex checked the girth and inspected the placement of the bit.

"Remember what I said about his mouth," Mr. Gow said. "Fair ruined, it is."

"We'll see." Alex mounted up and settled his heels low in the stirrups. Then he squeezed the horse with his thighs. "Walk on."

The horse plodded down the narrow street, his great head nodding in rhythm with the steady clop of his hooves. Alex chirruped and he broke into a brisk trot. Badgemagus did indeed have a sweet gait. Horse and rider fell into an easy rhythm with each other.

"Gow is telling tales on you, my friend," Alex crooned to the gelding. "You're biddable as a lamb."

Then he tried to turn the horse down a lane that forked off to the right.

Badgemagus let Alex swing his nose in that direction, but kept trotting straight ahead.

Alex hauled back on the reins, but the horse only gave his bridle a shake and picked up his pace. At the next side street, Alexander tried to turn Badgemagus to the left. The horse ignored the man on his back as if he were of no more import than a tick in his shaggy coat.

By the time they reached High Street, Badgemagus had stretched out into a full rolling canter.

"Oh, no," Lucinda said. "What are we to do?"

"Why we nip up to the roof so as to get a better view of the show, o' course," Mr. Gow said.

"But—" Since the hostler had already disappeared back into the tack shop abutting the stable, Lucinda had no choice but to follow.

"Dinna fret, lassie," Gow said. "Yer young man'll take no hurt ; . . . provided he knows how to fall. Come with me now and step lively."

Mr. Gow no doubt meant his words to be a comfort but Lucinda took none from them. She followed him to the rear of his shop, up three rickety flights and into the cobweb-festooned attic. Then they climbed a ladder to a narrow parapet perched along the spine of the steeply sloping roof.

"Och, there they are, lassie." Mr. Gow pointed into the distance.

Lucinda squinted in that direction. The streets of Edinburgh were laid out below her in a bird's-eye view. Alex and the gelding barreled down the main street, swerving wildly from side to side. Foot traffic and mounted travelers alike skittered out of their path.

"Watch now. Old Badgemagus will try to peel him off."

The horse hugged the left side of the street in order to bash Alex into the low-hanging signs that graced the shops' entrances. Alex leaned on one stirrup and flattened himself onto the plunging animal's side.

If he fell now, Alexander might roll beneath those huge hooves. Lucinda pressed a hand against her chest. Her heart threatened to pound right out of it.

"Are ye afeared yon laddie will kill himself afore he makes ye his Lady Bonniebroch?" Mr. Gow asked.

She hadn't been until that moment. Wounded pride or a sore head was as far as she'd allowed herself to imagine. Now she visualized the worst. Not only would Alexander Mallory's untimely demise ruin what her family hoped for in the match, she couldn't bear the thought of his fine strong body being trampled to a bloody pulp.

A sob escaped her lips.

"Och, I'll warrant he'll be all right yet. A lad as stubborn as your Lord Bonniebroch would take a heap o' killin'."

Then the horse streaked beneath the last of the overhead obstacles. Once they were past, Alexander righted himself and swung back up into the saddle.

"He's a bonny rider, Englishman or no'. I'll give him that," Mr. Gow said. "Your young man has kept his seat longer than any of the others. Most of 'em panic as soon as they realize they canna turn him. If not, that trick with the signs usually works."

"If you knew what the horse would do, why didna ye warn him?"

Mr. Gow bared his yellowed teeth in a frightful grin. "Where's the sport in that? But dinna fret. Yon laddie has an excellent seat on a horse."

"*The excellent seat of his trousers is not to be lightly dismissed either,*" she quoted the *Ladies' Guide* to herself as she leaned on the wrought-iron rail that framed the parapet. When Alex and the horse flew over an apple cart and landed on the other side without breaking stride, a thrill coursed through her. "The man's a veritable centaur."

"We'll see," Mr. Gow said. "Badgemagus has more one trick up his—och! Here 'tis and there he goes."

The horse bolted up to the edge of a hedged garden, then stopped dead at the last possible moment. Alex had evidently been gathering himself for a leap over the hedgerow, as he'd done when they jumped the apple cart, but this time, he made the leap alone. Momentum threw him over the horse's head and tail-over-teakettle into the garden.

The horse's whickering laugh floated all the way up to Lucinda on her perch above the tack shop. Fortunately, Alex's head popped back up from behind the hedge almost immediately. Thank heaven, he didn't seem much damaged. He only looked a bit ridiculous with several sprigs of juniper sticking from behind one ear.

But Lucinda had never seen such a look of fury on a man's face. Her betrothed was a storm about to break. She almost pitied Badgemagus.

"Weel, that's that," Mr. Gow said mournfully. "The horse'll run back to his stall now and I've lost the chance to sell him and buy him back by dealing too honest."

Lucinda cast him a tight-lipped grimace. "You failed to tell Lord Alexander of the horse's true faults. How is that honest?"

"I insisted the lad try to ride him, did I no'?" Mr. Gow headed for the ladder. "Handsomer than that, ye couldna wish."

Lucinda snorted. Then she looked back at Alex. The horse didn't seem to be running away. It stood by the hedge, ears pricked forward as Alex pushed through a gap in the greenery. He spoke to the gelding.

Instantly, the horse hung his head with every appearance of contrition. But to Lucinda's great relief, Alexander didn't try to mount the beast again. Instead, he collected the slack reins and began leading Badgemagus back to the stable at a determined pace, stopping from time to time to berate the horse with another verbal blistering.

Lucinda marked the fact that her betrothed had a black temper. Granted, the beast had warranted it, but she wondered what it would take for her to see that English storm headed her way.

She decided she didn't want to find out.

"I'll take him," Alex said once he and Badgemagus finished their uphill trudge to the stable.

Mr. Gow eyed him with suspicion. "Did ye suffer a clout to the head in yer fall?"

"No. I'm perfectly sensible."

The way Lucinda rolled her eyes, it was obvious she agreed with Mr. Gow.

"But the horse is no good to ye," she insisted. "Ye canna ride him."

"Not yet," Alex said. "But I will. What will you take for him?"

He haggled with Mr. Gow over the price long enough not to be thought a total dupe and bought the tack along with the gelding. Badgemagus might be no prize, but his saddle was crafted of fine-grained Spanish leather and the halter and bridle was its perfect match.

It didn't matter if Badgemagus was the worst example of a horse in equine history. It didn't matter if the sky opened in a downpour when they traveled to Dalkeith on the morrow. Alex was determined not to be trapped in an enclosed coach where he'd be outnumbered by the MacOwen females all the way to the Christmastide house party.

It was bad enough that his future was being outnumbered by them.

"Ye do seem to have a way with horses, even if he did unseat ye in the end," Lucinda said as they walked back to her great-aunt's house with Badgemagus trudging head down behind them on a tether. "What did ye say to calm him so after ye . . . well, there toward the end of your . . . ride?"

"I instructed him a bit about his namesake," Alex said. "The first King Badgemagus was attached to King Arthur's court, you see. He dearly desired to become a knight of the Round Table, but never quite cut the mustard. After many sorry misadventures, he was accidentally killed."

"And that story settled the beast down?"

"No. He settled when I promised if he didn't shape up, *his* demise would be no accident."

Chapter Five

"I'll no' be havin' me great-nieces spirited off in the company of an English heathen with no one to tend to the proprieties o' things," Hester exclaimed on the rare bright December day when all the Mac-Owen girls were finally bundled into the waiting coach that would take them to Dalkeith.

"Now just a moment," Alex said, taking a stand between her and the loaded coach. "I may be an indifferent churchgoer, but I'm no heathen."

Hester gave him her best impression of a gargoyle, but he wouldn't budge. "Cromwell banned Christmas ye know for bein' a pagan festival. Ye English have started up celebratin' it again with all manner of foolishness, but I dinna want me nieces tainted by yer foreign ways."

"I hardly think they'll be corrupted by a little wassail and mistletoe," Alex said.

"Still, they'll need a chaperone as they're motherless lambs, the poor dears, so it's me bounden duty to serve as such," she argued. "Lucinda, get ye out of that conveyance now and help me set the house to rights afore I close it up. The rest of ye may go on yer way. Only mind ye be at yer best comportment till I get there, Aileen MacOwen—aye, I'm lookin' at ye, girl—or I'll know the reason why. Mary, ye're the only one with a lick o' sense in the lot, so mind that yer sister doesna disgrace us with a lack of manners."

Lucinda had always prided herself on having a good deal of sense. *So much for "poor dears,"* she thought, bristling a bit. The MacOwen girls had degenerated from motherless lambs to ninnies who didn't know how to hold a spoon properly in one swift tongue-lashing.

As if Aunt Hester could hear her rebellious thoughts, the old woman cast a gimlet eye at her. "I used to think ye the most likely of the bunch till ye went and got yerself betrothed to an Englishman and a MacGregor to boot." Hester turned back to Mary. "Tend yer flibbety-gibbet sister for me 'til I get there."

Lips drawn in a tight line, Alex opened the coach door. Lucinda tamped down her irritation and supposed he was right to let Aunt Hester have her way in this. It was less trouble than trying to thwart the old biddy.

She slipped her hand into Alexander's as he handed her down from the carriage. Ordinarily, she'd have enjoyed his warm grip, but she sensed his frustration in that brief touch. He was as anxious as she to be gone from Hester MacGibbon's dictatorial presence.

They weren't the only ones.

"I thought we were rid of that auld harridan," Brodie MacIver grumbled in her ear as he held tight to her shoulder.

While Lucinda's ghost was charmed with the sound of his own voice often enough, he was less forgiving when others bumped their gums constantly. Or, as in Hester's case, so authoritatively.

Brodie had been upset at being left behind while Lucinda went with Alexander to buy his horse yesterday, so he wasn't about to be separated from her now. Brodie clamped a firm hold on Lucinda's shoulder with both hands as she waited for Aileen to hand her hatbox down.

It was deemed too frail to ride in the baggage cart. Lucinda couldn't chance anything happening to the delicate box or its precious contents before her wedding day.

"Discretion is the better part of valor," Alex quoted under his breath as he took the hatbox from her.

She shot a glance at Alexander from under her lashes. His face was a bland mask. She could well believe he was a masterful card player as he ordered the driver to take Aileen and Mary to Dalkeith Palace and then return to collect the rest of the party.

Badgemagus trotted behind the carriage, rolling his eyes and shying to one side when he passed Lucinda and Brodie. The hitched team hadn't responded to the ghost's presence at all, but the blinders with which they were fitted might have had a hand in that.

No worries about that blue eye at all, Lucinda thought. Badgemagus seemed to see Brodie just fine.

"Worthless beast," Alexander muttered.

He might have been of a different opinion if he'd been aware there was a ghost hovering nearby, but Lucinda wasn't about to tell him about Brodie. Certainly not before the knot was tied good and tight.

"Be sure to leave the gelding at Dalkeith," he called to the driver. Alex kicked at a stone in the road. "It'll make a good rest for him on the way to the glue factory."

"Ye dinna mean that," Lucinda said as she followed Aunt Hester's ponderous trudge back into the house.

"I almost do." Alexander fell into step beside her. "I tried several times yesterday evening to make that horse respond to the bit, but each time I wound up in a breakneck race that ended in an abrupt stop."

"Mr. Gow will buy him back from ye."

"I wouldn't give that old charlatan the satisfaction," Alex said, shoving his hands deep into his trouser pockets. "No, I mean to ride that horse if it's the last thing I do."

"Let us hope it doesna come to that."

"Lord Bonniebroch!" Aunt Hester called back to him. "I'm feeling meself a bit wobbly. Your arm, if you please."

"She seems disposed to forget I'm English and a MacGregor for the moment. I'd best take advantage of it," Alex said softly before he excused himself and trotted ahead to offer a steadying arm to the old woman.

Lucinda smiled, admiring the fine lines of the man as he walked ahead of her.

Excellent seat of his trousers, indeed. She made a mental note to consult *The Knowledgeable Ladies' Guide to Eligible Gentlemen* again to see if Lord Alexander was mentioned in any other entry besides the alphabetical listing.

"Ye see what he's about, dinna ye?" Brodie whispered in her ear. *"Dancing attendance on yer auntie like that. He's milkin' the cow to get at the calf."*

"Nonsense," she whispered since Hester had engaged Alexander in a loud tirade about the English and their overbearing ways. "He's only being a gentleman, something with which ye've little enough experience. Besides, the betrothal is settled. Lord Alexander already has the calf . . . I mean, he has me."

"He'd better no' have ye," Brodie said darkly.

"Let me be worryin' about that. Remember what I said. Ye're to leave Lord Alexander alone. No appearing in his chamber once we get to Dalkeith. No boiling slugs in his bathwater. No ordering spiders to converge in his boots. In other words, none of your usual tricks."

Her threat to never speak to Brodie again simmered in the air around them as they entered beneath the low lintel of her great-aunt's house. Hester's cantankerous complaints rattled through the residence as Alex settled her in the parlor, so Lucinda felt free to continue her conversation with the ghost for a moment longer.

"Och, as ye will then. I'll leave his precious lairdship alone," Brodie promised.

"And whilst we're on the subject, I want to thank ye for the restraint ye've shown in leavin' me alone over the years when I've had the need for privacy, when I dress and bathe and such like."

"Weel, o' course." If he'd been able to, Brodie would have blushed. *"To me, ye're still the little girl I met in the cellar. And I'm like the uncle ye never had."*

"You're like the uncle no one's ever had. But back to the subject at hand. A girl with her betrothed needs privacy too. I want ye to leave Lord Alexander and me alone should we ever chance to find ourselves, well . . . alone."

"Lass, ye dinna ken what men are."

"And I never will if ye dinna—"

"Who are you talking to?" Alexander stood framed in the parlor doorway, looking at her with a puzzled expression.

She gave what she hoped was a convincing little chuckle. "Myself. I do that from time to time when I've a good deal to do. Helps me organize me thoughts."

"Well, perhaps you can organize me too. Your aunt wants a tot of rum and I'm not sure where . . ."

"Ah! That'll be in the cold larder, back of the kitchen. Follow me." Lucinda glanced behind her to see that Brodie had heeded her wishes and wasn't tailing them.

Instead the ghost circled the iron candelabra in the vestibule so quickly, the fixture glowed as if every wick was lit.

* * *

"I must say, ye're taking Aunt Hester's change of plans with exceeding good grace," Lucinda said as she stretched and stood tiptoe trying to reach the bottle of rum on the top shelf. Alexander stepped close, pinning her between his body and the shelves, and retrieved it for her.

"Here you are."

He handed her the bottle but didn't move away. Their bodies weren't touching, but Lucinda fancied she could feel the heat of him in any case.

"You're patient with your aunt too," he said, still not moving to allow more space between them.

"Weel, o' course, I am. She's family," Lucinda said.

"What difference does that make?"

She turned and stared up at him as if he'd sprouted a second head. "Dinna ye ken that our family teaches us about the world and our place in it? Whatever we may know about the important things in life, we learn at our parents' knees. 'Tis said one may choose their friends, but God chooses a family for us."

Alex snorted. "The Lord must have a sense of humor to send you scurrying about trying to please someone who can't be pleased."

She smiled at that. "I'm sure we all give Him reason to chuckle from time to time. Oh, I know Aunt Hester may seem like an old bother, but how d'ye know she wasn't put into my life to teach me the patience ye see in me?"

"So you're saying we deserve the family we've been given?" He leaned a hand on the cupboard behind her. "If I'd known that, I'd have repented in sackcloth and ashes long ago."

"Is your family so terrible, then?"

"More like nonexistent."

Lucinda knew that wasn't true. According to *The Knowledgeable Ladies' Guide to Eligible Gentlemen,* Alexander's father and brother were very much alive. Of course, there was also that cryptic entry about madness in connection with his mother. Perhaps it was time to change the subject.

"Weel, I'll have Aunt Hester all packed up and ready to go by the time the coach returns for us."

"Speaking of packing, what's in that hatbox you've been so precious about?" he asked.

"Just a little something for me wedding," she said. The veil that her mother had worn for *her* wedding was tucked in the padded compartment. It was a delicious confection of lace that had been handed down through several generations of MacOwen women. Lucinda had never dreamed she'd actually ever wear it and wed such a handsome fellow in the bargain. She was still tempted to pinch herself each time she looked at Alexander Mallory. "I want ye to be surprised."

"No worries there. I've been surprised nearly every moment of the day since I arrived in Scotland. Even the word 'wedding' gives me a bit of a jolt."

She pressed down her disappointment. He was no closer to being a willing bridegroom than he was when he stepped off the *Agatha May.*

"Lucinda!" Great-Aunt Hester bellowed.

"A moment, aunt," she called back. Alex still didn't move away, so she tipped her chin up to meet his gaze.

"You've been patient about other things besides your aunt. Like finding those other three men to kiss.

There's been no chance for you to even meet any since we've been delayed in moving to Dalkeith," he said. "Unless of course you kissed Mr. Gow while I was otherwise occupied."

That made her chuckle. "He's no' exactly the sort of man who makes girls' pantalets twist, is he?"

"I suppose not."

He leaned toward her, a hand on the shelf at her shoulder. There was no need to imagine she could feel his warmth now. Their bodies were touching and it was as if a low fire had been kindled in her belly.

"What sort of man might affect a lady's pantalets like that?" he asked.

"As if ye didna know, Your Much of a Muchness." She couldn't resist naming him thus when the hard length of him was pressed up against her.

"I thought you wouldn't call me that till you knew if I deserved it."

"I'm making . . . an educated guess."

"If I'm the first man to ever kiss you, I don't think you may consider yourself educated in such matters. Not even enough for a guess."

"Then why dinna ye educate me?"

His expression grew as strained as if he were wrestling Aileen's big trunk down the staircase again. "You've no idea what you're asking."

He stepped back a pace and Lucinda's belly curdled in disappointment.

"Never mind, then. Surely there'll be a man at Dalkeith who'll be happy to fill in the gaps in my learning. After all, I do have three kisses to dispense

and I'll warrant more than lips may be involved
and—"

Alexander pulled her roughly to him, covering
her mouth with his in a possessive kiss. He cupped
her bum and lifted her a bit so she could feel the
feverishness of him through the thin muslin of her
gown, the length and the hardness of him pressed
against the apex of her thighs.

His smell, that disturbing, warm masculine
scent—all leather and fresh air and horseflesh—was
everywhere. Something dark and delicious fluttered
to life in her belly.

His hands flicked over her, sending sparks of pleasure trailing after them. Up and down her spine,
then around to trail under her breasts. Her nipples
ached and she arched herself into him.

He rocked against her and she rocked back, luxuriating in the flood of warmth pooling between
her legs.

Alexander straightened and looked down at her,
a smile slowly spreading over his face. Then the
smile faded and his gray eyes warmed to the color of
burnished pewter. He bent and claimed her mouth
again.

She didn't protest. He covered her lips with his for
a moment. Then he slanted his mouth across hers,
tasting her, teasing her lips open. His tongue toyed
with her and she made a little noise of impatience.

Then he took her hand and guided it between
their bodies, laying her palm over his groin and
pressing it against the hard bulge.

He wants me to feel just how Much of a Muchness he is.

Lucinda was equal parts shocked and intrigued.
There was something vulnerable about the way he

invited her to explore him. She ran an experimental hand over his length and he groaned into her mouth. When she gave him a squeeze, he thrust his tongue between her lips as if showing her how he'd like to thrust that other part of him into another place in her. He was long and thick and she ached to feel him without the layers of his trousers and undergarments between them.

"Lucinda!" Her great-aunt's voice sing-songed down the hallway and into the kitchen. "Dinna make me wait for me rum, girl!"

Alexander stopped kissing her and buried his nose in her hair. He drew a deep breath as if he might inhale her all the way down to his toes. She gave him one last stroke as he stepped back.

"Lucinda, I'm sorry. I shouldn't have—"

She pressed a finger to his lips. "We're betrothed, Alex. 'Tis only a matter of a few days and the bit of naughtiness we're about now will be Church-sanctioned naughtiness then."

A dark shadow seemed to pass over his face at that.

He still doesna want me. Not really.

The realization struck her with the force of a blow, but Lucinda swallowed back her hurt. However much her chest ached at the thought that Alexander still felt trapped by their betrothal, she still needed to make the match work. For the sake of her family's future. For her brother, Dougal, on the wrong side of the law. For too many reasons to count.

Not the least of which was the way Alexander Mallory twisted her pantalets.

It was early days yet, she decided with dogged determination. She'd *make* him love her, one way or another. Jealousy might be a way to goad him down the road. And he was the one who brought up their wager and the three kisses she was due before their Christmas Day wedding.

"Thank ye kindly, Alexander, for that little dollop of education," she said with what she hoped was a winsome smile. "Ye've given me ever so many interesting things to compare when I start kissing other men."

"As a general rule, a lady should never attempt to make a gentleman jealous. It is deceitful, manipulative, and unworthy of a gentlewoman's character. However, one should not underestimate its effectiveness if done correctly."

From *The Knowledgeable Ladies' Guide to Eligible Gentlemen*

Chapter Six

Once the carriage returned for them, Alexander and the driver loaded Aunt Hester's trunks in the boot and bundled the old woman into the equipage. Both were neat tricks because the lady and her luggage claimed a goodly amount of the available space. Alex and Lucinda crowded together on the rear-facing squab.

Ordinarily, he'd like nothing more than to be close to such a lovely young lady, but not this one who seemed more convinced than ever that he intended to marry her. He'd mentally kicked his arse up between his shoulder blades several times for kissing her in the kitchen like that when he ought to be looking for ways to end this sham betrothal.

Encouraging her to fondle his cock probably

hadn't been the best way to begin to break things off with her either. Usually, he took his mistress to dinner or dropped by with flowers and broke the news to her gently. He was always kind about it how he phrased it. Something on the order of "while their association had been memorable and oh, so pleasurable, it was now time for them to go their separate ways."

He rarely faced tears and recriminations because most of his light-o-loves had husbands to turn to. Or else they were worldly widows who collected men like some women collected Delft pottery. He had no objection to joining such collections temporarily, but when he was ready to climb off the display shelf, nothing could stop him.

Alex had never dealt with a virgin before and he wasn't sure how to proceed. So, he folded his arms over his chest and closed his eyes. With any luck at all, the weeping woman who'd plagued his dreams wouldn't find him in the rocking coach.

The back and forth movement was sensual, like the give and take of a vigorous swive and so, contemplating silken limbs and deep thrusts, Alex drifted to sleep.

The woman moved slowly across the room, shedding her night rail as she came. One button at a time. One more delicious inch of alabaster skin was bared with each unfastened seed pearl. The thin fabric slid off her shoulders and her breasts gleamed in the flickering light of the fire, but her face was still in shadow.

Not knowing who she was made it better somehow.

"*I've come for ye, Alexander,*" she whispered.

"*If you haven't come for me yet, you will,*" he promised, grinning at the double entendre. Then he plastered a stern look on his face. "*But you must stop moving right now and do nothing unless I give you leave.*"

"*Why?*"

"*Because I mean to give you pleasure and I mean for you to accept it without argument.*"

The faint light teased up her neck and chin to her lovely bow of a mouth, but he still didn't recognize her. She closed her lips firmly, accepting his mastery over her. A satisfied rush of power coursed over him.

"*Come and kiss me,*" he ordered.

Her night rail was hung up on her elbows. The hem trailed the ground as she approached, her neat little bare feet peeping from beneath the thin linen. Her breasts bounced a bit with each step, her berry-colored nipples drawn tight. When she bent to kiss him, her breasts fell forward, luscious fruit for him to pluck. He kneaded and squeezed and flicked her peaks with his thumbs till she moaned into his mouth.

"*Spread your legs.*"

She obeyed instantly. He undid a few more buttons and thrust a hand between her thighs. Her skin smelled of lilac, sweet enough to make his mouth water. He wondered if she must bathe in the stuff to so ingrain her flesh with the scent.

She was wet and soft and she whimpered when he touched her, little bleating sounds of distress and longing. They went right to his cock and made the pressure in his shaft rise to the tipping point.

He grasped her shoulders and held her at arm's length though she continued to strain toward him. "*Go lie down on the bed.*"

She straightened and obeyed him, though she did allow the night rail to slip off her arms as she went. He decided not to complain. It might have been an accident and she hadn't meant to disobey his dictum not to do anything unless he gave the word.

The globes of her heart-shaped bum undulated with each step. When she climbed up into the tester bed, her buttocks tipped up and he was treated to a glimpse of her glistening slit. Then she raised herself to her knees, faced him, and fisted her hands at her waist.

It was beginning to bother him that her face was still in shadow.

"On my stomach or back?" she asked.

"Surprise me."

She settled on her stomach. He rose and walked toward the bed, realizing for the first time that he was already naked. His cock led the way, bobbing merrily toward its goal.

She was a delight to his eyes. Her thick cloud of hair reached below her shoulder blades. He gathered it in one hand and forced her to raise up, arching her spine. He bent and planted kisses on the two dimples above her bum. He trailed a fingertip down her back and teased the cleft of her bottom. She quivered with delight. Then he flipped her over and settled between her legs in one smooth motion.

"You didn't really think I'd let you choose, did you?" he asked. "If I want your ankles over my shoulders or you on your knees like a dog, that's how you'll be."

He lowered his mouth and claimed hers roughly as he slid into her hot, tight channel. She hooked her ankles behind his back. It felt so good. So uncomplicated, this joining of bodies without any more promise than that of pleasure, given and received, between them.

Then suddenly, she rolled, pinning him beneath her.

"Dinna move without my leave, ye say." Her voice was thick with derision. *"Ye didna think I'd allow meself no' say in this matter, did ye? If there's anything on God's earth as takes two hearts deciding and doing together, it's this."*

She sat up on his groin, impaling herself on his thick cock. She raised her arms over her head in mock surrender, the long white length of her throat exposed as her head lolled back. Every bit of him strained toward her, even though she had disobeyed him.

"Love me, Alexander," she said throatily. "And I'll love ye right back."

She leaned down then and before he was engulfed by the thick curtain of her hair, the light finally reached her face.

It was Lucinda MacOwen.

The coach sank into a pothole and tossed its occupants upward so their bums left the tufted squabs for a moment. Alex woke with a start, but Aunt Hester merely grunted and burrowed deeper into the arms of Morpheus.

He glanced sideways at Lucinda, who was peering out the window, blissfully ignorant of the way she was about to be rutted six ways from Sunday in his dream.

As dreams went, that one was a close call. Another minute or two of it and he might have gone off like a fountain in his trousers. Alex took a handkerchief from his waistcoat pocket and wiped his brow.

"How much farther is it to Dalkeith?" he asked, willing his body to settle.

"Shh!"

Lucinda put a finger to his lips. "My aunt has

finally stopped grumbling and fallen to sleep," she whispered. "An' ye know what's good for ye, ye'll help me keep her in that state."

He nodded his agreement.

She lifted the heavy curtain to get her bearings. Despite the rare December sunshine, a cold draught washed over them before she dropped the curtain back in place.

"Not so far," she whispered. "Only a wee bit more now."

"You've been to Dalkeith before?" He matched her soft tone to keep from waking Hester. Lucinda was right. Best to let sleeping dragons lie.

"Only to walk the grounds," she admitted. "'Tis supposed to be ever so grand on the inside, ye ken. Queen Mary lived there for a time, but that was long before she ran afoul of her wicked English cousin Elizabeth."

Alex rolled his eyes. "Do you know any bit of history that doesn't involve allegations of English oppression?"

"I'd say lopping off a body's head is a good bit more than allegations of oppression."

She laced her fingers primly on her lap, those same lovely fingers that had danced over his hard length only that morning. He was forced to look away.

"Dinna blame me if your people have a history of mistreating the Scots in general and our queens in particular," she went on in a louder whisper. "Mary Stuart had as good a claim to the English throne as your Virgin Queen. Better, some would say."

"That all happened a very long time ago."

"Aye, but we Scots have verra long memories."

"And a misplaced sense of whom to blame for your past woes. I had nothing to do with any of it."

"I'm thinkin' ye and yer friends have more to do with our future woe. Ye're here to bring an English king to us, are ye no'?"

Alex ran his hand through his hair in frustration. "He's not just the English king. He's your king too, whether you like it or not."

"Whether I like it or no'," she repeated. "You're right. How daft I am. That doesna sound like oppression at all."

Hester MacGibbon snorted wetly in her sleep, a truly horrendous sound that reminded Alex of a wild boar thrashing in the brush.

"You're upsetting your aunt," he said. "Let's talk about something else."

"Maybe we shouldna speak at all," she said tersely and turned her face to the curtained window as if she could see through the heavy damask.

He folded his arms over his chest and closed his eyes again. Lucinda MacOwen couldn't start kissing those other men soon enough to suit him, he decided.

If only his gut didn't roil at the thought.

The pale stone of Dalkeith rose from its sheltered place among hundred-year-old Caledonian oaks. In high summer, it would be breathtaking. Now with bare limbs and a broad expanse of winter-brown grass, the edifice was just shy of forbidding. The palace was styled after William of Orange's Holland estate. The Continental influences showed in its sloped lead rooflines that sprouted over a dozen tall chimneys. The multi-paned windows spread across the front of the building in rigid symmetry.

There were footmen aplenty to help pry Aunt Hester out of the carriage and see her safely to one of the rooms that had been prepared for Lord Rankin's guests. The fact that Hester had invited herself probably never entered the old lady's mind as she supervised the unloading of her effects.

A cricket game was ranging over some of the grounds. The flock of sheep that kept the grass short scattered each time a batsman connected with the ball. Alex handed Lucinda down from the carriage, told her he'd see her at supper, and turned her over to the waiting servants.

He'd already lost too much time to feminine distraction. It was time to go to work.

Clarindon was standing on the sidelines watching the play, cupping his hands and blowing into them to warm them. As an Englishman, he was accustomed to a wet cold, but the wind that whistled down from the Highlands lent winter an extra bite.

Alex came up to stand beside his friend. The Scottish team was hopelessly unsure of how to field and sweep. The English batsman slammed another ball that skimmed the ground.

The English contingent erupted into a cheer as their man began to sprint to the opposite wicket.

"What's this?" Alex said. "Rankin's idea of building goodwill is pummeling the stuffing out of the locals?"

"Something like that," Clarindon said. "The mood's

getting a bit nasty on the Scottish sidelines. This clearly isn't their game. If Rankin keeps walloping them like this, the king's progression will be over before it starts. Are you going to play? Rankin's been asking for you."

Alex had been the top batsman on his cricket team at Oxford. Though it wasn't his greatest strength, he had a good spin on the ball when he bowled as well. "Yes, I'd better play, but not for Rankin."

He loped back to the carriage and found his trunk before the porters could cart it off to his assigned chamber. He removed his jacket and waistcoat and stuffed them into the baggage. Playing in his shirt-sleeves would give him more freedom of movement. Then Alex rifled through the contents of his trunk and came up with the MacGregor plaid sash.

The final score was 197 to 198. The English team did not win.

Alex had cajoled and encouraged the Scots and was astounded by how quickly they picked up the finer points of the game once someone took the trouble to explain it to them. Their natural balance and athleticism carried the day.

But they seemed to think it was Alex who tipped the scales in their favor. So once the winning point was scored a pair of the long-haired giants hoisted him on their shoulders and paraded him around the field. As they went, they growled out a fighting song in Gaelic. It sounded rather like a pack of dogs being butchered alive, but what the singing lacked in grace it made up for in enthusiasm.

Lord Rankin watched the celebration from the sidelines, his florid complexion paling to the color of rancid suet.

Toward the end of the match, Alex had been vaguely aware that more ladies had donned their pelisses and stood in the cold sunshine to cheer on their teams. From his perch on the pair of burly shoulders, he scanned the crowd, hoping to spot Lucinda.

He finally did, but he wasn't happy about it.

She was dancing around a shaggy-looking fellow with deep auburn hair and a beard and mustache to match. Then she threw herself into his arms and he twirled her about, her skirts billowing.

When they stopped, she palmed his cheeks and kissed him right on the mouth.

"Let me down," Alex demanded.

The fellows carrying him reluctantly allowed him to clamber down and then lifted the man who'd bowled out the final English batsman for a celebratory lap around the field.

Alex sprinted toward Lucinda and the hairy, unwashed brute who had her complete attention.

Of all the men she might choose to kiss, why this one?

"How long have ye been here at Dalkeith?" she was asking as Alex came alongside her.

"Since a few weeks after Michaelmas," the man said. "Word came that the English were set on coming to Dalkeith and the steward hired an army of folk to spruce up the place. Been working on the grounds and in the stable ever since."

"Oh, I'm so glad, Dougal—"

"Wait a moment," Alex said, positioning himself

between Lucinda and the broad-shouldered man. "You know this person?"

Lucinda smiled up at him with deceptive sweetness. "This is my land, Englishman. I know lots of people."

He grasped her elbow and led her away. "And out of all of them, *this* is the one you choose to squander a kiss on?"

"Is this Sassenach bothering ye, Lucy?" The Scotsman had crowded up behind them and stood with his ham-sized fists at his waist.

"No, Dougal. He's no' bothering me. No' the now, at any rate. I expect that'll change," she said with a saucy tilt of her head as she turned back to Alexander. "And that kiss didna really count."

Irritation stiffened Alex's spine. The kiss may have been lacking in passion, but it more than made up for it in exuberance. It definitely counted.

The bell in the palace chapel began to chime the hour. "It's time we were getting in," he said, determined to spirit Lucinda away from the big Scot. "Dinner is always served at eight. You'll be expected to dress."

The Scotsman laughed. "Dinna worry, English. We're no' the savages ye think us. No need to tell her to dress for dinner. Me sister willna come to the table in naught but her skin."

"Sister?" Alex said.

"Aye, Dougal's my brother."

Lucinda bade her brother farewell and promised to meet him in the stable on the morrow so they could catch up on each other's doings properly. Then she turned away without introducing Alexander to him. At the very least, he would have expected she'd tell her brother about their betrothal, but she merely hugged herself against the wind and headed for the grand entrance to Dalkeith Palace.

When Alex fell into step beside her, she lifted a brow at him. "Surely ye didna think I'd throw myself into just anyone's arms, did ye?"

"Given our brief history, yes." She'd certainly flung herself into his.

"Careful, milord. If I didna know better, I'd swear ye were a bit jealous."

"Of your brother?" Alexander snorted. "Don't be ridiculous."

"But ye didna know he was my brother. I saw the red haze in your eyes when ye joined us."

"I'd just finished a wicked cricket match," Alex protested. "What you saw was fatigue."

"Are ye certain sure?"

They passed through the broad doorway into the grand entrance hall that was fitted with enough pale marble to do justice to an emperor's residence. If the Duke of Buccleuch who owned the place wasn't careful, George IV would wangle Dalkeith away from him once he saw it next August. The bare alcove at the base of the grand curving staircase was begging for a statue of the English king.

But Alex shoved the king's visit to the back of his mind for the moment.

"Hang it all, Lucinda, all right. I'll confess it if you like. I'm frankly surprised that you'd kiss a man, even a relative, in such a public fashion."

"Oh, is that all?" She laid a slim hand on the smooth railing and perched on the first step so she could look him squarely in the eye. "Then just to put your mind at ease, let me assure ye I'll no' be kissing the next two men like that."

Surprisingly enough, relief swirled in his gut. "That's good to hear."

"Since public kissing isna at all the done thing"— she flashed him an impish grin—"I'll be sure to wait till I'm completely alone with the fellow. Next time."

"While it is tempting to consider only the gentleman when contemplating whether or not to accept a proposal of marriage, the wise young lady bears in mind that she is also joining herself to the gentleman's extended family.

And leg-shackling him to hers."

From *The Knowledgeable Ladies' Guide to Eligible Gentlemen*

Chapter Seven

Lucinda turned and fairly sprinted up the curving staircase. The look of dumbfounded surprise on Alexander Mallory's face was so priceless; staying a moment longer would have spoiled the effect.

He is *jealous.*

She hugged the knowledge to her chest as if it were more precious than pearls. If Alexander was jealous of her kisses it meant he had to feel *something* for her. Lucinda was beginning to hope that when she joined her bridegroom at the altar on Christmas morning, he wouldn't have to be dragged there kicking and screaming.

She hurried back to the room she'd been assigned. It was on the smallish side, almost an alcove off the larger one her two sisters had claimed, but at least she didn't have to share the space with Great-Aunt Hester. That worthy matron had demanded—and received!—a chamber fit for a dowager empress complete with its own sitting room and separate wardrobe.

Lucinda slipped through her sisters' room, not at all surprised to find it vacant. Mary had probably gone in search of the renowned library of Dalkeith and Aileen was no doubt in search of any available men with whom she could practice flirting.

Unlike Lucinda's life at present, everything in her sisters' chamber was neat and tidy. One of the upstairs maids had unpacked all Aileen and Mary's belongings and stowed them in the great trunk, capacious wardrobe, and a set of drawers in the tallest chest Lucinda had ever seen.

Lucinda's small cell was a different story entirely. Several of her gowns were splayed across the foot of the bed, hopelessly rumpled. Every drawer was open, stockings and stays and chemises draping from them. She was certain no lady's maid had a hand in this mess.

"Brodie MacIver!" she hissed. "Ye're petulant as a spoiled child. What do ye think ye've been doing?"

The ghost appeared hovering over, but not quite resting upon, the striped chintz cushion on the window seat.

"A spoiled child, is it? If I were child ye wouldna have left me."

Brodie had taken plenty of risks to accompany her to Edinburgh and Dalkeith. His relief at being safe inside the stone edifice where he couldn't be blown away was palpable. But he didn't relish being alone in a strange place.

"I canna stay inside with ye all the time," Lucinda said as she picked up one kid-soled slipper and knelt to peer under the bed in search of its mate. "Unlike some parties to this conversation, I have a life to live."

"No need to drag me unfortunate deceased state into it, but since ye've brought it up, those of us who dinna have a life have precious little to occupy ourselves with. The truth is if ye didna want me to meddle with yer things, ye ought to have stayed inside," he said tetchily. *"Bad enough I've been dragged hither and yon in a bouncing carriage—and let me tell ye I had no easy time of it crammed in next to yer fulsome auntie—but then once we finally arrive in a civilized location, ye leave me in the palace alone whilst ye trip blithely away to moon over that blasted Englishman and his cricket bat."*

"Lord Bonniebroch is not a blasted Englishman. He's my betrothed." Lucinda stowed her reunited slippers in the wardrobe and began to refold her stockings and place them in the lilac sachet-scented drawers. "'Tis no' considered mooning to admire a man I'll be marrit to in only a few days." Remembering the feel of the hard hot length of him sent a delicious tingle to her nether parts. "Besides, ye'd have approved of the way he handled his bat, I'm sure. The lad played for the Scottish team and they won."

"Hmph." Brodie floated up to the heavily beamed ceiling and did a leisurely backstroke across the room.

"Dougal is here," Lucinda said, trying to change the subject.

"Is he, now?" Brodie floated down and smoothed out the wrinkles he'd made in her gowns with a blast of his cold, ghostly breath. It was the closest thing to an apology Lucinda was likely to get, but since the pink taffeta was hopelessly rumpled, she'd take it. *"I like yer brother. There's a young man with a head on his shoulders."*

"And I'd like to see it stay where it is. There's still a price on Dougal's head, though I doubt there's a Scotsman alive who'd turn him in," she said. "But havin' to look o'er his shoulder every little whipstitch is no way to live. My brother needs a pardon. My marriage to Lord Bonniebroch will help Dougal."

Brodie frowned. *"I take yer point. An English brother-in-law might go a long way toward turning the eye of the law aside from any MacOwen."*

Dougal had been living rough in the Highlands since he'd been outlawed after the failed rebellion. Lucinda almost hadn't recognized him under that thick mat of hair and full beard. Even so, it was wonderful to finally be with him again, but she worried her lip as another thought struck her.

"There are other places where a wanted man might find work, places where he'd be less likely to run afoul of the authorities," she said. "Why do ye think Dougal is here at Dalkeith?"

Brodie was uncharacteristically silent for the space of several heartbeats.

"This is where the English king will come in high summer."

Her heart sank to her toes. "Surely Dougal isna so stupid. He wouldna dare try such a thing."

"When I said Dougal had a good head on his shoulders,"

I may have misspoken. But ye canna deny his heart's in the right place. Scotland's freedom pulses with every beat."

"That's no receipt for freedom for anyone." Lucinda wadded up the rest of her stockings and shoved them into the drawer. "'Tis a fool's errand. The English king will be guarded constantly."

"That's true." Brodie settled on the canopy above the bed, but since his incorporeal form had no weight, the damask didn't bow so much as an inch. *"But a trusted groundskeeper or handy groom stands a better chance than most of getting close to His Royal Majesty."*

"'Tis madness." She forgot all about righting her disheveled room and paced furiously instead. "No weapons are allowed in Dalkeith. Even my baggage was searched when we arrived."

"If the sin of Macbeth is Dougal's aim, I reckon yer brother has a way around that. O' course, there are those who wouldna count killing an English king a sin."

Lucinda stopped her ears with both hands. "No. He canna be plotting any such thing. Besides, even if Dougal were able to get close enough to strike down George IV, he'd never live to tell the tale."

"Living to tell it might not be Dougal's plan. There'd be plenty o' others who'd tell it though. Yer brother would be famous from one end of Scotland to the other," Brodie mused. *"Besides, take it from one who knows. There's worse things than dyin'."*

Lucinda looked up sharply at that, but Brodie had floated over to the window. The ghost complained often enough about being trapped between this world and the next, but he'd never shared why he'd been unable to find his eternal rest. All she knew was that it was someone named Cormag MacGregor's fault.

"*Let's no' borrow trouble before there's need,*" Brodie said. "*Yer brother may have no such ill-conceived thoughts in his head. And I'll no' fret ye any more about yer confounded marriage since it seems there's no help for it. But if that cursed Englishman gives ye a moment's grief—*"

"He won't," Lucinda said, thankful that the subject had been changed from regicide. "In fact, Lord Alexander has been a most amiable and liberal fiancé. He's even agreed that I may kiss three men before our wedding."

Brodie's feet levitated and he stretched out, head propped on his palm, as if he were reclining on the fainting couch in the corner, except that he was floating about four feet above it.

"*That doesna sound right . . . unless yer Lord Bonniebroch's planning on kissing three women his own self.*"

Lucinda hadn't considered that. There were any number of women at Dalkeith who'd jump at the chance to let Alexander Mallory kiss them.

And probably a good bit more.

Lucinda's chest ached at the thought.

"*Dinna fash yerself, lass. Ol' Brodie will keep an eye on the lad. He'd better no' play ye false or I guarantee he'll wish he hadna.*"

Brodie shot up in a sudden burst of white light and disappeared through the ceiling before she could order him not to tail Alexander.

Actually, she wasn't sure she'd give that order if it meant Brodie might keep her intended from dallying with other women.

But faithfulness that's forced wasn't really faithfulness, was it?

Lucinda breathed a sigh. It was the ghost, she decided, who had her all jumbled up inside. Brodie was not a restful spirit to have hovering about all the time. But just when she was ready to relax into truly being alone, he poked only his head back through the ceiling near one of the thick, blackened beams.

"I forgot to tell ye, lass. I felt another presence in Dalkeith Palace before ye returned to yer chamber. Seems I'm no' the only soul here who doesna have a life to live. Consider yerself forewarned. I didna wish ye to be surprised should the poor blighter try to speak to ye."

Then Brodie's disembodied head popped back through the ceiling. Lucinda sank onto the foot of the bed.

"Isn't that just what I need?" she said ruefully. "Another ghost!"

Alex waited until Lucinda disappeared around the curve of the staircase before he stomped up behind her. Who'd have guessed the girl was such an incorrigible flirt?

"Outstanding, Mallory," he muttered to himself. "Not only do you have a fiancée you didn't want in the first place, you're likely to be cuckolded before you're dragged to the altar."

The guests at Dalkeith had all been assigned rooms along a corridor that ran straight as a plumb line for more than the length of a cricket pitch. Since each door was marked with a placard indicating the occupant, he strode along the hallway looking for his name. Finally he found one whose small card beside the door had "Lord Alexander Mallory" worked in beautiful script on it. This designation had been crossed out and "Lord Bonniebroch" was scrawled under it in a much coarser hand.

Much coarser. Doesn't that sum up Scotland all around?

He pushed open the door and entered a surprisingly well-appointed chamber. The walls were paneled in dark oak and the six-point buck mounted over the stone fireplace lent a distinctly masculine air to the space. The bed curtains and linens had been freshly aired and the multi-paned windows looked out onto the broad lawn where Alex had lately led his cricket team to victory.

His foul temper improved slightly.

The valet who'd been assigned to him had already laid out his evening clothes in a neat row across the end of the bed. His trousers and jacket had been freshly brushed. His cravat was crisp and white and looked to have just the right amount of starch in it.

Water had been drawn in a great copper hip bath and when he tested it with his hand, it was still warm. A full kettle rested on the fireplace hearth so he'd have plenty more hot water when he needed it.

Alex crossed over to the pitcher and basin that rested on a walnut commode beneath a large mirror. He frowned at the dark beard shadow on his cheeks, splashed water on his face, and wondered if he had time for a shave before he dressed for dinner. The valet had laid out his shaving accoutrements on the commode.

"At least the Scots have servants who seem to know their business," he grumbled.

"Indeed, milord, we know a good deal more than that, which a body might learn if any took the trouble to listen to us."

A light flashed in the corner of his eye and Alex looked up sharply at his reflection in the mirror. There was an elderly gentleman standing behind him.

The fellow's beard and mustache were neatly trimmed, but the gold earring in the flange of one ear gave him the aspect of an old pirate. Brows like a pair of runaway scrub brushes hung above dark, piercing eyes. The man doffed a tam that was hopelessly out of fashion. The scant hair on his head had been scraped back into a neat queue. He was a little bird of a man, small-boned and sharp-featured, but he carried himself with exaggerated dignity that made him seem more substantial. The fellow flipped his hat with a flourish, and sketched an elaborate bow that belonged to another century entirely.

In fact everything about the man harked back to an older time, from the frilly lace at his cuffs to the vibrant plaid of his outlawed kilt.

"Who are you and what are you doing here?" Alex asked. The fellow was soft-footed as a cat. He hadn't heard a single footfall.

"Callum Farquhar, Esquire, at yer service, milord." His low Scottish burr was just on the edge of sound.

One of the Dalkeith servants. If this was the valet who'd laid out Alexander's things, he'd come in handy indeed. "Very well, Mr. Farquhar, you're just in time to give me a shave."

Farquhar drew himself up to his full, if unimpressive, height.

"Oh, no, milord. T'wouldn't be seemly. Ye see, word reached us that the new laird of Bonniebroch was come to Dalkeith so I took the liberty of hieing meself here to present meself to ye before ye take possession of yer estate." He puffed out his chest like a wren fluffing its feathers against the cold. "I am not attached to Dalkeith, ye see. I have the honor of being the steward of Bonniebroch and have been for many, many years."

"Steward, eh? So such simple duties as giving your master a shave is beneath you, I suppose."

"Ye may be me lord, but ye're no' me master. However, milord is correct." Farquhar gave a dignified nod. "A steward doesna give shaves."

There was a bell pull next to the commode and Alexander considered ringing for the valet to return, but all the guests were dressing for dinner now. That meant every available servant was trotting in circles trying to keep up with their demands. He spared a moment of sympathy for the poor lady's maid who was assigned to Hester MacGibbon.

Alex picked up his razor and began to strop it on a bit of leather to hone the edge.

"Och, I see milord isna the sort who's too fine to do for himself," Farquhar said approvingly. "That bodes well."

"It bodes well for servants who think they're too fine to serve," Alex muttered as he put the razor down and began to lather up his brush. "I assume since you rushed here from Bonniebroch—say, where the devil is Bonniebroch?"

"The fair estate of Bonniebroch is situated in a fine arable valley, surrounded by a forest filled with game. It rests in a declivity between two of the loveliest peaks in the Highlands. It's watered by the River Tay and—"

"No, I mean how is it situated in relation to anyplace that's civilized?" Alex said. "Not that Edinburgh counts especially, but let us reckon from there."

Farquhar frowned at this. "There are those who think the limits of civilization end at Hadrian's Wall."

Alex laughed in agreement. The old Roman fortification had been built to contain the warlike Picts, the predecessors of the Scots, who resisted the conquering force's efforts to bring them niceties like a legal system, a written language, and plumbing. Finally, the Romans threw up the wall and contented themselves with keeping the woad-daubed tribes behind it.

"You've the right of it there," Alexander said, contorting his mouth to one side, the better to scrape the day's growth of beard from his cheek. "Hadrian showed a good deal of sense when he drew a line between the savage and the civilized."

"I fear ye've missed me meaning, milord," the old man said. "The civilized side lies to the north of the wall."

Now it was Alex's turn to frown. "At least on the southern side, an estate steward does not insult his lord."

"My apologies. No insult was intended, since I merely spoke the truth," Farquhar said, not looking the least apologetic. "I see your valet has laid out the wrong ensemble for this evening's festivities. Surely milord will want the belted plaid ye have stowed in yon trunk."

"How did y—" It was plain to see how the steward knew about the blasted kilt. Callum Farquhar was a world-class snoop and had already visited his new laird's chamber without permission. "No, Farquhar. Leave the plaid. I'll wear the trousers and jacket."

"With the MacGregor sash, at least."

"Not tonight."

The man's shoulders slumped. He gave every appearance of releasing a long-suffering sigh, but

Alexander heard no snort of breath. For tuppence, Alex would give him the sack, but he needed to see the lay of Bonniebroch's land before he made any changes in personnel at the estate.

"If ye willna heed my advice on the matter of yer wardrobe, how else may I serve my lord?"

"Aside from giving me a shave?" Alex paused before starting another stroke from his chin to his cheekbone.

"Aye, aside from that."

Alex scraped the razor over his skin. "Well, I suppose you're here to give an accounting of your stewardship. Let's hear it then."

"No, that's no' why I'm here. No' exactly," Farquhar said with an intense gaze. "Mostly I came to see what sort of accounting *ye* would give of yerself so we'd know what kind of laird Bonniebroch might expect in ye. If I may make so bold as to enquire, how is yer health?"

Alex arched a brow at him. "Barring a few bruises from trying to ride that devil with four hooves called Badgemagus, I'm fine. Healthy as a horse. At least, I'm a damned sight healthier than that one will be if he continues to fight me."

Farquhar made a tsking noise. "Language, milord. Damnation is no light matter. But 'tis glad I am to hear that ye enjoy good health. We at Bonniebroch hope ye'll be with us for a good long time, it being unsettling to everyone when we have to break in a new baron. The last one wasna with us verra long."

Alexander shook his head in disbelief at the man's cheekiness as he swished the razor in the soap-scummy stand of water in the basin. "Heaven forefend I should discomfit the help."

"Aye, that's good of ye, milord," Farquhar said,

obviously missing the irony dripping from Alex's tone. "And yer sleep. How is that? No disturbing dreams, I trust?"

Alex's head snapped up sharply at that. He'd told no one about the dream of the weeping woman. He'd been plagued with visions of her every night since he became laird of Bonniebroch, but not even Clarindon knew of the recurring nightmare.

"A man's dreams, like his thoughts, are his own," he said stonily.

Farquhar rolled his eyes. "Verra well, but I canna help ye, if ye dinna trust me. On to other items of interest. I understand yer mother was a MacGregor—"

"That's of no import," Alexander said, irritated that the little man seemed to know so much about him already. "In fact, you will never bring up the subject of my mother again or you'll be seeking other employment."

"'Tis worse than I feared," Farquhar muttered, rubbing one of his temples as if to ward off a headache. "Still, we must work with that which we have been given."

Farquhar folded his hands before the sporran dangling from his belt. It was out of proportion with the old gentleman since it appeared to be fashioned from the skin of an entire badger.

"I understand felicitations are in order. Congratulations on taking a bride from the Campbell clan. A Miss Lucinda MacOwen, I believe. These are happy tidings indeed, milord."

"Perhaps for you—ouch!" A small bead of red blossomed on Alexander's chin. He held a cloth to the wound to staunch the bleeding. "But don't count on me bringing a Lady Bonniebroch with me when I come to claim my own. The wedding's not set in stone."

Farquhar chuckled. "Aye, lad. And the trout thinks the hook is no' set either just afore he finds himself flopping on the riverbank. But it makes no never mind. All will be in readiness for ye and yer new lady to celebrate the merriest of Christmastides at Bonniebroch."

"There's no need for you to go to any trouble." Alex lowered the cloth and inspected his bleeding chin. The wound wouldn't require stitches but it was a near thing. "Besides, I thought Scots didn't give Christmas more than a nod and a wink."

"Mayhap in other places that's true, but we at Bonniebroch celebrate it with a good will."

"It makes no difference," Alexander said, wondering if this botched shave was worth the effort. "I won't be heading for Bonniebroch till after the new year."

A flat smile widened Farquhar's lean face. "We'll see ye when we see ye then. But we at Bonniebroch will keep the Yule log burning for ye and yer missus in any case."

Alex dabbed the cloth in the water basin, but another strange flash of light made him glance sharply back to the mirror.

Callum Farquhar was no longer standing behind him.

Alex turned quickly, but the fellow was nowhere to be seen. There was no place for him to hide in the chamber either. Alexander had heard neither the clack of a boot heel on hardwood nor the snick of the door latch. The Scottish steward simply wasn't there any longer.

Farquhar was wickedly fast for such an old gaffer, Alex decided. Sneaky as a cat.

The man definitely needed a bell around his neck.

And Alex desperately needed a valet. He nicked himself again with the razor before deciding it was time to give up on a shave.

But it was not time to give up on his freedom. Farquhar could burn all the Yule logs he wanted. Alexander was not going to arrive at his new Scottish estate with a Lady Bonniebroch in tow.

And that was final.

"The new laird of Bonniebroch is not at all what I'd hoped. Lord Alexander Mallory is so far removed from his true self, I doubt he'd recognize his own soul were he to see it in a looking glass staring back at him. I'd confess myself totally dispirited, but I've misliked punning since I tried to talk Master Shakespeare out of using that low form of humor in his little plays."

From the private journal of Callum
Farquhar, Steward of Bonniebroch Castle
since the Year of Our Lord 1521

Chapter Eight

In the round chamber at the top of Bonnie-broch's tower, white light poured from the long stretch of silvered glass. Before the shaft of brightness flared and the flash blinked into nothingness, Callum Farquhar stepped through the mirror and back into the room.

"Ah, there ye are, sir," Lyall Lyttle said. "Welcome back. Did ye find Lord Bonniebroch?"

"Aye. I went to London and Oxford and a bawdy house in Brighton before I ran him to ground right here on Scottish soil. He's at Dalkeith."

"I must say, I had me doubts ye'd find him. 'Tis a long step to all those places and back," Lyttle said, mopping his furrowed brow.

"Nonsense. No' so far at all by this method." Now that he was with the estate's butler, Farquhar could simply project his thoughts. If Lord Bonniebroch only knew how hard Farquhar had worked to send an approximation of a human voice to his ear. He might have been far more sensible of the honor done him by Farquhar's visit. *"Unlike the workings of man, there are no moving parts in the realm of the spirit which may break down. Even though I've had no call to use them in a hundred years, the secrets paths from mirror to mirror run smooth as . . . well, smooth as glass."*

Of course, there was always the chance that some living person might shatter a mirror and destroy the spiritual conduit from that place to others. There was a risk to any ghost who traveled those invisible byways that the mirror through which he'd entered the system might be compromised while he was in another location. If that happened, he'd be forever barred from returning to his point of origin. To Farquhar's mind, the penalty of seven years' bad luck for breaking a mirror was extremely light.

"And you're sure no one saw you at Dalkeith?"

"Lyall Lyttle, you fret more than an old woman. No one but our new laird saw me, and even then, he only saw me when I was safely behind glass."

Of course, Farquhar had been careful not to step through the looking glass into Dalkeith when there was another soul actually in the room. He'd inspected Lord Bonniebroch's personal effects before meeting the man because there was no better indicator of what was important to a person than the carefully chosen items with which a body elected to travel. Farquhar had been cautiously hopeful when he found the belted plaid in the trunk.

After meeting Alexander Mallory, he had his doubts.

"What's he like? Will he do, d'ye think?"

"He'll have to," Farquhar said wearily. *"We've no time to wait for another. The curse is coming to a head one way or another and there's no help for it."*

Farquhar settled himself at the writing desk and picked up his quill. Since Lyttle was the only one in the castle who could see and hear him, he communicated his wishes to the rest of the Bonniebroch staff through detailed instructions in his daily log.

His personal fears and hopes he kept in another private journal. After he made each entry, he squirreled that one away behind a loose brick in the fireplace in the laird's bedchamber.

"How is the mood of the staff?" Farquhar asked as he began to assign duties for the upcoming Christmastide festivities.

"Hopeful," Lyttle said as he peered over Farquhar's shoulder at the neat script rolling from the tip of the ghost's quill. "Worried, too."

"That canna be helped. But the holiday season will lighten everyone's spirits. We must be ready to welcome the new laird and his lady—"

"His lady?"

Farquhar allowed himself a small smile. *"Aye. Lord Bonniebroch is set to wed on Christmas Day. And even though I've no' met her, she's the reason I'm optimistic. Nothing like a woman to show a man what he's made of, aye?"*

Lyttle rubbed his hands together in glee. "We

haven't had a Lady Bonniebroch for, oh, I forget how long."

"It may well be that's why none of the other lairds have been able to lift the curse. A woman is much like a mirror for a man, ye ken. She reflects back to him all his faults and strengths, both inside and out."

There was silence for a few beats. Lyttle didn't have Farquhar's aptitude for original thinking. Farquhar had to be careful not to overwhelm his living assistant with the knowledge it had taken him centuries to accumulate.

"All right," Lyttle finally said. "Let us hope the new laird is willing to heed the looking glass of his lady."

"Amen to that," Farquhar said. *"In the meantime, set the girls to sweeping the place clean. Tell Mrs. Fletcher to prepare the goose. Have the lads scour the wood for the biggest Yule log in Christendom. I mean for us to celebrate this Christmas in the jolliest way possible."*

Farquhar waited for Lyttle to leave and close the door to the tower room behind himself before he added, *"For it may well be our last."*

Bagpipes squealed out a strathspey tune. The first floor ballroom at Dalkeith Palace was a blur of color as a set of four couples stepped lively to a reel. Lucinda MacOwen and her sisters, along with one other Scottish lady, tripped along in time with the music. Some of the more intrepid members of the English contingent were willing to give the raw Scottish dance a go for the pleasure of bouncing around the room with such comely partners.

Sir Bertram Clarindon was the first to volunteer. He invariably turned the wrong direction and trod on his partner's toes, but all the dancers seemed to enjoy themselves.

Alexander Mallory was not among them.

Instead he'd been roped into sitting with Hester MacGibbon along the edge of the dance floor. In truth, it wasn't terribly onerous duty. Once he convinced a footman to lace the old lady's tea with a generous dollop of spirits, all he was required to do was make an occasional grunt of agreement with her. Hester was capable of pontificating on everything under the sun unassisted so long as she was given occasional encouragement.

No one who knew Hester MacGibbon wanted to be pulled into her garrulous orbit if they could help it. But the enforced social isolation gave Alex a chance to observe the crowd without interruption and take the measure of the local nobility who'd turned up to welcome the English envoys.

There were Beatons and Frasers and Bruces galore. But the Scot who surprised him most was Darren MacMartin, representing the Cameron clan. Now styling himself simply as "Sir Darren," he had no reason to remain in Scotland, unless he was up to no good.

Alexander hadn't thought much of the fellow when he bested him on the *Agatha May*. A man who could hold neither his cards nor his temper when he lost was not to be trusted.

Alex really didn't like the way the man was holding Lucinda either. The fact that MacMartin was her dance partner and the close holds were required made no difference to the clenching in Alexander's gut.

Her face was flushed that becoming shade of peach again. Her green eyes sparked with such inner fire he couldn't blame Darren MacMartin for being drawn to her. She was as light on her feet as a faery dancing on a dew-spangled flower stem.

Alex gave himself an inward shake. He wasn't usually so fanciful. *Faeries and flower stems. Clarindon would have a field day with that.*

The occasional flip of Lucinda's skirt revealed slender calves.

Alex forgot about faeries and wondered absently what her skin would taste like if he were to trace a circle around her delicate anklebone with his tongue. He closed his eyes and attempted without success to drive that idea from his mind. He tried actually listening to Hester to distract himself, but since she was waxing poetic about the efficacy of a new bunion cure, he gave that up in a heartbeat.

The couples on the dance floor moved in intricate patterns. When the dance called for the couples to move into yet another close hold, Alexander's gut tightened again.

Just because he didn't want Sir Darren to have Lucinda, didn't mean he wanted her.

Lord Rankin strolled by. "That's your new fiancée among the dancers, isn't it, Mallory?" Rankin said with the hint of a malicious giggle in his tone. "You see now why I insisted on adding a bit of local color to our gathering."

"Local color, is it?" Hester stopped Rankin cold with a clawed hand to his forearm. "I'll have ye know

the reel is a Highland tradition, no' just *local color*."
Her face twisted into a horrifying grimace. "I'll no'
have ye denigrating the reel so. This dance was old
when me grandmother was a girl and—"

"Lord Rankin, allow me to offer you my seat so
Mrs. MacGibbon can further illuminate you on
Highland customs."

Alex stood and held the chair for the man in a
move that made it impossible for him to refuse.
Rankin shot him an evil glare as he settled his bulk
onto the sturdy seat. Alex nodded to Aunt Hester
and excused himself with a wider smile than the old
harridan deserved.

"I assure you, madam, I meant no disrespect. No
indeed," Rankin sputtered as Alex beat a hasty
retreat. "Perfectly delightful country dance, what?
When His Majesty visits next August, I'm sure he'll
be charmed by it."

Alex prowled the perimeter of the ballroom,
keeping Lucinda in sight. At one point he tripped
over a long train that one of the ladies had draped
artfully before her. He righted himself before he
ended up in her lap, but it was a near thing.

Alexander swallowed back a curse. What was
wrong with him? He wasn't normally so clumsy.

He'd been forced to apologize more in these last
few days he'd been in Scotland than he had in the
previous ten years.

"Outstanding, Mallory," he chided himself as he
moved on more cautiously. "You're making a buffoon
of yourself over a girl you don't even want."

Then the music stopped with a final wheeze of
the pipes and Lucinda fell into Sir Darren's arms

with a laugh. A red haze settled over Alex's vision and he started toward them. Before he reached the couple, the music began again in a slower tempo and Clarindon claimed Lucinda's hand for the Scottish version of a minuet.

Sir Darren withdrew from the ballroom floor and cast a sheepish grin at Alexander. With Lucinda safe in Clarindon's hands, Alex decided to have a few words with MacMartin.

"I'm surprised you didn't return to London, Sir Darren," Alexander said. "Not much for you here now, is there?"

"Your new station as Lord Bonniebroch has made you look down on we lesser mortals, I see," the Scot said, his brogue less pronounced than in most of the other Gaelic voices around them. "Let me stand you to a cup of the execrable punch they're serving here and you can tell me how you're finding your new holding."

Sir Darren was far too cheerful for a man who'd lost a barony. Still, Alex couldn't think of a reason not to drink with the man he'd bested so thoroughly. It would be churlish to refuse.

"In truth, I haven't found Bonniebroch at all yet," Alex said. "You might have warned me when I won the estate that a betrothal came along with the barony."

Sir Darren laughed. "Consider your bride an added gift. I'm not ready to face the parson's mouse-trap myself." His pale-eyed gaze followed Lucinda around the room for a moment. "Though if I'd known the MacOwen lass was such a comely bit of muslin, I might have played my cards differently."

Alex cut a sharp glance at the fellow. He was almost suggesting that he'd lost Bonniebroch on purpose. "I intend to leave Dalkeith to inspect Bonniebroch after the first of the year."

"Not my place to say so, but I wouldn't wait that long if I were you."

"Really? Why is that?"

Sir Darren pulled a silver flask from inside his waistcoat and sweetened his punch with a generous dollop of amber liquor. He offered the flask to Alexander and the strong scent of spirits wafted toward him, but Alex declined the whisky with a shake of his head. If MacMartin had lost Bonniebroch on purpose, it wouldn't do to lower his guard around the man until Alex figured out his game.

"I suggest you ask Farquhar why you shouldn't wait," Sir Darren said. "Of course, you'll have to actually go to Bonniebroch to see him."

"No, I won't. The old fellow turned up here in my chamber this evening."

MacMartin choked on his punch and Alex had to thump him soundly on the back to get him to stop coughing.

"Callum Farquhar was here? The steward of Bonniebroch. He was here and you saw him? In Dalkeith?"

"Yes." Why was that such an astounding thing?

"You're sure it was him?"

"That's how he introduced himself." Alex slanted a dubious gaze at the man. "My eyes have never given me cause to doubt them before."

"That can change, believe me."

The bagpipes weren't playing for this dance, so

Alex was able to catch MacMartin's muttered reply. Yes, indeed. The man knew a great deal more than he was saying. Alex wished for a few minutes locked in a room with the fellow. He was adept at dragging information from the unwilling.

Sir Darren gave himself a small shake and then fixed Alex with a pointed glare. "You know, you look a good bit less rested than you were when you beat me in that poque game. A bit drawn and tetchy. Sort of like I was at the time. Tell me, milord, how've you been sleeping since you became Lord Bonniebroch? Any disturbing dreams?"

This time it was Alex who choked on his punch. Why did everyone in Scotland seem to want to know about his dreams?

"So," MacMartin said with a satisfied smile that was purely feline. "You have met her."

"Met who?"

"The weeping woman, of course," MacMartin said cryptically. Then he set his cup down on the sideboard and started to head back to the dance floor.

Alex decided not to wait for a locked room. He grasped MacMartin's lapel and swung him around, pressing the man's spine to the walnut-paneled wall and holding him up so that his toes barely touched the ground. "What do you know about this weeping woman?"

"Not a damned thing." Sir Darren grinned wickedly. "But I do know it's far better that she plagues your nights instead of mine. For the rest, you'll need to ask Farquhar."

Alex released him since the music stopped and

the attention of the party was no longer riveted on the dance floor.

MacMartin adjusted his jacket and smoothed down his waistcoat. "And now if you'll excuse me, I believe the next number is a waltz. I intend to dance it with the lass who got away."

"Gentlemen are blessedly predictable creatures. A little competition brings out the best in them . . . and the worst. The wise young lady rouses this competitive spirit in small, manageable doses."

From *The Knowledgeable Ladies' Guide to Eligible Gentlemen*

Chapter Nine

"Capital party, what?" Clarindon said as he joined Alexander by the punch bowl. "I say, that Lucinda of yours is quite the dancer."

Alex crossed his arms over his chest and forced himself to look away from his supposed fiancée and her current dance partner. "She's not my Lucinda."

"No? Well, that may be true given the way Mac-Martin is waltzing with her. Who knows? He may solve all your romantic entanglement problems by whisking her away to . . . hmmm." Clarindon swiped his perspiring brow with a clean, white handkerchief and then stowed it back in his waistcoat pocket. "Desperate couples back in England hie themselves to Scotland to marry in haste. Where do you suppose Scots flee to?"

"I don't know and I don't care. That's not why

we're here." Work. That's what he needed. Surely focusing on his mission would settle this blasted fire in his gut each time he caught Lucinda's eyes sparkling while she danced with someone else. "You've been at Dalkeith Palace longer than I. What have you learned about the locals?"

"The nobles have no use for the rebellion or any of the Radicals' causes. Interrupts trade, they say." Sir Bertram helped himself to a spot of punch. "Weak stuff, what?" he said with a grimace, but still managed to down the whole cup in one long swallow. "No, I think we may safely conclude that the landed Scottish nobility have calculated which side of the argument best suits their interests. They've decided to back the Crown."

"Even against their own countrymen?"

Clarindon nodded. "So it seems. No sense of national unity at all in Scotland, which is a boon for our side. Comes from all that clan nonsense, I suppose. Been their downfall since the time of Robert the Bruce. They're more loyal to their own tight little circle than to the country as a whole. But they do know where their coin is minted. Frightfully practical people, the Scots."

"Then that leaves the lesser nobility and the gentry who might give aid to the Radicals," Alex said.

"Oh, well done," Clarindon said with a sniff. "Now that you're a landed baron, someone who's *earned* a knighthood is merely a *lesser noble*."

"I don't mean you," Alex said. Clarindon had been knighted after he took a bullet meant for the king's cousin in France three years ago. It was his shining moment and Clarindon would happily untie his cravat and undo the top three buttons on his shirt for anyone who wished to see the scar near his clavicle. "Besides, let's not get carried away by the idea of me being 'landed.' I'm still fully expecting to find myself laird of a place with a roof that's open to the night sky and a flock of mangy sheep that are expected to fatten on rocks."

"It'd serve you right." Clarindon pulled a face at him.

"What have you learned about Sir Darren Mac-Martin?"

"Oh, very well. I suppose I'd ought to prove I haven't been wasting my time drinking and wenching. Not all my time at any rate . . ." Clarindon pulled a palm-sized journal from his waistcoat pocket and flipped a few pages. "Been compiling a dossier on all the Scottish chieftains. I'll do more research of course, but here's what I've gleaned from MacMartin himself. He's very proud of his family motto—'*Hinc Fortior et Clarior,*' which means—"

"'Hence stronger and more illustrious,'" Alex finished for him. "Thank you, Clarindon. I too studied Latin."

"Yes, yes, I was there at Eton with you, but I didn't think you were attending much at the time. As I recall, you were too busy devising ways of sneaking out to visit the girls in the nearby village after the headmaster and his minions were abed."

"And as I recall, you never turned down a chance to come with me. Now go on." Alexander ground his teeth as Lucinda and Sir Darren turned and dipped past them. "Why was MacMartin knighted?"

"That's the odd thing. He didn't bring it up. Most do, you know. When I tried to broach the subject, he turned the conversation in another direction."

Clarindon shifted to allow Lord Rankin to join them. "Good evening, milord. I was just saying to Mallory how well this first meeting with the local nobility has turned out. No doubt the credit redounds to you."

Lord Rankin puffed up under Clarindon's praise like a toad during its courtship season. Alexander's friend had a knack for flattery that bordered on genius. He'd often tried to teach Alex how to do it, but Alex proved a less than apt pupil.

"Yes, the evening does seem to be going well," Rankin said. "Of course, that blighter Lord Arbuthnott was trouncing me in a chess game earlier, but after this little break for dancing, I'll figure a way out of the trap he's set for me."

"Nonsense. I'm sure you're merely allowing Arbuthnott to win," Sir Bertram said.

Alex thought that was doing it a bit too brown, even for Clarindon.

Rankin harrumphed a couple of times. "Don't breathe a word of it and he'll never know I threw the game. After all, we are here to establish a foundation of goodwill for the king. It's just as I explained to Lord Liverpool," Rankin said, reinforcing the fact that he had the prime minister's ear. "If we are seen to honor and even embrace the Scottish traditions, their politics can't help but fall more in line with our own. I count on you two to jump in with both feet when it comes to ingratiating ourselves to the Scots." Then he skewered Alex with a glare. "But if you ever leave me with Hester MacGibbon again, you'll be on the first boat back to London, whether you're a Scottish laird or no."

Is that a promise? danced on Alex's tongue, but the waltz ended and he began to excuse himself so he could collect Lucinda from Sir Darren.

"No, stay a moment, Mallory. I want your opinion on something," Lord Rankin said. His tone was genial, but it was an order nonetheless. "I've arranged a special exhibition of the very thing I was talking about—a celebration of Scottish culture. Of course, I have it on good authority that it's a display of noble savagery, but the king is a devotee of Rousseau. If this demonstration goes well, we'll have them perform for His Majesty when he comes."

The bagpipes started up with a mighty wheeze that blossomed into a bone-chilling squeal. The hair on the back of Alexander's neck lifted. There was something both otherworldly and strangely familiar about that sound, as if it belonged to the realm of dreams. Or nightmares.

Or another lifetime . . .

Three kilted warriors entered the hall, two of them bearing a pair of long claymores each. The third appeared to be unarmed save for a wicked looking dirk at his waist.

"I thought we outlawed weapons in the palace," Alex said.

"We did," Rankin agreed. "But these blades are ceremonial."

"The edges look well-honed enough to ceremonially kill someone," Alex said dryly.

"Don't be such a pessimist, Mallory. Trust is the oil which greases the wheels of diplomacy."

Clearly, Rankin had lost sight of their directive from Lord Liverpool. They were supposed to search out and bring to justice any remaining Radicals, not join hands with the Scots and sing around a Maypole.

Alexander narrowed his gaze at the fellow who bore the dirk. His reddish-brown beard had been trimmed and his hair was clubbed back into a neat queue, but Alex still recognized him.

It was Lucinda's brother, Dougal.

Lucinda hissed a breath over her teeth. It was one thing for Dougal to tend the horses in the stable or prune the roses in the garden at Dalkeith. No one marked the humble servants who did those jobs. But it was quite another for him to stride into a ballroom wearing a belted plaid that had until very recently been illegal while gripping the hilt of a wicked-looking dirk.

He was bound to be recognized as one of the leaders of the Radicals, if not by the English, surely by the Scots. She'd told Brodie earlier that no one would turn him in.

Now she wasn't so sure.

As they waltzed, Sir Darren had told her everyone wished to make themselves agreeable to the English. What better way to do it than to turn in a wanted man who happened to be a Scot?

Dougal stood off to one side while the other two men laid out their claymores like prone crosses on the polished hardwood floor. Then they began leaping and dancing from one quadrant of the crossed swords to the next, their feet flying in perfect tandem, their arms raised in triumph.

"Ah, the sword dance," Sir Darren said at her side. "I haven't seen this performed since I was a boy."

Lucinda had never seen it. The masculine beauty
and grace of the dance and the terror of naked
blades so close to unprotected ankles fairly snatched
her breath away. The agility, the strength, the stamina
it took to dance with the blades and take no hurt
boggled her mind.

As soon as the sword dancers made their furious
finish, Dougal loosed a full-throated war cry and
leapt into the center of the ballroom, brandishing
his dirk.

"I've heard of the dirk dance." Sir Darren leaned
toward Lucinda to whisper in her ear. "It's supposed
to be the most primal thing a man can do short of
actually killing somebody."

Lucinda feared she might be sick. All of Dougal's
movements were stylized feats of arms, slashing and
turning, leaping and thrusting. It was as if he fought
an invisible foe in time with the wild squeal of pipes.

Dougal sparred with the air, hacking and plunging. After a particularly harrowing series of turns,
feints, and parries, the audience burst into spontaneous applause, even though the dance wasn't finished yet.

"Word is, come summer, they'll be performing
these dances for the king," MacMartin said.

Lucinda bit her lower lip. So that was Dougal's
plan. He'd be armed. He'd be close to King George.
The crowd was so mesmerized by the dirk dance,
Dougal could be on the king before they realized it
wasn't part of the performance.

And as Brodie had predicted, Dougal didn't plan
to live to tell the tale.

She swayed uncertainly on her feet.

"Are you well, Miss MacOwen?" Sir Darren asked solicitously. "You've gone quite pale. Come. I know of a little terrace off the ballroom. We'll step out and get you a breath of fresh air."

He shepherded her through the crowd and into a short corridor that led toward a set of French doors. Behind them in the ballroom, the screech of pipes went on, building to a frenzy.

Lucinda imagined how it would all play out when the king arrived next summer. Dougal's fine strong body would whirl in a dance of stylized death, and as the music built to its frenetic conclusion, he'd make a desperate leap toward the king to deliver the fatal blow.

Even if no one in the English contingent was bearing arms, they'd tear Dougal limb from limb before their sovereign's body grew cold. Lucinda swallowed back the rising bile.

"How could he even think about doing such a thing?" she mumbled. She and Sir Darren pushed through the French door and onto a slate-floored terrace. It was hedged about with a stone balustrade overlooking the expansive gardens, now pruned back and asleep for the winter.

"I know what you mean," Sir Darren said. "The sword dancers were pulse-pounding enough. That fellow with the dirk certainly seemed the dangerous sort. But he was only dancing, so don't let yourself be troubled by it."

"Aye, I'd expect you're right," she said. Better that Sir Darren think she was upset by the raw aggression of the dance than by what she suspected her brother was going to do with it. And while she was at it, she needed to keep the fact that Dougal was her brother from Sir Darren as well.

She leaned both palms on the stone balustrade and breathed in the crisp night. It was chilly enough that they wouldn't tarry there long, but the cool air blew away her queasiness. Light snow began to fall. It was the sort that melted as soon as it touched the ground, or a dry leaf, or an eyelash, but felt more than a little magical on its way down, as if each flake was the kiss of a frost faery.

Sir Darren came to stand beside her and rested his hand on the balustrade close enough to hers that they touched, lightly as the brush of a feather.

"Did you know that until an unfortunate incident on the voyage here, I was Lord Bonniebroch?"

"Really?" She'd figured she was well rid of a man who was reckless enough to chance losing so much on the turn of a card. Somehow, she'd never imagined the previous Lord Bonniebroch might be as young and engaging as Sir Darren.

"I was a fool to be drawn into that benighted card game," he said without looking at her.

"A man who can admit to foolishness is on the path to becoming wise," Lucinda said.

"Doesn't feel wise," Darren said with a snort of disagreement.

His attention seemed to be directed to the dormant garden, so she was free to study his profile.

MacMartin had a fine straight nose and deep-set, soulful eyes. If he'd kept the title, Lucinda supposed she'd have been grateful he wasn't the toothless, hairless wretch her sister Aileen had predicted for her and been satisfied to meet him at the altar.

If she'd never stumbled smack into Lord Alexander Mallory's arms.

"Well, then, it seems we would have been betrothed but for your lack of skill at the gaming table." She turned around and leaned the small of her back against the balustrade.

"It wasn't lack of skill. I—" He clamped his lips shut and his brows knit together as he obviously rethought what he was about to say. "I only want you to know if I'd met you beforehand, perhaps I wouldn't have been so quick to offer up the title and estate in a poque game. That English fiend Mallory doesn't deserve you."

The fiend in question pulled back a curtain in the ballroom and peered out at them. Pleased by the look of consternation on her betrothed's handsome face, she decided to needle him further by leaning toward Sir Darren.

"Flattering words are easily spoken, sir. They slide off the tongue and into the ear and mean next to nothing." She walked her fingers up his arm.

The curtain opened wider and from the tail of her eye, she saw Alexander's jaw drop. If she tempted Sir Darren into kissing her, Alex would have to pick his chin off the floor.

"I've always felt actions speak louder than words," she said with more boldness than she felt. After all, she'd only really kissed one man before, but she was owed the chance to try two others. Lucinda was eager to do it if she could flummox Alexander in the process. "Perhaps there's a way ye can show me the depth of yer esteem for me."

Lucinda tipped her face up, inviting MacMartin to kiss her.

She didn't have to ask him twice.

Sir Darren grabbed her and jerked her roughly to him.

"That's it, Sassenach," Brodie whispered into Alex's ear, though the Englishman gave no sign of having heard him. Lord Bonniebroch all but pressed his nose against the steamed up window panes, peering out at Lucinda and that other fellow. *"Are ye no' going to do something, man?"*

The blasted Englishman had been so intent on the dirk dance, he wouldn't have even noticed Lucinda leaving the room with Sir Darren if Brodie hadn't jostled him enough to make his gaze swivel in their direction. Then Alexander "High-and-Mighty" Mallory finally deigned to make his way around the room at entirely too slow a pace to suit Lucinda's ghostly protector. Brodie had to blow on the curtains over this window to make them part, as if from a draft, before the man thought about looking out onto the terrace where Lucinda was playing with fire.

When Lucy walked her fingers up Sir Darren's sleeve, Brodie nearly burst a gut, or would have if he'd had one, but Lord Bonniebroch stood rooted to the spot.

"Bollocks, man, do I have to shove ye out the door to make ye protect what's yers?"

Brodie would have gone himself. He imagined setting a small fire in Sir Darren's left boot. It was a neat trick and one he'd perfected with plenty of practice. Or perhaps he'd give the man a case of the prickly heat in his crotch that would have him sitting down in agony and peeing like a girl for a month.

Anything to take the fellow's mind off Lucinda, who's behaving like a strumpet, so she is.

Brodie would give her a stern talking to later that night once she was back in the safety of her own chamber. If such a thing were possible, he'd have liked to take her over his knee and tan her backside for the way she was flaunting herself before that MacMartin fellow.

But Brodie could do nothing at the moment.

There was a goodly breeze outside. Naked tree limbs swayed with it, their bare twiggy fingers scratching the sky's dark back. A spirit might be blown halfway to the River Tay before he could get in any serious licks on Sir Darren.

Then MacMartin suddenly pulled Lucinda close and covered her mouth with his in a kiss that was about taking, with not a smidge of giving at all.

Alexander Mallory cursed softly and streaked out of the ballroom and down the corridor to the French doors.

Brodie smiled after him.

"Well, Sassenach, ye may be the proud owner of a pair of balls, after all."

Satisfied that Mallory could handle matters on the terrace, Brodie turned his attention back to the assembled Englishmen. There wasn't much he could do if Sir Darren proved to be more than a match for Alexander.

At least a fight would allow Lucinda time to escape. Of course, women sometimes liked to stay and watch. And once in a while, they even sided with the loser in a contest of strength—an oddity in the feminine sense of fairness that never failed to baffle Brodie.

His gaze fell on the portly fellow holding court with the head of the Campbell clan. Lord Rankin, he'd heard him named.

One of Brodie's favorite tricks was to emit a noxious odor between two people he wished to separate. Both of them would assume the other fellow was to blame for the stench and they'd sidle away from each other in embarrassment.

Ah, just think what fun I'll have when George IV comes calling next summer. By the time I'm done with him, they'll be calling the English king "Ol' Thunder-Mugs."

Lucinda gasped, but Sir Darren showed no sign of letting her come up for more air. His mouth was so firm over hers, it reminded her of one of those glass cups physicians used to suction a patch of skin and draw out the ill humors that made a body sick.

She'd only goaded him into kissing her because Alexander was watching. Oh, how she wished she hadn't.

Kissing other men was highly overrated.

Alex's kisses left her light-headed. Darren's made her light-stomached. She felt all queasy and dirty inside. When he grasped her buttocks and lifted her into him, she nearly retched into his mouth.

Lucinda balled her hands into impotent fists and pounded his chest.

"Le' muh gaw," she said into his mouth.

"The lady wants you to let her go," someone said.

Oh, thank you, God!

The voice belonged to Alex. So did the hand that wrenched her free. Along with the fist that connected with Sir Darren's jaw.

Unfortunately, Sir Darren landed a punch as well. Alex's head snapped back, but he didn't go down.

"Don't be blaming me," MacMartin said, fists tucked under his chin, ready to lash out to protect his face. "That little tart all but begged for it."

"Aye, I know she did," Alex said, his body taut as a hound on point. "I was watchin' the pair of ye through the window."

Lucinda stared at him in wonderment. There was the slightest hint of a brogue in his voice, even more than in Sir Darren's. Where had that come from?

"Then you know she started it," MacMartin said as he circled warily.

"And I'm ending it," Alex promised as he launched himself toward the other man.

"While it may seem incredibly romantic for gentlemen to come to blows over which of them deserves a lady's favor, the knowledgeable miss will bear in mind the old adage:

'To the victor goes the spoils.'

The victorious gentleman may well enjoy his triumph.

The same cannot always be said for the spoils."

From *The Knowledgeable Ladies' Guide to Eligible Gentlemen*

Chapter Ten

Lucinda had seen enough male ferocity while she watched her brother perform the dirk dance to last her a lifetime. The naked aggression on Alexander's features as he whaled away on Sir Darren MacMartin made Dougal's stylized combat seem pale and toothless by comparison.

The men met with a furious exchange of blows and counterpunches, a strike to the midsection here, an elbow to the kidney there. Lucinda flinched at each thud of fist on ungiving flesh. The fight degenerated into a brawl with no observable rules.

Snow fell more heavily now, sticking to the slate

pavers and making them slick underfoot. Lucinda slipped as she backed away from the men and would have gone down if she hadn't grasped the dead vines crawling up a trellis attached to the great house.

She gasped when Alexander staggered back a pace after one of Sir Darren's wild swings connected with his temple. He ducked the next blow and came up with an undercut to Sir Darren's jaw. The force of the wallop spun MacMartin around and laid him out on the snow-covered terrace.

A dribble of red showed starkly on the gathering white.

"Damn you, Mallory." MacMartin rose to his knees, swiping his mouth with the back of his hand. "You've knocked out a tooth."

"Stay down or you'll eat nothing but soup for the rest of your life." Alex stood over him, chest heaving, fists still clenched. For good measure, he planted his booted foot on his foe's spine, pushing him back into a prone position. "You will give Miss MacOwen a wide berth for the rest of the time you remain here at Dalkeith. If you're seated next to her at supper, you'll excuse yourself and take a tray in your room. You will not dance with her. You will not speak with her. If I mislike the way you so much as look at her, we'll do this again and I won't stop with one tooth. Have I made myself clear?"

MacMartin nodded, but otherwise remained motionless.

Lucinda's heart fairly sang. Alexander *did* care for her. No man laid out another like that unless he had feelings for the lady.

Then Alex turned his steely gaze on her and she began to have a bit of a rethink. If his glower was any indication, the feelings he had for her now were not the ones she was hoping for.

He didn't say a word, but when he grasped her firmly by the wrist, she had no choice but to accompany him back toward the palace. Alexander pulled the French door open and then once they were inside, he threw the bolt behind them. Sir Darren would have to trudge all the way around the great house in the increasingly thick snow in order to re-enter by the main doors in front.

"You're going to make a terrible enemy," Lucinda said.

"Thanks to you, I already have." He tugged her down the hall. "Did it occur to you that I might have more important things to do than to make sure you don't come to grief through your own foolishness?"

She decided to let the "foolishness" pass unremarked. She had been foolish, but he was still her betrothed. Alexander owed her the protection of his body. "Most men find tending to the welfare of their future brides to be quite important, more important than other matters, in fact."

"Most men don't have their future brides forced upon them."

Lucinda swallowed back her hurt at that and settled for bristling anger instead. The man was being hateful for the sake of it. Very well. She could repay him in kind.

She hoped they'd return to the ballroom where a sprightly tune signaled that a country dance was in progress, but Alexander kept barreling down the corridor without slowing one bit.

"If I've pulled ye away from something so dreadfully *important,* far be it from me to keep ye."

"Trust me, madam, you now have my complete attention."

She didn't like the sound of that. And her wrist was beginning to ache where he gripped it.

"My sisters will wonder where I've gone." She broke into a trot to keep up with his determined strides.

"No, they won't. They're having far too much fun dancing to fret over your whereabouts," he said. "Besides, you should have thought of that before you left the ballroom with that blatherskite MacMartin."

"Aunt Hester will be looking for me."

"Your aunt Hester will be looking for her next tot of rum. She was working on her third when I left her. The drink may leave her drooling, but it makes the old bat more agreeable."

"That's no' verra charitable of ye. She's a poor old widow woman—"

"Who probably drove her husband to the grave with her incessant demands." He pulled her into the first available empty room.

A banked fire smoked in the grate, but it was enough for Alexander to use to light the lamp with a straw taper. Then he closed the door to the corridor, sealing them in.

The room turned out to be a study of sorts. There was a wall of bookshelves, but they were too sparsely filled to be called a library. Hunting trophies lined the other walls, disembodied heads of rams and stags glaring down with glass-eyed gazes of amazement at finding themselves in such a state. A bearskin rug, complete with a snarling openmouthed maw, was stretched out in the middle of the room.

There was no desk, but a pair of wing chairs done

up in scarred, worn leather flanked a small table where a game of chess was set up. The board was in a state of play, with the black bishop threatening the white king. Unless the player on the white side was willing to sacrifice his queen, the game would be over inside a couple of moves.

No players were in sight, more's the pity. Lucinda needed a buffer between herself and the man who seemed fiercer than the bear on the floor. She settled for crossing her arms over her chest and meeting Alexander's glare with one of her own.

"I hope you're satisfied," he said.

"You beat a man to first blood," she said. "Why do ye think that should please me?"

"Because you tempted him into kissing you so I'd do it."

"Sir Darren has no free will? That'll be a surprise to his vicar." The intense way Alexander looked at her made her tremble. She'd have a better chance at suppressing how he affected her if she were sitting. Lucinda crossed the room and sat in one of the wing chairs. "And how can I be to blame for you bursting out onto the terrace and picking a fight with the man?"

"It's clearly what you wanted. You purposely allowed him to kiss you in the hope of making me jealous."

"So you *are* jealous."

"Of MacMartin? You jest. I only intervened to save you from his ignoble intentions." He gave her a mocking bow. "I'd have done the same for any other silly female in similar circumstances."

Her chest constricted. How had Alexander divined her intentions so easily? If he had any tender feelings for her, he was making a good job of hiding them.

"I wasn't trying to make you jealous because you have no standing to be. The only thing binding us is a contract and I'm no' yours yet," she said tartly. "May I remind you that you agreed I should kiss three men before our wedding?"

"That wasn't a kiss. It was an assault," Alex said through clenched teeth. "Admit it. You were out of your depth and struggling to break free from him."

"No, I wasna." The lie tasted sour on her tongue. "And even if I was," she amended, "if I'd wanted to get away, I would have."

"Really? What would you have done if I hadn't arrived?"

"I was . . . I would have cried out."

"No one inside would have heard you and Mac-Martin is probably the sort who enjoys hearing a woman protest." Alexander paced before her, energy crackling off him like heat lightning. "Especially if there's nothing else she can do about it."

"There are other things I could do."

"Oh, do you mean the way you were pounding on his chest? If you weren't trying to get away, I have to assume you think men like being pummeled while they kiss you." He leaned on both arms of the wing chair, forcing her back into the tufted seat. "Most men don't relish being punched when they're trying to work their way into a woman's pantalets."

That made her breath hitch uncertainly. She wouldn't have classed herself a prude, but when he said "pantalets," she flushed all over. Maybe her reaction wasn't embarrassment though. Maybe it was something much different. Something darker and more dangerous. And tinged with wicked promise.

Alexander's face was so close to hers, his breath feathered warmly over her mouth. The scowl melted from his features as he looked down at her with an intensity that made her belly jitter. Her lips parted softly. She couldn't seem to help it.

"What . . ." she whispered, "what *do* men relish when they . . . when they're . . . ?"

"Trying to work their way into a woman's pantalets?" he repeated, his voice husky this time.

Drat the man! He must be able to tell how he's discomfited me.

Lucinda didn't think her voice would work so she simply nodded.

"You really want to know?" The sharp edge of irritation left his tone.

She nodded again.

"Trust," Alex said simply as he brushed his fingertips along her cheek and then tipped her chin up. "A man relishes a woman's trust."

Slowly, he lowered his mouth to hers.

This kiss was so far removed from the blistering taking of Sir Darren MacMartin, they couldn't be classed as the same act.

Alexander's lips caressed hers, warm, wet, and insistent. Even though she could still sense his bridled fury in the aftermath of his fight with Sir Darren, Alex's strength was controlled.

Designed to make me trust him.

She opened to him like a daisy to the sun and his tongue slipped in to explore her with tense gentleness. When their mouths finally separated a bit, she was aching in the tender place between her legs and desperate for more.

Lucinda draped her arms over his shoulders. "You win, Alexander. I trust you."

He kissed her again, long and slow.

It was wonderful, but it wasn't *enough*.

"What else does a man want . . . when he's working his way . . . into a woman's pantalets?" she asked breathlessly between kisses.

"Yes," he said and claimed her mouth again.

What? That makes no sense. But then she wasn't thinking terribly clearly. Maybe he wasn't either.

Alexander's kisses made her lips tingle and her head fuzzy. It was as if she'd sneaked into her great-aunt's store of rum and consumed the lot. When she inhaled, all she could smell was him, all leathery and male and with a light undernote of spicy bergamot. He made it hard for her to put a coherent thought together, much less voice it, but she finally managed to whisper, "Why 'yes?' I dinna understand."

"The only thing a man wants to hear a woman say is 'yes.'"

"Oh." She went all limp and liquid inside, lost in the heat, the yearning, the wonderment of his mouth. "Aye," she said, soft as a sigh. Then, for his sake, she amended it to the very English "Yes."

His hands moved from the arms of the chair she was sitting in to her breasts.

She jerked in surprise, but then his kiss deepened, his tongue gently exploring. She supposed she ought to find this all normal, his soft caress through the thin silk of her gown, the way her body seemed to melt in places. After all, folk had been doing this dance since Eden. A man seducing a maiden was the most ordinary thing in the world.

But now it was happening to her and that made the old dance new. Fresh as the Garden itself. No man had ever kissed a girl like Alex kissed her. No one had ever felt this jumbled up Oh-God-what's-coming-next anticipation that swirled in her belly. No one had ever made love before. Alexander and Lucinda were making it up as they went.

It was life-altering. Shattering. Inevitable.

The tips of her breasts peaked to hard points, each so sensitive and throbbing she groaned into his mouth.

His fingers dipped into her bodice, first a brushing, teasing series of strokes. Then he moved around the chair so he could tip her head against the seat back, run his palm over the length of her neck, and slide his whole hand down the front of her gown.

Oh! To be held so. The aching eased for a few heartbeats, and then began again in desperate throbs. He took a hard peak between his thumb and forefinger and gently squeezed. A jolt of desire zinged from that sensitive point to her soft molten core.

But it still wasn't *enough*.

She unbuttoned the seed pearls that marched down her bodice and unlaced her stays enough to tug the neckline of her chemise down. Still suckling his tongue, she helped him free her breasts completely from her layers of clothing so her skin lay exposed to his touch and his gaze.

"You're beautiful," he said as he kissed down her neck to her waiting breasts.

When he took a nipple in his mouth and sucked,

she thought she'd die of bliss. He tugged at her peaks, bit down on them till she moaned his name.

Even this delight wasn't *enough*.

The nameless longing moved down her body, raging into a stronger ache that settled between her legs in a steady pounding throb.

Want me, Alexander. Need me. Love me.

She was thinking it so loudly, she was sure he must be able to hear.

"I do want you, Lucinda," he growled in her ear as he thrummed her nipple.

Oh, dear Lord, I didn't say it out loud, did I?

She didn't have long to puzzle over whether or not he could hear her thoughts because he scooped her up then and carried her to the bearskin. Still kissing her mouth, her cheeks, her closed eyelids, he lowered her to the soft pelt.

Lucinda wasn't sure what he expected of her. Should she touch him as she had in her great-aunt's kitchen when she'd learned for certain sure just how "Much of a Muchness" he was? Should she simply lie there with her eyes squinched tight?

Trust, he said. That's all I have to do.

"There be three things which are too wonderful for me, yea, four which I know not: The way of an eagle in the air; the way of a serpent upon a rock; the way of a ship in the midst of the sea; and the way of a man with a maid."

Proverbs 30:18–19, King James Bible

Chapter Eleven

Lucinda decided on keeping her eyes open and she was so glad she did.

Otherwise she'd have missed the wholly unexpected look of tenderness on Alexander's face as he lowered himself beside her. She'd have missed the way his eyes closed in something like reverence when he bent to kiss her breasts and the way the corners of his mouth turned up wickedly when he reached under her hem.

When he slid his hand up her silky pantalets, it was as if the thin fabric disappeared entirely. Her legs fell open of their own accord. She couldn't have kept her knees together unless they'd been bound with a cord.

Then Alexander found the open crotch in her pantalets and cupped her sex with his whole hand.

"Oh," escaped her lips.

Her insides did several backflips, a fierce melding of need and joy. She'd never imagined wanting to be held like this. Now she couldn't imagine what her life had been like before he did it. He took that part of her she didn't know quite what to do with—the part that some had tried to teach her was shameful, not to be touched or fiddled with more than strictly necessary—and he held her as if that small bit of her was the most precious thing in the world.

"Can ye feel that?" she whispered. "My heart is pounding between me legs."

He smiled down at her. "Just wait."

Then he bent to kiss her again and as he slipped his tongue between her lips, he slipped a finger between her soft, moist folds.

The whole world fell away.

Everyone pronounced the sword and dirk dances an unmitigated success. Lord Rankin moved around the ballroom, dropping a few words into each little clump of revelers' conversations, and received nothing but glowing comments in return.

His talents were wasted playing sheepdog to men like Mallory and Clarindon. So much more could be accomplished through diplomacy. Once Rankin paved the way for a successful royal progression next summer through his own methods, surely Lord Liverpool would see that in the modern world, such old-fashioned spies as Mallory and Clarindon were as antiquated as knee britches and snuffboxes.

And how might the prime minister reward someone of his talents? An ambassador's post sounded good to Rankin. Preferably to someplace warm. Italy, perhaps. Tuscany was particularly lovely any time of year. Lord Liverpool could arrange matters for him.

Rankin was warming to a vivid daydream of dusky dark-haired maidens, their bare calves stained from stomping grapes, when Lord Arbuthnott interrupted his musings.

"Weel, milord, are ye ready to return to the chess match we started?" Arbuthnott said. "Though if ye didna wish to, I couldna blame ye. I left ye in a deuce of a pickle, an' I do say so meself."

"Don't be too hasty," Rankin said. "We English have had our backs to the wall before and emerged victorious." When Arbuthnott frowned, Rankin realized he'd steered the conversation in entirely too military a direction. "But no matter. The point of the game is stimulating conversation as far as I'm concerned. And I believe I saw a decanter of port in the study as well. Shall we?"

He waved Lord Arbuthnott ahead of him and started along the perimeter of the ballroom toward the exit. The musicians had launched into another set of dances and he noticed the comely MacOwen sisters had once again taken to the floor, this time with new partners. It had been a stroke of genius to include that family in the gathering. Not only were the girls highly ornamental, their presence seemed to irritate Mallory since they were a tangible reminder at every turn of his unexpected betrothal.

And serve him right!

Strange that he didn't see Mallory's fiancée dancing, too. Or Mallory himself, for that matter.

"Lord Rankin, I'm cravin' a word wi' ye."

Hester MacGibbon's croaking voice carried over the music and he wasn't quick enough to pretend he hadn't heard her. She rumbled along right behind him and Lord Arbuthnott. The old lady could be surprisingly spry when she wished.

Since it wouldn't do for him to be seen to be discourteous to a guest, even an uninvited one, Rankin stopped and allowed her to catch up to him, though every fiber in his being urged him to flee. The Mac-Owen girls were a fine addition to the party. Their demanding great-aunt was not.

"What is it, Mrs. MacGibbon?" He added a silent *"this time."*

"'Tis concerning me niece Lucinda's nuptials," she said. "The marriage contract stipulates that the wedding between her and Lord Bonniebroch be held at St. Giles, the High Kirk in Edinburgh, on Christmas Day. But I'm thinkin' we could bend the particulars of the agreement without disturbin' the intent. Not to mention that these old bones don't crave another carriage ride back to town for no longer than it'll take to say the needful words over the happy couple. The MacOwen family would be satisfied if the ceremony were held here at Dalkeith, in the St. Nicholas chapel."

Satisfied? She'd be merely *satisfied* to have her niece married in the very chapel where King George IV would make at least an appearance of piety next summer. The woman's pushiness had no limits.

"Surely this is not the time or place for such a discussion. Kindly make an appointment with my factor and I'll give your request full consideration tomorrow."

"I don't see as there's all that much to consider," Mrs. MacGibbon said.

"Nevertheless, I have a pressing chess match to

settle and I haven't time to attend to other matters at present." He turned to follow Lord Arbuthnott, who was well on the way to making good his escape. "Now, good evening."

"Aye, it's been that," Mrs. MacGibbon agreed with uncharacteristic cheer as she clasped his arm and tottered alongside him. "Chess, d'ye say? Not with Lord Arbuthnott, I hope. The man's a master. Why, he'll give ye such a drubbin' as ye'll never recover from. Best I go along and see can I offer ye some help. Many's the time I kept Mr. MacGibbon, God grant him rest, from castling his king when he ought to have charged across the board."

Rankin couldn't shake her without curtness. Perhaps acquiescence to her demands was the ticket. "On second thought, I believe a St. Nicholas chapel wedding is a capital idea. I don't see why your niece and Lord Bonniebroch shouldn't be married right here."

"Weel, that's grand then," she said, but showed no sign of turning him loose.

"Now that that's settled, there's no need for you to leave the evening's festivities," he said with fading hope.

"Och! In truth, all this music's beginning to give me a headache and I'm needin' a bit o' quiet. A good game o' chess will be just the thing," she said. "Tell me, milord, how stand ye on the question of using the King's Gambit for an opening?"

Lord Rankin slowed to match her pace and continued on toward the parlor. There was no help for it. He'd been short to the point of rudeness, but she hadn't even recognized the cut. He'd given in to her demands and she merely took it as her due. Short of peeling the woman's hand off his arm and fleeing for his life, he wasn't going to be rid of her.

Lord Rankin sighed.

A wise man knows when he's lost the skirmish, throws down his weapon, and lives to fight another day.

Alex thought he couldn't get any harder, but watching Lucinda's face while he played with her soft folds made him like granite. Her breasts were perfection and the sweet, wet heaven between her legs was worth dying for, but to watch first wonder, then need, and finally rapture parade across her lovely features was the finest thing he'd ever experienced.

He kissed along her jawline, then licked her earlobe. She shivered with delight, raising her arms above her head in surrender. Her eyelids fluttered closed and he knew she was so intent on simply feeling, she couldn't bear too many senses at once.

His were all on high alert. The fresh, musky scent of her arousal perfumed the small space. He longed to bury his face between her legs and wallow in her essence, to nibble on those sweet nether lips and run his tongue through her secret valleys.

But Lucinda was a virgin. He didn't want to overwhelm her.

Next time, he promised himself.

For now, he worshiped her soft wet petals with his touch. He circled and teased and stroked the little pearl that had risen under his fingertips. He slipped into her tight channel, first with one finger, then with two, while his thumb still tormented her most sensitive spot.

She writhed under him. She arched her back while he tongued her nipples. She moaned his name. She didn't hold back or beg him to stop. Lucinda accepted everything with heart-pounding delight.

She was a veritable queen. And her trust made him feel like a king.

Her breathing grew increasingly ragged. Finally Lucinda's eyes flew open and her whole body stiffened. She curled her fists into the shaggy bearskin.

"That's it, love," he said encouragingly. "Let it begin."

Her release started with a soft pulse in her folds, then a pounding around his fingers. Finally her whole body bucked with the force of the contractions and she cried out in a long thin sob of joy.

Alexander cradled her sex in his palm. It was as though her heart galloped in his hand. He kissed her again, intending it to be a sweet conclusion to her experience, but she pulled his head down and held it while she thrust her tongue into his mouth. Her other hand found his groin and she began rubbing him through his trousers in long, hard strokes.

So much for overwhelming her.

He undid his trousers, hiked up her skirt around her waist and settled between her thighs. He stopped, poised at her swollen opening.

"That was . . . there are no words," she said, squirming down to take him in. The tip eased into her warm wetness. "But it still wasn't enough. I'm so empty."

He kissed her breasts, then her chin, then her lips. "And I can't bear to see a damsel in distress."

She was going to be a tight fit. Should he go slow to avoid hurting her or shred her in a single hard thrust and get the business of deflowering her over with quickly?

But before Alex could do anything, fast or slow, the door to the corridor opened and Lord Arbuthnott walked in.

"God's teeth, laddie, are there no beds in Dalkeith that ye must defile your lass on a bear rug?"

Alex scrambled to yank Lucinda's skirt down as she rolled out from under him, away from the Scottish laird. Then he stood and refastened his trouser buttons, while she, faced away from Lord Arbuthnott, did up her bodice.

Blood started to flow back to Alexander's brain and sanity came with it. What on earth was he thinking? He didn't want to marry Lucinda. Wasn't that the whole point of their ridiculous "kissing three other men" agreement? And yet he couldn't bear to watch MacMartin slobber on her.

"This isn't what it looks like, milord," he began.

"If it isna what it looks like then the English really are a different sort of folk," Lord Arbuthnott said, arms crossed over his chest. Lucinda finished arranging her clothing, smoothed down her hair, and turned around. "Ah, there ye are, lass. I mind ye now. Ye're the MacOwen girl, are ye no'?"

"Aye, milord, an' it please ye."

The laird's brow lowered. "It doesna please me."

"What doesn't please you?" came Lord Rankin's voice from the hallway.

Wonderful, Alex thought. *Almost caught with my trousers around my ankles by the man who most wants me to fail my Scottish mission.*

"What's amiss, Arbuthnott?" Rankin's voice was

closer now. "Have you realized your mistake and seen the way I'm going to beat you?"

"Oh, I reckon it'll come to a beating," the Scottish laird said. "But it willna be me who'll be getting it. It'll be one of yer young gentlemen."

Rankin's bulk filled the doorway for a moment. "Mallory, what's going on here—oh."

Lucinda was blushing scarlet and fiddling with her bodice buttons as if to make sure they were all done up. Her hair was disheveled, her mouth kiss-swollen. There was no mistaking what had happened.

"Is this what we can expect from the English, Rankin?" Arbuthnott demanded. "Are ye thinkin' to break the spirit of the Scots by instating some sort of *droit du seigneur?* Ruining our women with no recourse! I'm telling ye, man, we'll no' stand for it."

"I'm no' ruined," Lucinda said softly. "No' quite."

"Quiet, Lu—" Alex began. Nearly shagging her was a mistake brought on by the heat of the brawl with MacMartin and the way her eyes went all soft in the light of the banked fire and—oh, hang it all, he was without excuse. But the last thing he needed was for her to try to defend him.

"Lucinda Ismay MacOwen!"

Correction. Great-Aunt Hester making an appearance behind Lord Rankin was the last thing he needed.

"Weel, now," the old lady said. "What have ye to say for yerself?" When Lucinda started to explain, Hester interrupted her. "No, lass, say what ye will, there's no excuse for behaving like a trollop."

"Now wait just a minute," Alex said, moving in front of Lucinda. "She wasn't behaving like a trollop. This is my fault entirely."

"Aye, it is." It may have been a trick of the soft light, but Alex could have sworn the ghost of a smile wafted across the old woman's features. "There's no help for it now, is there? The pair of ye must needs wed and with no more dallying. No need to wrangle over the details on the morrow, Lord Rankin. We'll have a wedding this very night."

Aunt Hester waddled toward them, grasped both their hands and pressed them together. "I ken as how the contract specified Christmas Day for the ceremony, but I'll be bound, I dinna trust the pair of ye to bide under the same roof until the knot's been tied good and tight."

She turned back to Lord Rankin. "Wake the vicar."

"By all means, a young woman should enjoy the preparations for her wedding day. Revel in lace and nosegays and a lovely trousseau. However, the knowledgeable lady realizes these are but pretty distractions from the awful seriousness of what is about to occur—a vow before God and man that ends rather ominously in 'till death do us part.'"

From *The Knowledgeable Ladies' Guide to Eligible Gentlemen*

Chapter Twelve

Lucinda was surprised her aunt allowed her a moment to run a brush through her hair, much less change into the gown and veil she'd planned to wear for her wedding. But Great-Aunt Hester insisted that though everything must be done with all speed, there was no reason why it couldn't be done correctly at the same time.

"It'll be a mercy to have this wedding over with, so I'll only have two eejits to watch over instead of three," Hester had added as she huffed her way up the stairs behind Lucinda and her sisters.

Aileen and Mary fluttered about Lucy, excited as a pair of butterflies flitting around a lily that had just unfurled its petals. Once Lucinda was stripped out of her ball gown and decently laced into the fine pink confection with seed pearls at the bodice and a discreet flounce of lace at the hem, Brodie appeared in her small chamber to wish her well.

Of course, she was the only one who could see and hear him.

"Ye look pretty as a speckled pup," the ghost said as he appeared in the mirror behind her reflection.

Everyone else was busy fluffing out the lace on Lucinda's veil on the other side of the room, so she pulled a face at him.

"Thank ye verra much," she whispered furiously. "What lass doesna wish to be compared to a dog before she marches down the aisle."

"I didna mean . . . 'tis only that ye look so . . . weel, ye're no' me little girl anymore, are ye?"

He sniffed, swiped his nose with an embroidered handkerchief edged with French knots, and blinked rapidly. If Lucinda didn't know better, she'd say the spirit was trying to hold back tears.

"Brodie," she said softly. "Dinna take on so. I'll always be yer little girl."

The ghost smiled, his pale face a wreath of satisfied wrinkles.

"Lucinda," Aunt Hester said sharply, "what are ye natterin' on about? Folk will think ye're nipped in the noggin if they hear ye mumbling to yerself like that."

"I'll be watching o'er ye in the chapel, just to make sure the knot's tied good and tight," Brodie said and then winked into nothingness. Only a faint wisp of white remained in the place where he'd been, hovering

next to her reflection like the last breath of a snuffed-out candle.

Aileen and Mary came skittering across the chamber, their mother's long veil billowing behind them. They settled it on Lucinda's head and pinned the lacy concoction into place.

"Just think, Lu," Mary said with uncharacteristic breathlessness. "This verra night, ye'll share a bed with a man. It'll be so strange, I'd think. If Lord Bonniebroch snores like Father does, I doubt ye'll get a wink of sleep."

"I should hope she doesna." Aileen rolled her eyes. "Ye're such a wee ninny, Mary. Do ye no' ken that when ye share a bed with a man the last thing ye'll be doin' is trying to sleep?"

Aunt Hester made a low growl in the back of her throat. "Dinna let me hear the pair of ye talkin' like that again or we'll pack up and head back for Edinburgh first thing in the morning. I've a notion to do me spring cleaning early and though I doubt ye'd be much help, I'll find plenty to occupy yer idle hands till yer father comes to collect ye in a few weeks."

The sisters protested that they had exhausted both their knowledge and interest about how one shares a bed with a man and their aunt would never hear a peep more about it from them if only they'd be allowed to remain at Dalkeith for the Christmas festivities that would stretch into Twelfth Night.

"Verra well," the old lady said. "Now get ye gone to the chapel and wait for us in the nave there. I'll be havin' a privy word with the bride, if ye please."

Lucinda swallowed hard. So far, Great-Aunt Hester hadn't berated her for the compromised state in which she and Alex had been found. That was about to change. Once Mary closed the door behind her and Aileen, Lu braced herself for the onslaught.

"Now, I ken as ye were far too young when yer mother died for her to have done the needful by ye on the matter of what passes between a man and his wife," Great-Aunt Hester began.

Lucinda blanched as white as her veil. This was worse than a dressing down. Aunt Hester was going to explain just how one *did* share a bed with a man.

"Auntie, I'm farm raised, remember," she said, trying to head Hester off before she mortally embarrassed them both. "I think I've an idea of what to expect."

"Judging from what passed in the study, ye've more than idea."

Lucinda sighed. Back to the dressing down. She supposed it was the lesser of two evils.

But to her surprise, her aunt palmed both of her cheeks, pulled her head down, and pressed her dry, papery lips on Lucinda's forehead in an awkward sort of benediction.

"I must swear ye to absolute secrecy," her aunt said solemnly. "If ye breathe a word of what I'm about to tell ye, I'll deny it with me dyin' breath. And I'll change me last will and testament so ye'll no' be getting the bequest of me mother's brooch when the time comes. T'was old when my grandmother's grandmother was a girl, all amber stones and silverwork, so it's worth a pretty price, ye ken."

Lucinda had no idea she was even in her aunt's will. Nor had she seen this valuable brooch. "I'll no' tell a soul."

Her aunt's face lifted in a ghost of a smile that made her almost pleasant-looking. "I just wanted ye to know ye're no' the first bride in the family to anticipate her wedding vows a wee bit," Aunt Hester said. "Mr. MacGibbon and I fairly led me poor parents a merry chase 'round several haystacks before they hauled us into the kirk to make matters legal. And nary a moment too soon."

"Thank ye, auntie." Lucinda threw her arms around the old woman. "Ye really are sweet, are ye no'?"

"Bah! Sweet is for tea and crumpets." She disentangled herself from Lucinda's arms with a self-conscious shudder. "Old women should be annoying. We've certainly earned the right. Now, let's get ye marrit to that strapping young man of yours."

The chapel must have been ancient at the time of the Flood. In stark contrast to the pale sandstone of Dalkeith Palace, the stone that marked this sacred spot might have started out light gray, but it had darkened over the years, black with soot from countless fires and damp with mold and candlelit sanctity.

Alex thought the depressing space fit the occasion.

"You can't say I didn't warn you." Clarindon straightened Alexander's cravat with disgusting cheerfulness as they waited in the transept. "It's a matter of physical science. Playing with the business end of a dirk will make you bleed. Playing with a loaded derringer will lead to a gunshot. Playing with one's fiancée accelerates the velocity at which a man is catapulted toward the altar."

"You're not helping," Alex said glumly.

"Sorry, old son, but you're beyond help now,"

Clarindon said. "If it were only Lord Arbuthnott and Lord Rankin, you might have had a prayer. Once Hester MacGibbon joined the fray, the hill of your bachelorhood was irreparably lost. You may as well smile and make the best of it."

"How can I do that?" Alex asked through clenched teeth. "You know what we do, the places we go, the risks we take. There's no room in that life for hearth and home."

Not to mention that at times, he'd had to seduce information from the wives and mistresses of well-placed foreign dignitaries. While Alexander's wife might be resigned to a husband who faced danger in performance of his duties for King and Crown, he imagined Lucinda wouldn't be amenable to his using his bed skills to complete his assigned work. The times he'd been forced to take that route weren't his proudest moments, but there was no limit to what he'd do for his country.

It didn't help matters that those amatory exploits were the only ones his father seemed to catch wind of. For example, the marquis wasn't aware he'd broken into a Barbary pirate's stronghold and extricated the king's cousin, saving the Crown a small fortune in ransom money. It was the nature of Alexander's business that he couldn't share the scope or details of his covert activities with anyone. As far as the world knew, he and Clarindon were part of King George's entourage of courtiers. Merely two more among the many sycophants and posers.

Just once he wished he could tell his father, "There, you see, sir. The incident with the King's brother in Cornwall where disaster was averted. The recovery of the Duke of Cambridge's stolen signet ring before it could be used to alter military dispatches. Uncovering the plot to murder the Russian ambassador and use his death as a pretext for war. That was me. I did those things."

But he couldn't. As far as the marquis knew, his second son was a wastrel who spent his days gaming and drinking and chasing every available skirt. And his father despised him for it.

It wasn't anything Alex could admit, not even to Clarindon, but the trust of Lord Liverpool began to make up for that lack of fatherly approval. Not that he'd had much chance to serve the prime minister's interests since he set foot in Scotland.

It was as if Fate had conspired to snatch the only thing in his life that made him feel worthwhile and replaced it with Bonniebroch and all the complications connected with his new Scottish estate and title. Not the least of which was about to corner him at the altar.

"You sound as if you wish to continue working for Lord Liverpool forever," Clarindon said, smoothing back his own hair. "I certainly don't."

Alexander's gaze snapped toward his friend at that. He'd always thought Clarindon was as addicted to the excitement, the challenge of covert action as he. "Never say your heart's been snagged by one of those Scottish maidens you were dancing with this evening."

"No. But my heart is certainly intrigued by the *idea* of being snagged by one." Clarindon clapped a hand on his shoulder and steered him to his place before the altar. "Face the facts, my friend. This is your last service to the Home Office. Your traveling days in Lord Liverpool's service are done unless you mean to make your wife a widow to your career."

"Not necessarily," Alex whispered from the side of his mouth. Now that they were beneath the spot where the highest arch vaulted over the cross-shaped design of the chapel, his voice carried further.

"What do you mean?" Clarindon turned to watch the MacOwen sisters precede the bride down the central aisle.

"Simply that annulments can be arranged," Alex said.

"Yes, but in order to be granted one, you'd need to prove that a true marriage never took place. Rather hard to do since you're only here now because you were within an ace of shagging the lass on a bear-skin rug."

"You think I can't control myself?" Alex glared at Clarindon as the vicar ambled sleepily from the door that led to the sacristy. "I have a will of iron."

"Which does you no good once another thing of iron rises as well."

The vicar shot the men a black frown that suggested if it were up to him, he'd happily cast the pair of them into the fiery pit. Never mind the scandal of a rushed wedding. The real crime was interrupting the vicar's sleep.

Alex turned and faced the rear of the chapel. The only witnesses in the pews were Lord Arbuthnott and Rankin on the bridegroom's side of the chapel, Great-Aunt Hester on the other. The old woman skewered him with an evil glare. Aileen and Mary Mac-Owen reached the choir, their faces surprisingly fresh considering the lateness—or the earliness, depending on one's point of view—of the hour, and veered off to their places to wait for the bride's arrival.

Lucinda appeared, framed in the doorway at the rear of the chapel. She hesitated for a couple heartbeats, then began to walk steadily toward him. The silk of her gown draped her form like water, conforming to her curves and spilling to the floor in pale pink folds. As she walked, her slippered toes peeped from under her hem, shyly disappearing again with each step.

The veil effectively obscured her features.

For a moment, Alex wondered what she was thinking. Was she happy? Resigned? As confused by everything as he?

Guilt flogged him with long heavy stripes. She deserved so much more than to be leg-shackled to a man who had one foot out of the marriage before the vows were even said.

Lucinda stopped long enough for her sister to push back the veil to reveal her face. She leaned to kiss Aileen's cheek, then turned and met Alex's gaze.

The naked hope on her features rendered her vulnerable and soft and undeniably appealing. His chest ached. He wished someone would swoop in to snatch her up and carry her away. Someone should warn her not to face the world with such an open heart, not to risk herself on a man like him. He couldn't love her as she deserved. He'd only bring her pain.

"About that iron will you were talking about," Clarindon whispered. "Good luck, old son."

"It is a saying, time out of mind, that whomever one weds, one discovers in short order that one is actually married to someone else entirely."

From *The Knowledgeable Ladies' Guide to Eligible Gentlemen*

Chapter Thirteen

The ceremony passed by in a blur. Lucinda supposed she gave the right responses at the right time, but she couldn't swear to it. The warmth of Alexander's hand when it closed over hers was glory enough for her to lose herself completely. She pretended everything was going to be all right.

After the vicar's final pronouncement and the chaste brush of Alex's lips on hers, she still felt as if she were sleepwalking through a dream. Even the procession to Alex's room, which would be pressed into service as their bridal chamber, had a hazy sense of unreality to it.

But once the door closed and she was alone with Alex in his room, the enormity of what they'd just done came crashing down on her.

Lucinda expected to feel a surge of triumph. After all, she'd secured her family's fortune with this match. Her sisters' futures were ever so much rosier because of it and Dougal might yet escape the hangman with a half-English brother-in-law to ease his way toward a pardon.

And contrary to her sisters' dire predictions, her new husband wasn't a toothless, hairless dotard. Instead, Alex was so handsome, it hurt to look at him. He was like a lightning bolt at sea or the searing flash of sunlight on the River Tay. She knew it would strike her blind if she looked long enough, but the urge to do just that was beyond her will to resist.

She had every right to feel as if she'd just run a race and won the prize. But she didn't.

Alex hadn't said a word to her since they were marched from the study where they'd been caught together on the bearskin. He'd never wanted the match in the first place. He made no secret of it. How must he feel toward her now that his hand had been forced?

He stood looking out the window where the frost-rimed grounds of Dalkeith sparkled with a million pinpricks of diamonds in the moonlight. His back was ramrod straight, his hands clasped behind him. He was the sort to shake his fist at heaven and declare himself master of his fate.

But now his silence made her suspect Alexander felt like a prisoner who'd been escorted to his cell.

She wanted to ask him what was wrong, but was afraid he might tell her and it would be horrible. Once harsh words were spoken, they could never be recalled. They hovered forever in the air, unrelentingly given and received. They settled into the heart of the hearer to fester and burn. It was easier, no, it was safer, to pretend that this silence was normal for a man who'd just been wed.

"Where is your dressing screen?" she asked, her voice much smaller than she wished it to sound.

He didn't turn around. "Don't think I have one. Not much call for modesty in a bachelor. Go ahead and prepare for bed. I won't trouble you."

Something inside her crumpled. She wanted him to trouble her. She wanted him to trouble her to pieces.

Lucinda crossed over to the commode where an age-spotted mirror hung so she could see to remove her mother's veil. It was so delicate, if she missed a hairpin, she might rip the lace.

An odd movement in her reflection made her blink hard. The room was dimly lit, but for a moment, she thought she saw a little old man's thin bewhiskered face peering back at her from over her left shoulder. She jerked her head around to look behind her, but there was no one there. A sudden flare of light reflected from the fireplace. A log fell off the triangular stack and spit sparks up the chimney. When Lucinda looked back at the mirror, the man was gone.

Then she remembered Brodie's warning about another ghostly presence in Dalkeith. If this spirit wanted to make contact with her on her wedding night, his timing was less than ideal.

It was a not-so-subtle reminder that she had several secrets she was keeping from her new husband.

Alex was still transfixed by the window. He had secrets of his own. He'd said several times that he had "important" things he'd ought to be doing.

What were they?

She plucked out the pins and removed the veil, trying to ignore the way her hands shook. Lucinda spread it out on the bed and folded it carefully. Aileen and Mary would want it for their weddings someday.

"May they wear it with more joy," she murmured.

"What was that?" Alex asked.

"Nothing of import." Lucinda began to undo the buttons that marched down her spine. There were five or six she couldn't reach between her shoulder blades.

A bell pull dangled beside the commode, but it was the middle of the night. If she gave it a tug, she'd be rousting a poor lady's maid out of her bed, just as they'd waked the surly vicar to perform the ceremony. Lucinda had been nothing but a bother to everyone this evening. She didn't want to add to the roll.

"Alexander?" He was already first on the "Inconvenienced by Lucinda MacOwen" list she'd composed in her head. A little more discomfort could hardly make matters worse. "I need a bit of help here, if ye please."

She turned her back to him so she didn't have to see his face as he walked toward her, but she wondered what it would show. A hint of lust? She'd welcome that. Irritation? She didn't think she could bear it. Or what if it was worse? What if he was indifferent to her?

His capable fingers made short work of the buttons and the back of her gown fell away, sliding off her shoulders. She held it up in front with both hands over her breasts.

"I'll need ye to unlace me stays too, please." Why, oh, why had she chosen a gown for her wedding that required help to get into and out of? She was a woman fully grown. She'd ought to be able to handle her own wardrobe without assistance.

He untied the knot at the base of her stays and worked the laces free. She hadn't been cinched particularly tight, but she drew a deep breath in any case, enjoying the freedom of expanding her ribs fully. As he pulled the ribbon free, his fingertips brushed against her spine. Only the thin muslin of her chemise separated her from his touch.

Her skin didn't seem to care that he hadn't stroked it directly. It rioted in pleasure at any rate.

"Thank ye," she said softly.

He didn't move away from her.

"It's no trouble."

Hope flickered in her chest. Perhaps she could strike his name from the "Inconvenienced by Lucinda MacOwen" list, after all.

"'Tis plain ye know yer way around a woman's garments," she babbled to keep the silence at bay.

"Do you really want to know more about that part of my past?"

She shook her head. His breath flowed warmly over her nape and down her back. She barely resisted the urge to lean into him. Instead she slowly turned around to face him.

"Ye say 'tis no trouble, and yet, I've an inkling that ye think I'm trouble to you." There. Maybe if she said it for him, he'd deny it.

"It's not that." His hands curled into fists as if he were ready for a fight, but she sensed it wasn't with her. It was with himself. "You have no idea who I am or why I'm really here."

"I would if ye took the time to tell me." Lucinda wished she could reach for his hand, but if she did, her gown and stays would drift to the floor and she'd be standing before him in naught but her shift. "I'm a verra good listener."

He looked at her so intently, she felt as exposed as if she were in only her shift. "That's just it. We should have had that talk long before we said words in church. This is all backward."

He strode over and plopped into the heavy-timbered Tudor chair near the dying fire.

"My parents didna ken each other at all before they were marrit."

"I suppose you'll tell me their marriage grew into a love match."

"That I'm no' privy to. Some things in a marriage should be only for the ones inside its circle, but ye can tell the kind of tree by its fruit, they say," Lucinda said, standing straighter. If there was one thing she was certain of, it was her family. "Erskine and Katie Mac-Owen were blessed with seven children, so there must have been some liking for each other. They buried two bairns and raised five. And my father never sought another woman to warm his bed after he laid my mother in the arms of God. They may have started as strangers, but they didna stay so. They made a life together."

We can too danced on her tongue, but he looked away from her, staring at the flickering embers in the grate. She forced herself to stop talking. If she let silence reign, perhaps he'd be moved to fill it.

"It sounds as if your parents were happy, but it doesn't always work out like that," he finally said.

The cryptic entry about Alexander in *The Knowledgeable Ladies' Guide to Eligible Gentlemen* flashed in Lucinda's brain. She couldn't recall the exact wording, but there was a mention of "unpleasantness" regarding his mother and the fact that neither he nor his brother exhibited signs of madness. If his mother had lost her wits, it stood to reason his parents' marriage wasn't the solid comfort Erskine and Katie had enjoyed. Alex hadn't grown up in the protected center of a circle of love as she had.

No matter. The future was meant to knit up the ragged ends of the past. A darned stocking was often stronger and warmer than one that had never been mended. She could make things better for Alexander.

Lucinda decided to grasp her marriage with both hands. She let her gown and stays sink to the floor in a pool around her ankles with a soft rustle of silk. The gesture might have been more effective if Alex had glanced her way. He continued to stare stonily at the fire.

In for a penny, she reasoned. Lucinda toed off her slippers. The floors were cold underfoot and the chill shot up her shins. Then she bent over and reached under the hem of her chemise to untie her garters and roll her stockings down. She stood upright and undid the drawstring at her waist that held up her pantalets. If Alex had looked her way, he'd have been treated to the sight of her bare calves since she had to hitch up the chemise.

He made no move toward her. She'd have to go to him.

Barefoot on the hardwood, she padded over in only her shift and knelt before him. "Ye asked me earlier this night to trust ye and so I did. Will ye no' trust me now, Alexander? I'll be a good and faithful wife to ye and do ye no hurt so long as I live."

He still refused to look at her, but she was close enough to see that his features were taut, strained to the breaking point. His handsome face was at war with itself.

Lucinda took one of his hands and pressed it between her breasts so he could feel her heart hammering. "Do ye no' see how fine I think ye are, husband?" When he still didn't respond, a sob closed her throat, but she managed to whisper, "I know ye feel trapped by our wedding, but can ye no' find it in ye to like me a little?"

"Oh, Lucinda." He reached for her then, pulling her up onto his lap. Her heart soared as he claimed her mouth and slid a hand down the low neckline of her chemise.

Soft. Biddable. Willing. She was everything a man could wish. It had taken every ounce of his will not to look while she'd slithered off her gown, but his imagination had been running at full tilt. In his mind's eye, he could see her alabaster arms bared in the firelight, the chemise a thin wisp of nothing, shadows of her curves wavering enticingly, the darker skin of her nipples plainly visible. When she'd bent to remove her stockings, the chemise would have fallen away and he'd have glimpsed the sweet hollow between her breasts.

Maybe he should have looked. He'd lost the battle

in any case. But who could blame him when she knelt before him? The sweet cloud of her scent wafting around her, the beating of her heart under his palm like some wild young thing, terrified, but willing to trust—she wore down his resistance with gentle persistence, like a drip of water hollowing out solid rock.

He crushed her to him, palming one of the globes of her bum, his fingers brushing the crevice between them.

"We'll do better," she assured him as she kissed along his jaw.

"Better than what?" At the moment Alex couldn't imagine anything better than this sweet armful of woman. Unless she were out of her chemise . . .

"Better than yer parents, o' course." She nibbled up to his ear and then latched onto the lobe to give it a quick suck. "I'm too thick-headed to run mad and ye show no sign of it."

He pushed her away and held her at arm's length. "What do you know of that?"

Her mouth formed a silent "oh," then she hurried on. "No' much. Only what I've read in a silly book full of gossip and questionable advice. Dinna worry. The writer said as yer mother's madness was no impediment to ye bein' considered quite the catch."

No impediment.

The memories of that distant time were cloudy, as if someone had pulled down a scrim on his life and rendered it hazy, etched softly in shades of sepia and wheat. But the sounds came through loud and clear, if the words were somewhat garbled. There was interminable shouting. That was from his father. And endless weeping. Those keening sobs could only have come from his mother. Then they turned to shrieks when strange men pulled Alex from her arms and took her away. He toddled after them, tripping and scraping his knee on the pavers, but he couldn't catch up.

That empty place in his chest ached afresh. It confirmed what he'd always believed. There was something broken inside him. Something elemental that made him what he was. Solitary. Driven. Unwilling to risk losing someone ever again. Like his mad mother, he was damaged. He was like a watch spring that had been sprung or a clasp that had been bent too far. Nothing could put it back to rights without breaking it completely.

"So I'm considered quite the catch," he said woodenly.

"Aye, truly."

"Well, that just goes to show you can't believe everything you read." Alex moved her off his lap, rose to his feet, and braced both hands on the mantel lest he be tempted to touch her again. Her heart might be hurt, but she'd heal. He didn't want his brokenness to corrupt her too. "Go to bed, Lucinda."

She stood stock still for a moment and he feared she was about to put up a fight. Then he was afraid she might do worse and begin to cry. When she turned away without a word, he could have kissed the curve of her instep in gratitude.

After he heard the bedclothes rustle enough to confirm that she was in the big featherbed, he sat back down in the chair. Even though his arousal had settled, the ache in his chest throbbed enough to keep him from sleep.

No matter.

On the morrow, they'd leave for Bonniebroch. Since he'd lost his usefulness at Dalkeith by nearly defiling a daughter of Scotland under the noses of the local nobility, he decided to turn to the countryside to try to flush out any Radical elements. Besides, once he and his bride were ensconced in his own home, he could arrange for separate bedchambers for them. It was his only hope of eventually obtaining an annulment and his freedom. The only way to return to a life that made sense, one that didn't keep dredging up his past or offering him glimpses of an unobtainable future he didn't deserve and could never have.

But the separate bedchambers were a must. One night listening to Lucinda's breathing, knowing she was near, knowing she was willing, would be more than enough.

"Never in all her years of matrimony will a woman have more power in the marriage than in those halcyon days immediately following the wedding. When preparing for one's honeymoon trip, the knowledgeable lady will pack lightly. If one suddenly discovers one needs another gown or reticule or just the right necklace to go with that darling little riding habit, one's new husband will be more inclined to spend on his bride then than at any other time."

From *The Knowledgeable Ladies' Guide to Eligible Gentlemen*

Chapter Fourteen

It was a damned long night.

Mercifully, Lucinda wasn't the sort to sob into the coverlet, though she moved restlessly every few minutes and pummeled her pillow into submission more than once. Eventually, she settled, but then her soft breathing was a different type of torment.

Alexander waited for dawn in the Tudor chair, not dropping off to sleep from sheer exhaustion till the darkest watch of the night. He woke with a sore back and a crick in his neck.

He cast a longing gaze at the still form in the bed, but there wasn't a moment to waste. Escaping the bridal chamber before Lucinda stirred, he made for the kitchen where he took a cold breakfast, breaking all sorts of protocol by eating alongside the help. News of the middle-of-the-night wedding had spread through the Dalkeith gossip mill, quick as a case of the measles. Alexander was treated to stifled giggles and knowing looks from the staff while he pumped the servants for information about Bonniebroch. The Master of Horse seemed the likeliest source of reliable information since he traveled often in search of new stock to keep up the palace's herd.

"I understand the steward of Bonniebroch is here at Dalkeith," Alexander said between sips of surprisingly good coffee. It was black and hot and stout enough to cause new hairs to sprout on his chest. "Callum Farquhar by name. Have you seen him?"

The horseman scratched his wire-haired pate. "Dinna know as I have. There be a powerful lot of new folk here the now, both above and below stairs. I mighta met the fellow and no' known it, but I'll leave him know ye wish to speak with him an' I see him."

"I haven't time to wait." One night of sharing a chamber with his new wife was all he could bear. "I need to get to Bonniebroch and I haven't found anyone who can tell me where it lies."

Farquhar had tried during their strange conversation, waxing poetic about hills and rivers and declivities, but Alex had cut the man off.

"Weel, in truth, the castle isna so far. Ye can reach it in a long day's travel," the Master of Horse said before he crammed a bite of day-old bannock slathered with butter into his mouth and chewed noisily.

Alex lifted a surprised brow. No one had named

Bonniebroch a castle before this. He revised his mental picture of the estate. "Castle, you say."

"Och, aye. *Broch* being Gaelic for 'tower,' ye ken, and as for *bonnie*, weel, I'll leave that to yer own judgment since beauty lies in the eye of the beholder, they do say."

Bonniebroch might not be a croft with sheep on the roof, but a castle could still be a crumbling ruin. Better to keep his expectations low. "You've been there?"

"Nae, but there's no' many as goes that way, ye ken. The folk what lives in Bonniebroch keeps to themselves. There's something a might queer about them. Only a few tradesmen venture up the River Tay to bring them goods and news from the outside."

Outstanding. The residents at his new estate had raised clannishness to an art form. They'd likely not be terribly forthcoming when he tried to gather information from them.

"What road do we take to get there?" Alex asked, feeling more certain by the minute that Sir Darren MacMartin had lost Bonniebroch to him on purpose.

"No road. The hills are steep 'round about the tower. Ye might make it on horseback, I suppose, if ye were to follow the game trails."

Alex still couldn't manage Badgemagus on a level patch of ground. He certainly wasn't going to trust his neck to a Highland game trail. And besides, he had no mount for Lucinda.

"I doubt my bride's luggage will fit in a saddle bag," Alexander said.

The Master of Horse laughed. "Nae, it willna. A man may make do with his plaid and his dirk, but women need a powerful lot of things to get them through their day. Ye'll have to take the ferry barge then."

He gave Alexander directions that would take them back to Edinburgh and then on north to the place where they'd find the ferryman on the River Tay.

"From there, ye'll have to trust the ferryman. Busby MacFee is his name, but his friends call him Beans."

Alex decided he didn't want to know why.

"The Tay is a tidal river so ye may have to wait for the water to be favorable," the horseman warned.

"Isn't there a towpath?"

"Part of the way. For the rest, ye must go when the river allows ye." The Master of Horse thanked Cook for his breakfast and crammed a disreputable tam on his head. "Godspeed, milord, and a Merry Christmas to ye and yer good lady."

My good lady. We'll see how good she is after I tell her we're quitting Dalkeith immediately. On Christmas Eve, no less.

Feeling a bit like Daniel re-entering the lion's den, he trudged back to his chamber. To his great relief, there was an abigail with Lucinda. A dressing screen had been found and moved into his room.

His bride stood behind it, her shoulders bare except for the long auburn locks teasing around them.

Lucinda in nothing but her skin. His imagination went into full gallop at the thought of heavy breasts, a supple waist, and heaven between her silky thighs. If he hadn't ever heard of Lord Liverpool and his web of intelligence gatherers or been convinced he was doing her a favor by not being a true husband,

Alex would have pulled down the screen and enjoyed the sight of his beautiful wife in the altogether.

Instead, he couldn't even tell her why he was really in Scotland. A marriage based on lies and half-truths had no chance at all. His head argued that he was right to keep his distance.

Another part of him begged to differ. Most insistently.

"Yer pardon, milord," the maid said, dropping a hasty curtsey. "I'll be on me way."

"No need." Alexander waved her back. It was safer to have the girl there as a buffer. Formality was preferable to honesty at this point. "My wife is clearly in need of your services. Carry on."

Lucinda shot him a questioning look, then raised her arms to allow the girl to slip a fresh chemise over her head.

"'Tis the day before Christmas," Lucinda said cautiously, as if she too were treading lightly around their frail marriage. She disappeared completely behind the screen and Alex's imagination rose up to taunt him with images of her rolling her stockings up her shapely legs and tying neat bows behind her knees. "I expect me sisters and I will take to the woods to gather boughs and mistletoe and such for the beautifying of the hall. Will ye be taking part in finding the Yule log before the Hanging o' the Greens?"

"No. I intend to leave before those festivities get underway."

Lucinda's head shot up at that. She peered over the screen at him, a burning question in her eyes. "Leave us, if ye please, Brigid."

As if the lady's maid sensed an approaching storm,

she skittered out without a word, taking Lucinda's clothing from the previous night with her.

"So, ye dinna intend to honor yer vows," Lucinda said, her voice deadly calm.

"I misspoke. I should have said *we* will be leaving. I intend to take you with me." He might be a cad, but he'd never embarrass Lucinda by abandoning her after one night. Since Alex figured he'd be stuck in Scotland at least until the king came and went next August, there'd be time enough for her to realize that they weren't suited—would never be suited—and she'd give him the annulment he needed without a qualm.

Her chin lifted and her eyes glinted coldly. "Then ye intend to stick to all the points outlined in the contract, my bride-price, the support of my father's invention, the herds and grazing rights, all of it, and not a farthing less?"

"Yes, yes, I'll honor it all." She was turning into quite the mercenary little wench.

Then her chin quivered a bit. "Ye just dinna intend to honor me."

Alexander was doing her more honor than she knew. This was about more than securing his freedom. He was giving her a chance to get away from him as well. He might not run to madness, but he still wasn't meant to be a husband. Not with his father's blood coursing through his veins.

"Be ready to leave within the hour."

Lucinda barely had time to pack a fourth of her belongings. Her sisters dragged themselves from bed and tried to help, but only succeeded in slowing her progress with unwanted questions and advice.

"Go wake Aunt Hester for me, so I can say good-bye," she'd finally pleaded in hopes that she'd have a moment alone to explain matters to Brodie. She'd heard once that ghosts didn't take kindly to crossing water. When Alexander told her that a goodly portion of their journey would be by ferry barge, she knew she'd have to persuade Brodie to remain with her sisters till he could return to the Mac-Owen farm with them. Sometime—it didn't matter when since Brodie had all the time in the world—she and Alexander would have to visit her family and she could be reunited with Brodie then.

She still expected him to pitch a fit over their separation.

As soon as Aileen and Mary left, bickering loudly over who would have the dubious honor of pulling back the bed curtains and rousting their aunt from sleep, Lucinda called Brodie's name softly.

He didn't answer.

She knew he enjoyed exploring out-of-the-way places within the safety of Dalkeith's stout walls, but his hearing was so preternaturally keen, he'd hear her whether he were floating near the rafters in the garret or skimming the dank stone of the deepest crypt. In all the years she'd known him, he'd never refused to show himself when she called, no matter how peeved he might have been with her.

Now he was simply . . . gone.

Lucinda sank onto the foot of her bed and let the gathering tears fall. She wasn't usually such a watering pot, but she had good reason now. Her husband didn't want to take her to wife. Alexander was pulling her from the bosom of her family on the day before Christmas and she'd lost her best friend in the world.

She'd have given anything to hear Brodie's scratchy brogue telling her *"Ye dinna have to cry so, lassie,"* just as he had when she was a little girl and he first found her shut up in the cellar. But when she held her breath, listening intently for him, there was only the soft sibilance of air currents flowing from one room to the next and the crackle of the fire in the grate.

Then there came a scuffle from the skittering kid soles of her sisters' slippers and the heavy clunk of her aunt's ponderous steps in the adjoining room. Lucinda wiped her eyes and forced an over-bright smile. No need to trouble her family with her woes.

There wasn't time to find Dougal in order to bid him good-bye. Alexander was in such a hurry to be gone, Lucinda wondered that he waited for her.

The carriage ride with her new husband back to Edinburgh was a study in awkward silence, so she feigned intense interest in the landscape scrolling past the isinglass windows. Thick hoarfrost coated every blade of grass, turning meadows into fields of short white daggers jutting upward. Trees scraped the sky with their icy fingers. The scenery matched the cold bleakness of Lucinda's new marriage.

Finally, she could bear the quiet no longer.

"I see ye've given up on riding Badgemagus," she said since Alexander had left him at Dalkeith.

"No, I haven't." He still didn't look at her, staring instead out the window with as much interest in the countryside as Lucinda had pretended to. "I arranged for your brother to bring him to Bonniebroch after Christmas. The horse will do better on the ferry with blinders and a knowledgeable groom to tend him along the way."

Lucinda sniffed. It was all well and good to care for one's animals, but she'd do better if *her* groom gave as much thought to tending to her needs as he did to his horse.

"I wonder if you might like to have some of your family close by." Alexander's gaze darted to her and then away to the window again. "Once your brother comes to Bonniebroch, perhaps he might want to stay on in some capacity. If you would like his company, of course."

Something fluttered in her chest. It was kindly meant of him. Getting Dougal away from Dalkeith where King George would be lodging next summer was an answer to prayer. Lucinda hoped never to see that dirk dance again.

"I would like that." It wasn't the loving conversation every girl hopes to have with her bridegroom the day after their wedding, but at least they were talking. "When Dougal comes, I'll see can I talk him into staying. He's a dab hand with horses and though he's no' the inventor me father is, he's Erskine Mac-Owen's son when it comes to building or repairing things. I'm sure ye'll find a use for him on yer estate."

"Our estate, as per the marriage contract," he corrected. "You're Lady Bonniebroch now."

Much good may a title do me when my bed's still cold.

"We couldn't hire your brother as a servant. That wouldn't be seemly," Alex said. "But perhaps he could help me with getting to know the tenants. Would he fancy being overseer?"

"Lording it over the crofters attached to the estate and collecting rents, aye, that's just the sort of thing

Dougal would fancy." Her brother always liked being in charge. The cellar incident rose in her mind and she added, "Ye'll have to keep an eye on him to make sure he doesna get too heavy-handed though."

"Don't worry. I intend to," Alex said quickly.

Her gaze snapped to him at that. She had her suspicions about Dougal. Did Alex have them too? And if he learned Dougal had been mixed up with the Radicals was Alex English enough to act upon his suspicions?

"The new laird will be among us shortly. We know not what may come if he succeeds. Only what will happen if he fails. Perhaps the Powers have ordained it so. Too much knowledge of what's ahead might quell a stouter heart than our new Lord Bonniebroch possesses."

From the secret journal of Callum Farquhar, Steward of Bonniebroch Castle since the Year of Our Lord 1521

Chapter Fifteen

"Beans" MacFee lived up to his pungent nickname. The garrulous ferryman reeked of the thick pottage he kept bubbling in the little boathouse on the bank of the River Tay near where his barge was tied up. A miasmatic cloud of onion, garlic, leeks, and legumes and their accompanying gasses oozed from the layers of his plaid with every swinging stride. However, as long as Alexander stayed upwind, Beans seemed a jolly enough soul and an entertaining companion.

"Don't get many wishin' to go to Bonniebroch, ye ken," he told them when Alexander bespoke their passage up river.

"Yes, we know," Alex said as he counted out the

coin into MacFee's grimy palm. "I've heard the people
there keep to themselves."

Beans laughed. "Aye, the castle's shut up tight as
an oyster most times. Nane go in. Nane come out."

That was an exaggeration surely. The people from
Bonniebroch couldn't stay behind its walls all the
time. After all, Callum Farquhar had called on Alex
at Dalkeith, however briefly.

"Why is it that the folk there dinna go abroad in
the wide world, d'ye think?" Lucinda asked.

"Because o' the curse, I reckon," Beans said as he
finished loading the last of their trunks and cast off
his lines.

"Curse?" Lucinda's eyes widened. "What curse?"

"Och, there's always two or three versions of it
floatin' about at any given time. The details are lost
in the past, ye ken, so it does nae harm for folk to
make up what they dinna know for certain." Beans
scratched his head, giving the lice that called his
gray, matted locks home an excuse to scurry around.
"Mostly, the gist of the tale is that because of some
sort of treachery, and I dinna quite know what it was
exactly, mind ye, but this particular foul deed was
committed back in . . . och, I forget how many hundred years ago . . . and as I said, nane can say for sure
what it was as happened, but in any case, it were a
most grievous thing as was done. Most grievous."

MacFee shook his head to accentuate his point
and, like any raconteur worth his salt, waited for his
audience to ask for more. When Lucinda obliged,
he favored her with an alarming black-toothed
smile.

"Since the guilty party wouldna step forward to
admit to the offense, the whole of the castle was set

to pay dearly for it. Then just when it appeared all was hopeless, a fellow who hadn't anything to do with the original misdeed took the punishment. And that great-hearted deed saved all the souls in the castle at the time."

"That sounds as if all's well that ends well," Lucinda said, her smile tentatively hopeful.

"It do, don't it?" Beans said agreeably.

Alex crossed his arms over his chest. "It ended well for everyone except for the poor blighter who paid for someone else's treachery."

"Aye, there's the rub." A cunning smile spread over Beans MacFee's weathered face. He tapped the end of his nose, and then pointed to Alex in agreement. "Even good deeds can bring down a sort o' punishment of their own. After all, they didna kill saints for evil-doing, did they?"

"No, I suppose not," Lucinda said as she settled on one of their traveling trunks. "What happened then?"

"The powerful sorcerer what set about to punish the original culprit was unhappy that the folk of Bonniebroch had escaped the end he'd intended for them, so he cursed 'em, each and every man, woman, and child what called Bonniebroch home."

"That's enough nonsense," Alex said crossly. "My lady doesn't wish to hear about curses."

"Aye, she does," Lucinda contradicted with a tart grin, then turned back to Beans. "What sort of curse?"

"Och, it'd be a wise man as knows that," Beans said. "Nane save the folk who bide there are privy to the particulars and they're no' sayin'. But so long as ye dinna intend to stay long, I imagine the curse will no' apply to the pair o' you."

"We'll stay there as long as we like," Alexander snapped, hoping to shut the man up. The next thing he'd probably tell them was that the castle was haunted or infested with boggles or some other Scottish demon. "We are Lord and Lady Bonnie-broch."

"Och, ye have me condolences then," was the last thing Beans MacFee said for the rest of the trip.

As they rounded a bend in the River Tay, a thick bare-limbed forest of black alder, ash, and silver birch crowded the declivity between two bleak hills. A stand of blackthorn hovered near the river's edge, gnarled and twisted. Like a coven of witches dipping their toes in the water, their threatening prickles were ready to snatch at anyone unwise enough to pass close by.

A gray stone castle rose behind these woodsy sentinels. Its crenellated top and lofty tower were the only visible evidence of human settlement, save for the listing dock toward which Mr. MacFee steered his craft.

"Here ye be," Beans said as he looped a line around a moss-furred piling. "Fetched ye up at Bonnie–broch, as promised."

Lucinda drew her cloak tighter around herself. The estate looked daunting enough from the ferry barge without the dubious bonus of a curse attached to it. After her experience with Brodie MacIver, she knew there were spirits abroad in the world, most of them trapped near the places where they'd met their end. And Brodie had warned her once that not all of them were so blithe a spirit as he. If she were to catalogue places that looked as if they were home to malevolent ghosts, Bonniebroch would make the top of the list. The raucous cry of a raven split the silence and made her jump.

Alexander's hand on the small of her back settled her somewhat as he helped her out of the craft. She waited on the dock while Mr. MacFee unloaded their trunks. No one seemed to be stirring inland, though she'd made out a trail broad enough to accommodate a small gig cutting through the trees.

"No one guards the dock?" Alexander asked.

"No need," MacFee said. "Your things will be safe enough here till the servants come to retrieve them. No one's daft enough to steal from Bonniebroch."

Since the sun was setting, Lucinda decided they wouldn't have long to wait.

MacFee liberated a small leather pouch that was tied to the dock. He fingered the contents, setting the coins clinking, and pulled out a folded piece of paper.

"An order for provisions," he explained though neither Lucinda nor Alexander had asked. Then Beans turned away, clambered back into his barge, and lost no time in slipping the cable. As he pushed off with his long pole, he tugged the brim of his hat. "I'll be back this way before sundown on Twelfth Night. Put up a flag if ye wish to leave. But watch ye for me. I'll no' wait long."

"Well, milady." Alexander offered Lucinda his arm. "Shall we see what sort of castle you'll be chatelaine of?"

"Ye dinna think we should wait with the baggage?" she asked doubtfully, eyeing the darkening forest.

"No." Judging from Lucinda's chattering teeth, it was high time they found shelter. And besides, he'd rather walk through this wood with a bit of daylight to spare. Wolves hadn't been seen in Britain since the reign of Henry VII, but this was Scotland and a wild bit of it to boot. Alexander wouldn't discount finding a pack of the slavering creatures in that shadowy forest.

Leaving their trunks on the dock, they started down the path through the wood. A thin skiff of snow crunched underfoot and the promise of more swirled in the frosty air. The last rays of daylight faded and the forest sank into twilight.

They hadn't gone far when Alex became aware of a low rhythmic thudding, like the tramping sound of an army on the march. The woods were too thick to see anything headed their way. Whatever it was, it was approaching rapidly.

There was no place to run. Not even a defensible outcropping of rock near the path. He didn't think Lucinda seemed the type to climb a tree. The forest floor was thick with brambles so they couldn't flee to the deeper woods to hide without being cut to ribbons by thorns.

"Get behind me," he ordered bluntly and positioned himself in front of Lucinda. His gut clenched. It was a novel sensation. Usually the hint of danger merely put all his senses on high alert and made him feel more vibrantly alive than at any other time.

Now he knew what fear tasted like. Hot and acrid, it burned down his gullet.

It wasn't fear for himself, but for *her.*

He swallowed back several choice swear words. This sort of thing just reinforced why he wasn't meant to be a married man. He was expected to venture into unknown places and face equally unknown danger during the commission of his work.

She was not.

He pulled out his pistol, thankful he'd decided to bear it on his person instead of packing it in his baggage. The flintlock was only worth a single shot and if the sound of stamping feet was any indication, they were about to be confronted by many. Still, an armed man was more intimidating than one with nothing but a handful of fingers, so he drew out his boot knife for good measure.

"Dinna ye think talkin' to them first would be better than waving yer wee gun at them?" Lucinda asked, gripping his shoulders and peering around him.

Wee gun! Did it mean nothing to her that his first instinct was to protect her with whatever he had on hand?

"Trust me, madam, I can talk to them just fine from behind the barrel of this 'wee gun.'" If he could convince the leader of the approaching band that his would be the head Alex would drill with a lead ball should it come to that, he might be able to hold the whole company at bay. "Now keep still. If I tell you to flee, I expect you to do so without argument. And don't look back."

"Every woman has dreams. We knit them up as girls, play with them as debutants, and pin them on the gentlemen we ultimately take as our husbands. But the knowledgeable lady realizes once she weds, she is no longer a child. No man on earth can be expected to equal those childish dreams."

From *The Knowledgeable Ladies' Guide to Eligible Gentlemen*

Chapter Sixteen

A splash of yellowish light broke through the trees ahead of Alexander and Lucinda. It spilled across the snow-covered trail like melted butter. A man holding a lantern at shoulder height rounded a bend in the path with a gaggle of folks at his heels. He stopped dead when he saw Alex and Lucinda. Bug-eyed and pug-nosed, his face would put a Notre Dame gargoyle to shame. Then a smile burst over his ugly features, rendering them honest and good-natured instead of off-putting.

"My Lord Bonniebroch, I presume. And my Lady Bonniebroch, a thousand welcomes!" The man gave an elegant sweeping bow and all those behind him followed suit. "Lyall Lyttle, head butler and yer servant, an' it please ye."

Mr. Lyttle didn't have a fighting force at his heels. It was a regiment of household retainers. Fortunately, they were not armed with pitchforks and cleavers.

There were footmen in full livery that made them look as if they'd stepped from a previous century. Housemaids in homespun with voluminous mobcaps and thick shawls crowded around men-of-all-work types in coarser garments, long tunics swathed with faded plaids, and argyle stockings tucked into heavy boots. Every face was alight with expectation, greeting, and more than a little curiosity.

Feeling foolish, Alex tucked his pistol back into the waist of his trousers and sheathed his knife.

"My lord is quite right to go armed in the woods," Mr. Lyttle said. "Never know what one might meet on these trails. But ye're quite safe now. If needs be, there's no' a man-jack of us as wouldna lay down our lives for ye and yer good lady." He turned back to the assemblage behind him to deliver orders. "Davey, take Jock and Angus and nip down to the dock for our laird's effects. Mrs. Fletcher, do ye take her ladyship and see to her comfort."

Mrs. Fletcher, who appeared to be the housekeeper, was a round, merry-looking woman. She greeted them with another bobbing curtsey and started to lead Lucinda away with promises of a hot bath and a hot supper, in that order. Alex almost rescinded Lyttle's command so he could keep her with him, but it seemed daft to mistrust such an open welcome. But the servants' very presence in the wood begged a question.

"How did you know we were on our way here?" Alexander asked. He'd spotted no guard, no lookout on the dock.

"Och, we've been preparing for yer arrival for days. Mr. Farquhar ordered us to come greet ye."

And how on earth could Farquhar have known? Maybe Farquhar was keen enough of nose that, if the prevailing wind was right, the odiferous Mac-Fee's mere presence on the dock was warning of impending guests.

"Where is Mr. Farquhar?" Alex asked, looking around. If he organized this welcome, why wasn't the steward leading it? "I don't see him here."

Everyone stopped in mid-step. There were several sharp intakes of breath, as if Alex had uttered the most heinous blasphemy. Mrs. Fletcher turned back to face him.

"Ye've *seen* Mr. Farquhar?" Her eyes narrowed to disbelieving slits, nearly disappearing behind her ruddy, round cheeks.

"Yes. I spoke with him at some length." It wasn't a very satisfying conversation though. Alex had never met a less servile servant than his new estate steward.

A buzz of whispers erupted around him though he only caught snippets of the conversations.

So, it's true . . .

There's hope . . .

Didna think we'd live to see it . . .

After that blasted MacFee's talk about curses and such, Alexander was mortally tired of all this strangeness. He was laird of the place. It was time he acted like one.

"I'm sure you all have duties which require your

attention. Apply yourselves to them immediately or
I'll find more work to keep you occupied." He strode
forward to Lucinda and the crowd parted around
him. He held out his arm. "Mrs. Fletcher, you may
see to baths and board, but I'll escort Lady Bonniebroch to her new home."

Lucinda hadn't expected joy in this homecoming,
but when she tucked her frigid hand into Alexander's elbow and he covered it with his warm one, she
felt cosseted and cherished and slightly feverish all
over. It was a nice change from feeling like part of
her husband's baggage all day, something to be
transported safely, but not concerned about over
much. As she and Alex passed, the servants dipped
in bows and curtseys.

So must a queen feel, she mused.

The path before them widened and they entered
a clear space where the castle rose behind a frozen
moat and a lowered drawbridge. A candle gleamed
in every window on the upper stories and light
spilled even from the arrow slits on the lower sections
of gray stone. The sun had set and the moon had
risen during their journey through the forest. Flecks
of mica in the granite of the castle glittered in a
million pinpoints of reflected glory. Bonniebroch's
proud tower stood to one side, straight as an arrow
aimed at heaven. Pennants flapped along the battlements, snapping in the stiff breeze.

"Now that I can see it clear, 'tis like a faery castle,"
Lucinda said in wonderment. How could such an
enchanting place be kept such a secret?

"Well, there are no sheep on the roof, that's for sure," Alex muttered. "Let's see if there are any pigs in the bailey."

There were, but they were neatly penned in one of the clean stalls that were pressed up against the outer wall, alongside all the other animals. A small herd of cows, assorted goats, three pairs of great draft horses, and a brooding flock of hens bided within the keep. The boys who tended them doffed their caps as Alex and Lucinda passed by.

There was a little jewel of a chapel set to the right side of the bailey, its steeple crowned with an ornate cross. The Great Hall rose on the other side of the courtyard. The tall double doors leading into the hall were twice a man's height. Someone had already adorned them with evergreen boughs and sprigs of holly.

"Just in time for Christmas." Lucinda ran a hand over soft needles of fir as they entered. The evergreens released a fresh breath of their crisp perfume.

Inside, the hall blazed with torchlight. Long tables were set up with benches on each side. Wooden trenchers and pewter mugs were arranged neatly at each place. A fireplace large enough to roast an ox whole blazed along one side of the room, banishing the cold.

A smaller table was positioned on a raised dais at the far end of the room. Fine porcelain, silver salt cellars, and goblets of dear Frankish glass graced this table. A festive kissing bough dangled above it with plenty of white mistletoe berries to ensure a generous number of kisses stolen beneath it.

"This way, my lord, my lady," Mrs. Fletcher said,

beckoning them to follow her up a curving stone staircase. There were no cobwebs, no grit in any corners. Everything was meticulously clean.

When they reached the second story, Mrs. Fletcher opened the first door they came to. "This is the laird's chamber. I'm hopin' it meets with yer approval."

"It'll be fine," Alex said without a glance through the open door.

"And yer room is just down the hall a wee bit, my lady, if ye'd care to inspect it." Mrs. Fletcher waddled ahead of them down the corridor, her boat-sized slippers shushing along on the thick runner that warmed the stone floors. "The girls have yer bath waiting, I'll be bound."

Lucinda held her breath, waiting for Alexander to say there'd be no need for separate chambers. They were on their honeymoon. He couldn't bear to be parted from her. He was her "Much of a Muchness" and she was his "soft little rabbit."

But Alex didn't say a word.

Separate chambers. An empty ache throbbed in her chest and Lucinda's shoulders sagged a bit. She supposed she ought to have expected it. The upper crust was required to maintain decorum at all times and private rooms for wellborn husbands and wives was part of the scheme of things.

As if having a "Lady" before one's name makes a body less likely to want a husband to snuggle with on a long winter's night.

But the promise of a bath was a potent lure and she followed Mrs. Fletcher without a backward glance to Alex. If the man wanted matters arranged differently, he'd have said so. She shoved her hurt down where no one could see it.

Her chamber turned out to be a full suite of rooms, a sitting room with a merry blaze in the hearth and comfortable stuffed chairs arrayed before it. There was a separate chamber that boasted nothing but wardrobes and storage for her trunks and a room with a bed large enough to accommodate a family of twelve. By far the finest thing was the bath with its own copper tub filled with steaming water and a toilet Mrs. Fletcher called a "garderobe" for Lucinda's personal use. The furnishings and tapestries smacked of the medieval but the suite was the finest the castle offered.

Barring the laird's, of course.

"Och, and here are Jane and Janet," Mrs. Fletcher said when two girls arrived in striped skirts and matching mobcaps. "I'm needed below the now, but they'll put ye to rights in time for the supper, my lady. Ring if ye wish for anything else."

The pair of lady's maids, who were as like as two peas, fluttered about Lucinda, helping her disrobe, bathe, and dress in a stiff brocade that might have been in fashion when Queen Mary was on the throne.

"Did ye ever see such a fine head of hair?" Jane asked Janet as they dressed Lucinda's tresses and cooed over her reflection in the looking glass.

"Never in all me livin' life," Janet agreed. "And did ye ever see such a handsome man—"

"As our own new laird?" Jane finished for her. They erupted in nearly identical giggles, a high irritating twitter that scraped Lucinda's spine.

Jane and Janet did everything in almost perfect unison, as if there was but one brain between the pair of them, which Lucinda began to suspect was the truth. When she finally dismissed them because she craved a little quiet, she wasn't the least surprised when Jane and Janet curtseyed as one and tripped lightly to the door in step with each other.

Once blessed silence settled in her chamber, Lucinda walked to the multi-paned window and looked out over the bailey and curtain wall to the forest beyond. Filtered through the green and violet glass, Bonniebroch was beautiful, in a stark, forbidding sort of way. Surely she and Alexander could find a way to be happy there.

Except that he doesna want me.

The hurt over Alex's dismissal rose afresh. The empty ache in her chest pounded. She was so very alone, more alone than she'd ever been in her life. Memories of her mother were hazy, but she'd always felt encircled by the care of her father and her sisters. Now she was cut off from those whose love she never doubted. At this point, she'd even welcome seeing Great-Aunt Hester.

But not only was she parted from her family, she had lost Brodie MacIver as well.

If Alexander had been prepared to be a husband to her, perhaps those losses wouldn't have stung so badly. She'd let herself hope for happiness with him when he'd moved to defend her so gallantly in the forest, but then he shuffled her off to the servants' care. The fact that he still didn't want to share her bed made her heart hurt, a low keening thrum that wouldn't be stilled.

Lucinda was so tired of hoping and then being disappointed. If only she'd kept to the spirit of this marriage as a mere contract, a gentleman's agreement between her father's attorney and Bonniebroch's lawyers . . . If she abandoned her desire for a normal life, for a husband who might love her a little and cherish the home and family they built together . . . If only she'd never tripped before Alexander Mallory and looked up into his damnably handsome face . . .

Unshed tears washed the view of Bonniebroch's forest from her vision, so she closed her eyes.

Lucinda couldn't bear to offer her heart and not have it accepted any longer. She decided to give up on Alexander, to force herself not to care.

She covered her face with her hands and wept. Broken dreams smelled of lime-washed stone and freshly aired bedding that would never see a night of passion. Gray, the color of Bonniebroch's granite walls, was the color of surrender and she laid aside her hopes. She folded them up, tucked them into the deepest corner of her soul, and resolved never to take them out again.

When Lucinda was all cried out, she looked up and saw a white handkerchief floating across the room toward her. A familiar voice curled around her ear.

"If that blatherskite of a husband o' yers is the cause of those tears, he'll find a spider in his coffee at breakfast." Brodie MacIver's pale form materialized behind the handkerchief.

"Brodie!" She ran toward him, wishing she could hug him and plant a tear-salted kiss on his pale cheek. Instead she snatched up the handkerchief and blew her nose loudly. "How did you ever find your way here without me?"

"Weel, now that's a good trick, an' I do say it meself." The ghost preened a bit, brushing his long nails on his jacket lapel and then examining them for a non-existent speck of dust. *"Ye'll mind how I told ye there was more than one spirit hoverin' about Dalkeith."*

She nodded, too happy to see him to trust her voice further.

"I chanced to see the bugger sailing through the upper stories of the palace and so I followed him on the quiet-like, just to see what he was up to. Bless me, if he didn't home in on yer husband's chamber."

"Why Alexander's room?" She sensed her husband had secrets. Maybe this ghost was one of them. Perhaps if she shared Brodie's place in her life with Alex, he would . . . no, she'd given up, she reminded herself. She wasn't going to try to make a real marriage any longer. She only made herself vulnerable with hopes like that.

"And then quick as a rabbit, this other ghost, he ducked through the mirror over the washbasin."

Mention of the looking glass triggered a memory. "Oh! What did he look like?"

"A wee little bird of a fellow. Old beyond reckoning if wrinkles have anything to say about a body's age. Why d'ye ask?"

"I may have seen him in Alexander's mirror . . . on our wedding night."

"Hmph! Peeping in on the happy couple, eh? And ye felt the need to warn me that ye need yer privacy! If I catch up to that blighter, I'll——"

"Never mind about that now. The other ghost didna stay long. But ye still havena answered my question." And she wanted to forestall any questions Brodie might have about how happy or unhappy she was in her marriage. "How did ye find yer way to Bonniebroch?"

Brodie smiled. *"Same way that other spirit did. Through the mirror, o' course. Tailed him all the way here, I did. I never knew it, but there's a whole other world behind that silvered glass, a web o' connections between looking glasses where those of us who're unencumbered with flesh can travel quick as a thought."*

"Truly?"

"Aye, and all those spirited roads lead to other mirrors in other places. Why, I could travel the world and never leave the comfortable insides of a sturdy structure once I decided it was safe to leave the looking glass at the other end."

"But ye dinna mean to leave me, do ye?" Panic tightened her gut. She didn't think she could bear to lose him again. "I mean, no' the now that ye're here and all."

"O' course no', lass. Ol' Brodie will stay as long as ye've need of him. Especially as there are other spirits about and I wouldna leave ye defenseless."

"I'm no' defenseless. Ye should have seen the way Alexander pulled out his pistol this evening when he thought I might be in danger."

"Hmph! I've yet to be impressed by yer new husband." Brodie's lip curled. *"Especially as I just caught ye cryin' when ye think no one sees. I know ye've a high opinion of yer laird, but, I dinna think yer Alexander is equal to the darkness I'm sensin' here in this Bonniebroch."*

"Darkness? What do ye mean?"

Brodie screwed his face into a scowl. *"I dinna ken exactly. 'Tis more a feeling than anything else, but so strong it is, I canna shake it. There's an old evil here in Bonniebroch. Something lurking in the dark corners and under the eaves. And to make matters worse, it's waitin' for something."* Brodie shuddered so that his spectral image wavered like a disturbed reflection on a pond.

A superstitious tingle raked Lucinda's spine. This mysterious entity had to be fearsome indeed if it gave a ghost pause. "What is it waiting for?"

Brodie shook his head. *"That I havena figured out yet. But one way or the other, I mean to see ye out of this castle before whatever it is breaks free."*

"Light the Yule log, laddies. Drink ye cup of cheer.

If the curse isna lifted by Twelfth Night, there'll be nae more merriment here.

B'Gad, that's as abysmal a bit of verse as ever I've penned. Make a note to Lyttle not to leave me mulled wine no matter how I plead. 'Tis not as if I can drink it and the mere memory of the sweet nectar leaves me too maudlin to be of any earthly—or should I say unearthly?—use."

From the secret journal of Callum Farquhar,
Steward of Bonniebroch Castle since the
Year of Our Lord 1521

Chapter Seventeen

The hall rang with laughter and song. The celebratory feast started with a rich cock-a-leekie soup, followed by tatties and herring, grouse and songbird pie, and a great haunch of venison with side dishes of rumbledethumps and curly kale. For dessert, a luscious Dundee cake was presented along with a sweet, sticky trifle called a "Tipsy Laird."

Alex had expected to see haggis, but nothing remotely like a sheep's intestine made its way to his plate. He began to revise his opinion of Scottish cuisine.

Mrs. Fletcher and her minions kept the meat and drink coming until the diners cried for mercy. The company was merry, as befitted the night before Christmas, and against all expectation, Alex enjoyed pleasant conversation with Lucinda while the meal ran through its many courses.

She was beautiful, decked out like a queen from an age gone by. Or a faery princess, who might vanish at midnight since one so fair was surely enchanted and couldn't remain in the mortal realm forever.

Alex snorted under his breath and gave himself an inward shake to banish such wayward thoughts. There he was off on another flight of fancy over his new wife. It wasn't at all like him.

He tipped back his horn and blamed it on the drink. In addition to the excellent wine served in pale green goblets, he was given an ancient drinking horn, all studded with silver work and intricately wrought. The footman who stood behind him never allowed either vessel to become empty for longer than a blink or two.

Still, there was no denying that his bride's eyes sparkled. Her laughter was a pleasing tinkle in his ear, not a nervous twitter or a mannish guffaw. After the way he'd treated her, it was a testament to Lucinda's pleasant character that she could bear his company at all, let alone laugh with him.

He was an unworthy wretch, but every man in the hall must think him the luckiest devil on earth to have such a wife.

Alexander found himself wishing he could take her hand under the table. Or better still, run his palm under her hem and up her leg. He'd sink his fingers into her wetness and pleasure her secretly with the whole of Bonniebroch none the wiser. He loved to hear those desperate little noises she made when he'd touched her. It would be exquisite torment to watch her try to stifle them. When he reckoned she could bear no more, he'd swoop her up and carry her off to—

Alexander drew a deep breath and forced that fantasy from his mind. He tried to focus on the epic poem being recited for their entertainment, but he'd lost the thread of the story somewhere between his imaginings of Lucinda's knee and her sweet secret spot.

There'd been so many toasts raised in his and Lucinda's honor that his lips buzzed. And of course, he was expected to drain either the horn or the goblet for each one. Maybe that's why his thoughts were darting around like a school of herring, flashing this way and that. The poem ended to thunderous applause and yet another toast was offered to the new laird.

"They act as if I'm Arthur come again," he said under his breath before he tipped back the goblet and swallowed it all to the accompaniment of renewed cheers and palms pounding on the long tables. The ale served at Bonniebroch was rich and yeasty with an alcohol content higher than most brews. But the wine was truly magnificent, full-bodied and complex with a bouquet that went straight to his head. The footman behind him refilled his goblet.

"Dinna compare yerself to King Arthur," Lucinda corrected. "He was an English king. Ye should aspire to Kenneth MacAlpin, the first king of Scots, or perhaps Robert the Bruce. He certainly put the fear of God into the English oppressors."

"Are we back to English oppression again? You're going to have to accept the fact that I'm half English, you know."

"As soon as ye accept that ye're also half Scottish," she said with maddening sweetness.

Earlier that evening, his valet had been adamant about laying out his MacGregor plaid, but Alexander overruled him. The tartan sash was a mere token of his Highland roots, but it was more than enough.

Anger boiled under his skin. Why did Lucinda insist he embrace the part of him he loathed most?

"My only claim to Scottish blood is through my mother," he said with a forced even tone. "And she ran to madness."

"I know." She nodded, her green eyes sad for him.

No, damn it, he didn't want her pity. He wanted her to understand so she'd leave him alone about it. So she'd realize why he held her at arm's length, why he wasn't any good as a husband and never would be. It was about more than the risks he ran in the service of his government or exposing her to them. It was about him and the broken bits inside him that no one but he should have to bear.

"I'm sure your mother loved you all the same," Lucinda said.

"That shows you don't know as much as you think." He downed the rest of his ale and signaled for a refill. The buzz had left his lips. He couldn't feel them at all anymore. "My mother loved her family so much she hung herself in Bedlam on my fourth birthday."

Lucinda flinched at the bitterness in his tone.

He never intended to tell her that. His father had hushed up the particulars at the time, but he made certain over the years that his sons learned every last gruesome detail. Alexander had never told anyone how she'd died.

Not even Clarindon.

It must be the drink, he reasoned, swiping a hand over his eyes. But perhaps it was best that he spill the whole sordid tale now. It certainly wasn't getting any prettier for being pent up.

"She might have gotten well, you see. My mother might have returned to us, if only she'd tried. But she *chose* to leave us." His father's words poured out his throat, scalding and bitter. Then he added softly, "To leave me."

Lucinda laid a hand on his forearm. "I ken ye've been hurt, but I dinna think yer mother meant to hurt ye. Madness is a terrible sickness. It makes a body do things they'd never consider were they in their right mind."

Or my mother weighed her options and considered her family wasn't worth coming back to. Alex drained his goblet and lifted it slightly so the footman would refill his glass.

Lucinda continued in a soft tone. "To do such a thing, she must have been in such unbearable pain, she felt there was no other way through it."

What of his pain? He'd been a child, a spare heir left to the untender mercies of a father who cared for no one but Alexander's elder brother. Young Alex was relegated to an ill-paid nanny who skimped on his food, pocketed most of the money for his clothing, and forced his growing feet into shoes two sizes too small. Then she'd switch Alexander with a stinging clump of birch whenever she knew his father was about to make one of his rare passes through the nursery. The marquis invariably found his younger son fussing and fretful and he stayed away even more.

His earliest memories were hazy, but he knew in his heart that things hadn't been so when his mother was there. The last bit of softness and ease in Alexander's life fled away on the day his mother was yanked from him. The fact that she hadn't even tried to come back for him was an ulcerated sore that never healed.

"I lost my mother when I was young too," Lucinda said gently. "Not in the same way as ye. Mother died bringing my sister Mary into the world. But a loss is a loss and none know the weight of grief but the heart that bears it. I only tell ye this, so ye know that a grief shared is a grief halved. As yer wife, I'll help ye bear it."

He snorted. As if he expected anyone to bear anything for him. He'd learned early that he was alone in this world. It was better not to love. Not to depend on anyone but himself. Part of him knew it was unreasonable to be angry with a dead woman, but rage was a safer emotion than grief. It simmered in his chest, ready to erupt into a full boil at any moment.

"Ye have a new life here, Alexander. A fresh start," Lucinda went on. "A whole castle full of Scots who have taken ye to their hearts. Ye're their good laird and they want to love ye. If ye let go yer stiff

Englishness and embrace yer Scottish self, if ye choose joy—"

"You mean delirium, don't you?" he said loudly. "That's the true legacy of my Scottish half, not joy. You want to know about my MacGregor pedigree? Here's the sordid truth. My mother was a bloody selfish lunatic who died raving and soiling her night rail while she took her own life. Now, isn't that a heritage to be proud of?" He was shouting by this time, but he didn't care. "There'll be a snowstorm in hell on the day I count myself a Scot."

Alexander became suddenly aware that the hall had gone quiet enough to hear a mouse fart. Every eye was turned toward the dais, a look of horrified fascination frozen on each face.

"Mr. Lyttle," Lucinda said with a catch in her voice as she dabbed her lips with her napkin and rose to her feet. "Would ye be so good as to light me to my chamber?"

The butler moved to do her bidding with all speed but no one else twitched so much as an eyelash. As the sound of her retreating footfalls faded, the weight of eyes on Alexander grew oppressive.

"Eat," he ordered as he scooped up another spoonful of the Tipsy Laird. *Singularly appropriate,* he mused with a grimace. *As God is my witness, I will never mix ale and wine again.* "You heard me. Eat!"

No one moved.

"You, boy." He pointed to the lad in the corner who'd been torturing a set of bagpipes off and on all evening. "Play something."

The boy stood and put the pipe to his lips, but all he managed was a shaky wheeze.

"What?" Alexander demanded of the assembly.

"Are there no more songs? No more dances? No more bloody interminable epics to recite? And here I'd heard the Scots were a race of warrior poets."

There was nothing warlike in the gazes that greeted him. He'd have welcomed that. He'd have picked out the biggest bloody Scot in the place and challenged him to fisticuffs on the spot. Instead, each face was fearful, filled with nameless dread.

Was he laird of a castle full of cowards?

Alexander could stand no more. He rose to his feet, swaying only slightly, and stalked from the hall. He hoped he could find his way to his chamber because he damned well wasn't going to ask any of them for help.

"Be merry, blast you," he shouted when the buzz of whispered conversations behind him began humming like an upturned hive. "Don't you know it's Christmas?"

Mr. Lyttle rang for Jane and Janet to help her ladyship to bed before he left Lady Bonniebroch at her door. Then he made a beeline for the tower, taking the winding stone steps two at a time. It was a measure of his distress that he didn't wait long enough to knock and receive Mr. Farquhar's permission to enter. He burst in as soon as he unwarded the door, wringing his hands.

"Och, this is terrible," Lyttle said, his chest heaving. "'Tis disastrous. Did ye hear—"

"*Aye.*" Farquhar didn't rise from his writing desk. He blotted the page with sand and shook the excess out as if nothing troubled him at all. As if all their fates didn't hang on the events of the next few days.

Lyttle knew the steward was preparing the roster of duties for everyone within the keep for the morrow, but they didn't have time to spare for such mundane things now. Not when their last hope was fading so quickly.

"I hear everything that passes in this castle, whether I wish it or no'," Farquhar said with maddening calmness. *"I take it his lordship is a bit in his cups."*

"He is," Mr. Lyttle admitted, "but that's a wee bit our fault. Ye gave orders that he was to have double portions of both ale and wine, the stoutest we have in the cellars. I'm thinkin' that were a mistake. All it did was make him angry."

"Nae, he isna angry. He's finally letting himself feel his old hurt and that's all to the good." Farquhar released his quill into the air and it floated over to the inkwell on its own. *"Like reopening a wound to let out the poison. Pain experienced fully has a way of purifying, of burning out old damage."*

"But he said he'd never—"

"He didn't say never," Farquhar corrected. *"He said there'd be a snowstorm in hell on the day he counted himself a Scot. That's not never."*

"As near as makes no difference."

"Ye're wrong. Did ye know that the Viking raiders believed in a hell of eternal ice and cold? Nothing is more likely than a snowstorm there."

"But we aren't Viking raiders," Lyttle pointed out.

"Ye might be surprised if ye were to go back far enough in yer family tree. But, no matter. His lordship is thoroughly foxed. Strong drink makes a man say many things, but

contrary to the old saying, there isna always veritas in vino. What his lordship says is of no import."

"No?"

"No. It's what he does as will make a difference for us."

Lyttle paced the room like a caged lynx. "So ye still have hope?"

"There is always hope, Mr. Lyttle," Farquhar said. *"To that end, might I suggest that the castle inhabitants leave the hall and gather in the chapel? 'Tis almost midnight and prayers are always heard on the night before Our Lord's birth."*

Lyttle noticed that the steward didn't say prayers were answered. Only heard.

"Please convey my compliments to the footmen and our sommelier. Their work has rendered his lordship in a highly suggestible state, which is precisely what I intended. If ye'll excuse me, Lyttle, my presence is required elsewhere."

"An' ye dinna mind me asking, what d'ye intend to do?"

"Simple. Lord Bonniebroch identified his sickness with his outburst in the hall this evening. I intend to make sure he knows where to find his cure."

"From time immemorial, men have needed women more than they need us. They soften our rough edges and knit up the loose threads of our ragged souls. They are our very breath, though we often don't realize it. Our first father, Adam, tried to blame his woman for his own failings. After losing Eden, I wonder how long it took him to understand what a mercy it was that he could still have Eve after the Fall. And that the Garden was never far from his heart, so long as she was near."

From the secret journal of Callum Farquhar, Steward of Bonniebroch Castle since the Year of Our Lord 1521

Chapter Eighteen

Alexander climbed the stone staircase and stumbled toward his room. He plucked a torch from the wall and lit his own way. Damned if he'd ask one of those pathetic souls in the hall to do it for him. They all looked as if they'd drop over dead if he so much as crossed his eyes at them.

To his amazement, the first door he tried turned out to be the correct one. His valet had laid out his banyan on the foot of the big bed, though the servant himself was nowhere to be seen.

Probably cowering in the Great Hall with the rest of them.

The chambermaid had left a banked fire in the grate. Alex stubbed his torch out into the fireplace and dropped it there. The pitch spit sparks up the chimney and the blaze roared back to life, banishing the chill in the room. Then Alex plopped into one of the rustic wooden chairs and started tugging off his boots. His head pounded.

Tea only, tomorrow, he promised himself as the first boot came free.

Finally, after much twisting and pulling, he yanked off the second boot and stretched out his legs. He shrugged out of his jacket and waistcoat. He removed his waterfall neck cloth. Then he unbuttoned his shirt. He forgot to take off his cufflinks before he started stripping. The sleeves became hopelessly hung up at his wrists and in frustration he ripped the shirt when he stomped a foot down on it to yank himself free.

In his current foxed state, that simple activity wore him out. He leaned back in the chair, wishing it was of a more comfortable design. If it were a tufted wing chair, for example, he might not even have to rise and stumble toward the heavily timbered bed where the counterpane had already been drawn back. Alex leaned his head in his hand, covering his eyes.

He'd behaved abominably in the Great Hall and he knew it. Once he started, he couldn't seem to stop. It was almost as if he were watching himself from outside his own body, saying all those horrible things, acting like a complete ass, and not able to do a single thing to end his diatribe.

He sighed. Lucinda had every right to hate him. He hated himself.

His breathing slowed. The crackle of the fire faded and even the tick of the ormolu clock on the mantel seemed to stop. He skimmed the surface of sleep, dipping beneath its deep blackness long enough for dream fragments to rise in his mind.

A cavalry charge in France, the stench of sweaty horses and equally sweaty men filling his nostrils.

Before the pounding line of horsemen met the opposing force, the images, sounds, and smells faded, blending into an entirely different scene.

A ballroom in Prague. A couple glided across the gleaming marble in shades of sepia and puce. The woman sent Alex a seductive glance over her partner's shoulder.

In a swirl of silk, the vision faded along with the spicy jasmine of the woman's perfume. In its place came a dimly lit chamber.

The crying was soft at first. Alex hardly noticed it. Then it began to build, pressing against his heart in wrenching sobs. The woman, whoever she was, threw back her head and howled out her grief.

God, make her stop. Please, someone—

The wood in the fireplace shifted and popped. Alexander startled in his chair and jerked awake, wondering for half a blink where he was.

Across the room, a man stepped from the long mirror. Not from behind it, but *from* it. The silvered glass wavered as he passed through and then coalesced behind him in shimmering circles, like a pond disturbed by a pebble.

I'm still asleep, Alex decided.

"*Good evening, my lord,*" came a soft Scottish burr.

Alexander knuckled his eyes and recognized the man as Farquhar, his long-absent steward. "It took you long enough to present yourself, man. Have you waited till I'm totally ape-drunk to show me the estate ledgers?"

"*Och, nae, my lord, there'll be time enough for that after Christmas. But trust me. You'll find everything in order so far as that's concerned.*"

Farquhar moved to the window with a surprisingly smooth gait for one of his advanced years and looked down into the bailey.

Alex hauled himself up and joined the steward there. Since this dream didn't seem to be fading or melting into another one like the others had, he figured he might as well become engaged in it. Strange as this night phantom was, with people popping in and out of looking glasses and such, he was grateful that at least the weeping woman was gone.

Below in the bailey, all the denizens of the keep were pouring across the snow-covered courtyard and into the well-lit chapel.

"Midnight service?" Alex asked.

"*Aye,*" Farquhar said in his papery, thin tone. "*To celebrate the birth of Our Lord and to pray a bit for the new laird of Bonniebroch as well.*"

"I didn't ask them to."

"*Aye, lad, ye did. No' in so many words, o' course, but yer outburst at the supper was a cry for help, whether ye knew it or no'.*"

Alexander's ears burned. Once again he was struck

by Farquhar's unservant-like demeanor. He was more like a tutor or an elderly uncle. Or a confessor.

It was time to change the subject.

"If you're not here to demonstrate the efficacy of your stewardship, why are you in my chambers instead of down there in the kirk with the rest of them?"

When Alexander gazed at the steward full on, he looked like any other aged Scot, wiry and tough, if a bit more diminutive than most. But viewed from the corner of his eye, Farquhar seemed frailer, as if Alex could actually see through his slight frame to the room beyond.

There. Wasn't that the coal hod showing clearly through the tail of Farquhar's old-fashioned frock-coat? And didn't the thistle pattern that framed the wall tapestry continue unabated along the edge of the floor through Farquhar's white stockings?

Alex closed his eyes and rubbed the bridge of his nose. *Drunk and dreaming. A bad combination.*

"I may no' attend services with the rest, but dinna fret about the condition of me soul, my lord," Farquhar said, his voice so soft, Alex strained to hear it. *"The Almighty and I talk with each other plenty. I simply prefer to do it when He and I are alone."*

It had been a long time since Alex had conversed with God. So long he wouldn't know where to begin. He scrubbed a hand over his face. He didn't want to think these thoughts. It was as if they weren't even his, as if Farquhar had planted them in his head.

Even if he hadn't, the steward had a bad habit of changing the subject when the current one didn't suit him. Alex turned to Farquhar in irritation.

"You still haven't answered my question. Why are you here?"

"Och, that's easy. To make sure ye're privy to the secrets of the laird's chamber."

Something hidden always pricked his interest. Against his will, Alex was intrigued. "What sort of secrets?"

"There are many of them. More than ye can bear at the moment, but for tonight, we'll start with the privy passages that lead to and from this room." Farquhar moved smoothly to the fireplace. *"Come, yer lordship."*

Alex ambled over, nearly tripping over his own feet. "In case you haven't noticed, I'm in no condition to wander far."

"Good. We'll no' be going far. Now, if ye'd be so kind as to reach up and grasp the statue of Kenneth MacAlpin on the right side of the mantel and pull it toward ye. . . . "

There was only one stone figurine on the thick slab of oak, so Alex reached for it. Surprisingly, he couldn't lift it off the mantel. Its base was attached at one side so he could only tilt it like a lever. As he did, the faint rasp of stone on stone came from beneath the tapestry that featured a trio of hunting dogs harassing a bristly-backed boar.

"Now, pull back that tapestry," Farquhar ordered.

It occurred to Alex that his servant was doing the commanding and he was doing all the obeying. Not what he expected when he became a "by-God Scottish laird," but he couldn't come up with a cogent argument against it at the moment. Alexander lifted the heavy tapestry and a blast of cold air whooshed by him, raising a raft of gooseflesh on his bare arms and chest.

It also cleared his head. His vision was honed to knife-edged sharpness, but without benefit of additional light in the dark corridor he couldn't see beyond ten feet.

"The passage hasna been used in a while. Ye'll forgive the musty smell. I collect as it's a mite dim for ye as well. Do ye light the first candle just there, if ye please."

There was a tin sconce inside the passage with tinder and flint in a wall-mounted container situated a respectable distance away from the sconce. Alex lit the candle, which threw a cheery circle of light. Now he could see that the passage was studded with sconces at intervals as it disappeared into darkness. The candles would banish the black, but did nothing for the cobwebs that draped over his head like lacy bed curtains.

"I take it you didn't give the previous Lord Bonniebroch this tour?"

"Nae. He wasna the right laird. No heart. No honor. We all kenned it from the start. T'was a mercy when Sir Darren MacMartin decided to lose the estate to the first man daft enough to engage him in a game of poque. Oh!" Farquhar seemed to realize he'd just insulted his new laird and had the grace to look chagrined for a couple blinks before he hurried on. *"I do beg yer pardon. We like to think Providence had a hand in ye being the daft man, ye see. All's well that ends well. At least, that's the hope. Now, if ye please, let us proceed."*

Alex was too intent on the secret passage to waste time over his servant's unintentional slight and ham-handed apology. He moved down the narrow way. He didn't hear the steward's footfalls behind him but the old man's voice tickled his ear, admonishing him not to turn off the main passage. A set of stairs going up disappeared to the right.

"Does that lead to the battlements?" Alex asked.

"Aye, in darker days, it was expedient for the laird to be able to show himself on the ramparts at a moment's notice. I mind the time when . . ."

"When what?"

"'Tis no matter the now, my lord. 'Tis a tale for another night."

Farther along the passage, another staircase led downward. "I suppose that leads to the deep dark dungeon," Alex said with a laugh. As if there still were such things in this thoroughly modern Year of Our Lord 1821.

"Aye, it does," Farquhar confirmed. *"But ye dinna need to trouble about that for another few days or so. What bides there is still contained. Mostly."*

Alex jerked to peer over his shoulder at Farquhar, but the passage was too dim, as if someone had guttered the candles behind him so they nearly winked out at that precise moment. Alex couldn't see the old man clearly. He decided not to ask for an explanation of that cryptic statement. Farquhar wouldn't tell him any more unless he wanted to in any case.

He stopped before a doorway outlined in faint light seeping through the cracks. "What's behind this door?"

"Yer treasure, lad."

Treasure? Alexander had never thought himself the sort to be motivated by gain, but his heart quickened at the adventure of finding a trove. He turned the knob and pushed the door open slowly.

The room was lit only by the banked fire, but his vision had become sharpened even further by his sojourn through the dark passageway. No barrels of coin or upturned, gem-encrusted goblets greeted his eyes. This was no dragon's hoard, no pirate's buried treasure.

It was a bedchamber.

He took a few steps into the room, his stockinged feet making no sound. Then there was a soft creak and the latch snicked behind him. He turned to see that the secret doorway had no knob on this side, no visible evidence that it even existed.

And no evidence that Farquhar had followed him into the room either. Which was just as well, because if he had, Alex would have had to toss him out the window.

The sleeping form in the big four-poster belonged to Lucinda. Alexander couldn't bear the thought of another man being in her chamber while she slept, not even a decrepit old soul like Farquhar.

She was only for him.

Lucinda was buried under a mound of coverlets, but he still knew it was her. Her soft lilac scent teased his nose and set all his senses on edge.

Somewhere along the dark tunnel, Alex had realized he wasn't dreaming. Starting from Farquhar's unorthodox entry into his chamber through the mirror, to Alexander's passage through the strange tunnel with its upward and downward staircases he was admonished not to take, to this moment of indecision in his wife's bedroom, not much of this benighted night made logical sense.

But he knew clear to his bones that all this was real.

For one thing, if he'd been dreaming, he wouldn't have hesitated. He'd have joined his phantom Lucinda on the thick feather tick and made sloppy-drunk love to her. He'd have spread her wide and plunged in, wallowing in the mindless animal joy of rutting.

If this were a dream, it wouldn't have meant anything but a stain on his sheets in the morning and an unexplained smile over his tea at breakfast.

But if he joined Lucinda in her bed now . . . if she *allowed* him to join her . . . it would change everything.

Slowly, he walked toward the bed. It couldn't hurt just to look at her.

But it did.

His chest ached at the sight of her, all limp and relaxed. Her mouth was softly parted, her hair spread in waves across her pillow, the peaks and valleys of her form only hinted at beneath the thick counterpane.

He yearned to touch her, to slide his fingers over her satiny skin. Without his conscious volition, he reached toward her cheek, but stopped himself before his fingertips brushed her soft skin.

If I touch her once, there's no going back.

It would mean surrendering his goal of reaching Lord Liverpool's inner circle. His father would never realize his younger son wasn't the wastrel he always took him for. He'd be stuck in Scotland for the foreseeable future. Probably forever.

Lucinda sighed in her sleep. He moved his hand another couple inches and stroked her cheek. Her eyelids fluttered open and she looked up at him wordlessly.

"I'm sorry," he whispered. The words seemed so small, but they were all he could think to say. He'd been nothing but a cad since he first laid eyes on her and discovered he was unexpectedly betrothed to her. She'd done nothing but try to make the best of a bad situation, while he'd hurt and embarrassed her at every turn.

Perhaps the words bore repeating. With emphasis. "I'm *so* sorry, Lucinda."

He braced himself for a long-winded lecture. A strongly-worded reproof, at the very least. Instead, she did the last thing he expected.

She lifted her arms to him in silent invitation.

"Contrary to popular belief, love does not manifest itself in hearts and flowers. It does not hang upon the cadence of sonnets or hide with sparkling jewels in black velvet cases. Instead, it is born in the whispered breath of a heartfelt apology. Even then, love doesn't truly live until it is given substance in the magic of 'I forgive.'"

From *The Knowledgeable Ladies' Guide to Eligible Gentlemen*

Chapter Nineteen

Angel woman.

Alexander didn't wait for more. He shucked out of his trousers and smalls in record time and sank into her embrace, covering her with kisses. Her neck, her chin, her closed eyelids—he lavished his wordless apology on each of the small freckles spattered over her cheeks and nose with a soft, questing mouth. Then he took her lips hard and she gave him absolution.

Lucinda opened to him immediately, receiving his thrusting tongue with a greediness that surprised and delighted him. He knew he'd ought to go slow. He should draw out this first loving till she could bear no more, till she screamed for release.

Unfortunately, he was already at the point where his own impending climax made his ballocks tense and his shaft pulse. To take the edge off the "Center of the Universe" between his legs, he started spelling random words in his mind, anything to ease the building pressure.

Nipples. N-I-P-P-L-E-S. Nipples.

He took the lace at her neckline in his teeth and ripped her night rail to her navel. Her breath hissed in suddenly, but she didn't complain. He lowered his head and began to suck one of her taut peaks. Oh, the feel of her nipple in his mouth . . . He sucked and sucked and sucked till his eyes rolled back in his head.

He was wrong. His cock wasn't the Center of the Universe, after all. The woman beneath him was.

When she made little sounds of distress, he switched to the other nipple and gently twisted the one he'd just left with his thumb and forefinger.

Lucinda writhed under him. She clutched his head, holding him close.

As if he'd try to leave.

Her helpless little noises grew more urgent as he kissed his way over her ribs to sink his tongue into her belly button. He decided to switch to spelling backward in order to keep himself under control.

Navel. L-E-V-A-N. Navel.

He forced himself to move with exquisite slowness as he pulled up her night rail to expose her sweet mound.

"Spread your legs, Lu," he said, his voice passion-rough. "I want to look at you."

"There?" She raised herself on her elbows to meet

his gaze as he settled between her legs and slid both hands under her bum.

"God, yes." She smelled like heaven—a musky, spicy heaven. "And I want you to watch me."

"Why? What are ye going to—Gracious Sakes!"

Alexander's mouth at her breasts had sent Lucinda into near delirium. The ache in her nipples shot through her body and settled in the spot she'd always secretly thought of as her *ruminella,* because no one had ever told her what the proper thing to think of it as was. She'd *ruminated* over its possible functions and uses and knew there was much more to it than she'd been told. Now she was learning what that part of her body was designed to do.

It was an instrument of torment.

She never thought it possible to want something so badly and not know exactly what it was she wanted. When Alex pressed his mouth on her, she ached. She throbbed. She wept moisture onto his lips.

He licked it up greedily. When he slipped his tongue into her tight channel, her head fell back.

There were no words. No concept for what he was doing to her. Possession was the closest thing that came to her mind. It was a claiming, a declaration that she no longer belonged to herself.

She was his.

Then his tongue found a tight nub that had risen at the top of the little valleys between her legs. He closed his lips over it and sucked.

Lucinda came apart from the inside. She convulsed. She bucked, but he gave no quarter. Bits of her soul were coming undone and floating away. She'd never be whole again.

She didn't care. She didn't care a lot.

Before the final pulse contracted her insides, Alexander raised himself over her, his "Much of a Muchness" poised where his blessed mouth had recently been. He kissed her lips and she tasted herself, all salt and musk. Lucinda wrapped her arms around his shoulders as he pushed into her slowly.

"More," she pleaded.

His eyes glinted wildly. "I'm afraid . . . if I go faster . . . I can't be gentle," he said through gritted teeth.

"I dinna want gentle."

Alexander shredded her then, thrusting his full length in one long stroke. The pain was sharp and quick, but it faded with the joy of holding him inside her. Fully seated, he drew back for another. And another. He hooked his elbows under Lucinda's knees and nearly folded her in two. He bore down on her. His ballocks slapped her bum with each rutting thrust.

She moved with him, caught up in the heat and friction and grinding joy. Her insides tightened again and this time her release pounded around something.

Him.

This time, she was the possessor. She claimed him, declaring that he belonged to her.

He stiffened and arched his back as he drove into her. The hot flood of his seed erupting inside her in rhythmic pulses. It went on and on and she hooked her ankles behind his back, determined not to release him until he'd given her everything.

She'd earned it.

Finally, he stilled and collapsed a bit onto her, his weight settling on her lower half, while he kept his torso balanced on his elbows. Still, his head sank onto the pillow beside hers.

His chest heaved as if he'd run a mile. Lucinda was more than a little breathless too. She'd thought she was permanently shattered, but, one by one, the little pieces of her that had sheared off while Alexander claimed her returned. They gathered together again, sparking a bit as they reattached themselves inside her. Her entire being was reinvigorated. Whole.

She stroked his hair, letting the world slide past them. Nothing else mattered but this precious moment, this joining, this afterglow of something so holy, she couldn't wrap her mind around the enormity of it all. When her sisters plied her with questions later, she knew she wouldn't have words for what had happened inside her, even if she'd been willing to share it with them.

She and her lover—her husband!—were wrapped in the silence of bonding, giving their souls time to separate again after they'd mingled. They needed a few moments to settle back into their own bodies. Everything else seemed to stop.

Then after a little while, the silence became oppressive.

She wished he'd say something. Anything.

How was it that she and this man had just been closer than she'd been to another living soul since she left her mother's womb, and she hadn't a clue what was rolling around in his noggin?

She'd gone to bed that evening sick at heart, and not only on account of the cruel display Alex had put on at supper. Despite his assurance that he'd honor the other points of their marriage contract, she'd been convinced that he meant to wait a decent amount of time and then turn her out, since their marriage hadn't been consummated. No more worries on that score.

'Tis done. I'm a wife in truth now.

But that didn't mean things would get any easier for the pair of them.

Especially since, yes, there it was again. She wasn't mistaken. The man was snoring softly.

She wedged her arms between them and heaved. "Get off me, then, ye great ox!"

He came awake with a snort as he rolled to one side. "What's the matter?"

"What's the matter, the man says," Lucinda fumed. "Ye fell asleep."

He knuckled his eyes and blinked slowly. "I don't know about Scottish customs, but sleep is a generally accepted pastime in England."

"But no' the now. No' when ye've just taken me maidenhead." She tucked the coverlet under her chin. "Have ye naught to say to me?"

"I said I was sorry."

"And?"

"I . . . thought you forgave me."

"Aye, I did, but have ye no words of—" *Of love,* she almost said, but she snipped off the words before they tumbled out. If the man had to be prompted to speak of love, he couldn't have many deep feelings on the matter. "Never mind."

He rolled onto his back and laced his fingers behind his head. "Now that I'm wide awake again, I have to say, you were . . . incredible, Lucinda."

"Aye?" No one had ever named her incredible at anything before. Her heart leaped up in hope, but she reined it in. There were too many highs and lows with Alexander. When would they find that calm center she so longed for?

"Aye," he repeated with a grin. Then he reached for her and tugged her close. He was so warm it was like snugging up to a banked fire. The embrace wasn't a declaration of undying affection, but her skin tingled where it touched his. She wished he'd ripped her night rail even more thoroughly so more of her would be flush against more of him with not a scrap of fabric between.

"I suppose I shouldn't have let myself go to sleep. Bad form," he admitted. "But I was so relaxed after . . . and it felt so good to sink into a sleep without dreams."

"Everyone needs to dream, Alex."

"Not the dreams I have."

"Do ye have night terrors then?"

"I don't know if I'd call it that. Besides, it's just the one. But it comes almost nightly."

She raised up on one elbow and looked down at him. He was so handsome, he made her feel unaccountably shy. She distracted herself by teasing the sandy hair that whorled around his brown nipple.

"If the night phantom comes to ye that often, 'tis of some import. Tell me yer dream, Alexander."

He rolled toward her, pinning her beneath his

body, and kissed her again. Languid and slow, he nipped at her lips and teased her with his tongue.

"Ye're trying . . . to distract me," she said between kisses. He covered her mouth and the ache that had been stilled between her legs so recently throbbed afresh. Lucinda reached around him and squeezed his tight buttocks.

Oh, aye, Knowledgeable Ladies' Guide, *the man has an excellent seat, for certain sure.*

But much as her body urged her to go blithely with Alex's lead, her head told her not to be so easily turned. She shoved against his chest again.

"Alex, I mean it. No more playing. Tell me the dream now."

"Then more playing?" He nuzzled her neck.

She sent him a smile full of promise. "Aye."

He gave her one more lingering kiss and then sighed. "Very well. Since I became Lord Bonnie-broch, I've been plagued with a dream of a weeping woman. The dream is dark, so I can't see her clearly. I've no notion who she might be. All she does is sob . . . until it breaks my heart and I wake in a cold sweat."

"And ye've only dreamed of her since ye came into yer Scottish title?"

He nodded.

An idea struck Lucinda, but she wasn't sure she should mention it after what happened at supper. Still, if she could help him understand what he was dealing with, she had to try. "D'ye think . . . I mean, could it be your mother ye hear weeping?"

He rolled off her and sat upright. "After all these years why would I start dreaming of her now? And trust me, if I decided to dream of her, I'd make every effort for it to be a more pleasant one."

"Ye may have no say in it. I've never met anyone who could direct their dreams. 'Tis too jumbled up with the spirits and memory and whether we had too many turnips at supper." She sat up too. "Ye see, when we dream, I believe the veil between this world and the next wears a bit thin. The departed can get our attention more easily when we're asleep."

He cast her a dubious frown.

"Truly. I mind the time right after my grandsire died. I was a little girl then, but he came to me in a dream, smiling in that twinkly sort of way he had as he sat on the foot of my bed. And then he said to me, 'Lucy-girl, tell yer grandmam I love her and that'll never die.' Then he winked at me and was gone." She snapped her fingers. "Just like that."

"And you really believe your grandfather appeared to you in a dream?"

"I dinna ken, but I do remember it pleased my grandmam out of all knowing when I told her of it the next day," she said. "And why shouldn't my grandsire speak to me so? Doesna the Scriptures say angels spoke to Joseph while he slept?"

Alex cocked a brow at her. "I bow to your superior knowledge of holy writ, but I'm not convinced. Besides, my mother has been gone for a long time. Why would she begin to trouble me now?"

"She was Scottish, aye? Now that ye're in the Highlands, ye're closer to where she spent a great deal of her life. It may be she can reach ye easier here. And I dinna think she means to trouble ye. Sounds as if she's sorrowing over something."

"She has plenty to be sorrowful over," he said

softly, then he shook his head. "But that can't be it. The previous Lord Bonniebroch had them too. It's doubtful my mother decided to visit *him* by night." He narrowed his eyes and cast Lucinda a sidelong gaze. "How is it you know so much about dreams and visitations from the dear departed?"

Lucinda swallowed hard. It was the perfect chance for her to tell him about Brodie MacIver. But the bridge she and Alexander had built between themselves was so tenuous, she didn't know if it would stand the strain of introducing her ghostly companion just yet.

So she arched up to kiss his jaw and nibble his earlobe. "So many questions. Are ye intending to talk all night, husband? I thought ye wanted to play."

> *"Never have our hopes been so high. Yet for all its bright promise, the felicitous state of Lord Bonnie-broch's marriage isna the only bolt which must slip if the curse is to be broken. I've yet to decide if our laird has the strength to lift the others."*

From the secret journal of Callum Farquhar, Steward of Bonniebroch Castle since the Year of Our Lord 1521

Chapter Twenty

"Lu—" Alexander couldn't seem to find the end of her name. It got caught in his throat while she tormented him with all the skill of an accomplished courtesan, teasing and stroking. She'd taken to love play like a spaniel to the water. He'd never have believed her a virgin if he hadn't claimed her purity himself.

Of course, the fact that she wanted to touch and taste every bit of him with boundless enthusiasm may have colored his perceptions a bit. Once she got him to agree to grasp the spindles in her headboard and not let go until she gave him permission, she began a thorough exploration of his whole body.

"How strange that ye should be so soft near to where ye're so hard," Lucinda murmured as she fondled his ballocks with one hand while stroking his cock with the other. As if to make a liar of her, his balls tensed into a tight mound. "Hmm. It appears I'm mistook. Do ye change so at will? Or is it like a sneeze and ye canna stop it from happening?"

Then she bent and licked him from base to tip. It was a good thing she didn't really seem to expect an answer to her question. He was incapable of speech.

Alex was also incapable of keeping hold of the headboard for another moment. He grasped her hips and pulled her up so he could slip into her. She was wet as waterweed, slick and welcoming and he slid into her tight channel with the rightness of a homecoming.

"Ye promised ye wouldna let go of the headboard," she chided, but she rocked her hips slowly, luxuriating in having him fully seated inside her.

He grasped the spindles again. "I'm sorry."

"Ye've been saying that a lot this night."

He grinned at her. "Only this time I don't mean it. I just couldn't wait any longer, Lu. I had to be inside you again. But now, I'm completely at your mercy. Do with me as you will," he said. "Only don't stop doing with me or I'll die."

"We canna have that, can we?" She cocked a brow and smiled down at him, beneficent as a Botticelli angel, wicked as his most lascivious dream.

Lucinda set the pace. She bent to allow him to rub his face in the sweet hollow between her breasts. He caught a nipple as she started to raise back up and held her there as he sucked. He thrust upward as she bore down on him.

He could go deeper. He had to. He longed to

release his white-knuckled grip on the headboard so he could press her hips down further. He'd rut her completely. He'd split her in two. He'd—

"Hold me, Alex," she pleaded and he let go of the spindles.

He grasped her hips and held her down, driving himself in completely. She arched her back, thrusting her breasts forward, her head falling back so her hair cascaded down her spine and tickled his ballocks.

She moved on him, building the friction and heat. He began his mental spelling bee again to keep from emptying himself into her before she came. She had to come again first. He longed to feel her fisted around him, pounding around him—

Lucinda. A-D-N-I . . .

Even spelling backward wasn't working. He was losing the battle with the pressure rising in his shaft. He decided to switch to French.

Amour. R-U-O-M—

There was no stopping it this time. His body demanded release. Just as he began to go off like a Roman candle inside her, she came with him. They rode the bursts of pleasure together till they were utterly spent.

She'd been waiting for him, the little minx.

He'd been waiting for her . . . all his life. As she collapsed on his chest, he held her close. It made no sense if he thought about it logically. He hadn't known her much more than a week and yet, there was something inside him that recognized her. There were myriad things for him to learn about her, but at some deep level, he already knew Lucinda down to the soles of her little arched feet. Strangely enough, she seemed to know him as well.

And she hadn't turned away.

That was a Christmas miracle in its own right.

But on top of that, she made him feel something he'd never felt before. He wasn't sure yet what this emotion or sensation or whatever-it-was ought to be named, but this hot lump in his chest was too uncomfortably real not to mean something. He buried his nose in her hair and inhaled her sweet scent.

"Thank you," he whispered. *Thank you for not turning away when you saw who I really was,* he finished silently.

"Ye make it sound as if I rendered ye a service. 'Twas no' like that. I rather think what we do together is a gift we give each other."

"It is. But thank you all the same, love."

Lethargy stole over him, that drowsy don't-give-a-tinker's-damn-about-anything sensation that followed a good hard swive, but he knew he dared not let himself drift off again. Not until she did, at least.

If he was going to stay awake, he needed to be upright. Alexander rolled her off of him and swung his legs over the edge of the bed.

"Ye're leaving me?"

"No, just stretching my legs." The odd passage between his chamber and hers rose in his mind. "Want to go on a bit of an explore with me?"

She wrapped one of the blankets around her shoulders and climbed out of the bed to join him. "Where to?"

Heedless of his nakedness, he wandered to the wall where the doorway had opened, trying to find it again. The secret passage was so cunningly disguised;

there were no visible seams in the richly paneled walls. Then he looked at Lucinda's fireplace. Another figurine depicting the first Scottish king stood sentinel on the mantel.

He tilted the statue and Kenneth MacAlpin opened the doorway again. The candles in the tin sconces were still flickering in the long stone passageway. Lucinda gasped in surprise.

"I do believe your MacAlpin is my favorite historical monarch," Alex said with a grin.

"Mine too, if he led ye to my chambers this night."

"That was actually Mr. Farquhar's doing." The disturbing vision of the old steward stepping from the looking glass still rang as true in his head, but it couldn't be. Farquhar had probably slipped in through the door in the conventional manner just as Alexander was surfacing from a dream of him popping from the mirror.

He gave himself a shake. It was hard to tell real from imaginary on a night like this. When Lucinda slipped her hand in his it seemed real enough. He'd have hated to wake if this was all just a dream.

"Much as I like seeing ye in naught but the skin God gave ye, d'ye think ye ought to put on yer trousers if we're to go wandering behind the walls?" she suggested.

"You're right. And you'd better put on something warmer too." Her ripped night rail was scant protection from the elements. "It's chilly in there."

While Alex tugged on his smalls and trousers, Lucinda donned a fresh night rail and wrapper. Alex draped the blanket around her shoulders for good

measure. They joined hands at the yawning opening
in her wall.

"We'll have to go single file." He kissed her
knuckles and then held her hand behind his back
as he led her through the opening. He wasn't surprised when the doorway grated closed behind
them, but Lucinda gave a little squeak.

"Might we no' get lost back here?" she asked in a
small voice.

"Oh, ye of little faith," he said. "We can probably
go anywhere we want once we learn the system, but
we'll just follow the lighted candles back to my room
for now."

He pinched off the burning candles as they
passed, throwing the corridor behind them into
darkness. Alex fancied he heard something as they
came even with the stairs leading to the dungeon.
He hurried Lucinda past the dark opening and then
stopped.

"Did you hear that?" he asked.

It was faint, barely on the edge of sound. He
might have imagined it completely. Nothing was
more likely on this most fanciful of nights.

"What?" Lucinda cocked an ear.

He strained to listen, but the sound didn't come
again.

"I dinna hear anything but me own heart pounding in me ears," Lucinda whispered.

"*Alexander Mallory, Laird of Bonniebroch.*" There it
was again, a whisper like a courtyard full of dead
leaves. Lucinda showed no sign of having heard it,
but the voice sent a ripple of dread down his spine.

Alex moved her in front of him, so he could keep his body between her and the stairs leading downward.

When they came to the staircase leading upward, Alex stopped. "Let's go this way. I'm in need of some fresh air."

The stone steps turned in a tight spiral but it didn't take long for them to come to a heavy plank door with a beam in a bracket across it. Alexander lifted the beam and pushed the door open. He and Lucinda stepped out onto the battlements under a sky blazing with stars.

There was no moon, no clouds, only a hazy path of dense fire trailing across the sky. Far to the north, lights danced along the edge of the earth in eerie shades of green.

"That's something you don't see in London." Alex wrapped his arms around Lucinda from behind so he could shelter her from the cold.

"Oh, aye? We see them often in the winter."

"I've heard of the aurora borealis, of course . . ." The green lights changed shape and wavered in long streams. "I never expected they'd be so full of movement."

"That's because they're dancing," Lucinda said. "We call them the Nimble Men. Look! That one just bowed to his partner."

The sky did seem to be hosting a great ball for the dancing lights with stars winking against the blackness beyond.

"Sometimes, there are red spots here and there in the northern sky as well," Lucinda explained. "When that happens, folk tell tales of great battles between the Nimble Men and their enemies. The sky is strewn with wound-stones and pools of faery blood."

"I'll wager it's even prettier when there are red lights."

"Aye, it may be fine to look upon, but I dinna like it when I think what it represents. Violence isna pretty. Why is it men must fight and kill?"

Her words took him back to the French battle-field where he'd hacked his way through a melee after his horse was shot out from under him. His senses were so acute, his memories of that time so vivid, he could still smell the metallic tang of blood and acrid smoke, still feel the burn in his sword arm from every thrust as his strength dimmed and the English trumpets sounded retreat, still remember the faint wisp of a mustache on the last young Frenchman he cut down before he made it back to the relative safety of the English lines.

"Sometimes," Alex said wearily, "disputes among men can't be settled by civilized means."

"But wars mean fatherless bairns and broken-hearted women who must carry on without them. Why are men so bloody-minded? Why not just walk away from discord?"

He shrugged. "I love peace as much as the next man, but there are some fights one can't walk away from, not without surrendering something even more important than peace."

She sighed.

"I don't see any red tonight," he pointed out.

"Nae, the Nimble Men seem happy the now."

He could hear the smile in her voice and bent to drop a kiss on her neck. "Why wouldn't they be if they have Nimble Women up there too?"

She leaned back into him. Wind whipped past, setting the pennants flapping.

"Share the blanket with me," Lucinda said, lifting it to drape around his shoulders. Then she positioned herself before him and he wrapped his arms around her again. "A warm man *and* a warm blanket. Handsomer than that a girl couldna wish, unless . . ."

"Unless what?" At the moment, with her soft bum snugged up against his groin, he was disposed to give her anything she wanted.

"Unless ye'd be willing to share a bit more." She gave a beguiling wiggle of that soft bum. "Ye've hinted that ye're here in Scotland for something important. Oh, I know ye're one of King George's envoys, but ye dinna seem the type to be overconcerned about protocol and precedence and all the silly things that are so important to a royal court. When ye say your work is important, I dinna think ye mean schooling the local gentry on how to bow properly when they meet your king next summer. What might that work of yours be exactly?"

Alexander's lips tightened in a hard line. His work for Lord Liverpool had flown clear out of his mind, lost in the wonder of this slightly fantastical night and the thoroughly fantastical woman in his arms.

He'd never told anyone about his covert activities before. It would mean breaking several rules and his own personal code to tell her.

But this was Lucinda, the woman who forgave him for being such an impossible ass. Who loved him, maybe.

She was his wife. His other, better half. Surely one hand needed to know what the other was doing. And she might actually be a help. Not that he'd ever let her do anything that might put her in danger, but she might know something that would put his investigation on the right track.

And he suspected Lucinda was the sort who'd put a leaky roof to shame if he didn't tell her. So between one heartbeat and the next, he put his whole future in her hands.

"I'm here to root out any remaining Radicals and bring them to justice before King George puts so much as a royal toe on the dock at Leith."

She trembled. And something told him it wasn't because of the cold.

*"If larking about the Continent is not possible, then
the honeymooning lovebirds ought to hide away in an
undisclosed location for two months at least. The wise
bride knows that nothing is less conducive to marital
bliss than the inundation of relatives upon the bridal
bower."*

From *The Knowledgeable Ladies' Guide
to Eligible Gentlemen*

Chapter Twenty-One

Christmas Day passed in unbridled merriment.
The unpleasantness of the previous night's supper
was forgotten as word spread throughout the castle
that Lady Bonniebroch's effects were being moved
into the master's suite of rooms. The change in Lucinda's marital relations lifted not only her spirits,
but the spirits of everyone in Bonniebroch. After the
morning service in the little chapel, the entire popu-
lace bent to work with a will to clean the already spot-
less keep for the more riotous celebrations to come.

When the company broke off their labor for the
midday meal, the boy with the pipes screwed up his
courage enough to torment his instrument again. A
trio of little girls did a sprightly pointed-toe dance
for their entertainment while the household ate.

Lucinda was told by one of the footmen that the dining arrangements were not unique to the holiday. Unlike the staid English custom of the family dining alone and the help eating below stairs, everyone in Bonniebroch took their meals together, with their laird and his lady presiding from the dais. She was inordinately pleased by this. It was as if she and Alex had a ready-made large family amassed around them.

When Alex reached under the table and took her hand, Lucinda allowed herself to hope, to believe that something of a Christmas miracle had taken place between them. If she could only put his true reason for being in Scotland in the first place out of her mind . . .

Mrs. Fletcher and her staff outdid themselves with a goose, roasted, stuffed, and drizzled with applesauce relish. There was a rich fish soup called cullen skink, followed by meat pies, and oatcakes. For sweets, there were trifles and shortbread and tattie scones galore. Everyone had a healthy portion of the Christmas pudding that Mrs. Fletcher had been working on since the first Sunday in Advent. It was declared her best ever by one and all.

"When will the holiday games begin?" Alex asked as he scraped his spoon along the bottom of his bowl.

"Not until after the Feast of Stephen, the day ye English call Boxing Day," Lucinda explained. "That's when we begin to celebrate Hogmanay leading up to Twelfth Night. What sort of games were ye expecting?"

"Oh, you know, Hot Cockles, Snap Dragon, and such like."

Mia Marlowe

"I dinna ken how to play those English games."

"Easy," Alex explained. "For Hot Cockles, one person is blindfolded. While he lays his head in someone's lap, someone else has to give his bum a whack. Then the blindfolded bloke has to guess who struck him."

"And ye think this fun?"

He cast her a wicked grin. "Having my head in your lap sounds like fun to me."

"That we can arrange without someone giving ye a paddling at the selfsame time," she said with a laugh. "I'm afeard to ask about Snap Dragon."

"It involves chanting a long rhyme while snatching raisins from burning brandy."

She rolled her eyes and shook her head. "How did your ridiculous kind ever conquer mine?"

"I'm not sure we have yet," he said, offering her a bite of his trifle. She took it from his spoon. A little of the sweetness trickled from the corner of her mouth, so he leaned over and licked it off. "But I'm looking forward to trying again tonight."

Then he gave her a lingering kiss that warmed her to her curled toes. Lucinda would have been perfectly happy if only her brother Dougal wasn't one of the Radicals her husband planned to "bring to justice."

Matters were made worse when her Radical brother arrived on the Bonniebroch dock, courtesy of Beans MacFee's ferry, in the middle of that afternoon.

Lucinda donned her wool pelisse and accompanied Alex through the woods to the dock. Somehow, she had to figure out a way to separate these two men before they realized they were at enmity with each other.

Dougal had brought Badgemagus as Alexander had ordered. He'd bound the gelding's eyes with a cloth to keep him calm during the ride on the ferry-barge, but the horse hadn't thought much of the process. When Dougal unwrapped Badgemagus's head, the horse stamped and reared and might have run off into the wood if Alex hadn't arrived in time to loop a second rope around his silly neck.

Once they subdued the gelding, Alex thanked Dougal for bringing him from Dalkeith on Christmas Day.

"'Tis no matter. One day is like another for a man who must work for his bread," Dougal said gruffly. "But I dinna think ye'll thank me for bringing ye this beastie in the end. I never saw a more stubborn horse in all me life."

"You tried to ride him, I'm guessing," Alex said as he paid Mr. MacFee's fare. The ferryman shoved off with all speed, but Lucinda didn't imagine the odiferous Beans had a family to hurry back to even if it was Christmas. Lucinda had invited him to stay, but he didn't want to spend any longer near Bonnie-broch than he could help.

Alex took the horse's lead rope as they started back through the woods to the castle. Lucinda followed, trying to step in the tracks Alex and Badgemagus left in the snow so as not to ruin her slippers. Unfortunately, her stride was much shorter than either man or beast.

"Aye, I did manage to mount the blighter a few times, but he wouldna let me keep me seat," Dougal said, rubbing his backside surreptitiously. "I'd heard ye'd had some trouble wi' him and thought as I'd gentle him a bit for ye. I was sure the evil things folk said about Badgemagus couldna possibly be true, but it seems they are. Never met a horse I couldna ride before."

"Me either," Alex said.

At least these two men Lucinda cared for had found common ground. Pity it was in a horse that was destined to be turned into glue.

"And so long as I don't give up, I still haven't met the horse who bested me," Alex said with dogged determination. "I mean to ride this beast, one way or the other."

"Meanin' no disrespect, milord, but me money's on 'the other.' Ye'll be pickin' rocks out o' yer backside if ye mount him again."

"We'll see," Alex said as they passed over the drawbridge, Badgemagus's hooves clopping loudly on the ancient wood. "I've been thinking about this stubborn old cuss and there's something I haven't tried yet."

As soon as they were inside the bailey, Lucinda put a hand on her brother's arm and pulled him aside.

"Dougal, ye must leave here," she whispered as Alex walked on. "Now."

Her brother's face screwed into a frown. "The ferryman's gone. I havena even had a chance to warm me frozen bum or take a nip o' Christmas cheer. Ye'd send yer own kin packing on this day of all days?"

"Trust me, 'tis for your own good. The Englishmen are looking for Radicals."

"I figured the ones at Dalkeith were sniffin' about. One of the reasons I left as soon as I could." Dougal glanced at Alexander's back. "Yer Englishman as well?"

Lucinda nodded miserably.

"Dinna fret. I've given up that cause and there's little to connect Dougal MacOwen with Dougal Dun." That was the name her brother had assumed when he began his idealistic crusade. Living rough since he went into hiding had etched itself on Dougal's face. There was a hardness in her brother that hadn't been there before. "The few who know Dun and MacOwen are one and the same know well enough to hold their tongues if they wish to keep them."

Something inside Lucinda shivered. Her brother wasn't exaggerating. He was a cold enough man to deliver on the threat. "And yet ye still remain hidden, only in plain sight the now."

"A man canna be too careful. I've but one neck, ye ken."

"Though I'm glad to hear ye no longer work for rebellion, I dinna understand how ye can set aside yer principles so easily," she said. "Ye were so over-wrought about the English and how they'd oppressed the Weavers Guild."

At their height, the Radicals had sought to echo the cries for freedom heard across the Atlantic in America and in France's revolution as well. However, when James Wilson, one of the leaders of the movement, was hanged before a crowd of some twenty thousand onlookers, the Radicals lost steam and went underground.

"Can ye give up something ye gave years of yer life to?" Lucinda asked in a frantic whisper. She wanted to believe it, but the Dougal she knew was as stubborn as Badgemagus once he set his feet.

"Aye, but 'tis hard. There's no denyin' we were in the right and had legitimate grievances. Dinna think me heart doesna still beat for Scottish independence, but we must use our heads lest we lose them," Dougal said with surprising practicality. "Times have changed. What with this royal progression, Scottish weavers have work and to spare. Now that George IV has decreed that all his subjects must greet him in the plaids of their clans, no one who owns a loom goes hungry."

"But what about the dirk dance and all? You weren't planning to——"

"Lucy, d'ye take me for a fool that would try to murder a king? I've no wish for martyrdom." A faraway look softened his eyes and eased the fine lines around the corners of them. "I've a less lofty goal than that now but 'tis one I'd come closer to risking me neck for. Has Enya MacKenzie taken a husband yet?"

"Hmph! That I dinna ken." Lucinda had been too caught up with her own family's doings to keep up with gossip in another village. Her sister Aileen would be the one to ask. "Ye ought no' expect a lass will wait forever. Somehow, we must see about a pardon for ye before ye think to go courting."

"Aye, and if wishes were horses, then beggars would ride," he quoted the old saw. "I'll believe a pardon will happen when I see yer husband riding that damned Badgemagus——"

"Then look, brother."

Alexander came riding across the bailey at an easy trot. About twenty feet from Lucinda and Dougal, he guided the horse in an easy figure-eight pattern, demonstrating complete mastery over the gelding, and then came straight ahead. For once, Badgemagus halted before them without throwing Alex over his head.

"Alexander Mallory, how did ye ever manage it?" Lucinda said as she reached up to pet the gelding's velvet nose.

"I remembered something Mr. Gow said about him. He mentioned that Badgemagus was broad enough to pull whatever I cared to put behind him. It occurred to me that he might have been trained to cart rein instead of neck rein." Alexander dismounted and gave the horse an affectionate pat on his arched neck. "If I pull back on one side as though I'm driving a cart, he responds perfectly. When I was neck reining, he didn't understand what I was asking of him."

"No wonder he was difficult," Dougal said. "All the men who tried to ride him were dunderheids who didna speak his language."

Alex laughed. "I hope to retrain him, but for now, we understand each other. Come warm yourself, Dougal, and help us celebrate Christmas."

Lucinda hoped she'd be able to keep the men sufficiently apart until she figured out a way for her husband not to help her brother into a noose.

Brodie MacIver liked Bonniebroch Castle fine. There were plenty of out-of-the-way places for a ghost to explore and lots of new people to play a few harmless tricks on.

Like the way he mixed up the Christmas pudding

helpings. The little serving maid had planned for the second footman to get the one with the message to meet her in the solar at sundown stuffed inside it. Instead, he was served a pudding with naught but the requisite twelve ingredients. At the other end of the table, the stable hand scratched his head over the bit of foolscap tucked into his dessert. From the way the lad scowled at the note, Brodie would bet he couldn't read a lick.

If Lucinda learned about his tricks, she'd do more than frown at him.

"What Lucinda doesna know willna hurt me."

Besides, his little lassie was so taken up with her new husband, she hadn't a moment to spare to scold a ghost. Still, he didn't feel the least neglected. Even without fretting over Lucinda's well-being, there was plenty to keep him occupied. Brodie was as happy as a fellow without skin had a right to be.

Of course, there were some oddities about Bonniebroch, as well. He was certain there was at least one other spirit wandering about the place. Most often he sensed its energy when he approached the tall tower. But that way was warded by a shimmering wall of glamour and he could only advance so far up the winding stone staircase that led to the top turret.

Then there was the sense of something foul hidden away in the deeps of the castle. Brodie hadn't screwed his courage to roam in that direction. He told himself it was likely warded as well, but in truth, he didn't want to be any closer to the source of uneasiness that bubbled up inside him.

And finally, there was the soft sobbing. He didn't hear it all the time. It came and went, but it pierced his heart each time. He didn't know why it should. He had no notion of who the weeping woman was.

Brodie had never told Lucinda how he'd died, because actually, he couldn't remember. Much of his life on earth was veiled in mist. A few snippets poked through from time to time, like the fact that Lucinda's new husband strongly resembled Cormag MacGregor, the man who'd had something to do with Brodie's demise. But the particulars were like flotsam frozen in the castle moat. He could see bits and pieces of them, but he couldn't dig them out of the prism of time.

Sometimes, he wondered if it really mattered anymore. He had the sense of being stuck, of not being where he was supposed to be, but at the same time, he was enjoying where he was.

"How many as has breath can say the same?"

While Lucinda watched her new husband ride his pesky horse again, Brodie floated along at ceiling height from one yawning chamber to the next on the second floor of the Great Hall. When he came to the library, he stopped. Unlike the feckless stable hand with the pudding message, Brodie *could* read.

He just had trouble turning pages. Brodie could manipulate objects in the material world, but it required intense concentration and no little effort on his part. A book would have to be a cracking good tale for him to flip through all those pages. Fortunately, there was a large book already laid open on the heavy oak desk.

Brodie hovered lower and took a peek. It wasn't a printed volume. It was an illuminated manuscript, copied out by a precise hand long before Gutenberg churned out his first Bible. The book was opened to a genealogical chart for the Lyttle family spread out on facing pages, decorated with curlicues and fanciful beasts. Sure enough, there was Lyall Lyttle, the current butler of Bonniebroch. . . .

"It canna be." Brodie sank down to make sure he wasn't imagining things, but the quill scratchings remained the same. He shot up and through the library ceiling, then made for the largest window facing the open bailey below.

"Lucinda has to see this."

"Every soul in the world has secrets that, if ye only knew them, would break your heart. Why should a castle be any different?"

From the secret journal of Callum Farquhar, Steward of Bonniebroch Castle since the Year of Our Lord 1521

Chapter Twenty-Two

"I dinna understand it. The book was right here." Lucinda scoured the floor-to-ceiling shelves that were full to bursting with leather-bound manuscripts. An astrolabe and sextant was propped on one shelf and a stuffed marmot was poised to pounce from another. Mr. Lyttle studied the tips of his shoes with absorption.

Alexander slowly circuited the room. "Was there a title on the binding?"

"I didna think to look. It was lying out here before God and everybody. Someone," Lucinda said, shooting an accusing glance toward Mr. Lyttle, "has gone to the trouble of putting it away."

The butler refused to meet her gaze.

"Did you move it, Lyttle?" Alex asked.

"No, milord, upon my word, I didna."

Alexander sighed noisily. "It'll take forever to find

if we have to go through all the volumes in this room. What was so troubling about this book that you had to drag me away from the stables?"

Besides getting ye away from my Radical brother?

Lucinda sighed too. Less noisily. "Ye'll no' believe me if I canna show ye."

He came across the room and took her into his arms, heedless of the fact that their butler was looking on. "I'd believe you if you told me the sun rose in the west and set in the east."

"But it would be so much easier if ye could see it with your own eyes. It was a genealogy chart for our Mr. Lyttle."

"Oh?" He turned back to the butler. "Do you know what this is about then?"

Mr. Lyttle worried his lower lip but didn't respond.

"Let me refresh your memory. 'Tis remarkable enough," Lucinda said. "The chart in the book shows ye were born in the year 1489."

Alex laughed. "Lu, names run in families. Likely our butler had a many-times-great-great-grandfather of the same name."

"One who was married to a lady named Dorcas, the same as our Mr. Lyttle? And sired a set of twins whom he named Duncan and Dorrel," Lucinda said. "Refresh *my* memory, Mr. Lyttle. What are your sons' names?"

The butler shifted his weight from one foot to the other. "Dorrel and Duncan."

"And they are twins, aye?"

Like all the chambers in the castle, the library was on the coolish side. The fire in the grate did little to dispel the cold, but Mr. Lyttle pulled a crisp white handkerchief from his pocket and mopped his brow in any case. "Aye, me boys are twins."

Lucinda crossed the room to stand directly before him. "When were they born, Mr. Lyttle?"

He swallowed hard. "On the sixth day of September, milady."

She arched a brow at him.

He dropped his gaze. "In the year of Our Lord 1514." Then he looked up, his eyes darting back and forth between her and Alexander. "But ye were no' supposed to learn about the peculiarities of Bonniebroch like this. Mr. Farquhar wanted to explain things to ye his own self, I'm sure."

"Good idea. I can't wait to hear his explanation for this. Oh, wait, I have one. You're all mad as hatters," Alex said, his voice tight. "Farquhar's made himself scarce enough this day. Go fetch him and tell him that he's to wait upon me in my study."

Mr. Lyttle's face crumpled in misery. "I canna do that. Mr. Farquhar doesna leave his chamber during the day."

"Then by all means, lead us to his chamber. It's time he and I had this out," Alex thundered. "I'm done tolerating servants who only serve when it suits them."

Mr. Lyttle rumpled the handkerchief into a wrinkled ball. Then he suddenly straightened his spine and looked Alex in the eye. "O' course, 'tis no' my place to say so, milord, but there's no another soul in Bonniebroch that serves the estate and its people as much as has our Mr. Farquhar."

"He just doesn't serve its laird," Alex said, stone-faced.

"I'm sure he didna mean to offend ye." Mr. Lyttle's meager store of courage deserted him and his shoulders slumped once more. "If it so please ye, follow me and I'll take ye to him. 'Tis near sundown, in any case."

All the talk of sundown and how Mr. Farquhar didn't venture out during the day made Lucinda wonder suddenly if their steward was a vampyre, like the strange creature from the legend of the Monk of Melrose Abbey. She suppressed a shudder as she and Alexander trailed Mr. Lyttle out of the library.

The butler led them back down to the ground level of the Great Hall and across the bailey to the round tower from which Bonniebroch took its name. When they reached the base of the tower, Mr. Lyttle took a large iron key from his pocket and opened the reinforced door.

A tickle of unease settled between Alexander's shoulder blades and he wished he could have persuaded Lucinda to leave this to him. True to form, she wouldn't let this mystery go without seeing it to its end.

"Mind how ye go," Lyttle said softly as he stepped aside to allow them to pass. Then he followed them in and relocked the door behind them. "No one comes into the tower but me, ye ken," he said in answer to Alexander's unspoken question.

"And Mr. Farquhar, one presumes."

"Oh, aye, he comes and goes as he will," Lyttle said as he lit a lantern and began to mount the narrow stone stairs that curved around the outer wall. The ceiling soared some fifty feet above their heads. At intervals, the dark remains of wooden beams jutted out from the gray stone. "In times past, there were several levels between the ground floor and the topmost. Back then, there were no stairs. Defenders would use ladders and pull them up after themselves at need."

"And you know this because . . ."

"Because I was there, milord," Lyttle said simply. "Mr. Farquhar will explain it all. In the meantime, do ye take care. Hug the wall, my lady. 'Tis a long drop and no rail to stop ye."

"Stay close," Alex whispered to Lucinda. He fell in behind Lyttle, but reached behind him with his left hand so he could hold Lucinda's.

They followed the butler up the round tower till the staircase dead-ended at a door. Here, instead of using a key, the butler made a series of stylized movements in the air before the latch.

"What are you doing?" Alex demanded.

"There's no key for this lock. The tower keep is warded with a charm," Lyttle said as if using magic were as natural as serving clotted cream with bread. Golden shimmers, like dust motes caught in a spoke of sunlight, trailed behind the butler's fingertips, leaving a clearly discernible pattern in the air. The pattern glowed red-hot then faded. Then, even though Mr. Lyttle hadn't touched the door, Alexander heard the latch give with a snick. Mr. Lyttle pushed it open and bowed from the neck to indicate that they should precede him into the chamber.

Alex pushed past him into the round room. It was lit by the light of a single candle, though narrow slabs of daylight sliced through the western arrow loops. The room was sparsely furnished. In addition to a bookshelf stacked with hide-bound ledgers, there was only a standing full-length mirror and a desk with a single chair.

Callum Farquhar was seated behind the desk, scratching away with a long-plumed quill. In the fading light, he seemed faded as well, as if he were no more substantial than a breath. He glanced up from his work, then back to the parchment to finish the sentence he'd been writing. Once he signed his name with a flourish, the steward laid aside his writing implements. He rose and sketched an elaborate bow to Lucinda.

"My Lady Bonniebroch, ye do an auld man honor to visit him in his humble home."

Alex frowned at the steward.

"Oh, ye too, milord. No, Lyttle, dinna pull such a face. 'Tis all right. I've been expecting them."

"Someone left out the book with—"

"Dinna fret, man. That was me. I sensed a new presence in Bonniebroch and wished to see what it would do. I see it reported the book directly to her ladyship."

"A presence?" Alex said. "What are you talking about?" He silently added, *"And while we're at it, why can I hear you when your lips aren't moving?"*

"Och, that's because I'm incorporeal," Farquhar answered as though he'd heard Alex's thoughts. *"I can make my voice heard by normal means but 'tis a great deal of trouble. Mind-speech is much more efficient for my kind."*

"Your kind?"

"Ask your wife, milord. I can see from her lovely, if somewhat bumfuzzled, expression that she understands completely."

Alex turned to Lucy.

"He's a spirit, Alexander. A ghost."

Farquhar clapped his hands but it made no sound. *"Brava. Tell him how ye know this."*

"The presence Mr. Farquhar sensed is *my* ghost. His name is Brodie MacIver and he's been with me since I was a wee lass," Lucinda said.

"You have a ghost?" What other secrets did his bride hide from him?

She nodded. "I didna tell ye because I thought ye'd believe me daft. Brodie is why I never had a beau before ye. He ran off every lad who tried to court me."

Alex's mouth twitched in a smile. "I think I like this Brodie MacIver."

"He's beginning to like ye, too. A bit."

Alexander glanced back at Mr. Lyttle, who was standing sentinel at the door. "So, is everyone in Bonniebroch a ghost? That would account for the strange reputation of the place."

"Nae, they're all as much flesh and blood as ye and yer good lady." Farquhar's bushy eyebrows drew together. *"But they're cursed."*

"How so?"

"Mr. Lyttle was indeed born in 1489, just as the geneal-ogy chart says." Farquhar drifted across the room, his movements mimicking walking, but with his feet a few inches above the thick slats of the floor. *"But he's been stuck where he is now since 1521."*

"Stuck?" Alex and Lucinda said in unison.

"Aye," Mr. Lyttle said from his post at the door. "That's when the curse caused the change to happen and all the folk at Bonniebroch stopped aging."

"So everyone in the castle is over three hundred years old?" Alex asked.

"Aye."

"The children too?" Lucinda asked.

Mr. Farquhar nodded.

"Three hundred years to practice and that boy still hasn't learned to play the pipes," Alexander muttered.

Farquhar chuckled. *"Aye, but ye must give him high marks for persistence."*

"I still dinna understand. How is it a curse not to grow older?" Lucinda asked.

"Ye'd think it might be the opposite, would ye no'?" Mr. Lyttle said. "I confess we all thought so ourselves for the first seventy or eighty years. Then it grew tiresome for the folk to try to explain themselves when they traveled to Edinburgh to trade or simply went to market in the nearest village. We hadn't aged a day and that marked us as peculiar. People dinna trust those who are different and we are that. The last time one of us went abroad in the world, the villagers were so leery, it nearly came to a burning for witchcraft."

"So the folk of Bonniebroch learned to keep to themselves," Farquhar said.

"Then other problems became apparent," Mr. Lyttle said. "The children didna grow up. They no' only didna age physically, they didna grow up on the inside either. They didna learn anything new. And poor Meg Liscombe! She was with child when the change happened and she's been big-bellied all these years, expecting a bairn that willna be born."

"When folk get stuck, there's trouble at the other end of life as well," Farquhar said.

"After a couple hundred years, those who were older to start with began to realize they had no heaven to look forward to," Mr. Lyttle said. "My mother-in-law reminds me often that 'tis no great blessing to wake day after day as the ages roll by with aching joints and dim eyesight and no' enough teeth to do damage to more than a bowl of parritch. She's weary to her bones and has no hope of real rest."

"Brodie MacIver says there are things worse than death," Lucinda said. "And I suppose a ghost should know."

"And being stuck means even those in the prime of life dinna grow and change as they ought. Some of the husbands and wives who might have mellowed into comfortable old age together became tetchy when neither of them moved on. They may have the years, but the wisdom that should have come with them isna there," Farquhar explained. *"If a fellow willna listen to his wife of thirty years, imagine her frustration when she's wed to the lout for three hundred and thirty."*

"I always listen to Mrs. Lyttle," the butler piped up.

"For which, I'm sure Mrs. Lyttle is grateful." Farquhar hefted a ledger book and levitated it above his hands till it came to rest upon the desktop. He waved his hand and the pages flipped until the book fell open to the last entry. *"On a positive note, ye'll find the accounts of the estate in excellent condition, milord. Three hundred years of accumulated interest will do wonders for a balance sheet."*

Alex strode over and inspected the ledger. His eyes flared in surprise. "My Lord, we're rich as Croesus."

"Aye."

"Will this curse affect us—Lady Bonniebroch and me?" Alexander asked.

"Nae. It'll no' touch either of ye. We've had many lairds over the years. Some for their whole life long. Others for only a bit. But none of them was troubled by the curse. They grew older and wiser and eventually went on to their reward."

Farquhar shrugged eloquently. *"O' course, a few simply went on."*

"Did Sir Darren MacMartin know about all this?"

"The previous laird? Och, nae. We knew he wasna long for Bonniebroch right from the first. When he went fair mad over how the weeping woman disrupted his sleep without a smidge of concern for her sorrow, we knew he didna have an ounce of compassion in him."

"Who is the weeping woman?" Lucinda asked.

"That's a tale for another time, though I believe milord has an inkling of her true name," Farquhar said.

Alexander frowned at him. How could he know who she was? He'd never seen her face in any of the dreams.

"But we were speakin' o' the curse just now. There's some other things that—"

"Can it be lifted?" Alex interrupted.

Mr. Farquhar gave him a sad smile. *"Aye. We have hope that it may. But it might be more difficult than ye think."*

"To break the curse of Bonniebroch, the lost son of Scotland must reclaim his heritage by accomplishing three tasks before Twelfth Night has come and gone. First, he must forgive an old hurt. Then, he must defend a new foe. And finally, he must be willing to kill an old friend.

Unfortunately, Lord Bonniebroch must do these things of his own volition without being told he must."

From the secret journal of Callum Farquhar, Steward of Bonniebroch Castle since the Year of Our Lord 1521

Chapter Twenty-Three

"Will ye bear me company, milord? I'll show ye as much as I may." Farquhar moved toward Alexander. When Alex nodded, the old ghost laid a spectral hand on his arm and led him toward the looking glass. *"Dinna become separated from me and all will be well."*

Farquhar held his other hand in front of them and his fingertips sank into the mirror as if it were malleable as water. "Alex." A whisper was all Lucinda could manage. Her feet were rooted to the spot. Her husband and the ghost passed through the silvered glass, leaving only a few ripples in the mirror in their wake.

"No!" Shock gave her additional strength. She tore herself from her place by Farquhar's desk and ran to the mirror. When she touched it, the glass didn't give a bit.

"Alexander," she wailed and drew back her fist to strike it. Mr. Lyttle grasped her hand, stopping her before her blow could connect.

"With respect, milady, I wouldna do that. No' only will ye have seven years bad luck, ye'll close this portal forever and they willna be able to come back here."

That logic rang true in her mind and she stepped away from the looking glass, lowering her hand. "My friend Brodie said he used the paths behind the mirrors to come here, but he's a ghost. Alexander is a mortal man. How can he travel them?"

"On his own, he couldna, no more than ye or I can. That's why his lordship needs to stay with Mr. Farquhar," Lyttle said. "Dinna fear, milady. Farquhar willna let any evil befall Lord Bonniebroch. We need him too much."

"But where have they gone?"

"That I canna say, but I know where we must go." He squinted in the direction of the setting sun. "The supper is laid by now. Everyone waits for ye. Will ye no' be pleased to serve as a chatelaine ought and signal that all may eat their Christmas supper?"

She'd never felt less like celebrating. Lucinda looked once more at the mirror, wishing with all her heart that Alex would step back through it. There was nothing she could do but act as the lady of the

castle ought and carry on in her laird's absence. She
wanted to believe the butler when he said Farquhar
would keep Alexander safe. They needed him too
much, he'd said.

Didn't Lyttle know she needed Alex too?

What the folk of Bonniebroch might need him *for*
gave her pause. Her association with Brodie had
taught her that ghosts were wont to play fast and
loose with the facts. Farquhar had probably told the
truth so far as it went. However, he was likely leaving
a good bit unsaid.

When Mr. Farquhar brought Alexander back—
and he would! He simply must!—she resolved to tell
her husband everything about Brodie MacIver.
Then she'd demand her ghost appear to share what
he'd learned about Bonniebroch since he began
haunting its gray walls. Perhaps between the three of
them they'd be able to puzzle out what Farquhar
wasn't telling.

"Lead on, Mr. Lyttle," she said with a sinking heart.
"Christmas supper willna wait."

Alexander had never been so cold in his life. The
hairs in his nostrils froze with every breath. Frigid air
bit his cheeks and made his fingers and feet go
numb, but he kept a grip on Farquhar's bony arm.
The ghost felt as substantial as a live person in this
realm beyond the mirror. Together, Alex and the old
steward floated along a corridor-like tube that was
alive with light. They seemed to be moving quickly,
judging from the pulsing, nearly transparent walls

surrounding them, but Alexander's hair didn't ruffle and his jacket didn't flap.

He tried moving his feet, but his body wouldn't respond. He couldn't even blink. It was as if he were a statue.

Darkness pressed around them. Beyond the narrow beam on which they traveled, Alex saw other small lights in his peripheral vision, flashing and zipping in myriad directions. He wondered if they represented other travelers in this odd place, but all he could make out were shimmering spots.

Then suddenly, he and Farquhar sank into a gelatinous mass that both slowed and warmed them. In a blink, Alex found himself stumbling out of a large pane of silvered glass, finally able to move again. His grip around Farquhar's arm closed suddenly on nothing but vapor, as the ghost's form lost the solidity he'd had a moment ago. Alex kept his feet while he came to a shuddering stop and brushed a layer of frost off his lapel and eyebrows.

A strange smell, a mix of old blood and offal, burning pitch and rusting iron, surrounded him. It was the stench of ancient misery. A single torch lit the dank chamber. The mirror he and Farquhar had come through occupied the center of the room, suspended from the high ceiling by a pair of long chains. The looking glass was so veined with dark spots Alexander's reflection wavered in disjointed chunks.

"Aye, 'tis old beyond reckoning. A wonder it still works, is it no'?" Farquhar said. Alex suspected his steward was a mind-reader as well as a ghost.

"Are we still in Bonniebroch Castle?" Alex asked.

Farquhar nodded. *"Ye might come here by the secret*

tunnel from your chamber, but the path through the mirrors is quicker and we've nae time to waste."

"This is the dungeon, then." Moldering leather straps attached to iron rings jutted from the gray stone and a gibbet hung in one corner. "I trust there aren't many inmates," he added as an afterthought, hoping to lighten the mood.

"Only two at present. Come."

There were three barred cells giving off the larger chamber where the mirror was. One appeared to be empty. At first Alex thought the next one was as well, but then he noticed a black shape against the back wall. If it hadn't moved he'd never have seen it. The darkness gathered itself into the form of a man and moved toward the bars. A sudden flash of brilliant light sprang from the bars and the shape slunk back into the corner.

"Settle, then," Farquhar told it gruffly. *"Yer time isna come yet."*

"What is it?"

"That is what's left of Morgan MacRath, a sorcerer of no little power."

The shape glowed like a glossy piece of obsidian at Farquhar's words.

"Why is he held here?" As Alexander stepped nearer to the bars, unbridled contempt rolled over him. The shape of Morgan MacRath seethed with hatred, directed at everything and nothing.

"Morgan's in a prison of his own making, ye might say. The result of a magical backlash. Ye see, he's the one who cursed Bonniebroch all those years ago. He's a fine canny sorcerer, ye ken, but a bit sloppy. If he'd read a bit further in his grimoire, he'd have realized that his curse carried a hefty price."

The shape seemed to shrink a bit, but Alex wasn't disposed to pity it. Anything so filled with rage was due a healthy wariness, but no empathy.

"So if the curse is lifted, what happens to the people of Bonniebroch?"

"They become unstuck. They'll grow and age naturally from that day forth and eventually die as God intended folk should." Farquhar joined him near MacRath's cell. *"Now they're like insects trapped in amber, frozen in time. Believe me, there's no' a soul in the castle as doesna long for a normal life and a normal death at the end of it."*

"And what about Mr. MacRath?"

"If the curse is lifted before Twelfth Night, he winks out entirely, never to trouble another soul again."

The dark shape rose and swelled to twice its size and then deflated like a child's balloon.

"And if the curse isn't broken?" Alex asked.

"Then Morgan MacRath will be strong enough to take corporeal form again. He'll be loose and abroad in the world to wreak whatever mischief his wicked soul chooses." Farquhar's narrow shoulders slumped. *"And the people of Bonniebroch who've been unchanging as stone all these years will finally become stone. They'll turn to statues where they stand when the chapel bell rings midnight on Twelfth Night."*

Alex turned away from MacRath's cell. "How do we end this?"

"We canna. At least, I canna. Ending the Bonniebroch curse must be your doing, milord, or no' at all."

"Very well. What must I do?"

"That I canna tell ye either."

Farquhar raised his hands before himself in a defensive gesture even though Alexander had made no threatening move against him. He only felt like wringing the ghost's scrawny neck. Evidently, Farquhar was as sensitive to intent as action.

"I didna make the magic, but we must live by its rules. But I can tell ye that in the coming days, ye'll be faced with some pivotal choices. How ye choose to act will decide what's to become of us all."

Alexander snorted. "Oh, good. No pressure." He strode toward the remaining cell. "Who's in this—"

He stopped to listen. Very softly, on the thinnest edge of sound, the sobbing began. "The weeping woman. Why is she being held here?"

"She isna held except by her own will. As ye can see, the cell door is open. She came to us some twenty odd years ago and hasna stopped mourning since."

"Who is she?"

"Search your heart, lad. Ye know already."

The woman stood in deep shadow at the rear of the cell. Then she turned and walked toward the open door. The shade stopped at the threshold. She was dressed all in black with the broad panniers of a generation ago extending the width of her hips so that she'd have to turn sideways should she decide to pass through the opening. He'd never seen her so clearly in his dreams. She'd always presented as a diaphanous shape that seemed to vanish when he came too close.

Her sleeves were festooned with furbelows and her petticoat was thick with obsidian ruffles. Her hat was large enough for a stuffed black pigeon to blend in almost unnoticed among all the other frufurrah. Reams of veils trailed over her shoulders and down her back. One swath of black netting was caught up so it obscured the bottom half of her face. Only her eyes were visible above it.

Storm-gray eyes that were mirror images of his.

In all the nights when his dreams were invaded by her sobbing, she'd never spoken to him. In a broken voice, the woman said the first intelligible word he'd ever heard from her.

It was his name.

"Take me away from this place, Farquhar," Alexander said quietly. He barely contained the tremble that threatened to take him.

"Will ye no' listen to her side of things?"

"She has no side. She chose to leave." The old keening ache in his chest throbbed afresh. The bitter venom his father had injected into Alex over the years coursed hotly through his veins. "Turns out she taught me well because that's what I choose, too. Now either take me back through the mirror or point me to the stairs leading up to my chamber."

"But, milord——"

"Now, damn it. Am I laird of this place or not?"

"The stairs are over there, milord," Farquhar said with a sigh and extended a spectral arm. *"Mind how you go."*

Alexander stalked toward the steps and started climbing. He had to stop halfway up to cover his ears. The farther away he was, the louder her sobs seemed to grow.

It wasn't fair. Wasn't it bad enough that he had to face her weeping in his sleep? Hearing her in the waking world made him doubt his sanity.

Well, that was fitting. Madness was all he might expect to inherit from his mad mother.

"'Love covers a multitude of sins,' or so says holy writ. But what are we poor souls to do when love has been long absent? Or seems to have been?"

From the secret journal of Callum Farquhar, Steward of Bonniebroch Castle since the Year of Our Lord 1521

Chapter Twenty-Four

Lucinda pushed her food around her plate until the rest of the company was served. The Great Hall fairly buzzed with excitement. The fact that conversations stopped abruptly as she passed made her strain all the more to overhear them.

"Mr. Farquhar has taken him . . ."

"Does anyone know what the first task . . ."

"Wouldna it be wondrous if . . ."

Snippets of gossip about their laird's absence in relation to the Bonniebroch curse sparked through the assembly with the unfocused energy of heat lightning.

'Tis fine for them to be stirred up over what Alex is doing, but I wonder how the other ladies here would feel if it was their husband popping through a mirror with an old ghost, Lucinda thought crossly.

As soon as she was decently able, she rose and

admonished the others to continue their Christmas feast. Mr. Lyttle lit her to the laird's chamber. She dismissed him at the door, telling him not to send a maid to help her to bed.

Lucinda wanted to remain dressed, ready to accompany Alexander if Mr. Farquhar decided to take him on another trip through any more looking glasses. Her heart lurched when she saw Alex in the darkened sitting room, his still form lit only by the fire in the grate. She hurried to him and knelt by his side.

Wordlessly, he pulled her up and settled her on his lap, but continued to stare into the flames as if mesmerized by them.

First things first. Aunt Hester had always told her the best thing a woman can do for a man who has a problem is to tend to his basic needs while he sorted the rest out for himself.

"Ye missed supper. Shall I ring for a tray?"

He shook his head. Perhaps the problem was more than he could sort out on his own.

"Alexander, what happened?" She kissed his neck and nuzzled his earlobe.

"My world is upside down, that's what," he said softly as he stroked her arm absently. "This sort of thing would never happen in England, you know. I suppose it's because we don't regularly consort with ghosts and curses are only the stuff of faery tales."

Lucinda wished he'd look at her. It'd reassure her to see his soul shining behind his eyes. "Brodie would say that's because there's more magic in one foot of Scottish earth than in all the land south of Hadrian's Wall."

"He'd probably also say it was time I learned to

listen to my wife. You were right. The weeping woman *is* my mother."

"You've seen her?"

"Aye," he said, not bothering to correct the Scottish-ism that slipped through his lips this time. "She's set up housekeeping in a cozy little cell in the dungeon."

"The dungeon? Whatever she may have done, you canna mean to keep her there." Lucinda tried to sidle off his lap, but he held her fast.

"I'm not. She keeps herself there when she's not bedeviling my dreams." He shook his head. "Doing penance, I expect."

"Oh, Alex. I dinna know much about these un-earthly things, but somehow, ye must release her."

"Since you have your very own pet ghost, you must know something about it. Certainly more than me. Where does your Brodie MacIver stay?"

"Pretty much wherever he wants. However, he's been verra good about giving us privacy when we are alone."

"Thank God for small favors." He finally met her gaze and she saw his eyes were clear, if still distracted by his trip through the mirror.

The man wants distracting in an entirely different way.

She brushed his lips with hers and he answered her by claiming her mouth in a bruising kiss. She melted into him. He held her so tightly, she had difficulty drawing breath, but she wouldn't complain. She wanted to be close to this man, so close their souls would mingle and stay mixed together forever. For several glorious minutes, neither of them thought about ghosts or curses or anything beyond the wonder of a shared breath.

Alex was the first to pull back.

"Before we get completely off the subject, will your ghost come when you call him?" he asked.

"Usually." She laid her head on his shoulder and wished she could take the pain of seeing his mother's shade from him. "Why do ye want Brodie?"

"It might be interesting to find out if I can see him."

"Ye canna. Ye've been in his presence dozens of times. He even shared the coach with us and Aunt Hester all the way to Dalkeith and ye didna notice him once. Brodie was being fair obnoxious that day too, as I recall."

"You'll have to tell me what he says then." Alex spit the next words out, which showed they cost him dear. "I need his help. Summon him."

"Let me up, then. Even though we're wed, he's still a might possessive of me." She slid off his lap. "Brodie MacIver!"

Almost instantly, the ghost came headfirst down the chimney and rolled onto the hearth rug with a laugh. *"Just sweepin' out the soot for Father Christmas. Cromwell should have been boiled in pudding for banning the celebratin' part o' the holiday. I've always loved Christmas!"*

"I thought you didna remember much from your natural life, Brodie." Lucinda stared down at him. She glanced at Alex, but his bewildered frown told her he still couldn't see her ghost.

"I dinna, but it'd be a poor spirit indeed as forgot Christmas entire, would it no'?"

"Mr. MacIver." Alex stood and looked down at the hearth rug as Lucinda had, but by that time, Brodie had already floated up to the ceiling and was doing barrel rolls along the sturdy beams. "I've need of your help."

"Indeed his lairdship does, since he doesna even know where I am."

"Keep a civil tongue in your head, and listen to the man, Brodie." Lucinda tipped her chin so she could follow the ghost's antics and show Alexander where he was now. "Go on, Alex."

"There's a female spirit in the castle. I need for you to speak to her and find out . . . well, whatever it is she wishes to say to me."

"If he knows she's here and she's tryin' to communicate with him, why does he no' talk to her himself?"

"Because some things are hard to hear firsthand," Lucinda explained. "Ye'd be serving as . . . as an ambassador of sorts. A mediator."

"Hmph!"

"Please, Brodie, this is important," Lucinda said.

"Don't beg," Alex interrupted. "If he's unwilling, he's not going to do it very well. I'll figure out some other way."

Brodie made a rude noise, the kind that made Lucinda grateful she couldn't smell her ghost. Then she cocked her head and listened while Brodie whispered to her.

"He says he needs the spirit's name."

Alexander crossed his arms over his chest. "Why?"

"It's how he'll find her. Just as I used his name to call him, he'll use her name to locate her. It's their way."

"Finding her is not a problem. Tell him she's in the dungeon."

"'Tis no' so simple a thing. Apparently, if ghosts dinna ken each other's names, they canna recognize each other. They slide by each other, like wind that ruffles a pile of leaves and passes on unheeding. He could look right into her cell and never see her, nor she him." When Alex shot her a dubious scowl, she added, "Ye remember how Mr. Farquhar said he sensed a new presence in Bonniebroch so he laid out the book with Mr. Lyttle's family tree to draw the other spirit out. Since he didna know Brodie's name, that's all he could do."

"And ye thanked me for bringing it to yer notice, did ye no'? This castle is peculiar and no mistake. Tell him I need her name or I'll be no help at all."

Alex huffed out a noisy breath. "Very well. Her name is Finella MacGregor Mallory."

"Finella," Brodie repeated, his tone suddenly thick with emotion.

Alexander's head jerked toward the sound. "I heard that."

Brodie suddenly shot through the floorboards at Alexander's feet with a burst of white light, but Alex must not have seen it. He didn't bat so much as an eyelash.

"He's gone," Lucinda said.

"Will he help me?"

"That I dinna ken, but he's on his way to talk to your weeping woman. He was headed straight down."

"Finella," Brodie chanted. Memories rushed back into him along with her name. The prettiest girl in ten parishes. Stolen kisses and furtive trysts when she'd sneak out of her brother's house by night. Riding bareback with Brodie. Galloping on the heath. Wind in her unbound hair. Oh, the feel of her arms

around his waist and her breasts pressed up against his back as they bounded through a burn in full spate. Her legs were wet. . . .

More slices of the past slammed into his mind. He remembered a hated contractual marriage with an Englishman. Brodie tried to steal her away, but her brother Cormag MacGregor found them out. Brodie was arrested and Cormag locked Finella in the tower till her Englishman came and claimed her.

Then Brodie was taken, bound and gagged, to a dank cellar. Finella was lost. He no longer cared what happened to him. He was dead inside already. The rest of him followed suit in time, though he couldn't say how long the dying took. Days and weeks blurred together in unremitting misery.

Sorrow aged his soul before it flew free. But he couldn't fly far. Anger chained him to earth. Other passions burned out, but seething rage remained. Little by little, his former life faded like a rose past its prime till all that was left was a wisp of what had been a sweet scent.

By the time a wee lassie crying in the dark pulled him out of his self-pitying stupor, Brodie had forgotten almost everything but his own name.

Now his first love's name called him back to himself. Back to her.

"I'm coming, Finella."

Alex sank back into the chair and leaned forward to balance his elbows on his knees, head in his hands. "I'm going mad."

"Nonsense." Lucinda knelt before him and kissed him. "Ye're the most sane person I know."

"Sane people don't send ghosts on errands. They don't pop through looking glasses or agree to some benighted campaign to end a curse."

"If it makes ye feel any better, ye've pleased your people here at Bonniebroch out of all knowing for it." She covered his hands with her own, framing his face. Her touch was cool and soothing. "They seem to know something's afoot and they're right proud of ye."

"Aye, they're all odd enough, they'd be the sort as would warm to a mad laird." He was sounding more Scottish by the moment, but he appreciated Lucinda for not pointing it out. He couldn't seem to help it. "I dinna—don't know what's come over me. They always say these things don't necessarily run in families, but I think . . . I think my mother's madness is finally beginning to tell."

"Ye've had a surprise this evening and no mistake. Several by my count." She smoothed back a shock of hair that had fallen across his forehead and then pressed a kiss there. "If ye didna doubt yerself, I'd be more worried about ye. The fact that ye wonder about being mad tells me ye're not."

He snorted. "There's a certain amount of sense there, but if the original premise is flawed, a thing can be logical and still be untrue. I could be quite rationally out of my mind."

"Then it comes to this. If ye're mad, I'll just be mad right along with ye."

He gathered her into his arms. In a world of shifting reality and ghoulies and ghosties, Lucinda was the only true thing he could count on at the moment. He longed to sink into her and draw the curtains closed on the rest of the world. It was more than lust, though he couldn't deny he was far hungrier for her than for his missed supper. Lucinda was his touchstone, his lighthouse, his promise that somehow all the odd thoughts scrambling in his brain—thoughts that hadn't been there a fortnight ago—still didn't mean he was insane.

"I can keep going no matter what," he whispered into her neck, "so long as you keep looking at me the way you do."

Her eyes shining, she pulled back to meet his gaze. "And how is it I look at ye?"

He shook his head in wonderment. "As if I'm Hercules and Hannibal and William the Conqueror all rolled up in one."

"For shame, Alexander." She made a tsking noise. "Ye're far better than that. None of them were Scottish, ye ken. Besides"—she sent him a sidelong glance—"ye know I always think of ye as 'Your Much of a Muchness.'"

He threw back his head and laughed in spite of everything. His career in Lord Liverpool's service was in tatters. His mother's ghost hovered in the dungeon. He somehow had to figure out what was required of him to break the Bonniebroch curse without Farquhar's help. And yet this woman could make him laugh.

He cupped the back of her head and pulled her toward him. He kissed her smiling lips, not nipping and teasing this time, but deeply. Honestly. His soul leaned toward hers. It was enough to simply feel her open under him, to welcome him.

Her hands moved over his head, his neck, his shoulders. His heart quickened along with his body.

The strange sensation in his chest confused him. It was an ache and a warmth and an unsettled yearning.

Love?

He tried to thrust the idea away. After witnessing the wreck of his parents' marriage, he'd never believed in love.

"A man should never place his heart in a woman's keeping. She'll only devour it like a she-spider," his father had often complained with bitterness. The marquis had given his Scottish bride his name and his trust, but she hadn't returned his gift. All Finella did was shame him by going mad and doing away with herself.

"Love leads to misery all around," his father said whenever the subject came up. Which the marquis made certain was often. He didn't want his sons to be unprepared for the wiles of the female of the species.

But with Lucinda, Alexander found himself wanting to imagine love was possible. That he could trust her with everything he was and she'd do him no hurt.

In this strange land of magic and mayhem, what spell was she casting on him?

If it was witchery, Alex decided he didn't care. He picked her up and carried her to the waiting bed.

Chapter Twenty-Five

Anticipation pooled in Lucinda's belly. Alexander stood over her and unbuttoned his shirt, baring his muscled chest. She mirrored his movements, starting to undo her own bodice.

"Let me do that," he said. "I like undressing you. It's like opening a present."

A sudden pang struck her. "Oh! I dinna have a gift to give ye for Christmas."

"Nor I you."

"Oh, aye, ye did. Ye gave me the 'lady' before me name and made me chatelaine of this wonderful old castle."

"If we're reasoning like that, you've far outgiven

me." He tugged off his boots, then shucked out of his trousers and smalls and peeled off his stockings.

"How do ye reckon that?"

He stood upright before her in nothing but his glorious skin and Lucinda thought the sight might fair strike her blind. He was so fine, this broad-chested man of hers.

Hers. Her own "Much of a Muchness." Her husband.

Alexander leaned down and cupped her cheek. "You outgave me because you gave yourself, Lucinda. Don't you know how beautiful and brilliant you are? You make me ache for you every time I see you."

"Oh." Her mouth went slack. Then she raised herself to her knees. "Best ye get busy with the unwrapping of yer present then. 'Twill be midnight before ye know it and Christmas will be over."

A shadow passed over his face.

"But dinna fret. We still have Hogmanay and Twelfth Night and, believe me, the celebration of Christmas is tame by comparison to those two."

He still looked a shade grim, as if the passage of time were a worry to him. So she reached for him, exploring the warm expanse of exposed skin. He bent to kiss her while he finished unbuttoning her bodice. The nearness of his fingertips was torture for her breasts as he worked down the hollow between them. The hard tips ached for his touch. He peeled back the bodice of her gown and gave attention to her stays, freeing her breasts beneath her chemise.

She pulled away from his kiss for a moment. "Dinna tear my clothes this time. It fair scandalized Mrs. Fletcher when I asked her to see if that chemise could be mended."

He chuckled, a low rumble in his belly that set his "Muchness" ajiggle. Lucinda reached to cup him, caressing and stroking. She wouldn't have thought it possible, but he seemed to grow even harder and stronger under her touch.

As she stroked him, he toyed with her breasts through the thin muslin of her chemise and Lucinda began to regret telling him not to rend the fabric. But she was giving as good as she got, fondling him in smooth, sure strokes. He was all hot and hard and strong and it gave her a thrill of feminine power when he groaned softly.

However, when she looked up at his face, she sensed something was still wrong. There was a bit of sadness around his eyes. A weight at the corner of his mouth.

A thoroughly wicked idea of how she might distract him from his burden danced through her mind. She remembered how she'd fairly unraveled inside when he put his mouth on her *ruminella*.

What's sauce for the goose . . .

Lucinda bent down to place a soft wet kiss on the tip of him.

His breath hitched over his teeth.

"Did that hurt ye?"

His eyes squinched tight in an almost pained expression. "No, Lu. No . . ."

"Shall I do it again, ye think?"

He looked down at her, the wild light of a stallion in his gaze. "Do what you will. All I am is yours. But for God's sake, do something."

All the heaviness she'd sensed in him burned away in the intense wanting she saw behind his eyes.

She wasn't sure she'd carry out this experiment rightly, but she was bound and determined to try.

Alex held his breath, waiting for what she'd do next. Watching her bend down to press her lips against him was the most erotic thing he'd ever seen in his life. Her innocent licks and kisses made his gut clench and he fought the urge to move.

Then she took him into her mouth.

"Aye, Lu . . . just like that."

His world dissolved in the wetness, the softness, the warmth of her sweet lips. He held her head, directing her gently, but she seemed to need little encouragement. She suckled and stroked him with her tongue. His hips moved without his conscious volition.

He was desperate for her to continue. Desperate for her to stop before it became too much to bear. The lavishness, the grace of her loving was more than he could ever have hoped. More than he deserved.

If she doesn't stop soon . . .

He had to stop her. The strain of holding back was nearly killing him. He couldn't accept this from her. Not without giving her pleasure. He'd always had a firm policy of "ladies first."

How much more should that apply to a wife.

Alexander lifted her up and held her flush against his body, burying his face in her hair. She smelled of evergreen and cinnamon and warm woman. A Christmas gift, indeed.

"Was I doing it wrong?" she whispered.

"No, love, you were doing everything right. It was the best . . . I never thought you'd . . ." Words failed him and he kissed her instead till they were both breathless. Then he left her lips only long enough to gather her gown in his hands and pull it over her head. He kissed her again. The urge to see her naked made him hurry as he pulled off her chemise.

The sound of ripping fabric made him stop for a second, then he peeled the rest of the garment over her head.

"Mrs. Fletcher will just have to be scandalized." He bent to capture the tip of her breast in his mouth and worried that sensitive bit of flesh with a gentle suck, a skillful tongue, and a light scrape of his teeth. Lucinda's longing escaped her lips in wordless cries.

He reached between her legs where her pantalets left her sex bared and softly invaded her nest of curls. He circled. He stroked. When her desperate gasps rent his heart, he laid her down and focused on her tender little spot.

Lucinda writhed under his touch. She arched her back. Her eyes, usually so bright, went out of focus and he suspected she saw nothing. Her brow furrowed with wanting, her face caught in an expression that was equal parts pleasure and anguish. He kissed her neck and suckled her earlobe.

"Come for me, sweeting," Alex urged. "Dinna ye see how I love ye?"

His words released her and her whole body bucked with the force of her climax. He held her as she came, riding the waves of joy.

As soon as she stilled, he kneed her thighs farther apart and settled between them. She was so ready he slid into her snugness without resistance. Then he began to move, looking for the right angle, the right speed and motion that would build her pleasure again.

He ran his hands along her hips, the sides of her ribs, and breasts. Little by little, he rolled so she could be on top. He let her control their rhythm.

It was torture to hold back when part of him wanted to plunge in and take her like a rutting beast. When she found the right combination of friction and speed, her breathing changed. Her short gasps and the way her head fell back told him she was close.

He slipped a hand between them to stroke her over the edge.

"Look at me, Lu," he urged.

Her eyes fluttered open and she met his gaze as her first contraction began.

"Say my name," he commanded.

She practically sang it. He couldn't hold back any longer. He rolled over, fully seated inside her, and emptied himself into her, driving in deep. All his hopes, all his fears, all he was. For better or worse, he was hers.

He collapsed on her and they sank deeply into the feather tick, gasping in unison. Time unraveled around them and the world might have spun a rotation or two without their notice. Their breathing settled and the only sound was the soft rustle of the fire in the grate and the barely audible whoosh of air moving around the cavernous room.

Lucinda finally broke the silence. "I've heard that men sometimes say things in bed that they dinna mean in the parlor."

He lifted himself on his elbows. "I meant every word I've ever spoke to you."

"Then ye love me."

"Aye, lass, I do." He kissed her again and decided not to fight the brogue any longer. Somehow, his brain had been touched with a Scottish spell and expressing himself this way was as natural as breathing. Why it had come upon him was as mysterious as the rest of the doings at Bonniebroch Castle and just as beyond his will to question. "Do ye no' have somewhat to say to me?"

"Aye." She draped her arms around his neck and grinned up at him. "As husbands go, ye'll do, Alexander Mallory. Ye'll certainly do."

The dream felt so real, he couldn't be sure he hadn't sleepwalked down the long staircase behind the walls to the dungeon. Alexander found himself in the dim cell as usual only now he recognized where it was. The weeping woman wasn't there this time. He didn't hear any sobbing. His mouth formed the word "Mother" but he couldn't bring himself to say it.

At the sound of *his* name, he turned around. The ghostly sibilance washed over him in diminishing echoes. There she was, standing at the doorway, on the outside of the reinforced bars.

"What do you want of me?" he asked.

"Only to talk to ye. Brodie says this is the best way, better than if he delivers me message to ye. If ye're asleep, ye can listen with yer heart instead of yer ears."

With one graceful hand, she reached up and removed the veil that obscured her face. She was as pretty as he remembered, with fine even features and a sweet smile.

Pity she was also completely dotty.

"*No, son,*" Finella said. "*I'm no' mad.*"

He was past surprise that yet another ghost seemed able to peer into his thoughts. "But Father says—"

"*Your father is a good man, but he's used to his own way and once he sets his feet on a matter there's no changing him. He decided I was mad because he didna care for the alternative explanation.*"

Alexander's hands bunched into fists. It felt like a betrayal of his father to even listen to her. But she hadn't really said a word against his father, which was something the marquis couldn't claim. He'd spouted poison about his mad wife whenever he had the chance. "What was the alternative?"

"*That I still cared enough for the beau I left behind in Scotland to weep for him when word came to me that he'd died. Dinna mistake me, son. I was a good and faithful wife to the marquis. But then news finally reached me that Brodie hadn't been living a happy life in the Hebrides as I'd been told. So of course, I grieved for him. Deeply. And for a long while.*"

She turned and floated away from the cell toward a brighter spot on the horizon. Alexander couldn't help but follow. Why had he never heard any of this before?

"*Yer father was angry when I started wearing black. So he had me taken from ye and put in Bedlam so I wouldna taint ye and yer brother with my supposed lunacy. I wasna mad when I got there, but I feared I'd become so if I stayed.*"

His mother's face brightened and color began

to return to her lips and cheeks. Even her black clothing began to subtly shift to soft gray with lavender piping.

"I began to make plans. The doctors at Bedlam told me if I was good and made what they considered progress, I'd be allowed to go home."

"Father always said you could have come back to us if you'd wanted to," he accused. "You just didn't want to badly enough."

"I wanted more than anything to be reunited with you and yer brother, but I wasna going to return to a man who'd have me sent away again if the notion took him. I knew yer father would hunt me to the ends of the earth if I took yer brother, but I thought perhaps he'd not come after me if I only stole ye away. I had a bit of money laid by in a place yer father knew nothing of and planned to take ship for the Americas with ye."

Alex thought his father probably would have come after them even if she'd taken only him. Not that the marquis was overburdened with familial feelings, but he regarded both his sons as assets to be controlled. He wouldn't allow one to slip away while there might be some use for him.

"My room was always locked by night, but the windows were not." She allowed herself a small smile. *"I'd convinced them that I didna believe I could fly, ye ken. So I tore up my bed linens and fashioned a rope to let meself down from the window of me third-story room."*

Her face crumpled and tears started to flow. Alexander steeled himself for the sobs that were sure to come, but she contained herself.

Brodie appeared suddenly and stood behind her,

his hands resting on her shoulders in a gesture of support. *"Go on with yer tale, lass."*

"I tied one end of the rope to me bed and started to climb down the side of the building. But I was never the tomboy, aye? And I was weak from months of eating nothing but the maggoty gruel they served at Bedlam. I got meself tangled up in the line and somehow it looped around me neck."

Alexander looked away. His chest hurt too badly to continue meeting her gray gaze.

"I didna mean to end meself. My death was an accident. I was coming for ye, Alex. Ye must believe me. I was never separated from ye by choice."

Unshed tears pressed against the backs of his eyes. He'd been carrying this old bitterness so long, he didn't know how to let it go.

"And now I've been grieving all these years. Not only for me lost love, Brodie MacIver, but also for ye, Alex. Ye and yer brother. I'm sick at heart that ye believed I chose to leave ye. Never." She moved closer to him and stretched out a thin hand in entreaty. *"Never would I do such a thing."*

If she was telling the truth, it changed everything he believed about his childhood. About his father. About himself.

"Will ye find it in yer heart to forgive me?"

His mother had loved him, after all. And he had a wife who loved him now. Lucinda hadn't answered his declaration in so many words, but love poured from her actions. If she didn't love him, she was doing a damned good imitation of it.

Love and bitterness wouldn't fit in the same heart. He had to release one. Alexander drew a deep lungful and breathed out all his old hurt.

It had no hold on him. Or on his mother.

"There's nothing to forgive, but if it makes you feel better, I do forgive you," he said and then added, "Mother."

She couldn't embrace him, so she washed over him instead. Her essence passed through him, radiating love and bone-deep peace. His mother left a benediction in her wake, the gathered force of all the good she wished for him. It smelled soft and powdery, sweetly infused with attar of roses and honeysuckle—all the scents he associated with her. Then the fragrance faded. When he turned to look for her, she wasn't there.

"She's gone on, lad," Brodie said. *"Ye released her. And now that she's moved on, I must too. Where Finella goes, there I'm bound. Tell my wee lassie I'm sorry I canna say good-bye to her meself, but me time is short now. Remind Lucinda that she'll always be the apple of me eye."* Then his expression turned stern. *"But dinna ye think for a moment I willna come back to haunt ye if ye bring my girl a moment's grief."*

A smile twitched the corner of Alexander's mouth. "I'd expect no less. Go with God, Brodie MacIver."

The ghost cast him a lopsided grin. *"If I do, it'll be Finella's doing. They'd never let the likes o' me into heaven elsewise."*

The ghost faded, becoming more and more transparent, till he finally winked out entirely.

Then the floor of the dungeon opened beneath Alexander's feet without warning and, turning end over end, he tumbled into the void.

"I'll not lie. Of course, I'm encouraged. The first of three tasks is accomplished. Our laird has laid aside an old hurt. But forgiving an offense is a small matter compared to the next hurdle Lord Bonniebroch must overleap. 'Tis one thing to defend a friend. Every man worthy of the name will do that. But not many will defend a foe. Time will tell if Lord Bonniebroch has that rare heart as can protect his enemy."

From the secret journal of Callum Farquhar, Steward of Bonniebroch Castle since the Year of Our Lord 1521

Chapter Twenty-Six

Alexander woke with a jerk, his heart pounding, his lungs starved for air. He gasped noisily and blinked hard, taking in his surroundings.

The banked fire had burnt down to glowing embers, but he knew immediately where he was. And with whom he was. He pulled a sleeping Lucinda close. She nuzzled his neck, settled her head on his shoulder, and snugged her naked body against his without waking. The feather tick enveloped them in a deep, soft embrace.

His heart rate began to settle as the sensation of falling receded.

It was just a dream, he told himself. And yet, it had seemed as real as the woman in his arms. After all these years, he'd spoken to his mother. His questions had been answered. The root of bitterness in his soul had been yanked out.

Even if it wasn't real, he decided to pretend it was. The conceit would hurt no one. He hadn't felt this light of heart in years.

As he gazed up at the high ceiling, a pinpoint of light began to flicker. At first he thought it was his imagination, the product of a mind still on the edge of dreams. But then the single light multiplied, spreading across the distant beams, in a thousand shimmering bits. They began to drape down from the ceiling like falling stars, drifting to settle over Alex and Lucinda.

Since Farquhar told him the fate of Bonniebroch was in his hands, Alexander had felt as though he carried a boulder on his back. As the twinkling lights trickled down the bed frame to cover them, a part of that weight was lifted and, in its place, came the glowing warmth of peace.

He didn't need the old steward to tell him. He knew. Somehow, he'd chosen the correct path for the first of the three mysterious tasks that would come to him before Twelfth Night.

The lights around them began to fade, so Alexander closed his eyes.

One down. Two to go, Farquhar, you old rascal. If that was the worst that sorcerer of yours can do, this curse is as good as lifted.

* * *

The mid-morning sun burned brightly through the unshuttered windows, setting dust motes swirling in bright slabs of light. Lucinda finally rolled over and opened her eyes. Alexander's pillow was cold, but he'd left a note on it that said he was off to ride Badgemagus. He admonished her to get plenty of rest. She'd need it when he joined her in bed again.

A satisfied smile stretched her lips till her cheeks hurt.

Alexander finished the note by saying he'd see her at the midday meal. She ran a fingertip over the simple "A" which served as his signature. It was like him. Strong. As aggressively male as the tip of an arrow it resembled.

Funny how even his handwriting made her feel softly feminine by comparison.

Lucinda rose, stretching. All her joints were pleasantly loose and a little achy. The price of a night of loving, she supposed as she slipped into her wrapper and rang for breakfast.

It took longer than she expected for the tray to arrive and the girl who brought it was breathless. It was either Janet or Jane. Lucinda hadn't much luck telling the two girls apart.

"Beggin' yer pardon, milady," the maid said as she swooped in with the energy of a whirling dervish. "But the whole of the castle is in sommat of a state on account of the visitors. We havena had anyone come to stay at Bonniebroch for ever so long a time, so naturally, everyone is all in a kerfuffle."

"What visitors, Jane?" She thought it was worth a

guess. She had an even chance of being correct, whichever name she chose.

The girl's eyes sparkled with excitement.

"Beans MacFee turned up at the dock a couple hours after dawn with the first load," the maid said. "I was down by the river hopin' to meet up with Seamus Abernathy and—"

"Wait a moment." Lucinda stopped the girl with a raised hand. "What do you mean, 'the first load'?"

"Oh, that." Jane trotted to the big bed and straightened the linens as she talked. "There wasna room on the barge for all of them and their baggage, ye ken, so Mr. MacFee had to make several trips."

Lucinda sank into one of the chairs. It was one thing to be a chatelaine. It was quite another to play hostess to an unexpected party in a big rambling place when she really hadn't found her feet yet. "Who's here?"

"Oh, there's more than I can count. Once ye get past me fingers and toes, numbers dinna mean much to me, aye? But the main ones ye'll be wantin' to see, I reckon, claim to be members o' yer family, milady."

Jane set out the tea things and served Lucinda a steaming cup with just the right dollop of milk and a single lump of sugar. "There's two of yer sisters and yer father—"

"My father is here?"

"Aye, that he is. And taking on something fierce to anyone who'll listen about how he missed yer wedding to his lairdship too. Seems he was in Edinburgh on Christmas Day, waitin' at St. Giles to give ye away, but ye and Lord Bonniebroch didna ever arrive."

Lucinda's father had signed the contract that stipulated the Christmas wedding in Edinburgh right enough. But as absentminded as Erskine Mac-Owen was, she never dreamed he'd actually make an effort to be there to see the deed done.

"We wed in the chapel at Dalkeith instead," Lucinda explained. "I'll send a letter to my aunt Hester asking her to assure him that she witnessed our vows."

"Is that Hester MacGibbon ye're meaning?"

When Lucinda nodded, Jane made a moue of distaste. "Then ye can save yerself the trouble of a letter, milady. Mrs. MacGibbon is here too. There's no missing her. She's as here as ever anyone was."

Lucinda smiled into her teacup. Aunt Hester would keep Jane and Janet both hopping. Seamus Abernathy would simply have to wait by the river by himself so long as Hester MacGibbon was in residence.

"Besides my family, who else has come?"

"Oh, there's more Englishmen than we've seen around here since the reign of Edward Longshanks." Jane helped herself to a dish of tea, oblivious to the fact that a servant and her mistress wouldn't take tea together as if they were bosom friends. If Lucinda were the fashionable sort, she'd be affronted by the girl's innocent presumption. Instead, she was charmed.

"The fellow makin' the most noise is someone named Lord Rankin," Jane said.

"Oh." Lucinda set down her tea. She sensed without being told that Rankin did not have Alexander's best interests at heart. "Why is he here?"

"I dinna know all the particulars, but word is he's looking for a little sport in the woods. He heard there are wild boars hereabouts and expects Lord Bonniebroch to accommodate him with a grand hunt. Seems he thinks it would be a fine entertainment for the English king when he comes and—"

"Are there boars?"

"Oh, aye. And water horses and boggles and all manner of creatures. That's why we never venture through the wood save to meet Mr. MacFee's ferry. And I never linger by the river, no matter what Seamus says. So long as we keep to the path and stay well back from the water, we're perfectly safe."

"Water horses aren't real, Jane."

The maid snorted. "Aye, they are. Ask old Audra Cruikshank. She'll tell ye about the one she saw when she was a girl near Loch Ness."

"Nonsense. Those are only faery stories." Even though Lucinda was sure she was right, a superstitious tingle crept down her spine.

"Nae, milady. Me hand on a Bible, Auld Audra saw one her own self. Reared its head out of the water it did, whilst its body trailed along behind in snaky coils." Without being told to do so, Jane buttered a scone and placed it on a plate for Lucinda. Then she helped herself to one. "Now kelpies, them's the river spirits, ye ken," she said with a full mouth, "are no' so big as a water horse, but they can still do a body plenty of mischief if they're so minded."

Lucinda let the girl rattle on. Someone who'd spent the last three hundred years squirreled away in this castle with little contact with the outside world was bound to have some odd notions. As soon

as she and Alexander were settled, she'd arrange for
a school for the children of the keep.

And for the adults too.

Water horses and kelpies weren't real. But wild
boars were and they were dangerous to hunt.

"Who else wants to go hunting for the boar?" she
interrupted Jane as the girl was winding up for a big
finish about someone named Balor, a one-eyed
fellow who was supposedly king of the Formorians,
a whole tribe of misshapen folk.

"Och, all the English I suppose. Besides Lord
Rankin, there's Sir Bertram Clarindon and any
number of servants they brought with them." Then
Jane's eyes took on a misty, slightly daft gloss. "And
o' course, there's Sir Darren."

"MacMartin?"

"Aye." Jane bobbed her head so hard it was a
wonder it didn't wobble off her shoulders. "Turns
out he's English on his mother's side. Now that I
think on it, that's just the opposite of our laird now,
is it no'? Is that no' the strangest coincidence?" Without waiting for agreement, Jane rattled on. "Ye ken
as Sir Darren was Lord Bonniebroch for a time, aye?
Hardly so long as it would take for a body to notice
there was a new baron, but me and Janet thought as
he was grand to look upon. Come to think on it, the
boar hunt sounded like it was his idea."

Which made Lucinda all the more certain that it
wasn't a good one. "Help me dress, Jane."

"Oh, aye, will ye want to be on the ramparts to
watch when they start beatin' the woods tomorrow?
I heard Sir Darren say it was as sure a way to scare
up a boar as a royal progression was like to scare
up Radicals."

Lucinda froze in mid-step. She'd stopped worrying about Dougal and his Radical past since he'd told her he'd foresworn the movement. Still, any mention of the doomed rebellion boded ill for him. Even if his motives were pure now, there was still a price on his head. "Where did ye hear Sir Darren say this?"

Jane tilted her head to one side as if the information might spill out her ear. "Let me see . . . Sir Darren was heading out of the Great Hall after the breakfast and I heard him in passing."

"Who was he speaking to?"

"Yer brother, Dougal, milady. Most intent Sir Darren was on it too, which strikes me odd as 'tis a most peculiar riddle. How is a boar like a Radical? And what is a Radical, in any case?"

Lucinda set a record for dressing, insisting upon a serviceable gray muslin instead of the woefully out of fashion sack dress and stomacher Jane wanted to cinch her into. She bolted from the room and clattered down the stairs.

She skidded to a stop at the ground floor when she saw Mr. Lyttle. "Have ye seen Lord Bonniebroch?"

"Aye, milady. He's riding in the bailey, putting that demon horse of his through its paces."

Thank heaven. Alexander hadn't left the castle. She hurried to the door.

"Wait, milady," Mr. Lyttle said as he trotted after her with a thick cloak. "Ye'll catch yer death if ye go abroad in naught but yer day gown."

Nae, 'tis Dougal who's like to catch his death if he goes about Bonniebroch Castle much longer.

Sir Darren MacMartin was exactly the type who would turn him in for the price on his head. A cold wind whistled through the door that opened to the bailey, so she paused long enough to allow the butler to drape the cloak over her shoulders. She pinned it closed with a silver brooch as she strode outside.

Somehow, Sir Darren had realized who Dougal was. Why else would he direct that comment to him?

She'd hoped to put this off till much later. While she and Alex had forged a bond in the marriage bed, outside it their union still felt tenuous, a house of straw that might tumble down in the slightest breeze. Now she needed to tell Alexander about her outlaw brother before Sir Darren did something about it.

A goodly crowd had gathered to watch Alexander work Badgemagus through a series of controlled turns and leaps. While the laird of Bonniebroch on horseback was a sight to quicken any woman's heart rate, Lucinda wished she'd caught him before he climbed into the saddle. Private speech with him was going to be a good trick.

"Lucy-girl, there ye are!"

She barely turned in time before her father caught her into a great bear hug.

"What d'ye mean by marryin' the man without yer father to give ye away?" His broad grin told her the scolding words weren't serious.

"I'm sorry, Father." She planted a quick kiss on his cheek. "Things didna go as planned, but at least they went. Alex will be pleased to support yer invention." Thinking of the incredible sum the estate had invested with the bank in Edinburgh, she added, "In fact, after Alexander settles yer accounts, if ye need more workshop space, I'll see that it's built for ye."

Her father tut-tutted at that suggestion, but the flash of excitement in his eyes told her he wouldn't decline the offer. "Weel, that's no never mind. The important thing is I'm here now with me girl to celebrate her marriage. We may have missed Christmas together, but we'll have the Hogmanay festivities and Twelfth Night." He sighed. "I only wish I had all me children gathered round."

"Maggie is still off with her new husband, I suppose," Lucinda said, making a mental note to write to her older sister and thank her for running off with the man-of-all-work at the neighboring estate. Without that happy accident, she'd never have had Alexander. "But ye have all the rest of us. Dougal is here too."

"He may have been before, but no' the now," her father said with a doleful shake of his head. "He left shortly after breakfast. Said something about someone recognizing him as a Radical. Heading back into the Highlands, he was."

Even though her father was clearly distressed about it, Lucinda was relieved. Her brother might be in for a cold, comfortless time in the wild, but so long as Dougal wasn't taken by the English authorities, his neck was safe.

But before she could console her father over Dougal's absence, Alexander rode up next to them.

"Good morning, my lady," he said. A glint of something hard flashed in the gray depths of his eyes, but it vanished so quickly, Lucinda decided she had imagined it. "Would ye be pleased to come riding with me?"

"I never learned to ride." Horses had always scared her more than a little. They were so big and so unpredictable, shying at a leaf or rearing to rid themselves of a rider if the notion took them.

"That is something we shall have to remedy. There's a sweet little mare in the stables that should do nicely for you, but for now, I meant *with* me. Put your foot on mine." Without waiting for her to comply, he leaned in the saddle, grasped her waist, and hefted her onto the saddle before him.

She was barely settled with her legs on either side of the horse's wide body, when Alex dug his heels into Badgemagus's flanks. The gelding burst into a gallop. They careened across the bailey, through the portcullis and over the drawbridge.

The forest rushed by in a gray and black blur as they pounded down the path. They ducked as one under a low-hanging branch and leaned together on the turns. Lucinda's heart crowded her throat, making it difficult to breathe.

"Stop," she chanted. "Please stop."

Alexander reined in the big gelding so hard, the horse nearly sat on its haunches. Badgemagus stamped and snorted, wanting to continue his gallop, but he obeyed, dancing in a tight circle.

"You're trembling." Alexander's voice rumbled in her ear.

"Aye. I'm no' accustomed to horses."

He dismounted and then lifted her down, none too gently. "And I'm not accustomed to being thought a fool by my wife."

Lucinda blinked in surprise. "How have I done that?"

His eyes hardened like burnished steel. "You didn't bother to tell me your brother is a Radical."

"Beige is the color of unintended betrayal. One wouldna think it, beige being such an unassuming shade. Blood red springs to mind, but that garish hue is more fitting to purposeful duplicity. Unintended betrayal hurts all the more for the way it hides in plain sight with a clear conscience. Treachery at its most beige."

From the secret journal of Callum Farquhar,
Steward of Bonniebroch Castle since the
Year of Our Lord 1521

Chapter Twenty-Seven

Alex clenched his fists to keep his hands still. Lucinda's mouth gaped for a moment. Then the muscles in her throat worked beneath her pale skin as she swallowed hard.

"You knew why I was here. You knew I was tasked with flushing out Radicals and yet you didn't think to warn me about Dougal," he said, barely bridling himself.

"I couldna betray him," she finally said. "He's my only brother."

"And I'm your only husband."

The urge to plant his fist in the nearest tree trunk was fast building to a head. Protecting his king from

men who fomented rebellion against him was so
ingrained in Alexander's character it was unthink-
able that he wouldn't act against a known Radical.

Yet, Dougal was Lucinda's brother. How could he
guard the Crown's interests without hurting his wife?
There were too many conflicts, too many competing
demands on his loyalty.

Damn it all. This is why I'm not fit to be a husband.

"There's no cause for concern now," Lucinda
said, wringing her hands. "Dougal has left the
movement . . . and Bonniebroch."

"At my order." Alex scrubbed a hand over his hair.
"As soon as MacMartin—and it had to be Mac-
Martin, damn it!—told me what your brother was, I
found Dougal in the stable and advised him to make
himself scarce."

Her face brightened and she visibly relaxed. "Ye
helped him."

"I helped myself," Alex said, his voice low and
controlled lest he roar at her. "So long as your
brother is nowhere to be found I'm not required to
act on what I know."

The tension was back in her cheeks. "And . . .
would ye act?"

"I'd have to."

Her eyes glistened with unshed tears and he
fought the urge to look away from her. How could
she expect him not to move against a traitor to his
king? How could the king expect him to turn in his
wife's brother? His gut twisted in a furious knot.

"I'm a new laird here. What I do sets the tone for
years to come. If I can't garner respect, I'll settle for
fear. If I don't suffer a Radical, even to protect a
family member, that'll do it."

Tension gave way to panic in Lucinda's face. It glinted in the whites of her eyes and the way her mouth tightened at the corners.

"Your people here already respect ye, Alex. Ye've nothing to prove to them."

But what about to himself? If he was no longer an agent for the Crown, what was he? He'd come to Edinburgh despising his Scottish half but now everything was upside down. London seemed a million miles and another lifetime away.

Bonniebroch still felt like a strange dream with its resident ghosts and looming curse. The only thing real in his entire life was the woman standing before him.

The one he made cry. One by one, tears spilled over her lower lids and streaked her cheeks, but she didn't say a word.

If she'd rant at him, he could defend himself. If she'd beg, he'd explain why he couldn't make an exception for her brother. Instead, she merely wept.

And he was the cause.

"Christ, Lu, you're tearing my guts out."

Alexander reached for her and was relieved beyond words when she came to his arms. He buried his nose in her hair and inhaled her clear to his toes. He found her mouth and took it hard. She met his rough kiss with urgency of her own. Then he pulled her away from him and held her at arm's length so he could look into her wide eyes.

"Ye didna trust me enough to tell me the truth," he said, not even noticing the brogue that crept into his speech anymore. His voice was thick with emotion.

"Aye. That's true." She nodded miserably. "I'm

sorry. I should have told ye. I'll no' keep secrets from ye again."

She moved close and stood tiptoe to reach his mouth again. He savaged her lips for a moment, then became aware that she was working the buttons of his trousers. He pulled back once more.

"Are ye doing this so I'll protect your brother?"

"No. I trust ye to do what ye must about Dougal." Her chin quivered when she lifted it. "This is only about you and me. You're my husband. I owe ye my first loyalty."

"And I owe you," he said. No, he shouldn't say that. He might still have to turn Dougal in. But at the moment all he could think of was the soft warmth of her mouth, of the feverish workings of her hands at his waist, and the haven that waited for him inside her.

And he couldn't wait another minute. Alex walked her backward to the broad trunk of a smooth-barked arbutus and lifted her skirts. With her spine pressed against the tree, he hooked an arm under one leg and raised her knee so she was open to him.

She whimpered into his mouth with need, so he took her. Thank God she was more than ready because he couldn't hold back, couldn't be gentle.

Lucinda couldn't either. After only a few thrusts, her insides fisted around him in quick pulses, while she clawed at his back and cried his name. He followed quickly in a heart-pounding release that made him arch his spine and caused his eyes to roll back in his head.

Alex pressed into her, unwilling to withdraw. He knew who he was when he was with Lucinda. Once they separated, his sense of himself would become murky again.

Whatever else his wife was, whatever secrets she might withhold from him, he'd lay money she was part witch. He'd intended to have a shouting row with Lucinda to rival anything his father had ever launched against his mother. Instead he'd rutted her in a quick impassioned taking that left him wondering what their fight was about in the first place.

She stroked his head and kissed his cheek. "I may have no' shown it well, but I do love ye fine, Alexander. In the days to come, dinna forget that."

If he lived to be a hundred, he never would.

But then, as the blood left other parts of his body and returned to his brain, he wondered what she meant about "the days to come." Keeping mum while she let her husband harbor an enemy of the king was bad enough. In the fresh rush of loving, Alexander didn't have the heart to ask her what other secrets she might be holding.

If she was planning to betray him again, he decided he didn't want to know. But as he smoothed down her skirt and refastened his trousers, he promised himself that he'd walk wary around his wife.

Just in case.

"Well, since Lord Bonniebroch sent Dougal MacOwen off instead of arresting him, does that count?" His round face expectant, Lyall Lyttle leaned over Farquhar's shoulder, but the old ghost closed his private journal abruptly.

Early yesterday, one of the stable lads had overheard the laird order his brother-in-law away so he didn't have to bind him over to the authorities for being a Radical. The news had spread through the castle grapevine like bedbugs through a new straw tick. It seemed as if the laird had protected someone who might be considered an enemy, so now every soul was hopeful the second knot that bound Bonniebroch's curse had been loosed.

"*Nae, it doesna affect the curse,*" Farquhar said wearily. He too had hoped the laird's action—or inaction—in the matter of his Radical brother-in-law would meet the enchantment's requirement. Unfortunately, the old steward had felt nothing stir in the realm of the spirit, no release of the talon-hold grip of the curse.

"But I thought his lordship only had to defend a foe—"

"*Only defend a foe?*" Farquhar repeated tetchily. He rarely let Lyttle's naiveté bedevil him. One of the good things about being pure spirit was that the passions that afflict the flesh had dissipated in the old steward over the centuries. Still, a little irritation bubbled up inside the ghost. Surely Lyttle couldn't be that much of a simpleton! "*D'ye ken how rare a thing it is for a man to protect his enemy?*"

Lyttle's guileless eyes blinked slowly. "But, as an Englishman, Lord Bonniebroch must count a Radical his enemy."

"*Aye, nae doubt, he does. But as a Scotsman, he also counts this particular Radical a brother-in-law, which doesna lend itself to enmity. At least, it shouldna.*"

It was such a tangled mess. Watching his laird stumble about trying to make the right decisions when Farquhar couldn't even tell him what the three needful deeds were or offer advice about how to fulfill the requirements of the spirits—it was the most onerous burden Farquhar had ever shouldered.

The steward floated over to the round window that looked down into the bailey. A heavy fog had rolled in during the night, obscuring the dozens of men who were checking the tack on their mounts or sharpening the wicked boar spears. Voices were muffled or amplified in turn depending on the shifting currents of thick haze. Then the order to mount was given. The sound of pounding hooves as well as the plodding tramp of the beaters who would venture out on foot echoed off the stone castle walls.

"It appears the English willna wait for the sun to burn off the mist before starting their hunt," Farquhar said.

"And they swear no' to return without a pair of tusks. They mean to stalk the boar all day, even by dusk and then by torchlight if needs be." Lyttle shook his head. "Are all Englishmen so daft?"

"Nae more nor less than other men. Though I'm hoping a Highlander would show a bit more sense in this case." Farquhar stared down at the men as if it might allow him to peer into their secret hearts. While he could occasionally read men's faces with uncanny accuracy, he wasn't truly privy to their thoughts. *"'Tis bound to be a dangerous enterprise. Fortunately, his lordship probably has plenty of enemies to pick from in yon crowd, should he choose to protect one."*

"And should he decide no' to?"

"We'll climb that stile when we get to it, aye? Sufficient unto the day, Mr. Lyttle." Farquhar drifted back over to his desk and eyed his journal with speculation. *"Let us no' borrow trouble from tomorrow. Lord*

Bonniebroch cleared the first hurdle. We may hope he clears the second and third as well."

"'Twould be better if we could do more than hope," Lyttle said grumpily. "Is there naught ye can do to show him the way?"

Farquhar ran a spectral fingertip over his private journal, wishing he could still feel the grain in the Cordovan leather. A fresh idea quirked up one of his wiry brows. *"Aye, mayhap there is."*

Mr. Farquhar wasn't the only soul watching the hunters fly through the portcullis. Lucinda used the secret corridor to make her way up to the battlements so she could stand in the brittle chill while Alexander led the party out. The pack of hunting dogs raised a cacophony of yelps as they trailed the riders. The feral sound made all the small hairs on Lucinda's body stand on end.

"If I were a self-respecting boar, I'd head for the hills about now," she muttered as she pulled her cloak tight around her and wished for thicker boots.

"Och, there y'are, milady." A maid who was either Jane or Janet made her way along the battlements toward Lucinda.

She bore a mug of something warm enough to send steam into the cold. Lucinda accepted it gratefully and wrapped two hands around the mug.

"Thank ye . . . Janet."

"I'm Jane, but it makes no never mind. We often confuse people."

"Where is Janet?"

"Meeting Seamus Abernathy down by the river."

Lucinda frowned. "But I thought he was your beau."

"He is. And Janet's as well. We're just after confusing him a bit. A confused man is a biddable man, me old mam always says."

Alexander might be confused from time to time, but there was nothing the least biddable about him. Memories of the quick taking in the forest yesterday brought heat to Lucinda's cheeks. Their marriage was still filled with awkward silences and moments of mistrust, but their bodies spoke the same language.

Lucinda wished their hearts did as well.

She brought the mug to her lips. It was filled with coffee, black and hot, but she scented a whiff of alcohol too.

"Aye, milady," Jane said as if she'd heard Lucinda's unspoken question. "Cook thought as ye'd need summat more than coffee to warm ye whilst ye watch the hunt."

Jane leaned over the crenellated edge to point out her father who was on the march with the beaters. Lucinda wondered at the excitement dancing in the girl's eyes.

"Seems to me that a man afoot is in more peril than one who's mounted," she said. "Are ye no' the least scared for him?"

"Och, no. Weel, I suppose I might be were it no' for the curse, ye ken. Me father might take a wound and be in pain for a time, but eventually he'd heal. I mind the time when young Davey Drummond broke his arm falling out of a tree. Took him the better part of a decade to heal, but when one of us is injured there's no question of it being mortal. We canna die, remember."

Lucinda wondered if Mr. Farquhar had told the residents that they'd turn to stone if the curse wasn't lifted. The prospect of becoming a statue was daunting, but the folk of the castle didn't seem panicked by it. "If ye canna die and always heal, I'm surprised ye wish the curse to be broken."

Jane's smile faded a bit. "I know ye dinna understand the way of it, but we are mortal tired of being stuck. I used to wish to become a bride and have a husband and bairns of me own, but that canna be so long as the curse prevails."

"But what about Mr. Abernathy? You might at least wed."

"Ye'd think so, but no. I canna make up me mind to have him and it's such fun for Janet and me to bedevil the man." Jane leaned her cheek on her palm. "O' course, after three hundred years of the chase, he still doesna seem to be able to decide which of us he favors either."

In the woods below, the riders had far outpaced the beaters and taken their station in a frost-kissed meadow at the base of a rising peak. The beaters thrashed through the underbrush. If there was a boar hidden among the brambles, they'd drive him to the men armed with spears and crossbows.

"Truth to tell, I'm more worried for Lord Bonniebroch during this hunt," Jane said artlessly. "He's no' touched by the curse, so we must hope the boar doesna touch him either."

"Scriptures admonish us to obey the spirit of the law instead of the letter. Since the Bonniebroch curse doesn't rise to the level of holy writ, I may have thought of a way to tell his lordship what must be done without actually 'telling' him. At this point, 'tis worth a try."

From the secret journal of Callum Farquhar, Steward of Bonniebroch Castle since the Year of Our Lord 1521

Chapter Twenty-Eight

Clarindon had bowed out of the boar hunt, deciding instead to spend the morning chasing a charming upstairs maid about the castle, hoping to catch her beneath a kissing bough. Alex wished he could have done the same with Lucinda.

As Alexander shifted in the saddle, the creak of leather sounded preternaturally loud.

Of course, one of the best things about this blasted hunt was that everyone was forced to be quiet lest they warn the quarry of their presence. Lord Rankin couldn't pontificate on everything under the sun. Sir Darren MacMartin couldn't make sly remarks, laden with innuendo and half-truths. As they waited for the beaters to flush out the boar,

Alexander was alone in the crowd of English nobles and their retainers with only his thoughts to keep him company.

As he looked down the line of hunters, bristling with weaponry, he mostly pitied the boar.

Then their quarry shot out of the woods in a black blur with a pack of baying hounds nipping at its heels. The boar was of monstrous size, almost four feet at the shoulder and his back measured more than six. Alex estimated its weight at over five hundred pounds. It turned in the center of the clearing and one of the hounds leaped up to grasp it by the ear. With a toss of its massive head, the boar ripped open the dog's guts, sending it keening and writhing in agony.

Alexander revoked his pity for the boar in a heartbeat.

Forewarned, the rest of the pack circled at a respectful distance and took turns rushing the beast, harrying it with nips on the heels and keeping it turning in tight circles to face new threats.

Lord Rankin was first to raise his crossbow. Alex clamped a hand on his forearm to stop him. "You're likely to hit one of the hounds. Those dogs are facing enough danger without our adding to it."

Rankin's lip curled in distaste. "Never figured you for squeamish, Mallory. Very well. Spears, it is. Likely more sport that way, in any case."

Lord Rankin strapped his crossbow across his back and untied the long spear that had been affixed to his saddle. Alex held Badgemagus still as he watched Rankin barrel across the clearing toward the beleaguered pig. Between the racket from the beaters who ringed the clearing, the tearing teeth of the hounds, and the dozen or so mounted hunters, the boar had no chance.

Nothing sporting about this, he decided.

Alex wouldn't have minded the boar hunt if the castle was short of meat and needed to fill its larder so that people might eat.

But to kill another creature merely to watch it die made his stomach turn.

Rankin cantered around the boar, looking for an opening. After circling once, he hefted his spear and lofted it into the air. It struck the boar's shoulder, penetrating the tough hide deeply enough to embed the blade, but not far enough to damage any internal organs.

In an instant the momentum shifted between hunter and quarry. The spear shaft quivering from its shoulder, the boar squealed with rage and charged Rankin's horse. As it streaked past, it slashed the gelding's belly with its long tusk. The horse reared and toppled, kicking and screaming. When the gelding landed on the iron-hard ground, Rankin's leg was trapped beneath it. He bellowed for help.

The boar turned, its piggy-eyes flaring red, and began to dash back toward the fallen man.

"Do something, Mallory," Sir Darren demanded, his voice shrill enough to make his mount dance sideways in nervousness. "This is your hunt. Your responsibility."

A number of the other mounted Englishmen quit the clearing and headed into the woods, fleeing back to the castle as quickly as their horses would take them.

For the first time in his life, Alex was ashamed of

his English blood. The dogs had fallen back, so he raised his crossbow and loosed a bolt. Because of the angle, he could only strike the boar in the flank, which only served to madden it further, but slowed it a little.

Alex kicked Badgemagus into a full gallop, but knew he'd never close the distance in time to save Lord Rankin, who was swearing the air blue above the screams of his dying horse and the grunting pants of the advancing boar. Both Rankin and his mount were doomed.

Then suddenly a man leaped from the woods and danced across the path of the boar.

It was Lucinda's brother, Dougal.

He was unarmed, save for his dirk, but he spread his arms wide, to make himself as large a target as possible and shouted to the boar in Gaelic. It swerved to focus on him instead of the fallen Rankin. At the last possible second, Dougal stepped to the side with the same masculine grace he'd exhibited in the dirk dance and buried his blade in the boar's back, hoping to hit the spine.

He missed his target, leaving his embedded dirk in the beast's back. Red streaming from its wounds, the boar ran past Dougal, but instead of turning this time to charge its attackers, it made a beeline toward Sir Darren and his horse.

MacMartin panicked and caused his mount to rear instead of bolt away. He slid off the horse's rump and landed on the frosty ground with a thud. The horse cantered away and the boar followed it for a few yards before stopping to turn back toward Sir Darren, who seemed frozen in place.

The boar seemed to be considering its options.

It glared back in the direction of Lord Rankin, whom Dougal was helping out from under his dead horse, then toward the unhorsed MacMartin. Even Alexander could tell which was the easier target, so he galloped to Sir Darren.

"Get up, man!"

If MacMartin stood up, he might have faced the boar down, but all Sir Darren could do was whine and scrabble backward toward the trees.

"Help me!" MacMartin wailed.

The boar lowered its head. If Alex waited for it to charge, he'd be too late. For a large animal it was wickedly fast and light on its absurdly tiny feet. He had to guess where it would go and take his chances.

He leaped from Badgemagus's back and gave the gelding a smack on the rump to send him fleeing back to the stable. Even though Badgemagus had been nothing but trouble, Alex didn't want to see him gutted like Lord Rankin's mount. Then he waved his arms to attract the boar's attention and strode to meet it, pulling his loaded horse pistol from his deep jacket pocket.

There were few kill spots on a boar, especially from head on. And Alex had only one shot.

White-knuckled, Lucinda leaned on the balustrade. They could see the clearing in the distance, though rising mist obscured their vision enough to make the women wonder what became of the first man who charged the boar on horseback. Many of the hunters were fleeing so Lu figured that wasn't a good sign.

The men were far enough away that she couldn't

make out their features, but she recognized Dougal by his blue and green Black Watch plaid. She held her breath as he danced with the boar and escaped untouched. She'd finally begun to breathe again when he ran toward the fallen horseman.

Then another Englishman lost his mount, but Lucinda hadn't seen how.

"Ooo!" Jane said, her cheeks painted with an excited flush. "Would ye look at that? Someone else is going after the boar afoot."

It wasn't just someone. It was Alexander. Lucinda would know that determined stride anywhere.

Her knees threatened to buckle, but she forced herself to stay upright and not look away. She covered her mouth with her fingertips to keep from crying out.

Oh, God. Help him, God, she chanted in her mind. She couldn't make her voice work, but surely the One who weighs hearts knew what was in hers.

Alex extended his arm and a flash erupted, followed by a loud bang. Billowing smoke combined with the swirling mist. Both the gunman and boar disappeared from her sight.

A whooshing noise rushed through Bonniebroch Castle, as if a howling wind were suddenly loosed inside. It roared through the corridors, billowed the tapestries as if they were mere bed curtains, and shot up the chimneys. Every fire in every grate flared. The kitchen blaze ruined the brace of pheasant Cook was roasting on a spit. She began shrieking for the bootblack boy to fetch a pail of water to put it out, but then the flames suddenly dissipated as quickly as they had flared.

The sound grew louder. It wrapped itself around every soul in Bonniebroch, trapping them inside the eye of a personal squall. Then as if someone had grasped the noise by the tail and given it a shake, the sound abruptly stopped.

An awestruck silence fell upon the castle. No one moved. No one spoke.

Except for Mr. Farquhar and Mr. Lyttle.

"Did ye feel something?" Farquhar asked.

Lyttle nodded shakily as he helped Mr. Farquhar replace his secret journal behind the faulty brick in Lord Bonniebroch's fireplace. "Aye, it was like a gale had been loosed inside me."

"Wish I could have felt it," Farquhar murmured. His was the only head of hair in the castle not standing on end. *"Three hundred years we've waited."*

"Ye mean . . ."

"Aye, the second requirement to lift the curse has been met. Our laird has defended a foe."

Mr. Lyttle did a jig, pirouetting in place. Then he shoved Farquhar's journal into the secret alcove in the fireplace and jammed in the brick till it was flush with the others.

"Nae, Lyttle. Dinna be so particular. We want his lordship to notice the brick is out of place, aye?"

Lyttle scraped the brick forward so it canted out drunkenly from its fellows. "Why can we no' just leave the journal out on the end of his bed for his lordship to find? We could even leave it open to the proper page."

"Because we canna cross the rules binding us. We canna

*tell Lord Bonniebroch what may come. We must only hope
he chooses aright when the time comes."*

"But we're hoping he finds yer journal and reads it?"

"Aye. There's nothing in the curse that precludes his
lordship discovering things for himself. Nor strictures
against us giving him a nudge in the right direction so long
as we dinna tell him directly."* Farquhar floated toward
Lord Bonniebroch's long mirror so he could return
to his tower room by the most direct method. *"The
last task is the hardest. And I'm thinkin' he'll need to ken
the stakes if he's to make the right choice this time."*

"When a lady is being courted, her beau will share a goodly amount about himself, his expectations in terms of future elevation and business dealings. Once one is a wife, the knowledgeable lady must accept the fact that there are things her husband will keep from her, be it a mistress or an investment failure. Such is our lot. The wise woman accepts it as the way of the world."

From *The Knowledgeable Ladies' Guide
to Eligible Gentlemen*

Chapter Twenty-Nine

"In a pig's eye!" Lucinda closed the *Ladies' Guide* with a snap and hurled it across her bedchamber. It splatted on the far wall and landed on the polished hardwood, rumpling the open pages and cracking the binding.

It wasn't right. Alex had no need to keep things from her, especially now that Dougal had won the favor of Lord Rankin by saving him from that charging boar. Rankin was so grateful, Dougal's royal pardon was all but assured. Of course, she hadn't heard about that from Alexander or from her

brother either. It had come to her through Jane or
Janet, she wasn't sure which, the fresh gossip spilling
out of the maid like sausage from a meat grinder.

Lucinda's husband didn't seek her out after returning from the hunt to reassure her that he was
uninjured either. His valet had informed her that
the laird was hale and hearty when he met her at
Alexander's door, along with the fact that his lordship was enjoying his bath and didn't wish to be
disturbed.

By anyone.

So Lucinda moved back to her own chamber,
grateful she'd left enough of her things there to
muddle by.

"Heaven forefend I interrupt Himself at his bath
because I need a fresh pair of stockings," she muttered tetchily.

She paced the length of the room, trying to look
on the positive side of matters. Alexander had
helped her brother by sending him away instead of
arresting him. Once the promised pardon came
through Dougal would be able to resume his normal
life. Maybe even court Enya MacKenzie, if she wasn't
already promised. By protecting Sir Darren Mac-
Martin during the boar hunt, Alexander had satisfied
the second requirement for the curse to be lifted. So
all in all, things were looking up at Bonniebroch.

Except for the state of the laird and lady's marriage.

After that frenetic coupling in the woods, they'd
barely spoken a dozen words to each other. Their
bodies seemed to know how to join, with predictable

frequency and devastating effect, but their hearts . . . that was another matter entirely.

Lucinda was sick over it.

Alex only seemed to seek her out when he was either angry with her or wanted to bed her. He'd even left her to play hostess to their houseguests while he remained closeted in his chamber for the rest of the day and into the evening.

Again, with orders that he wasn't to be disturbed.

His barred door was a crippling blow to her heart. *Verra well,* she decided as she slid the bolt and climbed into her cold bed. *My door can be locked too.*

Lucinda blew out her bedside candle and stared into the dark. Blood coursed in her ears like retreating footsteps as she waited for sleep to claim her.

It never came.

Her eyes adjusted to the dark and she followed the dancing shadows cast by the banked fire, small gray parodies of the Nimble Men she and Alex had watched in the northern sky. She'd been so hopeful that night on the battlements, so sure their made marriage would grow into a love match and they'd be happier than any two people had a right to be.

Lucinda sighed. *So much for hopes.*

Still, she wasn't entirely surprised when long after midnight, the secret panel in her wall whirred open and Alexander stepped through. She sat up in bed.

"I didna invite ye here," she said, pulling the coverlet to her chin.

He came over and sat on the side of her bed. "I don't need an invitation to enter my wife's chamber."

"But I need one to enter yours apparently."

He sighed. "I was busy."

"In your bath?" A horrid thought struck her. There were any number of housemaids she hadn't met yet and likely a few wouldn't mind a tumble with the laird. "Or maybe ye had company ye didna wish me to discover."

Alex swore so vehemently Lucinda was surprised the Almighty didn't blast him with a lightning bolt on the spot.

"I was alone all day." His eyes blazed at her. "What do you take me for?"

"I dinna ken, Alex. One moment ye're cold and distant. The next ye're hot as a furnace. I never know who ye'll be when ye come to me."

"No need for you to wonder now. I've come as your husband and I need you to be my wife."

He reached for her but she straight-armed him.

"Nae, ye only need me to soothe the urges of your body, but ye willna let me know what's going on in your head and your heart. That's no' a wife." She steeled herself to resist him. "Ye have me confused with a light-skirt."

He stretched out on the bed beside her without touching her again and laid a forearm across his eyes. "Well, you're right about one thing. I'm confused."

Against her better judgment, she asked, "What about?"

His chest rose and fell in a deep sigh. "The curse."

"Seems to me things are going well on that front. Everyone is delighted with the progress ye've made." If she wasn't going to offer him the comfort of her body—and she absolutely wasn't till he'd offered more of his heart—the least she could do was encourage him about the Bonniebroch curse. "There were so many toasts over it at supper, 'tis a wonder anyone was able to leave the tables upright."

He peered at her from under his arm. "I'm glad they enjoyed themselves this night because there won't be any more progress."

"Why not?"

"Because I found Mr. Farquhar's journal behind a brick in my fireplace. I've been reading the blasted thing all day. Three hundred years' worth of rumination takes some concentration, but now I know the final task to lift the curse," he said wearily, "and I can't do it."

"What is it?"

He sat up. "I have to kill an old friend. The only person in this castle who qualifies is Clarindon. He and I have saved each other's lives a dozen times over the years. I'd sooner cut out my own heart as hurt him, let alone kill him." His eyes wells of sadness, Alex met her gaze. "I won't be able to lift the curse."

"Then everyone in Bonniebroch is doomed," she whispered.

"I know. And there's nothing I can do about it."

Her chest constricted and she felt his despair as if it were her own.

"It's plain you want nothing to do with me," he said, "but would you . . . do you think you could bear for me to hold you for a while?"

His ragged tone crushed her heart. *So much for withholding meself to punish him.*

"Only if ye join me under the sheets," she said as she lifted the coverlet. He crawled under it and snugged her close against him. When she settled her head on his shoulder, she felt the tension leave his body.

As good as his word, he only stroked her hair, her arm, and occasionally down the length of her spine in slow caresses. His breathing slowed and eventually his hand stilled, fingers splayed on the small of her back.

Sometimes, she decided as sleep began to snatch at the edges of her mind, *love doesna have to proclaim itself with flowery words. It doesna always blaze in quick passion. Sometimes, 'tis plainest and sweetest in the sharing of a pillow and shutting out the world.*

Even though each day was very like another for Morgan MacRath, sometime-sorcerer and sole occupant of the castle dungeon, he gained strength with every dawn. The laird of Bonniebroch wasn't the only one who was glad to see the weeping woman gone from the other cell. She'd disturbed Morgan's concentration and set his plans back by keeping him from growing in power while she was there. Now, unimpeded by the distraction, he fed on his hatred for the residents of Bonniebroch who were counting down the days till Twelfth Night with riotous celebration in the castle above Morgan's head.

He seethed with loathing. He wallowed in spite for the people who'd inadvertently trapped him all these years. And with each malevolent thought, Morgan MacRath's strength returned.

He was no longer a black blob of amorphous goo. The sorcerer was now able to assume a spectral body like the one inhabited by that infernal pest

Farquhar. The bars of his cell no longer held him, but the exits to the dungeon were still warded against him. He could only wander the deepest reaches of the old keep.

That wasn't necessarily a bad thing. He discovered some subterranean spaces he was sure no living person knew existed. They would suit his purposes well, provided he could find a way out of the dungeon.

He couldn't assume physical form yet, but that wasn't a total impediment to his plans and what with the setback caused by the weeping woman he probably wouldn't be able to become corporeal by the appointed hour. Of course, he could always borrow a body, provided he could get close enough to one. The trick was to escape the dungeon and do it before Twelfth Night was over.

Morgan made another circuit of the large central chamber, hoping to discover a secret unwarded exit through the gray stone. From the tail of his eye, he caught his reflection in the long mirror hanging in the center of the room. He was drawn to the looking glass to admire his own face for a moment.

After three hundred years trapped as an entity with roughly the same consistency as a raw egg, it did his heart good to see himself again. He stroked the beautifully tended chin whiskers that had been his pride when he was alive. He was a damned handsome man, if he did say so.

Damned handsome . . . whatever I am now, he silently amended.

Then he noticed a flicker in the mirror, a streak

of light that hadn't come from behind him. It was from inside the looking glass.

"I wonder . . ." Morgan lifted a hand and touched the glass experimentally. To his great surprise and delight, instead of skimming over cool silvered glass, his fingers sank into a gelatinous substance. He'd seen Farquhar come through the mirror with the new laird of Bonniebroch some days ago. Morgan cursed himself for not trying this sooner.

So, the question of what he'd become was answered. He was pure spirit, like Farquhar, capable of projecting whatever image he wished. Morgan concentrated all his energy and morphed his spectral shape into an exact replica of the old steward.

"Ye wee bird of a man," Morgan said to his own reflection, looking back at himself through Farquhar's calm eyes. *"How did ye ever best me all those years ago?"*

Then he relaxed and returned to his own tall, devilishly handsome form.

"Things will go different this time."

It wasn't too late. By his reckoning, this was the day. Epiphany. Twelfth Night. The last day those dupes above his head might hope to end the curse. Perhaps it was fitting that he hadn't found the way to escape until now.

Besides, he hadn't learned the name of the body he'd be assuming until very recently. Like Farquhar, he heard everything that transpired, every conversation spoken in Bonniebroch, and he'd been paying particular attention to the new laird's pillow talk with his young wife. Lord Bonniebroch couldn't kill his old friend.

Morgan pushed through the surface of the mirror

and found himself moving steadily down a corridor of light. He paused briefly before each looking-glass exit he chanced to pass, looking for the right one.

"Where are ye, Englishman? Come out, come out, wherever ye are," he almost sang. It was only a matter of time until he found him.

Sir Bertram Clarindon had to be here somewhere.

"Here at the end, I wish I had something profound to say, some bit of wisdom to leave for whoever finds this journal in the days to come. Instead, I am poured out, a dry husk, beyond hope or help. Having done all I can, I watch and wait. For good or ill, the die is cast and the fate of Bonniebroch hangs upon the luck of this throw."

From the secret journal of Callum Farquhar, Steward of Bonniebroch Castle since the Year of Our Lord 1521

Chapter Thirty

The torches had never burned brighter in the Great Hall. As Twelfth Night revelry built to a fevered pitch, the folk of Bonniebroch ate as if there was no tomorrow. They played like children and drank like lords. Some of the younger and more foolish had been coaxed into the English game of Snap Dragon. The chanting and cheering made burnt fingers and mouths seem almost worth the trouble of trying to snatch raisins from flaming brandy.

Alexander had donned full Highlander regalia for the occasion. Some men didn't have the legs for a kilt. Lucinda was sad to admit that her father was one of them. Erskine MacOwen's belly protruded almost as much as Meg Liscomb's, the eternally pregnant member of the Bonniebroch household. In stark contrast, her father's legs were so skinny one of the wags in the hall had asked Mr. MacOwen if those were his shins peeping beneath his kilt or if he was riding a chicken.

But Alexander's legs were magnificent, heavily muscled and sturdily straight. As he moved around the room, laughing and talking with his retainers, his plaid swirled about him. If Lucinda half closed her eyes, she could imagine him as King of the Fair Folk, magic sparking from the folds of his tartan with every step. His stiff Englishness was gone.

To one who didn't know about the curse, this night would have seemed an idyllic culmination of Christmastide. But when Alexander's gaze met Lucinda's, she saw the carefully hidden misery in them. He knew what he must do to save these people.

And it wasn't in him to do it.

However, the folk of Bonniebroch didn't know that. Sure their laird would complete the third task, whatever it might be, they threw themselves into celebration with a will, singing and pushing the tables aside so they would dance furious reels down the length of the Great Hall. Even the young piper was less wheezy than usual.

After two sets, Lucinda begged off further dancing and retired to her place on the dais. Alex led the rotund little Mrs. Fletcher out onto the floor to wild cheering and stomping as the piper launched into a comical rendition of "The Maid I Adore." All eyes were on the pair, but Lucinda's were drawn to a flicker of movement at the far end of the room.

Sir Bertram Clarindon leaned on the double-door jamb watching the dancers with the rest of the party. Then he looked over their heads to Lucinda and smiled.

She'd been more than relieved when Alexander's friend had made himself scarce during supper. Charming, if not classically handsome, he'd reportedly been cutting a wide swath through the ranks of the upstairs maids. Anything that kept him out of her husband's path this night was cause for rejoicing. If Alexander wasn't confronted with his friend's presence, he wouldn't have to make the horrible choice before him.

Lucinda felt terrible for the people of Bonniebroch, but her heart ached for Alexander's wretched choice even more. She rose and, squeezing around the tight knots of revelers, made her way across the room to Clarindon.

He bowed beautifully, as always. "My lady, you are the moon and the stars this night."

"Good even, Sir Bertram," she said, taking his arm and leading him into the vaulted vestibule outside the feasting hall. "I wonder if ye'll take a turn with me."

"Delighted," he said, covering the hand she'd slipped into the crook of his elbow with his warm one. "In fact, you're the one I was coming to see."

"Really?" Sir Bertram had been correctly cordial to her but had never sought her out before. "Why?"

A wicked glint flashed in his usually mild eyes. "Well, there's a new game I'd like to introduce you to."

"Not another like Snap Dragon, I hope. Mrs. Fletcher will be doling out salve for burns for a month." *Or she would if the folk of Bonniebroch had another month.*

"Oh, no. Nothing like that." He laughed as they stopped before the long mirror, propped against the wall opposite the tall double doors that led out to the bailey. "This game is sort of like hide-and-seek. It's called . . ." He clamped a firm grip on her forearm. ". . . Capture the Chatelaine."

Then Clarindon stepped through the silvered glass and yanked her behind him. She was enveloped by a clear substance with the consistency of jelly.

Once they cleared that gelatinous layer, Lucinda sucked in a surprised breath and coughed at the frigid air that met her lungs. Alexander had tried to describe what the trip between the mirrors was like, but he'd failed to mention the bone-chilling cold. She was too stunned to resist Clarindon's hand on her arm and too frightened to pull away. She might tumble out of the tunnel of light through which they seemed to be traveling and into the abyss she glimpsed beyond the transparent walls.

Just as she was convinced she'd freeze into a solid block of ice, they passed through another jelly-like layer, which was mercifully warmer. She held her breath till they tumbled out of another mirror and into a dank chamber that smelled of rot and mold and ancient decay.

"Is this the castle's dungeon?" she asked in a small voice.

"You might call it that." Clarindon's eyes flashed in the darkness, golden orbs with no soul behind them. "I called it home for the last three hundred years."

Lucinda pulled a name from her memory of Alexander's recounting of his visit to this misbegotten place. It belonged to the sorcerer behind all of Bonniebroch's woes. "Morgan MacRath."

"In the flesh." MacRath sketched a bow, a less elegant one than Clarindon customarily offered, and cast her an oily smile. "Well, in someone else's flesh, at least."

"What's happened to Sir Bertram?"

"Oh, he's still in here." He thumped his chest with a closed fist. "Just a bit . . . submerged at present. The weaker mind will always yield to the stronger, ye see. Ye'll yield to me as well, milady."

Then he dragged her screaming into the dark.

Callum Farquhar leaped up from his desk and flew to the looking glass. He didn't pause before plunging into its silvered depths. For the first time in three hundred years, something was urgent.

He hadn't sensed MacRath in the secret passageways behind the mirrors. He'd had no advance warning that the sorcerer had escaped the dungeon and taken possession of Sir Bertram's body. It wasn't until Farquhar overheard the conversation between Lady Bonniebroch and Clarindon outside the Great Hall that he began to sense something was amiss beyond the fact that midnight was fast approaching.

Lady Bonniebroch's ripping trek through the mirror with Clarindon leading the way was proof positive that another spirit was involved. No human could travel those secret paths on his own. Farquhar felt such cold malevolence emanating from Clarindon, he realized MacRath had taken charge of Lord Bonniebroch's friend.

Quick as thought, Farquhar zipped through the passageway and shot out the looking glass near the Great Hall. He didn't slow his pace, streaking through the closed doors and finally coming to rest in the center of the long room. He manifested a good ten feet above the ground and several times larger than his size in life.

"Lord Bonniebroch," Farquhar thundered in mindspeech, casting a wide net so that everyone present could hear his voice echoing in their heads.

The assembly froze. None but Lyall Lyttle and the various lairds over the years had been able to see Farquhar. The residents of the castle knew he was there, of course. They were pleased enough to take orders from the old steward since he had more sense than any of the living, but they were also grateful he kept to his tower and relayed his instructions through Lyttle and his meticulous journal. It was one thing to be aware of a disembodied spirit in their midst. Quite another to see one in full fury.

The long case clock chimed a quarter to midnight.

"The hour is almost come, milord," Farquhar said.

"You will not force my hand in this, spirit." Eyes blazing, Lord Bonniebroch stepped toward Farquhar. "You know the intent of my heart. I canna kill my oldest friend."

"Even if he's about to murder yer wife?"

In the thick of merriment, the laird had lost track

of his lady. Alexander's head jerked around and he
scanned the hall for some sign of Lucinda. He bellowed her name, but when the last echo died, there
was no response. "Where is she?"

"Arm yerself, milord." Farquhar held out his ghostly
hand. *"I'll bear ye company as far as I may."*

When they emerged from the looking glass in the
dungeon, Farquhar was still talking, still explaining
that Morgan MacRath meant to use Lucinda for
some magical rite to unward the gates of Bonniebroch. MacRath was yet bound to the castle, but if he
undid the spell, he'd be loosed upon the world.

"And that's bad enough no' to bear contemplating,"
Farquhar said as Alex drew a deep breath and shook
off the effects of the trip between the mirrors. *"If
MacRath is disembodied a second time, it'll be all up
with him. The only way to save the Lady Lucinda now is
to kill . . ."*

"My old friend," Alex finished for him, his voice
hard as the stone of the castle. "Hurry up, man.
Where are they?"

Farquhar cocked his head, listening. *"This way."*
He vanished down a dark corridor that led off from
the central chamber of the dungeon.

Alexander broke into a mile-eating trot to keep
up with the spirit. Fortunately, Farquhar cast a lumi-
nescent glow so Alex could clearly see where he was
going. The stone beneath his feet had been polished
smooth by thousands of feet over hundreds of years.

Then at the end of the tunnel, the ghost stopped
abruptly. The corridor opened into a large vault
sparsely lit with torches crammed into fissures in the

gray rock. A subterranean lake glinted in the dark, its surface black and oily. The place smelled of centuries-old dust and bat guano and magic. Alexander half expected a water horse to rear its snaky neck from the depths of the lake.

"Why have we stopped?" Alex demanded.

"The way is warded against my kind." Farquhar brushed a hand toward the opening and golden sparks trailed his spectral fingertips. *"I canna go forward, but ye must. They're no' far from here now. Tread carefully. While MacRath bides in the body of Clarindon, his magical powers are suppressed, but what he can do is give yer friend more strength, more speed, more cunning than ever he had in times past."*

The old ghost laid a palm on Alexander's chest and the cold of it sank into his marrow, freezing his insides. *"Nae matter what ye may see, what ye may hear, remember 'tis no' truly yer friend ye meet here in this evil place. Banish mercy from yer heart, lad, for ye'll receive none."*

"Friend or no, if he's harmed Lucinda, he's already outlived mercy from me." Alexander drew his claymore and bounded into the large chamber, calling his wife's name.

"Alex!" Her tone was shrill. "I'm here! He—"

He moved toward the sound. Relief that she was still alive and panic over her cut-off voice vied for first place in his heart. He fought the urge to run toward her. If MacRath had set a trap, he didn't want to fall into it before he had a chance to confront him.

Alexander followed the edge of the body of water, staying away from the obsidian surface of the becalmed underground lake. It was brighter ahead.

When he peered around a rock outcropping, he saw Lucinda. She was bound to a tall stalagmite that rose to within an inch of joining the corresponding stalactite dripping from the distant roof.

A gag kept her from calling out, but Alex could see the whites of her eyes all around. She was alive, but terrified.

With reason.

Clarindon stood before her, muttering some incantation while brandishing a wicked-looking sword tip in strange patterns before her midsection. Alex took another step and a rock gave beneath his tread, sliding toward the lake. Alexander kept his feet, but the scraping noise made Clarindon turn toward him.

"Ah! There you are," his friend said.

"Step away from her."

Clarindon's familiar expression of mild annoyance turned to one of undisguised loathing for a couple blinks. Then he smiled. "It's only me, Alex. We're playing a little game here, your lady and I. We expected not to be disturbed. If you don't leave at once, I shall be very put out."

The voice was still his old friend's, with the same inflections, the same means of expression, but the way Clarindon's eyes flared in the dark reminded Alexander that there was really nothing of Sir Bertram here.

"Consider yourself more than inconvenienced, MacRath." Claymore raised above his head, Alexander charged. When he was near enough he brought the sword down in a lethal arc, meant to cleave the sorcerer from neck to navel.

MacRath met the blow with his sword, turning

Alex's blade harmlessly to the side. Then he launched into a blistering attack that had Alexander giving ground, something that had happened so rarely when he sparred Clarindon in practice that he could count the number of times on the fingers of one hand. The strokes came furiously and Alexander whacked solidly back at him, but none of his blows connected.

Clarindon had never been this accomplished a swordsman.

It's not him, Alex reminded himself as he took a wicked swipe at his friend's middle, which missed by inches. *It's MacRath.*

The fight boiled over the stark lakeshore, each fighter making use of the odd rock formations to give cover or provide an advantage in leverage. The world sizzled down to the next thrust, the next parry, the next desperate lunge.

Alexander's arms were tiring. Sweat rolled down his forehead and stung his eyes, but Clarindon's blows came with the regularity of hammer strikes. From the corner of his vision, Alex caught Lucinda struggling against her bonds, but he forced himself not to look at her again. Distraction would mean death for them both.

And for all of the folk of Bonniebroch.

He couldn't think about that either.

MacRath was smiling. Alex couldn't tell if it was his friend who was enjoying besting him for once, or the sorcerer peering out through Clarindon's eyes. The pair of them stumbled into the shallows, their footing uneven in the dark water.

With a grunt of exertion, Alexander swung the heavy claymore around and connected with his enemy's blade. Sparks spit as the swords' sharp edges kissed. The force of the blow reverberated up Alexander's arm and he twisted his wrist to flick his opponent's blade. Both swords flew out of the fighters' grips and sank into the black depths.

The men dove after them, but came up empty-handed, sputtering and blowing. Clarindon threw a bare-knuckled punch at Alexander that snapped his head back. Stars exploded across his vision and he staggered in the waist-deep water, but didn't go down.

Alex grabbed Clarindon and rolled under the surface with him, grappling for a good hold. When he found his feet, he planted them and stood up, forcing his friend's head beneath the water.

"Die, damn ye," Alexander bellowed.

Clarindon thrashed and kicked and tried to rear out of the surf, but Alex tightened his grip and held him down. Tears coursed down his cheeks, but Alexander didn't give even when Clarindon's movements slowed and finally stopped. He held steady, blood pounding in his ears like an army tramping through his head, waiting to make sure his friend was truly gone.

Then without warning an amorphous black shape rose from Clarindon's body with an unearthly scream. In the middle of the lake, a vortex began to swirl and the shape that was all that remained of Morgan MacRath was sucked into its twirling center. The scream rose in pitch until the vortex suddenly collapsed on itself and the lake went still as a sheet of glass.

Heartsick, Alexander dragged Clarindon's body to the shore. Then he sprinted to Lucinda to free her.

She pulled off her gag and ran back toward his dead friend. "Hurry. There's no time to lose," she yelled.

She knelt beside Clarindon. "Help me roll him onto his back."

"Lu, there's no need."

"There's every need. Now do it!" she snapped. "Get down here and press your hands against his chest like so."

Clarindon stared lifelessly up into the vault of the cavern, but Alex stacked his palms on his friend's chest and pushed rhythmically as Lucinda instructed. He was too numb to argue with her.

"My father is a verra canny man," she said as she turned Clarindon's head to the side and ran two fingers inside his mouth. "He's interested in better ways to do most everything and one of them was how to revive a drowned man. He read a whole treatise on it to me when I was a wee lass and he was trying to teach me my letters."

Alex pumped Clarindon's chest while flashes of their life together exploded behind his closed eyes. Becoming best friends at Eton after Alexander thrashed a pair of bullies who were tormenting the smaller Clarindon. Chasing the same debutant for one ridiculous Season, then getting roaring drunk together when she accepted the suit of an aging viscount instead of one of them. Going to war on the Continent together. The time Clarindon took a musket ball meant for him . . .

He swallowed back rising bile. "I killed my friend," he said through clenched teeth.

"Ye had no choice . . . but for now . . . keep the rhythm . . . steady."

Lucinda sounded winded. When Alexander opened his eyes it seemed she was kissing his friend.

"What are you doing?"

"Giving him me breath." She paused long enough for Clarindon's chest to collapse as the air escaped. She frowned down at him. "'Tis no' working."

Of course, it wasn't. Dead was dead. Alexander reached for her but she straight-armed him.

"Hit him." She bent to pinch Clarindon's nose and blow more air into his mouth. "Hard . . . right on the center . . . of his chest."

Alex bunched his fingers into a fist and brought it down on his friend's sternum. The body jerked with the force of the blow, but Clarindon still stared straight ahead.

"Again!" Lucinda ordered.

Rage at the damnable choice he'd had to make boiled out of him and Alex slammed his fist on Clarindon's chest with all his might.

Sir Bertram made a choking noise and Lucinda rolled him quickly to his side so water could spill out of his mouth. Then he sucked in a noisy breath. Then another.

"Where . . . where am I?" he said hoarsely.

Alex couldn't answer his friend. He was too busy kissing his wife. His wonderful, soul-completing, Christmas miracle of a wife.

"The only certainty in life is that life is most uncertain. A title is no proof against adversity. Great wealth is no guarantee of happiness. But love is proof against the dark days that are sure to come to all flesh. In spite of all evidence to the contrary, the knowledgeable lady chooses the right gentleman with her heart."

From *The Knowledgeable Ladies' Guide to Eligible Gentlemen*

Chapter Thirty-One

The long case clock chimed half past midnight as Lucinda and Alexander made their way back to the Great Hall, helping Clarindon along between them. Farquhar was nowhere to be seen, so they couldn't zip back through the paths behind the mirrors. They had to climb the steps to the secret corridor off the laird's chamber and then back down to the hall.

Lyall Lyttle saw them from his post near the doors to the Great Hall and came skittering across the long chamber. "Oh, well done, milord," he said. "Well done. The curse is lifted."

"How do ye know?" Lucinda asked.

"Weel, we're all still here and moving and 'tis after midnight," Lyttle said with a laugh. "And then there's Meg Liscombe."

"What about her?"

"The midwife reports that she gave birth just before midnight." Lyttle grinned. "Twin boys, God help her."

"Oh, that is good news," Lucinda said.

"O' course, we've also had a loss," Lyttle said, his smile fading a bit. "Granny MacNair drifted off to her reward in her sleep, but after three hundred years of rheumatism, her family says she'll be ever so happy to wake up in heaven."

"So life has returned to normal in Bonniebroch," Alexander said.

"Aye, milord, as normal as ever it was."

The people noticed their laird had rejoined them and broke into a rousing cheer. They wouldn't be satisfied till Alex led them in yet another toast, followed by spontaneous dancing and piping.

Lord Rankin pushed through the effusive crowd. "Lord Alexander, I was wrong to order you here. I see that now. Anyone who can move people like this should be closer to Lord Liverpool's inner circle. If you still want to accompany the prime minister to Verona, I can arrange it."

Alex tugged Lucinda closer. "Ye've mistaken me for someone else, milord. The name's Bonniebroch and I'll no' be leaving Scotland anytime soon. Consider this me formal resignation."

Rankin's face flushed the color of the scarlet table runner as he stomped away.

"You burned that bridge and no mistake," Clarindon said at his side. Sir Bertram was still pale, but he was gaining strength with every breath. "If you're not chasing about in Lord Liverpool's service, what are you going to do?"

"Do? I plan to stay right here and raise Blackface sheep." Alexander winked at Lucinda. "And, if this lady will help me, a castle full of red-headed bairns."

In answer, Lucinda draped her arms around his neck and pulled his head down for a long kiss. When she finally released his mouth, she whispered, "I thought I married a man of action. Ye'll get no bairns simply by talking about it."

Alexander laughed, swung his wife up over his shoulder and carted her, bum-first, out of the hall and up the stairs. His people were still cheering below when Alex kicked open the door to his chamber and carried Lucinda to their bed.

"No' so fast, milord," she said, her green eyes sparkling. "I'll dress for bed first if ye please."

"But what if I prefer ye undress?"

"Please, Alex." She pouted prettily. "I didna get to wear the chemise I intended for our wedding night and I thought to please ye with it the now."

"As long as ye dinna mind me tearing another one."

Lucinda made a tsking sound. "What will Mrs. Fletcher say?"

She popped out of the bed and disappeared behind the dressing screen. Alexander wandered over to the chair by the fire to watch his wife discard items of clothing. One by one, gown, stockings, ribbons, and stays came flying over the screen to land on the floor.

Then Alexander noticed that Farquhar's secret journal wasn't in its hiding place behind the faulty brick in his fireplace. It lay open in the center of the chessboard. He picked it up and began to read.

My Lord Bonniebroch,

When you were successful in lifting the curse this evening, I fully expected to find myself in another plane. One might argue that my work here is complete and 'tis high time I moved on.

Apparently, the powers that be aren't in agreement. Against all expectations, I find myself still in my tower as usual. If I can be of help to you or your good lady, I stand ready, as always, to wait upon the pleasure of Bonniebroch.

> *Your obedient servant,*
> *Callum Farquhar, Esq.*

"Well, Mr. Farquhar," Alex murmured, "I can no doubt use your help."

Lucinda stepped from behind the dressing screen. Her shining hair unbound, she was a vision in creamy lace.

"But no' the now, Mr. Farquhar," Alex said softly. "No' the now."

In his tower room, Callum Farquhar threw back his ghostly head and laughed.

Books by Bestselling Author
Fern Michaels

___The Jury	0-8217-7878-1	$6.99US/$9.99CAN
___Sweet Revenge	0-8217-7879-X	$6.99US/$9.99CAN
___Lethal Justice	0-8217-7880-3	$6.99US/$9.99CAN
___Free Fall	0-8217-7881-1	$6.99US/$9.99CAN
___Fool Me Once	0-8217-8071-9	$7.99US/$10.99CAN
___Vegas Rich	0-8217-8112-X	$7.99US/$10.99CAN
___Hide and Seek	1-4201-0184-6	$6.99US/$9.99CAN
___Hokus Pokus	1-4201-0185-4	$6.99US/$9.99CAN
___Fast Track	1-4201-0186-2	$6.99US/$9.99CAN
___Collateral Damage	1-4201-0187-0	$6.99US/$9.99CAN
___Final Justice	1-4201-0188-9	$6.99US/$9.99CAN
___Up Close and Personal	0-8217-7956-7	$7.99US/$9.99CAN
___Under the Radar	1-4201-0683-X	$6.99US/$9.99CAN
___Razor Sharp	1-4201-0684-8	$7.99US/$10.99CAN
___Yesterday	1-4201-1494-8	$5.99US/$6.99CAN
___Vanishing Act	1-4201-0685-6	$7.99US/$10.99CAN
___Sara's Song	1-4201-1493-X	$5.99US/$6.99CAN
___Deadly Deals	1-4201-0686-4	$7.99US/$10.99CAN
___Game Over	1-4201-0687-2	$7.99US/$10.99CAN
___Sins of Omission	1-4201-1153-1	$7.99US/$10.99CAN
___Sins of the Flesh	1-4201-1154-X	$7.99US/$10.99CAN
___Cross Roads	1-4201-1192-2	$7.99US/$10.99CAN

Available Wherever Books Are Sold!
Check out our website at www.kensingtonbooks.com